Shadows Fall
Book Two of the Morhudrim Cycle
by A D Green
1st Edition – 18th September 2020
Release version 1.4 22nd June 2022
© Andrew Green (A D Green)
ASIN: B08KPXM1RC
ISBN: 9798654775573

All characters in this work are fictitious and any resemblance to any real persons, living or dead is purely coincidental.

All Right Reserved.
No part of this publication may be reproduced or transmitted in any form or by any means, without prior permission in writing of the Author.

Cover artwork by Vikncharlie

Map artwork by A D Green

Edited by M.C. Green, BSc and Graduate Diploma in Arts (English)

For Michelle Green
You are my muse, my sounding board. You make everything better than it was before – Thank you

"You can make anything by writing."
— C.S. Lewis

# Contents

| | |
|---|---|
| Map of the Rivers Kingdom | iii |
| Map of the Nine Kingdoms | v |
| Map of Kingsholme | vii |
| Prologue | 1 |
| Chapter 1: Moving Up In the World | 3 |
| Chapter 2: The Shade Within | 12 |
| Chapter 3: The Marker | 16 |
| Chapter 4: Decisions | 25 |
| Chapter 5: Old Man | 32 |
| Chapter 6: The Loud Water | 43 |
| Chapter 7: Bloodlust | 49 |
| Chapter 8: The Hard Way | 54 |
| Chapter 9: More Questions than Answers | 64 |
| Chapter 10: The Roaring Cave | 70 |
| Chapter 11: Grim Times | 78 |
| Chapter 12: Greentower | 89 |
| Chapter 13: Your Will, Father | 99 |
| Chapter 14: The Essence of Things | 108 |
| Chapter 15: The Ugliest Children | 121 |
| Chapter 16: The Lake to Longstretch | 130 |
| Chapter 17: Reflections On The Road | 139 |
| Chapter 18: Into the Storm | 147 |
| Chapter 19: Red Cloth | 157 |
| Chapter 20: The Good Father | 168 |
| Chapter 21: Burnt Man | 176 |
| Chapter 22: Wraith | 186 |
| Chapter 23: Hunted | 196 |
| Chapter 24: The Defile | 209 |
| Chapter 25: Burning Woman | 222 |
| Chapter 26: He Came, He Whent | 232 |
| Chapter 27: Dead Metal | 243 |
| Chapter 28: Honour Be Damned | 262 |
| Chapter 29: Tae'al | 270 |
| Chapter 30: Ironside and Castigan | 279 |
| Chapter 31: Tankrit Red | 291 |

© 2020 A D Green

| | |
|---|---|
| Chapter 32: The First Rule | 299 |
| Chapter 33: Carvathe Shit | 305 |
| Chapter 34: Barden Vale | 312 |
| Chapter 35: The Holes | 324 |
| Chapter 36: Sparrow, An Observation | 337 |
| Chapter 37: Reunions | 352 |
| Chapter 38: The Kiss | 371 |
| Chapter 39: Winter Road | 382 |
| Chapter 40: A River Divides | 396 |
| Chapter 41: Not All Is As It Seems | 411 |
| Chapter 42: Knowledge Seed | 421 |
| Chapter 43: A Flame Of Hope | 430 |
| Chapter 44: The Easy Path | 434 |
| Chapter 45: Redwing | 444 |
| Chapter 46: A Glass Half Full | 458 |
| Chapter 47: Conclave Of The Cardinals | 463 |
| Chapter 48: The Red Queen | 476 |
| Epilogue | 492 |
| Principal Characters | 494 |
| Ilf dictionary | 501 |

© 2020 A D Green

## Map of the Rivers Kingdom

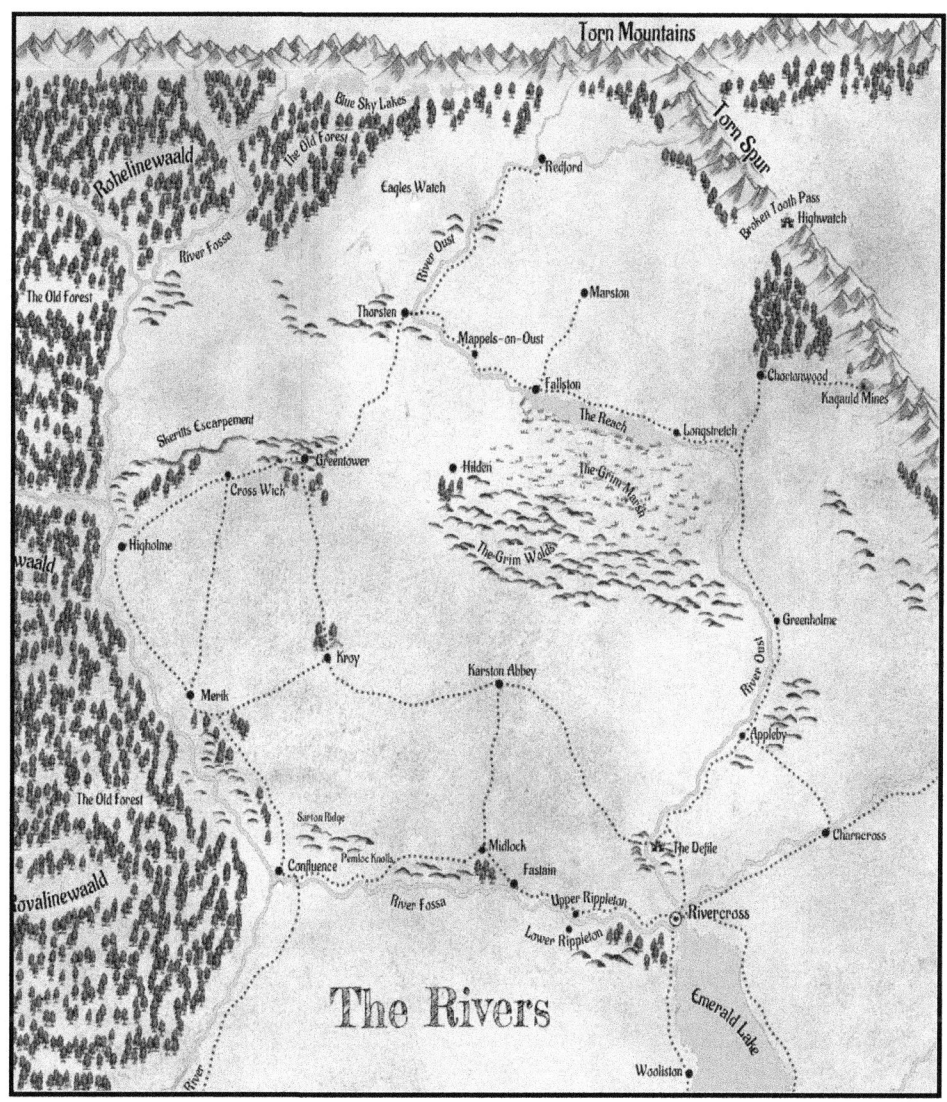

© 2020 A D Green

## Map of the Nine Kingdoms

© 2020 A D Green

## Map of Kingsholme

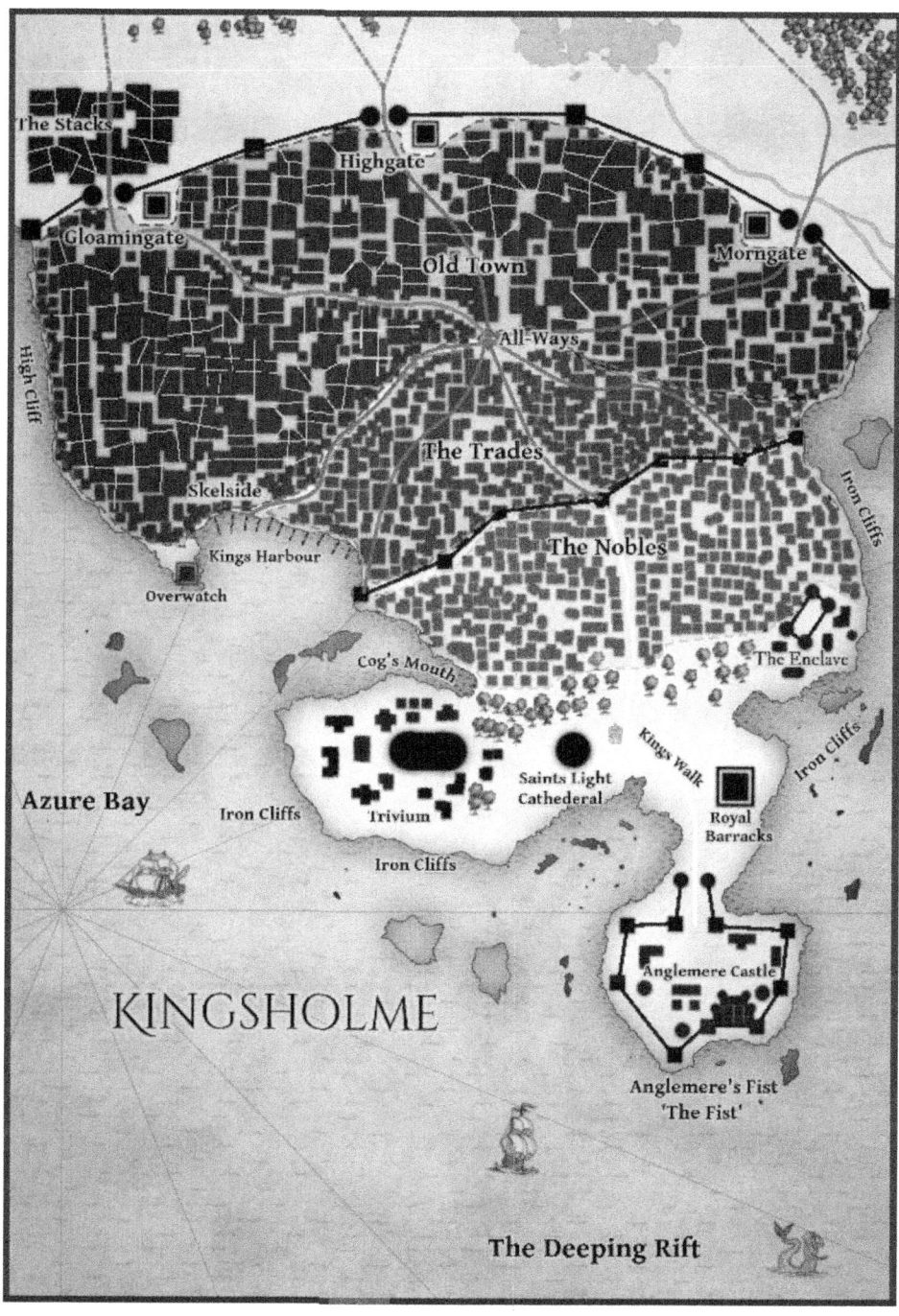

© 2020 A D Green

*When the Forgotten One returns, then shall the rivers run red and the shadows fall. And where the darkness resides there too shall chaos reign and all shall end, lest the light that was lost be found again.*

*Excerpt from the Gnarhlson Prophecies*

© 2020 A D Green

# Prologue

**1006 cycle of the 4th Age**
**1st Cycle of Ankor (The Return - Spring)**
**Karston Abbey, The Rivers**

Her screams broke his heart. High pitched and full of pain, they reverberated around the town square. The boy sobbed, fighting against the bars of his cage, his hands lacerated and bleeding. Tears streaked his face as he watched his mother burn.

She was bound naked to a stake, arms tied high. Blonde hair matted red where she'd beaten her head against the wood. Blood dribbled from mouth to heaving breast as she strained in panic against her bindings. Flames licked her feet. She thrashed, but there was no escape and in moments her lower legs were engulfed in fire.

The boy turned to his father, caged alongside, and saw the horror on his face as he knelt watching in silence. His rage was gone and his eyes dead, the life behind them snuffed out. He was broken and the boy couldn't bear to see it.

He looked back to the pyre and his mother. She was still alive, still shredding his heart with her suffering. Then nothing.

The crackle and spit of the flames filled the space her cries left. The boy wept as he stared at her burning husk and beyond to the hushed ranks of the town folk, illuminated by the fire's light. He saw fear and shock on many faces but none had stepped forward to save her. People he knew just stood, watching. Pity, anger, shame; they wore it all and he hated them for it.

His eyes stole back to his mother, unrecognisable now. He mashed his face against his hands but couldn't escape her. Wood smoke carried the stench of burnt hair and the sickly sweet aroma of charred flesh to assail him. He let go of the bars collapsing to the floor; his shoulders shaking as grief and fear overwhelmed him.

A figure, silhouetted by the firelight, stepped in front of his cage.

"Your mother was a heretic who refused to recant." The priest crouched in the dirt and the boy raised his head, glaring his hatred through tear-filled eyes. "But it's not too late for you. Save yourself. Repent…"

There was a crash and a scream. "Get away from him. Don't you touch him!" The man's arm flailed, grasping for the priest but not quite reaching.

The boy glanced at his Da, could see his own anger and grief mirrored there, and a tiny hope kindled. There was life in him still.

The priest smiled, unmoved. Reaching a hand through the bars he placed it on the boy's head. It seemed almost like a benediction. Then he patted him like a dog.

A madness he couldn't control filled the boy and he lashed out through the bars. The priest moved, but not quickly enough. A nail gouged into the flesh of his cheek narrowly missing his right eye, tearing a bloody strip.

Falling back the priest roared. Then, standing slowly, he took several deep, calming breaths and brushed his cassock down where dirt had soiled it. Blood tracked like a teardrop down his face and he dabbed a hand to his cheek. He looked at the blood on his fingers then glared at the child.

"You'll burn in hellfire boy but not before I have the skin stripped from your back." The words were spoken softly, only the priest's eyes gave lie to the calmness in his voice.

Afraid, the boy crawled to the back of the cage, his small act of defiance spent. Piss soaked his trouser leg.

"A whipping, a night of contemplation for your sins, then tomorrow it will be your turn at the stake." The priest turned to the man, swearing and spitting still.

"You can save him. It's too late for you but you can save your boy." He cocked his head to the side. "No? Nothing to confess?" He pouted his lips in mock sadness. "At least have the courage to admit you are of the Order?"

The man lapsed into silence, nostrils flaring.

The priest shrugged. "I'll ask you once more in the morning. Your answer will determine if your boy accompanies you to the fourth hell or not. Until then make peace with whatever it is you worship, heretic."

Daubing at the blood on his cheek he turned and walked away, back straight, his red cassock seeming alive as the light from the burning pyre played across it.

© 2020 A D Green

## Chapter 1: Moving Up In the World

**1017 cycle of the 4th Age**
**3rd Cycle of Ankor (The Wane - Autumn)**
**Kingsholme, The Holme**

Thieving was a dangerous business at times. Well, all the time really, thought Tomas 'the mouse'.

Leaping from the rooftop, he sailed over the narrow alley. Small and nimble he landed almost noiselessly on a tiled roof, hands gripping the edges of a stone chimney stack for support. He had just entered the Noble's, the southernmost district of the city, that bordered the High Kings castle Anglemere, where the wealthy and well-to-do lived.

As Tomas steadied himself, he waited for any sign his passage may have been detected.

Nothing.

At least nothing out of place, which meant sweet fuck all. The biggest danger, other than making a mistake and falling fifty feet to the cobbles below, was another thief. The city guard didn't patrol rooftops and none of the city's residents would be up here. Just cats, birds, and the occasional thief and a rival would hardly reveal themselves, so the nothing meant nothing.

Tomas spent the next half hour moving over rooftops. He had entered the Nobles' from the point closest to his destination, the Enclave.

The Enclave, as all in the Kingdoms knew, was home to the council of mages. It was where they lived, worked and taught people who exhibited talent. The Enclave itself consisted of four large squat towers, linked by long wide buildings forming a wall of sorts. Tomas had only ever seen it from afar before. The Nobles was not his stomping ground.

To break-in was both a bold and foolish endeavour, for it was said, 'none may pass uninvited into the Enclave'. None, excepting a skilled and talented thief, the Mouse smirked.

There was a tacit, unspoken rule that the Enclave was off-limits to his kind. So this job held an extra degree of risk. Should he be caught it would mean his death.

© 2020 A D Green

Still, he'd been commissioned for this by the Syndicate, the largest of the city's crime gangs. Chosen, in person no less, by the legendary, Bortillo Targus. So really, he had no choice in the matter. You didn't say no to Bortillo and expect to see the next dawn. Besides, it was his ticket off the streets, if he could pull it off. Tomas felt a certain pride that he'd been chosen; that despite his youth, word of his thieving skills had reached Bortillo.

The roof Tomas perched on lay directly opposite the Enclave. He stood where instructed, in front of the long building abutting the south tower, two chimney stacks to its left. He surveyed his surroundings. He was twenty feet away and slightly below the Enclave roof he faced. It was not a jump he could make.

Shrugging his pack from his shoulders, Tomas took out a small grapple and rope from within. The rope was woven of gossark fibre, strong and light. It was the finest quality and worth a princely sum. He'd lifted it from a rope-maker's shop the previous night and spent most of the day practising with his grapple to get the weight and feel of it.

Tomas cinched the ropes loose end around a brick embrasure near where he stood before taking the grapple and twisting it in a long loop around his head, slowly building momentum. It whistled as he spun it, the sound seeming loud in the still night, but Tomas was unconcerned; there would be no one to hear it up here. He released and watched the grapple as it was swallowed by the dark.

It missed the far chimney breast, flying past and over the crest of the roof before landing with an ominously loud clatter. Tomas crouched low into the shadows; it wasn't an ideal night for burgling, the clouds were too few and two of the tri moons were out, casting a pale light. He waited, unmoving for ten minutes. It was a patience he'd taught himself. Any thief needed it if they expected to live long and with all their limbs still attached.

Tomas detected no change to the sounds of the night, certainly no alarm or magical discharge as the grapple breached the Enclave's boundary. So much for those rumours.

Slowly, Tomas drew in the slack on the rope until the weight of the grapple was felt on the other end. Hitting the chimney would have been bad luck. He'd aimed high to make sure of clearing it. Tomas had always been lucky but Chancy the beggar told him once, 'luck is a fickle lady, never trust her' and he'd taken the advice to heart.

The grapple scraped back up the tiles on the far side of the roof until its hooks caught on the stone block that held the roof supports and joists in place. It was an old design from ancient times; a more modern roof crest would have held his grapple but maybe not his weight when he crossed. Luck, he smiled.

Leaning his full weight on the line, Tomas pulled the rope taut, feeling the grapple bite hard into the stone. Deftly, he re-tied his end around the embrasure, looping it over so that it held fast. As weight was applied the rope loop would only tighten its grip. Satisfied, he tested the line, it was firm.

Shrugging his pack back on, Tomas climbed out along its length. The rope was more than strong enough to support his weight but even so, it felt too slim in his hands.

Veins pumping with nervous energy he shimmied out over the yawning gap, the drop it promised pulling at him insistently. Tomas wasted no more thought on it. Now wasn't a time for thinking, now was a time for doing. Crossing the twenty-foot canyon between the buildings, Tomas pulled easily hand over hand, legs crossed over the rope for support.

Safe on the Enclave rooftop, Tomas took a moment and a few deep breaths. He felt nothing, no magic, no sixth sense saying he was discovered.

Moving quickly to the designated chimney stack, he smelt the waft of old smoke in its flue. Whatever fire had been lit had died out earlier in the night. Tomas took a second gossark rope out of his pack, this one weighted at one end. He lowered the weight down the chimney, slowly, hand over hand, until he felt it settle then pulled up an arm's length before tying the rope off. Hopefully, that should clear any fireplace, he thought.

Taking a deep breath, Tomas climbed into the chimney and braced his feet and back against the internal breastwork. It was a tight fit but he was small for his age and slender. Carefully, he lowered himself down into its dark maw.

Twelve hands of rope he'd measured out, so Tomas knew how far to descend. It took him five minutes of inching and edging his way down, through cobwebs and soot-blackened stone. Unavoidable bits of detritus broke loose pattering down the chimney, preceding him. Each time it happened, he grimaced, hoping no one was in the room below to hear and see it.

Approaching the mantle, Tomas met his first real obstacle. Two metal bars, rusted and pitted black from the fire, blocked his passage. Standing on the near bar he bounced on it a few times, before taking the weight off his aching back and arms. Fumbling his pack off, awkward in the tight space of the chimney, he pulled a small vial from a pouch. Crouching, he un-stoppered the vial and dribbled its contents over both ends of the far-side bar and immediately an acrid smell wafted up to him. He waited.

The sound of a door opening made its way up the chimney. Tomas held his breath, unmoving, as a light showed through the fireplace below, followed by voices and the door slamming shut.

"Taran won't go for it. He gave you a year and the year is done and you've made no progress, Korban."

"How can you say that, Harrick? I've made such progress. I've unlocked two artefacts, two vessels and both contain demons." Korban stressed. "I understand the nature of the vessels and how they work."

"Luck! Trial and much error for the most part, Taran is right. You play with things not fully understood. Until you can decipher the texts you're no closer to opening a pathway, or understanding how to call forth a demon, let alone control one." Harrick paused, then, "What's that smell?"

Tomas's heart flipped as footsteps grew louder. Someone moved across the room drawing closer.

"What have you been up to?" It was the one called Korban and he stood right next to the fireplace. Tomas almost launched himself back up the chimney thinking he'd been discovered but instinct held him in place. He breathed slowly, calming his nerves. The acrid stench as the acid burnt through the iron bar was strong. This didn't bode well. Surely the mage would discover its source.

"Well demon, answer me," Korban snapped.

"Why? Your question's so banal, it tires me so just listening to it," said a voice. It was soft and sounded bored to Tomas.

"What is that stench and why do you make it? Answer me or shall I banish you back inside your vessel?" Korban said.

"If it spares me from listening to your whining voice I would count it a favourable result. Honestly, how you ever got to manipulate tae'al I'll never know. By rights you should have self-combusted by now," the voice replied.

"Schniétrakor," Korban muttered, followed by silence.

"I hate that one. Really think you'd do better with the big," Harrick offered. "What do you think it was doing and how did it make that stench?"

"I don't know. Smells like brimstone doesn't it?" Korban mused. "In any event, we need some leverage against them. They are the key to unlocking these manuscripts I am sure of it. Still, it's late; let's try again on the morrow."

"With the big?" Harrick asked.

"No, the little one. It's cunning, I know, but I sense it hides a weakness of character. It's more self-serving. That gives me something to work with."

Tomas listened as the two men moved across the room. The door opened then closed, a key turned in the lock, then footsteps retreated, fading into silence. Tomas was gifted, he knew when a room was empty and this one was but he waited. The acid still had its job to do in any case.

Once the acrid burning smell started to dissipate, Tomas judged it time and kicked his foot at one end of the iron bar. Metal flaked off in a cloud as the end snapped clean off.

Bending low, Tomas grabbed the bar near the break and straining, bent it up and away. More debris broke free and there was a groan as the weakened bar moved but didn't snap. Holding the rope, Tomas lowered himself, squeezing through the gap he'd created. Clearing the mantle, he placed his feet on the edges of the fire grate, it needed cleaning out and chances were someone would come to do it before sunrise but he didn't expect them in the dead of night, he should have plenty of time.

Tomas ducked beneath the fire lintel and into the room. A sconce burned on the wall casting a weak light. Eyes roving, he surveyed his surroundings with practised ease. It was not quite what he expected for the Enclave. It looked almost drab in its ordinariness.

There were bookcases and several tables and chairs but that was it. At first glance, there was nothing magical looking at all. The largest table was near the fireplace and was too tall to sit at. There was an assortment of glass vials and containers on it and a thick, leather-bound book.

The book drew Tomas's eye, he liked books. He'd never written, didn't rightly know if he could or not but he could read. He wasn't sure how; for damn sure no one had ever taught him. It wasn't like he'd a Ma or Da to teach him.

Lifting the volume from the table, Tomas read the title. It was written in a strange script and it took him a moment to work it out, 'Sházáik Douné Táak, by Ellis Von Baxtuz'.

"The Book of Demons." He translated out loud. Sounds interesting, he placed it in his backpack almost without thought before turning his attention to the table.

On closer inspection, it had an intricate pattern drawn upon it in large swirls and curves. The pattern was studded throughout with small iron rivets and the whole design itself was ringed by an iron circle, beaten and pressed into the wood.

To Tomas, it looked magical and therefore ominous. At the centre of the pattern was an iron-bound wooden box. A lot of iron going on here, Tomas thought.

Bortillo had told him what to look for, a bracer and a ring, and that they would be in this room this night. Tomas looked at the box, knowing that what he was sent for lay within. He surveyed the container for several minutes but could discern no traps guarding it. Even so, he grabbed a poker iron from the fireplace and gently nudged the box until it lay outside the pattern. Nothing happened.

Encouraged, Tomas lifted the box and examined it. It wouldn't open and there was no latch or keyhole to pick. It was solid and heavy and had been inscribed in a strange script. Squinting he read the swirls and scratchings deciphering them in his head.

"Open here." He muttered. A small circle punctuated the strange writing. It didn't belong. Pressing his finger against it, Tomas repeated the words and tried the lid, which opened easily at his touch. He grinned, pleased with himself. Looking inside, a bracer and ring rested on a felt bed.

This is too easy, Tomas thought with a grin.

The box holding the trinkets was too bulky to comfortably fit inside his small pack, not unless he removed the book he'd lifted.

© 2020 A D Green

Reaching out, Tomas picked up the bracer. It was wide, maybe three fingers deep but it looked small, too small for a man to slip over his hand, was it a child's? It was delicate to, the metal thin and of a type unknown to him. It was soft, too soft for the rigours of his pack.

He'd seen twelve summers, so was hardly a child, but Tomas was small for his age. Scrunching his hand tight he managed to squeeze the bracer over it and slip it onto his lower forearm. It looks quite good, he thought, holding it up to the dull light.

He heard something and Tomas twisted his head. Distant footsteps, low voices growing louder.

Snatching the ring up, Tomas twisted it without thought onto his left index finger. Thinking quickly, he gathered a small charred piece of wood that had escaped the fire and placed it inside the box before shutting the lid and laying it back inside the centre of the pattern.

The footsteps stopped outside the door. A key turned in the lock and the door swung open.

* * *

Harrick entered and surveyed the room. Satisfied it was empty, he moved to the tall table and the wooden box at its centre. He lifted it gently and turning, handed it to the man who'd followed him in.

"The trinkets are inside, Taran. Korban will not be happy when he finds I have turned them over to you," Harrick said.

"He can take it up with me. How do you open the box?" Taran asked.

"Don't know. Korban doesn't trust anyone, never showed me how it opened. But I saw him place the ring inside with the bracer, not twenty minutes past," Harrick said.

Taran shook the box, gave a dissatisfied grunt, then turned and strode from the room. Harrick followed in his wake, stopping briefly to lock the door behind him.

* * *

© 2020 A D Green

Tomas blessed his luck and quick thinking. He was stood once more inside the chimney flue, resting on the lone iron bar. Smiling at his good fortune and the relative ease of the job, he reached up, grabbed the rope and began inching his way up and out to freedom. Bortillo would be indebted to him for this he mused, he was definitely moving up in the world.

Back on the rooftop, Tomas expertly pulled up the gossark rope. Untying it, he packed it away, squeezing it around the book he'd stolen. Slinging his pack over his shoulders and cinching it tight, he climbed out onto the aerial tightrope that stretched still over the chasm between the Enclave and the Nobles.

"Beware."

Tomas startled, almost losing his grip. He saved himself in a mad panic, scrambling to secure his hold. The yawning drop below was into darkness but Tomas knew it was a long fall onto hard cobbles. It would mean almost certain death. Tomas stilled himself. Hanging upside down, he took a moment and several calming breaths to slow his racing heart.

The voice had come unbidden, like a ghost of wind in his ear but there was no one there. He was suspended halfway between buildings, how could there be. A sudden thought struck him. Was it a magical warning he'd triggered inadvertently? His young mind flipped through the possibilities. It didn't make sense, why would he trigger it on the way out but not on the way in.

*"You plan on hanging here much longer? Only that man waiting for you doesn't look the patient type,"* the ghost whispered from just past his right shoulder.

A shiver of fear tickled his spine. "Who are you?" he hissed. "What are you talking about?"

The ghost's words had seeped into him though and Tomas was already scanning the dark of the far roof. It was a black mass, still and silent. There, he locked onto a darker shade of black, unmoving in the shadows. Tomas knew it was not part of the building.

*"Answers later, if you live. I suggest you head back the way you came."*

Tomas hadn't lived to twelve by being indecisive. Whether the voice told him true or not, he didn't know, but it gave warning and the dark shade on the roof was definitely not good news. He started to inch his way back to the Enclave roof.

© 2020 A D Green

Watching for it, Tomas saw the black shade detach and move, crouching ominously at the edge of the roof.

"You've sharp eyes to spot me little Mouse. But come, there's nowhere for you to go." The voice was soft yet foreboding. "Come lad, or better yet throw me the pack."

"Bortillo?" Tomas hissed. Relief momentarily washed through him before his young brain kicked in.

*"He means you murder,"* The ghost whispered, affirming his own suspicions.

Fear rinsing his blood, Tomas inched backwards away from the king of thieves.

"Ah lad, tis a shame I had to use you like this." Bortillo chuckled. "Alas, the mages will be hunting for a thief and bathed in their magic as you are I'll have to give 'em one."

There was a snick and the rope parted with a snap. Tomas held on but there was no tension on the line and he was suddenly flailing as he plunged into the black sea below.

Bortillo stood and, leaning out over the roof edge, peered into the inky depths. The thud of the boy's body as it impacted the ground was short and dull followed by a sullen crump. He grimaced, he'd have to get down there quick to recover his commission before the city guard happened by.

It was regrettable cutting the boy loose, but necessary. He could hardly pursue him onto the Enclave roof; that would have sealed his own fate. Still, he mused, I must be losing my touch for the boy to have spotted me like that, and hanging upside down from a rope no less.

Turning, Bortillo climbed back up the roof with a sense of urgency. The way down was arduous and it had been entirely too long since he'd last used the thieves' highway, he'd have to hurry.

## Chapter 2: The Shade Within

**Marston, The Rivers**

The town of Marston was three days ride southeast of Redford and two north of Fallston. A hundred years ago it had been little more than a village when it was awarded to Sir Merrill Trant, for services to the High Lord in a war forgotten by most.

The intervening century had seen Marston grow and prosper. It was walled, like most border towns were, but located as it was behind Thorsten and Redford, and given there had been no major conflict in over a hundred years its now Lord, John Trant and his forebears, saw little reason in maintaining them. Its castle too was more a fortified manor house than a true castle and was situated in a plush estate surrounded by low stone walls. It was ideal for entertaining, something Lord John was renowned for.

Word of an urak incursion started drifting in several days after the disaster at Redford. Two days later missives arrived from Lord Richard Bouchemeax, the Black Crow, Lord of Thorsten, confirming Redford's fall. Marston's people started evacuating that same day.

Lord John expected no help. The Black Crow's brother, William and his whole family had perished at Redford, and Lord Richard would look to Thorsten and his own people first. So he prepared, knowing at least what was coming. Lord John had assembled five hundred men at arms to join High Lord Twyford for his spring campaign and held another two hundred seasoned guardsmen in reserve. It wasn't enough. Not by a long way.

The urak came out of the rain misted morning a day later. To Lord John, they appeared a vast, seething horde of red-painted savages in numbers beyond count. And they were savage. The town fell in less than two hours. Many died but those that did not were bound and herded to the north and east.

*  *  *

It had been an easy victory. Krol was both pleased and disgusted by the battle if he could call it that. The dark shade that lay within him, that touch of the Morhudrim, was satiated by the carnage. But it left Krol feeling hollow, disgruntled at the fight and the lack of challenge. It was beneath them.

Krol supped from a blackened skull, newly taken that day, purportedly the local lord's. It had been hacked from his head and rendered down before being seared in flame to serve as a gourd. Hard nuggets of flesh still clung to it in places. Krol cared not as he gave thought to his purpose.

He was one of the Shackled. Taken over ten years past, Krol possessed a part of the all-consuming and pervasive essence of a Morhudrim. He'd learnt though that the shade's control over him wasn't absolute. The fact his mission lay further east was proof of that. He, Krol, had ordered the attack on Marston and further south to the Reach, not the Morhudrim. The Dark One used him as needed, its compulsions couldn't be ignored, but Krol found they could be worked around.

As well, when the Morhudrim was not directly controlling him, Krol found that its shade could be influenced. The shade was driven by an insatiable hunger. It fed on raw emotion, primarily fear. And, like an urak who took too much knorcha weed and craved it to the point of dishonour, so too did the shade crave. Krol fed it plenty and in doing so gained some semblance of control, at least when the Morhudrim let him be. The Dark One's compulsion drove him east and east he was going - just not directly.

His adversary Mar-Dur, warchief of the White Hand, was to the west. Taking these easy victories from Mar-Dur would cause him trouble and much loss of face. Enough that Mar-Dur could face a leadership challenge. Win or lose a challenge would leave the White Hand weaker. It wasn't much but it was the best he could manage, for now. He imagined Mar-Dur's anger when he found out and it made him smile. The shade within suckled.

In the past, Krol would have taken pleasure in what he'd achieved. He had accomplished much. Instead, his deeds sat like bitter seeds in his stomach. How could they not? These were not his actions alone. Everything he did now was tainted by the Morhudrim.

Sharp lancing pain stabbed through Krol's head. Lord John's skull rolled out of his fist and onto the ground, cracking and spilling its bloody contents. Krol dropped to his knees, nauseous, his balance gone.

The Morhudrim's presence was paramount within him and it was angered. He could feel it, or rather the lack of it. That part of his shade's essence that he passed to the manling, was gone, severed. The pain was as if a finger had been ripped from his hand, only it was not his pain he felt but the Morhudrim's.

Krol bared his teeth, pleased. That the Dark One could feel pain meant something. Holding that thought, Krol shielded it, afraid suddenly of what the Morhudrim would subject him to if it read his mind. If it fed on his emotion, would it wonder at the taste of pleasure it found?

<He is lost. He has failed me,> Came the sibilant hiss in his mind. The shade writhed, agitated. Krol's eyes clouded over until they roiled like black storm clouds. The Morhudrim's anger was palpable and Krol's fear could not be denied. He shook uncontrollably with it and was shamed at his weakness.

<You are south of where you should be.> Fresh pain, this time his own. His nerves felt on fire as if his body burned. Rigid, back-arching, Krol screamed and the shade within fed. Then, blessed relief, as the pain abated.

<Go, find who did this.> An image of a town appeared in his mind. It sat on the edge of a lake beneath a waterfall. The compulsion was strong. He felt it dragging on his mind and body. Urgent, insistent, it directed him south and west.

Krol lifted himself off the ground. The bloody contents of his drink were vomited down his front but Krol had no memory of it. Energy infused his body. He felt invincible. Unbidden, his hand rose to his face and wiped the blood and sick from his mouth. He smiled and it was grim.

"Chief, you okay?" asked Nartak, first of his Hurak-hin. He stood uncertainly to Krol's side. His chief often had dark fits, each bad but this past year they seemed to increase in intensity and frequency. It was a weakness, but not one any saw fit to challenge. The fits made Krol unpredictable and violent, at least more so than usual. Nartak felt a deep discomfort. He'd only been first a few days. A huge honour for him and his tribe but he wished it had fallen to another. There was something badly wrong with his warchief.

Krol turned slowly to face Nartak before exploding into him. His hand swept Nartak's spear aside and stepping in close he smashed his forehead into Nartak's mouth.

Blood erupted and Nartak dropped back, stumbling to his knees with a cry of pain. His hand reached for his knife but it never cleared his belt as with a crunch, Krol's fist punched into his throat. Nartak fell, hands grasping, knife forgotten. His pain a distant agony, as suddenly he was gasping for breath.

Krol walked away, leaving his first gaping like a landed fish, and turned to the Hurak-hin arrayed before him. The Dark One left him then, leaving behind only a lingering sense of amusement. It left Krol disoriented. Shaking his head, he looked back to where Nartak lay dying. It was a dishonourable end, and one not deserved. His anger roiled inside and the shade fed.

"Tar-Tukh, I name you first again." Krol motioned to his oldest of friends. "See you do not dishonour me as Nartak did."

Tar-Tukh stepped forward, a slight incline of his head his only acknowledgement.

Hurak-hin bonded like brothers. Krol could feel his friend seething, understood it, but he was warchief of the Blood Skull. The best he could do for Tar-Tukh was to ignore the harshness in his eyes and the tension in his body.

"Gather the tribes, we head south for the Reach," Krol ordered.

© 2020 A D Green

## Chapter 3: The Marker

**Kingsholme, The Holme**

"Ren," Edward Blackstar waved the Order ambassador into his chambers.

"Your majesty." Renix bowed as the Kingsguard left, banging the door closed behind him.

Edward smiled warmly. "You should come more often. I've missed your council."

Renix's eyes creased, "You're difficult to reach these days. The Lord Chamberlain is tenacious of your time."

Edward chuckled. "Ai, my lady Queen makes a similar complaint. Come sit; take some wine before Lord Malcolm bothers me with more business."

"Yes majesty," then at the high king's furrowed brow, "Edward. Trying times but you've not lost your humour I see."

"Ai, trying times and a hundred people quick to tell me what I should be doing," Edward complained. "If I wanted their advice I would ask for it."

Lifting a jug he poured wine into a silver goblet, one of a matching pair, and slide it across the table.

"Trouble has ever been food for the ambitious," Renix replied.

He sat, casting a critical eye over the High King. The hair was thinning and shot through with grey. It would lose the last of its black lustre in the next year, two at the most. The lines in his face were deeper and there were more of them than Renix remembered and the energy that usually suffused him seemed subdued.

"You look… worn, still think you're up to it?" Renix challenged his face deadpan.

"Hah!" Edward laughed, remembering the first time Renix had asked him that question. He shook his head, had it really been thirty years gone.

"Show me someone who's up for ruling nine fractious kingdoms and I'll show you a liar."

"True enough," Renix said, "though you've been good and fair. You can ask no more of a king than that."

"Ah, but they do. It's never enough. You've been around longer than I to know it."

Whilst they bantered, Renix sipped his wine. A robust red from Olme, it was really very palatable.

"Over thirty years we've been friends and you've aged not a day," Edward said. "When I look in the mirror I see what you see; a tired old man who's losing his hair." He tapped his skull with his fingers. "But it doesn't reconcile with the man I am in here. So yes, I'm up to it, gods be damned."

The door to the chambers burst open and a young man strutted in unannounced.

"I must speak with you," he said. He came to a halt on seeing Renix.

"I'm sorry father, I had no idea you were entertaining."

"Now you do," Edward drawled. "Well Herald, if it's so urgent it can't wait till the morrow, out with it."

"Mattie's killed my stallion," Herald said, then at his father's bemused expression. "You know. The one you and my step-mother got me for my name day last year, King's Champion."

Renix saw the consternation on Edward's face but had little sympathy; this was of his own making. His friend doted on Herald as a child. Now seventeen, spoilt and indulged beyond measure, he was flawed; encompassed by the foppery of his elaborately embroidered tunic and rich hose.

A knock and the door opened again, this time by a Kingsguard.

"Sire, Princess Matrice." He announced.

The Princess entered. Two years younger than her brother she was in stark contrast. Her long black hair was tied back in an elegant weave but wisps had managed to escape its confines giving her a playful air, accentuated by her clothing. She wore no dress to match Herald's finery. Instead, she was clad in riding breeches, leather boots and padded tunic; all expensively made but functional rather than fashionable.

"Sorry to intrude, father." Her voice was soft and lilting. "But you can't listen to Herald's skewed accusations. You know how prone to melodrama he is."

"I shall wait outside your majesty." Renix rose to leave.

"Sit, sit." Edward signalled and Renix sank back down. "You're my guest and they the interlopers. Now let us see what this is about, eh!" He turned to his son waiting for an explanation.

"Mattie had Gart Vannen kill King's Champion. She's jealous of me," Herald shouted, looking vehemently at his sister. "She wanted him for herself. Took him without my leave and now he is murdered. Sir Elwin is set to feed him to the hounds," Herald said, his face full of outrage.

Edward held a hand up, forestalling the next tirade. He turned to his daughter. "What have you to say?"

"It's Herald's fault the horse is dead," Matrice said.

"You lying bitch," Herald roared.

"Silence!" Edward said, his voice rising. "Apologise, Herald. I will not stand for your language or lack of self-control. Now contain yourself; you're the crown prince and she is your sister."

"I will not," Herald rasped back.

"It's alright, father. He's upset and rightly so," Matrice said.

Edward's gaze settled back on his daughter. "Then explain and be quick. And you," he snapped at Herald, "interrupt again and I'll throw you out. Understand?"

Herald's jaw clenched.

"King's Champion has sat in the stables all year. Herald commanded no one but he was to ride him. Given my brother never rides anywhere, excepting in a carriage, King's Champion lost conditioning. Herald likes to boast about his stallion like some trophy but never rides him. It's not fair on the horse. So I took him out," Matrice said.

"I had already gathered that much from your attire." Edward said, "Now what happened?"

"He was in worse condition than I thought."

"That is not what was asked," Edward glared.

Renix saw a flare of anger cross the princess's face. But it was gone almost as soon as it appeared. She shrugged.

"King's Champion panicked. He wasn't used to being ridden. He stumbled, I fell. The horse injured himself bolting through the streets. By the time Sir Vannen and I found him, King's Champion had sustained several wounds; the worst was a break to his leg. There was no choice but to put him down. Sir Elwin arranged his recovery when I explained. Feeding him to the hounds is just simple economics."

"Simple economics," Herald blustered. "And when was the last time you fell from a horse?"

"Okay, I've heard enough. Out, both of you," Edward commanded, rising from his chair.

"But father…" Herald protested.

"I'll speak with Sir Elwin in the morning and sort this out then. Now out."

Matrice gave a curtsy to her father. She spared Renix a curious look that lingered overlong, before turning and leaving.

Seeing the stern expression on his father's face, Herald gave an exaggerated sigh. He bowed, ignored Renix altogether then stomped out.

After the door had closed, Edward sank back into his seat. "Ruler of Nine Kingdoms yet I can't manage my own children. I should've listened to you years ago and shipped the boy out to Atticus for his schooling. I'm afraid Margot and I have spoilt him."

"It's not too late to send him. Matrice seems capable at least," Renix said.

"Would it were the other way round," Edward replied. "Come, let's change the subject. My children are not the reason I called for you."

"No indeed. I presumed from your missive it was to discuss the urak invasion of the Rivers?" Renix said. Then, upon seeing Edwards guarded look. "Though, maybe my presumption was presumptuous?"

Edward smiled. "I'd like your advice in that regard, of course. The Order's view on matters is valued."

Renix knew Edward well enough to know he prevaricated. He was worried about something.

"May I?" Renix circled his hands. Then at Edward's nod of assent, his eyes glazed over.

Edward felt his ears pop and the faintest shimmer of air brush against his skin, so light and quick he wasn't sure he'd felt it at all.

"We may talk freely, but Edward this is the first I have deployed my art in your chambers?"

"Eyes and ears are everywhere and not all belong to me," Edward confessed. "Now to business. Almost half the Rivers is lost to the urak, though Rivercross remains untouched. This morning a bird arrived from High Lord Janis. Urak have been sighted approaching Highwatch. They are pushing east and seek to cross the Broken Tooth into Norderland."

Renix looked grim at the news. "Tannon Crick is the Order Knight there and is held in high regard. Last he reported Norderland was mobilising. Highwatch is highly defensible."

"Bah, it's little more than a watchtower," Edward said, waving his hand dismissively. "Janis is a stubborn headed fool, does things his way, always has. Norderland will pay the price for his laxity."

Renix stroked a hand over his neatly manicured beard and shook his head. "No Edward. He's no fool, obstinate yes, but no fool. Crick reports the High Lord is sending a strong contingent to reinforce Highwatch. If they cannot hold it, if it is lost… it bodes ill. It will open up Norderland and the land, all the way to Deepwater."

"Deepwater is a long way off…" Edward paused, "I see." His eyes hardened.

"Yes, Deepwater damn you but not just for the reasons you're thinking. It is a distance away but, if they make it that far, it secures their flank."

"Ai, and opens the crossing to Tankrit Isle as well," Edward snapped. "After all these years, are you really no better than these sycophants in court?"

Renix pushed his goblet away and stood, leaning over the table. "Two urak clans are involved, the White Hand and the Blood skull. That we know of. The last time two clans invaded, the entire North was lost from Westlands to Eosland. So yes, I am concerned for the North but also for my own people."

"That was four, five hundred years ago if I remember my history lessons. We defeated them then and will do so again." Edward replied.

Renix didn't raise his voice, but his tone was clear. "You've learnt your histories poorly, majesty but at least you recall your lessons. Your people do not. Your people recall what the harvest was like last year. Was business good, did they have work and could they put food on the table?"

"They know nothing of urak, only the tales the bards tell and then only the glory of dead heroes. Back then it took forty years and four different High Kings before the urak were pushed back over the Torns. Don't make the same mistakes as your forebears."

Edward smacked his hand on the tabletop rattling the wine jug and goblets.

"You dare lecture me. Just… sit your ass back down." Spit flecked his lip. Gritting his teeth, Edward waited while his friend was seated, allowing his temper to cool. It had been entirely too long since someone had spoken so to him. Renix though appeared unflustered and he admired him for it. Wasn't so long ago it seemed he held the same self-control and he wondered briefly where it had gone.

Raising his cup he took a slow sip of wine and savoured it, feeling his blood calm.

"What mistakes am I about to make?" Edward asked.

"Who can say?" Renix said, a ghost of a smile gracing his face. "But you need to take control, personally. Do not tackle this piecemeal. Call a congress. Summon the High Lords and Ladies of the Nine Kingdoms or at least those who can come. Demand the High Cardinals of the Trinity and the Magus Supreme attend. This urak invasion is a threat to the whole of the Kingdoms. If it's not met in unity you will fall in singularity."

"The council of mages have already sent a contingent of twenty to Rivercross. They should be in Cumbrenan by now. I also met with the High Cardinal of Kildare. Five thousand of their Faith Militant have been ordered to Rivercross under Archbishop Whent. The other kingdoms are mobilising as we speak."

"Too abstract and not enough," Renix said. "The council sent a party of twenty but only five are full magus. Another five apprentices, the rest guards or servants. It's too little to have any real effect. As for the Red Priests, they play their own tune and follow their own council. I'm sorry Edward, but you need to get a grip on this. Call a congress, seize the initiative rather than letting others decide what they will or won't do. This moment, this time in history will be your legacy."

Edward supped his wine while he considered. Though Renix gave sound advice, his observations were a little too close to the bone. Had he lost his edge? A few years ago, his friend would not have needed to tell him these truths.

"Very well; missives will be sent tonight by bird and messenger." He paused, calculating distances and dates. "I will call an assembly for Winter's Fall. It will take that long for all to reach here. You will attend for the Order. In the meantime, I will dispatch what aid I can to Norderland and the Rivers."

"I'll consult with Keeper. The Order can be of great help. Though, we should acknowledge it may also prove problematic." Renix frowned before continuing.

"The Order is not held in high esteem as you know, thanks in large part to the Trinity. Some, like the Rivers, have rescinded the Order Accords that were signed and sworn and I've word this morning that High Lady Arisa Montreau of Cumbrenan has followed. It is also rumoured High Lord Costa Ostenbow of Branikshire will do the same."

"So I hear. Would that I could command them differently, but as you know, the Order Accords predate the Nine Kingdoms. Each signed and swore an oath. I cannot change that. Your point though brings me to mine and the reason I called for you."

Renix took a quaff of wine but the taste lay forgotten on his tongue.

"The Church of Kildare holds its conclave at Winter's Fall. My sources say they'll sign a charter, formalising and calling on the faithful to reject the Order and rescind the Accords altogether," Edward said. "I also have a report that the Council of Mages has lost something. My agent knows not what, but that you have their interest. What can you tell me?"

"Your agents are well placed in both regards. Though it comes as no surprise," Renix replied. "The Red Priests have openly opposed the Order for a ten year or more though it was not always so. As for the Council, our relationship has always been fractious."

Edward scowled. "The Trinity's influence grows, Ren; especially the Red Church. A lot of money has been spent, red money. Worship of the old gods is no longer tolerated. Kildare's truth is an unforgiving one these days."

Nothing Edward said was new to him. The king was leading to something. "What else?" Renix asked.

"There's a contract out on you, a death mark for a hundred gilders against your name."

"I see." It was a huge sum, eye-watering. A single gilder was a hundred gold marks. It was more money than a commoner could earn in a hundred lifetimes. Surely only the church or council could lay such a marker. Renix was aware that Edward scrutinised him for a reaction. Intrigue warred with concern on his friend's face despite his best efforts otherwise.

No, the Red Church or Council might be likeliest but the list was by no means a short one. Though Renix failed to see any immediate connection, half the great Lords in the Kingdoms could get thrown into the possible mix. High King included or at least the Blackstars.

"Why?" Edward asked, his intrigue winning out over his patience.

"Without knowing who placed the marker everything is conjecture," Renix said, with a shrug of his shoulders. He waited but the High King did not answer. After a brief moment, he nodded acceptance. Edward had nothing else to offer.

"Thank you for your warning." Renix drained the last of the wine in his goblet then stood.

"I will look further into this my friend," Edward assured him. "It may take some time. In the meantime, let me assign Kingsguard to protect you."

"Thank you but there is no need, majesty. The Order protects its own."

"It's outrageous. I will get to the bottom of it," Edward promised. He stood abruptly, chair scraping loudly against the stone. Reaching across, he laid a hand on his friend's shoulder. He looked as if to say more but muttered instead. "Take care, Ren."

"You've bigger concerns than my welfare." Renix patted Edward's hand where it lay; uncomfortable with the emotion he felt when he did so. It felt like a final goodbye.

Renix closed his eyes and carved a pattern in the air with his fingers. Nodding once to his friend he left.

## Chapter 4: Decisions

**North of Fallston, The Rivers**

There was a distortion in the flow, an abscess in the swirling colours of life, Hiro observed to himself. The event had happened a day or two past, he judged. A lot of energy had been discharged, eddying and rippling in the aether but it should have dissipated reasonably quickly, so the distortion was out of place. With sudden clarity, Hiro realised it was an absence of aether rather than a distortion, a knuckle of death in the bright kaleidoscope of life.

Hiro snapped back, his senses returning to the mundane world. Shapes emerged, the curved lines of leaf and plant, river and road. Smells percolated, of horse and grass, seed and flower. He felt the wind kiss his skin and ruffle his hair and the weight of his seat upon the saddle. Sound; of bird song and the swish of the tall grass in the breeze, even the distant rush of water as the river flowed. The change was abrupt, dramatic, and all in the space of a moment. Hiro, as ever, found it both exhilarating and disappointing, as for a split instant the two states meshed, one overlaying the other.

Blinking his eyes, Hiro looked at what had piqued his interest to begin with. The meadow grass lay bent and broken, leaving a beaten track from roadside to river; towards the knuckle of death. Hiro followed the trail to its end before dismounting and leaving his horse to graze in the long grass.

Here at the riverbank, Hiro saw that the grass had been flattened in many places and a fresh mound of earth had been raised, the sods still wet and pale in the sun. He walked the outside of the flattened area, eyes sharp, assessing. Most immediate and obvious was a large patch of wizened and blackened grass and bush. Someone had drawn aether and excessively. A black stalk of meadow grass crumbled in his fingers, turning to dust at his contact.

This doesn't feel right, Hiro thought. This wasn't like the power Keeper described sensing. This was darker, more familiar. It brought memories rushing back. Black memories, from a distant past that sat, still, like splinters in his mind. Time had not faded their touch. Hiro could recall them as if he'd stood witness just yesterday. Memories of whole swathes of land as far as the eye could see, withered and dead just like this small patch. Ice lanced through his veins, there was no doubt. A Taken had been here.

© 2020 A D Green

Hiro was old and had done much in his life, studied many things, and even mastered a few. The Chezuan Nomadi had taught him to track and read the ground but the art didn't come naturally to him. So it was that he spent much time huddled, inspecting the scene. He didn't have the skill with which to draw definitive conclusions but a battle had taken place that much was clear. Four, maybe five against one as he read things, the one being the Taken.

A line of singed grass led into the meadow where someone had lain or fallen in the long stalks and too he found a rust-brown patch on the ground by the river's edge. Blood!

Walking back to his horse, Hiro returned with his pack. He withdrew a short wide blade and screwed a wooden handle to it before scraping and digging at the mound of sods and earth until he found the body. It wasn't quite what he expected. A dirt-covered blanket was laid over it and as he pulled it free it revealed a dog of all things, a big one at that, more wolf than a hound. A wolfdog was unusual to see, hard to tame and harder to train, he knew. That it was buried told him it had been both.

It had been fifteen years since he'd seen Darion and Marron but they kept a wolfdog. Bear, it was named if he recalled rightly. A sinking feeling started to form in the pit of his stomach. Maybe they still did.

Hiro's mind drifted back to the evening before and the sick girl. The sick girl with two wolfdog's flanking her, one mottled black the other a dirty white. The girl had been watching too when he'd left camp earlier that morning, well before the sun was due to rise. She'd intrigued him but not enough to spark his interest. She was one amongst a crowd of humanity all escaping south and to his eye looked ill and frail.

Looking now around the battleground, his mind reasoned that maybe her frailty wasn't due to illness. He cursed himself for his lack of foresight. His curiosity often stood him in good stead or got him into trouble, one of the two. His lack of it though in regards to the girl had cost him valuable time. Whether she or one of her companions was the source of power Keeper detected, he didn't know but they'd survived a fight with a Taken. Intuition told him he'd missed his quarry and that she travelled the road south.

Hiro covered the dog back over with the blanket and shovelled dirt back on top. Superstition as much as sentiment, he conceded.

Done, he stood and wandered back to his horse, holding a sweet treat out for her to nibble as he gathered her reins. Hitching his pack on the back he pulled himself into the saddle with a languid ease that belied his age.

Riding back to the roadside he turned east. He'd pick Renco and Maohong up at Fallston along the way. With luck, he would catch the girl and her companions before nightfall.

\* \* \*

Hiro had ridden barely an hour when he picked out a smudge on the horizon. He should have seen it sooner but grey clouds crowded the sky and the smoke was well disguised. A distant rumble of thunder rolled out, quiet but deep. Trepidation filling him, Hiro urged his mare into a gentle, ground eating canter.

Senses ranging ahead, Hiro searched for trouble. At each bend in the road, he would phase briefly, studying the flow of aether for any tell-tale. All the while the smoke grew thicker and heavier. The noise, clearly drum beats, came and went intermittently. Urak he knew now, not that he'd been in any real doubt.

Hiro was a few leagues distant from Fallston when the first hint of trouble arose. Instantly, bringing his horse to a stop he dismounted. The distant life flows were too big to be human and the wrong hue. The white swirls of aether merged with threads of purple and red, standing out like lonely idris flowers in a green field. He'd seen their like many times before, though not for many years, urak. They were a distance away, hopefully too far to have seen him.

Thick bushes followed the path of the river and Hiro led his mare off the road and through the meadow grass towards them. Tying her reins up behind a stand that was tall enough to hide them both, Hiro assessed his options. They were few and none were good.

The urakakule must have taken Fallston he reasoned, sparing a thought for Renco and Maohong. Had they escaped the trap? Whether or not they had, there was nothing to be done about it now. He would find what he would.

The urak attack raised many questions and doubts in Hiro's mind; it was unexpected and certainly unheralded. How had the Lord at Fallston not known of their approach? Word surely would have reached him? What of the towns and villages to the north, if Fallston had fallen what of them? Both questions were largely redundant. The most pressing ones now were to find out what had happened at

Fallston, without discovery, and how best to locate his companion and charge. After resolving those questions, maybe then he could turn his attention to finding the girl.

Hiro absently patted his mare's neck as he thought things through. Stealth was needed rather than speed, he'd have to abandon her, he decided. Removing his pack and staff he laid them on the ground before unfastening the girth straps on the saddle. Pulling it from the mare's back he placed it under the cover of a bush, then slipped the halter and bit from her head and mouth. She was free to roam where she would.

Slinging the pack over his shoulder, Hiro gripped his staff in his right hand and stepped out of the bushes. The mare's gentle brown eyes followed Hiro with a lazy disinterest, watching as he walked away.

Hiro didn't look back. Keeping low in the long grass, he followed the river. He focused his senses. Up ahead, the distant urak hadn't moved and they'd be difficult to avoid; they had dogs with them.

Looking at the swirls and eddies of the river his expression turned grim. His robes were light and loose. Hiro removed them and then stripped out of his undergarments until he stood naked, his body sparse and lean with muscle. Folding his clothes into a tight roll, he squeezed them into his pack. Then, knotting his boots together cinched and tied them beneath. Finally, he lashed his staff across his back with a tie.

Ready, Hiro lowered himself down the bank and into the cold embrace of the river, hugging the side until the icy shock of the water relented. Then, pushing out into the river, he drifted along in the current. Kicking, he propelled himself across and towards the far bank.

The river was wide and the water deceptively fast. The bite of it was invigorating at first, familiar too, Hiro having bathed in the Oust every morning for the past ten-day. However, after a time the cold numbed, seeping into muscle and bone. By the time he made the south bank he was blue, his muscles spasming with chill. Dragging himself quickly up and into the shrubs and long grass, he vanished from sight.

* * *

Hiro checked the flow of the aether. There was nothing untoward nearby. The urak were close, the river had made it so, but they were on the opposite side and there was no sign they'd detected him.

Sitting cross-legged in the tall grass, Hiro emptied the contents of his pack, laying things out to dry in the breeze and weak sunlight. His body soon dried and the trembling in his limbs faded but he was weary and sapped of energy.

With no time to rest, Hiro closed his eyes and concentrated. He felt the wind on his skin and the pale warmth of the sun on his body. Sensing the flow, he gradually and carefully drew from it a slither of aether. It was just a hint but his body absorbed it hungrily, energy infusing him.

Opening his eyes, all was as it was before. Donning his damp clothes and lacing his boots, Hiro repacked his bag before shouldering it. With a firm grip on his staff, he stepped into the undergrowth.

The ground on the south side of the river was soft underfoot. The grass was coarser, their blades wider and darker than on the northern side. Accacha and needle bush grew thick all around and swamp willows sprouted along the side of the embankment.

Following the trees, Hiro kept them and the soothing sounds of water to his left. There were plenty of signs of wildlife and he tracked along an animal trail that looked well used.

* * *

It was after midday when the distant thunder of the falls could be heard and Hiro moved away from the river, trailing south to find what he was looking for. He reached the edge of a plateau, where the grass and bush tumbled down in a sharp, rambling descent, forty feet or more.

The view afforded was inspiring and beautiful. The blue-green sparkle of the Reach extended away before him. The lake was long and narrow and its southern shoreline was indistinct, fading and blending into a rambling mix of water grass and reeds that marked the border of the Grim Marsh. In stark contrast, its opposite shore was clearly defined and Hiro could make out the eastern fringes of Fallston.

Here, the rumble of the falls was loud as the waters of the Oust crashed over and into the lake below, sending a faint mist into the air that created a rainbow of colours in the sunlight.

The old monk cast an eye over what he could of Fallston. Smoke plumed the air from its eastern perimeter and there was movement out past that, too far and indistinct to make out clearly. He phased, his consciousness merging into the tapestry of the flow, and shifted through it. His heart sank as he detected thousands of tell-tale white points of aether, twisted through with the purple and red of urak. Curiously though, only a dozen or so appeared inside Fallston itself.

Hiro sensed many people still in the town and those same black memories from earlier in the day resurfaced. Urakakule usually roamed in nomadic tribes and hunted their food. The people here were penned in like cattle and Fallston nothing but a hunting ground, a place to blood their young.

Chewing on dried meat, still wet from his river crossing, and a handful of Accacha berries he'd picked along the way, Hiro rested. It had been a long time since he was last in this part of the world. It had changed a little, but he knew it well enough and hoped what he looked for existed still. Time would tell.

Hefting his pack, Hiro turned south and followed the bluff. After twenty minutes of searching, he found what he looked for, the way down. He regarded the path thoughtfully; it wasn't as well hidden as it used to be. Clearly, it saw regular use, for the ground was trodden enough that nature had not claimed the space back for its own.

The descent proved steep but not difficult, the path switching back and forth as it descended. By the time Hiro reached the base the sun had edged a hand further to the west. The ground here was damp and loamy underfoot and the waters of the Reach, barely a dozen strides away, were hidden by the tall grass and bulrush. A non-descript track could be discerned heading south, deeper into the Grim but it was north that Hiro turned, towards the falls.

All things change in time, the marsh, the lake, even the land. He hoped what was hidden was still there.

## Chapter 5: Old Man

**Fallston, The Rivers**

Nihm observed the old man with interest. He looked in a bad way. One side of his face was a marbled riot of blacks and purples and his forehead was livid, the skin raised where Mercy had stitched it. Blood still welled from it in places. His broken nose looked painfully swollen where it had been set but at least it had stopped bleeding.

They were in Fallston, in an abandoned house they'd broken into near the main docks and situated on the waterfront; the owners having had the sense and good fortune to have already left.

Earlier that morning it had been a chaotic scramble, as people panicked at the sudden appearance of urak. Most had made for the Uppers but Mercy had steered them to the docks where they'd found the empty home. They'd had to take refuge there; the old man needed seeing to or he would have died. In any case, Stama had quickly spied people from the Uppers stumbling back down the high road towards Fallston and surmised the road west was sealed as surely as the road east. So here they were, trapped with no immediate escape possible.

Nihm looked on as Mercy removed the cloth she used as a bandage, replacing it with a clean one she'd boiled and cooled. It must have pained him but the old man made no sound; simply glaring back with gritted teeth. He'd said nothing since regaining consciousness.

Nihm didn't think him broken as some were when they suffered trauma to the head or that he was incapable of talking. His eyes were too focused and alert for that; she could see him taking everything in.

He held a certain fascination, Nihm admitted to herself. She'd seen lots of different folk at Thorsten market over the years, mostly traders and a few mercenaries and hired guards. They came from all across the Nine Kingdoms and beyond but none looked like the old man. He was slight and his skin, aged and lined as it was, was the colour of golden oak. His face was long and angular and his eyes had a slight cant to them. He certainly wasn't from the Kingdoms.

The old man was unshaven and, together with his beating, gave him an unkempt appearance. Ancient, he was easily the oldest person she'd ever seen.

© 2020 A D Green

Older than Bess Cob at the Encomas who was grizzled and wrinkled like a dried-up apple. His eyes though weren't rheumy like Bess's were. They were clear, sharp and watched her back, no doubt making their own assessment. Uncomfortable under his scrutiny, Nihm turned to Mercy.

"Where do you s'pose he's from?"

Mercy glanced at Nihm then the old man. "East, out past the Great Expanse. Chezuan Imperia, seen a few like him before, in Kingsholme; none as old as this one though or as scruffy."

Mercy's comment brought a grunt from the old man; the first sound he'd made that wasn't a groan of pain. Nihm had the distinct impression he was amused, although it was hard to be sure given his bruised and swollen face.

The dogs suddenly rose from where they rested and faced the door, ears erect, and alert. It opened and Stama strode in banging the door firmly closed behind him.

Rising, Mercy moved to his side. "What's happening?"

"Far as I can tell we're surrounded. Can't step foot outside the town limits," Stama said. "Plenty of folks stuck here with us and ain't none of us going anywhere soon. Urak have us penned in like sheep."

"Why? Why not sack the town and slaughter us? Bunch of savages," Mercy spat. Stama shrugged in response.

"Waste not." A voice cackled before breaking into a hacking cough. Everyone turned and stared at the old man.

Nihm reached for a water skin and slowly, her movements careful and precise, slipped an arm about his shoulders. Raising him, she let him drink from its neck. The old man gulped a couple of mouthfuls before leaning heavily against Nihm's chest.

"Ah, better. Mao thank you," he cuddled into her breast.

Nihm dropped him back on his pallet with a thump. Her face colouring up in a mix of shock, indignation and embarrassment. She didn't know what to say or do.

The man cackled again, louder.

His amusement rankled and Nihm stood glaring at him before turning away.

The old man's laughter ceased as suddenly as it started.

"Girl want knife back?"

It stopped Nihm dead in her tracks. Her hand patted her hip. The knife was gone. Spinning about, she glowered angrily as he held her blade out handle first.

The stupid grin on his face was the final straw and Nihm snatched her knife back. It was the fastest, most precise she had moved since Thorsten market and she would have been pleased with herself if she'd stopped to think on it but she was too mad.

With a yelp, Mao sucked his hand to his mouth.

Mortified, Nihm's anger fled. "I'm so sorry. Did I cut you?" Her eyes flared wide in sudden concern and she knelt anxiously by his side.

He snorted, beamed a huge grin then wiggled his fingers in front of Nihm's face. "Mao make joke."

"Enough," Mercy stomped over pulling Nihm to her feet before edging her firmly away from the old fool. "Explain what you meant before."

Mao sniffed and with a disgruntled look turned his head away.

"In case you missed it, we saved your life back there," Mercy said, "so if you have something useful to say, say it. Otherwise, shut the hell up."

The old man gave no acknowledgement. Shaking her head, Mercy turned away.

Nihm was intrigued though. He was the strangest man. <Sai, you have any thoughts on him?>

<He is cunning. He used distraction to remove your knife. He engaged with you but not Mercy. I have insufficient information to form a proper analysis.>

<Forget the analysis, what do you think?>

<He was giving a lesson. He is intelligent and you interest him. That he spoke out earlier indicates he knows something. You should talk to him.>

<Really…> Despite her reticence, Nihm moved back to the old man's side.

*<And Nihm, he did not respond positively to Mercy's tone. Use a different one,>* Sai suggested.

Nihm rested a hand on the old man's shoulder.

"You said your name was Mao?" Nihm offered. "Mine is Nihm."

Cocking his head a little to the side, Mao waited.

Nihm wasn't sure what for but his eyes held hers. Something clicked. Some intuition kicked in or more likely her Ma's endless instructions on convention and courtesy.

"My name is Nihmrodel Castell, daughter of Darion and Marron Castell and I am of the Order," Nihm said, even if it wasn't exactly true. Nihm had given no mind to the Order a ten-day ago.

There was a sharp intake of breath from Mercy. Nihm could feel the mage's displeasure. The old man for his part just laughed until he started coughing again and Nihm had to give him more water, this time paying close attention to her knife.

"Agh, head hurts to laugh," Mao said, pressing fingers to his temples. "Ah, what Mao give see Master's face," he chuckled, shaking his head. After a moment, he gathered himself and turned to Nihm with a beaming smile. He touched a hand to his chest. "Tasao Maohong, formerly of Maritq'ha, son of Tasao Honsuh, third Kan of Maritq'ha."

"Why formerly?" Nihm asked before she could stop herself, not sure why she even asked the question.

"Story for another time," Maohong waved his hand dismissively.

"Ask him what he meant," Mercy interjected.

*<From your exchange I would extrapolate that Tasao Maohong, formerly of Maritq'ha, son of Tasao Honsuh, third Kan of Maritq'ha, would engage directly with Mercy, were she to make a formal introduction,>* Sai prompted.

"Maybe if you introduce yourself, Tasao Maohong will talk with you directly," Nihm repeated, detecting in her periphery a slight nod from the old man, his wizened face still scrunched in a crooked smile.

Glaring at Nihm, Mercy reluctantly conceded the point and gave a curt acknowledgement. Striding back, she towered over Maohong who reclined on his pallet.

"Forgive my bad manners. These are trying times," she said. "I am Mercy Duncan, daughter of Atticus and Morgenni, of Hawke in the Nine Kingdoms."

The old man chuckled gleefully, his crooked grin growing even wider. Then, as Mercy's ire grew, he moved. With a groan of pain and wincing at the effort, Mao propped himself up on his elbows making to rise.

Nihm held an arm out and taking it Mao struggled to his feet. Once steady, he sketched a bow that was little more than an incline of his head and shoulders.

"Tasao Maohong, formerly of Maritq'ha, son of Tasao Honsuh, third Kan of Maritq'ha," Mao intoned formerly. "You may call me Mao." He smiled, flashing crooked teeth.

"Well then, Mao…"

"You have look of mother yes, and temper. But have father eye, neh," Mao said, "Not patient though. Father patient, clever like Master Hiro."

Mercy stared, silent a while as she considered her response. "It's said I have my mother's fire and my father's wit. How do you know them?"

"Story for another time," Mao repeated.

Watching, Nihm could see Mercy suck her cheeks in and bite her lip. Mao, for his part, looked unperturbed.

"Man say already," Mao waggled a finger in Stama's general direction. "Penned like sheep, neh! Many urak, need much food. Now urak not need hunt so much!"

"You're saying we're cattle?" Mercy spluttered.

Mao shrugged his shoulders nonchalantly then cocked his head to one side as if listening. Turning, he looked to the door at about the same time the two dogs did. Ash and Snow's tails wagged. A double knock sounded and the door swung wide. Morten's face appeared around its frame looking breathless and excited.

"Lucky says come see. People are launching boats out onto the Lake."

Stama didn't wait and pushed out past Morten as Mercy went for her staff.

"Stay!" Nihm commanded.

Ash and Snow obediently sat, their eyes never leaving Nihm as she followed behind Morten who, message delivered, had disappeared back the way he'd come.

Nihm caught up with him outside on the dock looking out across the lake. The sun wasn't far off setting and the light was golden and red across the water.

The slow tamp of Mercy's staff sounded as the mage joined them and glancing across, Nihm saw that she half propped and half carried Tasao Maohong. He should be resting, Nihm thought, turning back.

The smell of burning and wood smoke was heavy in the air and, if Nihm had chanced to look up, she would have seen the thick brume drawn out over the town as the slight breeze off the lake pushed it away.

"They launched just a while ago," Lucky said, his hulking shape blocking sight of where he pointed.

Edging around his large frame, Nihm made out eight of the small two-man fishing skiffs, though there looked to be many more than two people aboard each of them. Sails raised, they glided slowly across the water, eastward, away from Fallston.

"Lakeside town, it stands to reason most folk would have a boat of some kind," Morten enthused. "Might be we could find one ourselves and get the hell out of here. Might even be one where we're holed up!"

A streak of fire and a burst of flame erupted on the water, as one of the skiffs exploded, making them all jump. One moment it was engulfed in an inferno, the next it was broken and falling apart, the waters of the Reach dousing the flames aside from a few errant bits of debris that burnt like floating candles.

"Saint's light!" Lucky exclaimed.

They watched as another finger of flame whipped across the lake, faster than an arrow. It missed its target, or else was a warning shot, either way, it landed next to the lead skiff, erupting in a hiss of vapour and water.

Another firebolt launched, this time striking the vessel true. It burst into flames before disintegrating like the first. They could see no survivors from either boat.

The remaining skiffs started turning and weaving in the water, but they were slaves to the wind and two more exploded in quick succession. The surviving boats turned back, running for town and its relative safety.

"Guess that option's off the table," Morten muttered, his face pale at the sudden violence and destruction.

They watched the skiffs a while. When it was evident no more death would be unleashed they trudged, disconsolate, back inside.

\* \* \*

The mood was sombre. Only Maohong seemed unaffected by their predicament, snoring quietly on his pallet. The brief interlude outside had obviously taxed him.

"We ain't stayin' here," Lucky said. "We're like fish in a barrel to those fuckers."

"You got a plan? If so, we're all ears," Stama replied.

"Shoulda rode south when we had the chance." Lucky glanced momentarily at Nihm and then the huddled form of Maohong.

"We all had the chance and none took it. Bitching about it now won't help none," Stama said.

"I ain't bitchin," Lucky squared up, temper rising, "Just statin' a fact."

"Sure sounds like bitchin to me. Sound like bitchin to you, Red?" Stama turned to Morten but his eyes never left Lucky, as the big man took a step towards him, rolling his shoulders. Anger pulsed off him.

Mercy interposed herself between them, glaring at both. "If you boys have got nothing useful to contribute then go play outside."

They said nothing but glowered at each other.

"Well?" Mercy demanded her voice like iron.

With a shrug of his massive frame, Lucky turned and stomped across to the only table in the room where he threw his prodigious weight down on one of the chairs. It groaned under his bulk. With a sudden crack, a leg snapped and the chair gave way, sending him rolling off the back and into the table with a loud thump.

Nihm couldn't help herself and burst out laughing as Lucky sat up wincing and rubbing his head. The moment broke the tension as Mercy started chuckling too. In the end, it was Stama that hauled the big man up and back onto his feet. They didn't say anything to each other, just clasped forearms, but the incident was done.

"I might have an idea, I don't know though," Morten muttered, scratching at his stubble. Everyone barring Mao turned to look at him.

"Spit it out Red. What ya got?" Lucky said.

"Look, I don't know if this is right or not, but I heard it said some folk do business with the Grimmers, trade and the like… black market trade," Morten started.

"I mean it does happen, right? The Black Crow posts about it all the time, it bein a hangin' offence and all. Seems to me the Crow wouldn't put those flyers up if it didn't. So, if'n it does, Fallston is right on the northern edge of the Grim, prime location and big enough to hide that sort of thing. So, if folks is trading with the Grimmers it makes sense they have a way of getting in and out discrete like." Morten stared at the watching faces. "It was just a thought."

"It's a good one," Mercy said. "Best we got right now." She glanced at Stama and Lucky then back to Morten.

"Stama, take Morten. Go ask around, see what you can find out. No need to tell you speed is of the essence."

Stama nodded then glanced at Morten who had only a long knife on his belt. "Bring your staff Red, just in case."

Morten grabbed it from where it lent against the wall before facing Nihm.

"Bye," he mumbled, "I'll bring it straight it back."

Nihm's eyes crinkled and her lips curled. "Just make sure you bring yourself back, idiot."

© 2020 A D Green

"Ay, right ya are." Morten grinned; turning away he followed Stama out the door.

Once they were gone, Mercy waved Lucky close. "See if you can find one of those boats we saw. Failing that anything that floats. Worst-case and we're stuck here we'll take our chances on the water. Leave at the dead of night and pray for some cloud cover."

"What about the old man? He ain't fit to travel and don't seem too worried none by it," Lucky said.

"Doesn't have much choice, does he," Mercy replied. "He can come with us or stay here."

*<Maohong feigns sleep,>* Sai told Nihm suddenly.

Nihm turned to look, watching the slow rise and fall of Mao's body as he breathed. She could detect the faint pulse of his heart and marvelled at it. How could she hear a heartbeat from two paces away? was it Sai?

*<It is always you, Nihm. You are my host. Everything stems from you. I just pay more attention,>* Sai answered.

Nihm smirked *<A joke Sai, you're getting a sense of humour.>*

*<It was an observation but I am glad you found it amusing.>*

Nihm shook her head, still grinning *<You had to ruin it didn't you.>* Kneeling next to Mao she poked him in the shoulder.

There was a grunt then a snort.

"Let him rest, Nihm. He needs it," Mercy said, eyeing her.

"If he was sleeping I would," Nihm replied. "But you're not asleep are you Mao?" Nihm prodded him again.

With a groan and feigned annoyance, Mao turned onto his back. "What you want? Mao rest."

"I want to know why you laughed when I told you my name and why you wished to see the look on your Master's face. Who exactly is your Master?" Nihm said.

A chair scrapped on the wooden floor as Mercy dragged it out from the table and across the room. Turning it around, she settled into it.

Mao and Nihm both turned at the noise.

"Don't mind me, they're all good questions," Mercy said, "Got a few of my own for good measure as it happens. Like, how'd you know my parents and why don't you seem bothered at our predicament?"

Mao looked at them both, crunching his face up as if he'd just sucked a lemon. He waved his hand in annoyance; then, as if reluctant, turned to Nihm.

"Not your name. Father's name, mother's name."

"How do you know my Ma and Da?" Nihm asked. Mention of them choked her up momentarily. One was gone the other missing.

"Bah, Mao this Mao that. Give answer, get more question," he grumbled. Then suddenly, "I see you as baby. Very noisy, strong lung yes and bad smell," Mao waved a hand over his nose.

A memory flittered through Nihm's mind. It was one she couldn't recall having. In it, she saw the same wizened face, just as lined and aged as it was now, peering down at her. She was crying and Mao was beaming at her with a toothy grin and making cooing noises.

Nihm muttered, "You were in our house."

"Yes, that what Mao say. Bad smell, big noise. Mao, not like baby."

"So, you know my parents," Nihm said.

"Yes, Master Hiro old friend. He look for father and mother. So very funny see his face, neh?" Mao grinned. "He walk but not see you. Mao find you." He tapped his chest proudly.

"Actually, I found you, beat up and dying," Nihm retorted unable to resist a grin of her own. She found she liked the old man and his funny way of talking.

"Same, same," Mao chuckled.

"Glad you're enjoying yourself elderly father but who exactly is Master Hiro?" Mercy interrupted.

Mao stopped abruptly. Looking Mercy in the eye, he growled. "Nooo patience."

He grinned again, "Just like mother."

Nihm watched the exchange, amused. Mercy though looked ready to punch him. As if coming to the same conclusion, Mao put his hand up.

"Master Hiro, friend of Order, yes? Know Atticus long time, since young man. Master Hiro explain. Be here soon," Mao stated. "Now question. Why you save Mao?"

## Chapter 6: The Loud Water

**Fallston, The Rivers**

They were in the poorest part of Fallston; known as the Hang. Those that lived in the Hang named it so because it sat wedged between the falls and the shadow of the overhanging cliffs, above which sat the Uppers.

No one wanted to live in the Hang. The rumble of the falls was a backdrop noise for everyone living in Fallston but here it was so much louder, a roar. But the noise was only half the reason. The other was the wet. If the wind blew across the lake, misty dew from the falls hung in the air and the buildings were all damp because of it.

It hadn't taken Morten long to find the place. In Thorsten, the Hang was often bantered about because of its name and the proclivity of its inhabitants to get hung for all manner of misdeeds. He guessed people liked the irony. This though was the first time he'd been in it and he didn't much care for the experience. The whole place had a wet musky stink to it, causing Morten to screw his nose up at the smell.

He closed the inn's big solid door with a bang. The two men found themselves in The Loud Water; a disreputable-looking tavern built up against the cliff face and set a hundred paces back from the lake. Its name was obvious if not a little lacking in imagination, Morten considered, peering into the gloom of the inn.

Stama moved ahead of him, wandering across to the bar. The tavern was mostly empty. The half dozen or so people it held looked rough and watched them with hard, suspicious eyes. In contrast, the barkeep was almost jovial.

"Fuck off, we're closed." He was a large beefy man who leant his thick forearms on the bar top as he spoke. There was nothing friendly in his manner.

"Door was open," Stama countered, "Could murder a whiskey."

There was a scrape of chairs on floorboards and Morten glanced nervously about as the inn's occupants rose as one. Stama though seemed unmoved and waited patiently where he stood. This might not have been such a good idea, Morten thought, his mouth suddenly dry.

"Double-shot, one for me and one for my friend here," Stama said, "In fact, get the room one. I think we all need it after today, eh!" He produced a coin and flipped it neatly in the air, caught it then slammed it down on the counter with a bang that made Morten jump. "Keep the change."

Stama removed his hand revealing a gold mark. Morten gaped, he'd seen one once in his life. A whole bottle of whiskey was worth five copper bits at best. A hundred coppers to a silver kern, twenty silver kerns to a gold mark. It was a fortune. It was a statement.

The barkeep's eyes flashed to the coin then back to Stama, staring at him as if by looking hard enough he could intuit who this man was. How dangerous. Nobody walked into a tavern and flashed gold, let alone in a tavern like his.

A moment passed by, then another. Stama held the man's eyes, not blinking, not saying another word. The next move wasn't his to make.

Finally, the barkeep stood tall, his hands on the bar. Coming to a decision, he turned, reached down, and opened up a cabinet behind him. He pulled out a bottle and expertly grabbed three tumblers in one hand. Casting the tumblers onto the bar top, he uncorked the bottle and poured its amber contents into each, spilling nothing. He banged the bottle down and scooped up the gold bit in the same motion, casting his eye over it before pocketing it.

"It's the best I got, not that cheap crap off the top shelf. Keep the bottle." The barkeep rumbled his flash of teeth yellow and dirty in the low light.

Stama smiled back. He slid one of the tumblers across the counter to Morten, then another towards the barkeep. Reaching for his own he raised it. "To life and living,"

Silence.

Feeling the need to fill it, Morten reached for his glass, cast a glance about the room and the men stood watching, "To life and living."

Finally, the barkeep lent forward, picked up his shot and downed it in one. Smacking his lips, he held the empty tumbler in one hand, his guarded eyes never leaving Stama. "To life and living." He slammed the glass down.

Morten felt himself flinch at the noise. But Stama didn't so much as twitch. He drained the contents of his glass, swilled it in his mouth then swallowed it before carefully placing the tumbler on the counter next to its companion.

All eyes were on Morten. Self-conscious he downed his drink. The taste was strong and oaky but held a stinging, bitter aftertaste. It burnt on the way down and he couldn't help but cough as his throat constricted. Eyes watering and trying to maintain his composure, Morten set the tumbler down. If that's his best shit I'd hate to try the top shelf, he thought.

The barkeep smirked at Morten, before addressing Stama. "Nice toast. A suspicious man might construe it as a threat. You threaten me, Kingsman?"

Stama laughed. "I like the sound of that. Kingsman. Makes me feel important. Why don't you tell your boys to take a seat, then maybe we can do some business, friend."

"Fuck you. They stay where they are." The barman's eyes glinted in the half-light. "I know your business and the answer's the same as for everyone. Can't help you, 'friend'." He growled this last implying Stama was anything but. He wasn't finished though and lent forward again. "If'n I could help you, I wouldn't. You stink like a Kingsman, walk like one and talk like one, and sure as fuck, no one I ever knowed has ever come in here having seen a gold bit let alone slap one on my counter like it was a n'er nothing more an a copper."

Morten felt his heart beating loudly in his chest. A silence permeated the room, no sound but the muffled ever-present roar of the falls. His back itched and he could almost feel the men behind step closer to them.

If it bothered Stama, he didn't show it. "Told you, friend, I ain't no Kingsman. Her Ladyship sent me to negotiate passage out of Fallston. Now, I know you can help me and you will. Choice you got is whether you want to help me easy or help me hard." Reaching for the bottle he refilled the three shot glasses.

"What'll it be?"

The barkeep laughed, his belly shook with it. "I like your balls. Even if you can use that fancy blade on your hip, you wouldn't last twenty seconds. Your boy with the stick, I give him ten at most. Now, I was willing to let you walk since you kept things civil." His grin turned to a menacing jeer. "But you gone threatened me in my own place. I can't tolerate that."

Morten's itch in the middle of his back got really strong. There was a sudden rasping of drawn steel behind and fear pumped through his veins. He was scared, and mad at himself for it. He had never feared for his life before this last ten-day but this was the third time now in as many days. It was paralysing. Heart palpitating, he watched Stama sip from his glass unconcerned. How could he stand it?

Stama smirked. "Stick, I like that. You like that, Red?" He spared a glance at Morten and slipped him a wink, much to Morten's horror.

"It is said, only old men and mages carry a staff," Stama said to the barkeep. "Red here, look like an old man to you?"

Morten stood, rigid and unmoving. Staring blankly at the barkeep, his eyes felt suddenly dry and he blinked them.

The barkeep looked again at the young man, unsure. The lad looked too young to be a mage but what did he know. Mages were rare in these parts. Some noble might have a mage he supposed and they were here at the behest of some great Lady.

The gold bit made more sense. It felt suddenly heavy in his pocket. Mage or not he was a cool one. Hadn't said hardly a word and stood there still as a statue. Possibilities ran through his mind. If'n he was a mage could they knife him before he could cast? Maybe, maybe not. Fuck! What the hell did he know about mages?

"Lad's young granted, still an apprentice truth be told," Stama continued. "He won't mind my telling that he ain't got the finesse yet of his master. Hell, he's as like to burn this whole tavern down and me in it as singe your hair and who wants that right." Stama smiled as if he'd just made a bad joke.

The barkeep looked past Stama and Morten and nodded his head. There was another rasp as steel slide back into sheaths and, with a scrape of wood, men took their seats.

Morten let out a breath he hadn't known he was holding.

Stama gave an encouraging nod. "Stay calm Red, nothing to burn today. Take a seat." He spoke, loudly enough for all to hear.

Morten licked his lips, his mouth was so dry. He reached for his refilled glass and took a swig, coughed again at the taste, and promptly sat on a barstool.

"You calm, Red?" Stama asked.

Taking his lead, Morten sucked in a deep breath. "I'm calm, nothing to burn here." He repeated. He thumped the butt of his staff on the floorboards, his knuckles white where he gripped it.

"That's good." Stama turned back to the barkeep. "No names. You know what I need? I want to know your price."

The barkeep sniffed. "You need what everyone in this town needs. A way out. What makes you think I can get you past them urak?"

"You're still here for one thing. That means either you can't get out or you got stuff here to shift. I'm betting on the latter," Stama said, sipping his whiskey.

"How many?"

"Six."

"Five gold." The barkeep didn't hesitate. His voice low enough that the sound of the falls masked his words from all but the two men at the bar.

Even as he blanched at the price, Morten could see the benefits of dealing with business in a place like this. It would be hard to overhear a normal conversation, impossible if it was a discreet one.

"Given the circumstance, five seems reasonable," Stama replied.

"Each."

Morten's eyes flared at the outrageous sum. He saw Stama keep his smile, only a slight tightening around his eyes gave lie to the fact he was happy about it. The barkeep must have seen it too.

"Your friends must be worth at least five bottles of whiskey." He grinned, flashing his yellow teeth again. "Figure a man foolish enough to buy a bottle of whiskey for a gold bit wouldn't have no issue with that."

Stama leant over the bar, spat on his hand then held it out. Laughing, the barkeep spat on his and slapped it into Stama's, sealing the bargain.

"Deal," Stama said.

"Done," Replied the barkeep. "It'll be darkening in an hour. Be back in two. Any later and you'll not find us here."

Stama nodded in return. "We'll be here. Come on, Red."

"Oh, and don't forget your whiskey," jeered the barkeep, sliding the bottle across the bar.

Grabbing it by the neck, Stama gave a curt nod before sauntering casually out of the Loud Water, Morten on his heels.

## Chapter 7: Bloodlust

**Fallston, The Rivers**

"Why does it stand?"

Krol stood on the high road looking down at Fallston as darkness descended. Burnt wood and death tainted the air and he could see, surrounding the town, hundreds of Manawarih campfires. Smoke rose from the eastside of town but it was clear from the pinpricks of light from deep within, that many of its inhabitants still lived.

The urak that Krol questioned was big, of a size to match his own. He was formidable and his reputation fierce. Tribal chieftain of the Manawarih, one of the five great tribes of the Blood Skull, he was Karth-Dur and there was enmity between them.

"The humans are weak. Soft. Their tupiks are made of stick and stone. They will fall when I say," Karth-Dur growled.

Krol was being provoked. He felt his rage building. His Hurak-hin bristled at the implied insult and challenge in Karth-Dur's tone. They were ready to fight.

It brought joy to Krol's heart. For a moment, it made him feel almost urakakule again, normal. But, his Hurak-hin were outnumbered two to one by Karth-Dur's own and the dark shade he carried within wouldn't let him throw his life away, insult or no. The Morhudrim's compulsion burned strong inside him and it cared nothing for honour.

"Good, I have need of it. You please me, Karth-Dur," Krol goaded. This time, he sensed the tension in the Manawarihs Hurak-hin, as they drew themselves up taller, shoulders back. Bloodshed was close.

Krol hocked, spitting a wad of phlegm on the ground. "Mar-Dur moves east and will be here in a turn, two at most. I will leave him nothing. No victory, no battle, no supplies. I order you east, to the human settlement of Longstretch. Take what you will but stay no more than a turn. Raze it, leave nothing."

In a show of bravado, Krol left the ranks of his Hurak-hin and stalked closer to Karth-Dur. "My warbands are near. I will take over here." He spoke quickly to hide his anxiety. For his warbands were half a turn behind. They would arrive by sunup or heads would roll but until then, Krol knew he was dangerously exposed.

Karth-Dur gazed at the clan's warchief, murder in his eyes. "Grimpok will lead the White Hand, I know it. I would make war upon him."

Krol knew of Karth-Dur's death feud with Grimpok. As much as he wanted his rival to weaken himself against his enemy it did not suit his purpose. He shook his head. "The clan moves east, Karth-Dur. Do not get left behind. After Longstretch, move the Manawarih north to the human settlement at Chortonwood."

"Do you fear real battle, Krol? We could crush them." Karth-Dur challenged.

"I made accord with Mar-Dur. I'll not break it. Do as I command or give battle, here and now." Krol challenged calm menace in his voice. He felt an overwhelming urge to draw his blade and strike Karth-Dur down where he stood. But it was a barb Karth-Dur had set to bait him. If he drew blade without formal challenge, Karth-Dur and his Hurak-hin would fall upon them.

The darkness inside Krol writhed, agitated, and hungry. He watched Karth-Dur carefully. They would fight, he was almost certain of it, and, much as that would please him, it was not what he desired. It would weaken the Blood Skull.

"Your first bloods are no doubt hunting. Pull them out. Go," Krol ordered. It was a distraction. Given a simple order to follow, Karth-Dur could step back. It was a last chance if he chose to take it. Krol rolled his shoulders prepared either way.

A moment passed, tense with the threat of violence. Then, with reluctance, Karth-Dur bowed his head a fraction and stepped away.

"Your will, warchief," There was nothing agreeable in his tone. North of the Torns, in the Norde-Targkish, blood would have been spilt and they both knew it. When he judged himself safe enough, the chief of the Manawarih spun and disappeared into the gloom, his Hurak-hin melting away with him.

Krol watched them go. Behind, he sensed the tension leave his own Hurak-hin. His first, Tar-Tukh stepped to his side. He said nothing but Krol knew his friend well enough to know he seethed with anger. "Speak."

"His head should be in the dirt, his blood feeding the earth." Tar-Tukh spat after the disappeared back of Karth-Dur.

Krol smiled. "It will happen but not now. A weakened Manawarih does not suit me or the clan. Not at this time."

Tar-Tukh made no response.

"Come, let us hunt." Krol set off towards Fallston. Tar-Tukh signalled his brothers and the five-score Hurak-hin at his back followed after their warchief, blood lust building.

\* \* \*

They entered Fallston from the road they had followed south from Marston, passing through a camp arrayed just to the north of town. Many warriors left their campfires and tupiks to watch them, mostly in silence as their warchief passed. They were armed and a sullen animosity hung about them. They were Manawarih; the warchief Sartantak. Ancient feuds existed between their tribes. Feuds held in abeyance since the clan's call for war. In abeyance maybe but they were not forgotten.

His Hurak-hin sauntered indolently past as Krol took it all in. Though he feigned indifference he was pleased. The Manawarih camp was well organised and they were armed and ready for war, as they should be.

At the edge of Fallston, Krol gave his orders to Tar-Tukh. They would split into twenty hands, each building would be raided. Any humans found were to be slaughtered and the houses fired. To the urakakule, it was a waste. Roaming the vast plains of Norde-Targkish life was harsh. Nothing was wasted in the north.

"And Tar-Tukh," Krol called out, as his first turned away to convey his chief's commands. "If you find any that fight they're to back off and report to me. Make sure all understand this."

Death notes, loud but short-lived, filled the night soon afterwards and flames licked against the black sky. Fresh smoke from the burning town billowed unseen into the darkness above. Whisked north by the wind it would choke the Manawarih camp they had passed through.

Closing his eyes, Krol listened to the screams and the crackle of flames, louder even than the rumble of the waterfall. He smiled, relishing the destruction, all visited by his hand, his command. The shade fed on his euphoria but it wanted more.

Opening his eyes, dark tendrils swirled in them. Krol stepped deeper into town. He could feel the life about him, the shade sensing which homes held it.

Blood surging in his veins, he kicked a door from its frame. Pausing on the threshold, Krol peered within. He struggled to cross the entrance and grunted, pressure building, as he pushed against its invisible barrier. The life inside though did not belong here. It was not their home and the boundary was weak. In the end, it wasn't enough. With a bestial cry, he prevailed, stepping through it. Blood dribbled from his nose but he gave it no heed, eager for what lay inside.

Krol found them in the next room; a man and woman with two younglings.

\* \* \*

The man struggled to remove a beam from where it sat across closed shutters, fear making him clumsy. He turned at the sudden crash of noise but an eerie silence followed it. With mounting dread, he turned back to his task. Another sound, he twisted around in time to see the door fly, broken from its hinges. His wife and children screamed in terror as an urak squeezed through the door's frame and into the room. He saw his death at that moment and his trousers darkened as they stained with his fear.

\* \* \*

Krol leered, enjoying the terror he elicited. The man stank of piss but nevertheless moved to meet him. The woman too stepped towards him, shielding her young. She screamed abuse and brandished a knife.

Laughing, Krol bared his teeth in pleasure. The mother recalled another to mind and he touched a finger to the puckered scar around his eye socket. He struck, so swiftly the woman was dead before she had time to register the fact. Brushing her arm aside, his fist drove into her sternum. Bones snapped and blood ruptured from her mouth as she flew backwards, skittling the younglings.

Mad with rage, the man leapt forward swinging a battered-looking blade. It was a sword but looked small to Krol, more like a long knife to an urak. The potency of his fear lent the man a wild urgency as he attacked.

Krol swayed and the blade hissed as it cut the air, missing him. Stepping in as it swung by, Krol punched the man in the face, once. It was a heavy blow and the nose folded as cartilage gave way and blood exploded. Head snapping back, the man's face seemed to cave in. He crumpled to the ground, body twitching in its death throes.

The shade eddied like smoke in his eyes. It was exhilarated, energised. It infused Krol, urging him on, demanding more.

Krol walked to the younglings lying scattered on the floor. The woman had carelessly killed one when she collided with them. The youngest, a female, lay with her tiny head at an obtuse angle and he could smell no life in her fragile body.

Disappointed, Krol turned to the other child. This one was male and very much alive; eyes filled with tears his face ashen.

The boy tried to scramble away and reaching down, Krol grabbed an ankle and dragged him back. He lifted the boy to his feet, the child shaking and screaming his terror all the while. The noise was pleasing, but that part of him that was Krol; pushed back and hiding in the shadows of his mind, was shamed.

Gripping the boy about the neck with one hand, Krol lifted him like a newborn pup into the air. Eyes bulging, he kicked uselessly in Krol's grasp.

Squeezing gently, he watched as the boy was starved of air. The youngling made no mewling cries now but Krol savoured the distress and panic he could see and feel. The boy struggled longer than expected, but eventually, his legs kicked no more. Nonchalant, Krol flicked the lifeless body away, flopping like a ragdoll to land across the woman.

Satiated, Krol roared. He felt good, felt fulfilled. He turned back to the door.

Tar-Tukh stood outside its threshold, watching. The face of his First was inscrutable but his eyes couldn't hide the distaste at what he must have witnessed.

Squeezing back through the doorframe, Tar-Tukh stood aside for him. Brushing past his friend, Krol paused, feeling the weight of his unspoken judgement.

"Burn it."

## Chapter 8: The Hard Way

**Fallston, The Rivers**

Nihm didn't much care for the Hang, it was damp and dirty with a stench to match. Everywhere she looked it was run down and ramshackle. Mould grew on walls and detritus littered the streets. She saw little sign of life, but what there was made her grateful for Ash and Snow's comforting presence. Feral dogs, ragged and skinny, eyes glinting in the dark as they prowled the alleyways, slunk off after a rumbling growl from the big wolfdogs.

The few people encountered looked not much better than the mutts. The contrast between the Hang and the rest of Fallston was stark. The shift from one to the other so abrupt, Nihm felt she was in an entirely different place.

Stama led them unerringly to a large tavern called, The Loud Water. It was backed up against the cliffside and looked in better repair than most buildings she'd seen in the Hang. This only served to give it a more sinister air, as if the Loud Water was the rotting, beating heart of the place.

Mercy didn't like it any more than Nihm. "We trying to get out or get our throats cut?" she complained at Stama.

"Oh, it has a certain charm to it, eh Red?" Stama grinned back.

"Oh I," Morten replied. "Wait till you meet the barkeep, salt of the earth."

The banter was light-hearted but Nihm could see Morten was tense. It made her nervous. Seven hells the whole place made her nervous.

"We're being watched," Nihm advised. Her eyesight was extraordinarily good; another of the improvements, Sai had made. She hardly need think about it and her eyes just seemed to adjust to the bad light. It was like a window suddenly thrown open, only the light here was greener in aspect, though crisp and clear. As clear, almost as if she stood in sunlight. "Second floor left window."

They walked on, only Morten looking up to see. Lucky jostled him. "Try not to stare kid. No point letting them know we seen em, eh," he whispered.

*<There are two men in the alley to the right of the building ahead.>* The thought from Sai was so seamless and Nihm's awareness of the men so instantaneous that it felt as if the thought was her own.

"Two in the alley, right side," Nihm repeated.

Morten couldn't help himself and stole a glance before realising it and forcing himself to look away and stare ahead.

They reached the tavern's door without incident. Stama lifted the latch but the door didn't budge when he pulled to open it. Bolted. He banged a hand against the wood, loud.

"I don't hear nothing," Stama had his ear to the door. "Then again, I can't hear nought over this din."

Nihm could. She tuned out the incessant rumble of the waterfall. Concentrating, she heard footsteps from within. "Someone's coming."

Mercy stared at Nihm and Stama glanced back.

"You're gonna have ta tell me how you do that?" He muttered. Mercy looked like she agreed with him.

"You just have to listen for what you want to hear is all. You're hearing everything and listening to nothing," Nihm said.

Stama gave her the strangest of looks, clearly not happy with her answer but the moment was broken when Maohong hobbled forward and slapped on the door. "Open, open! Mao need drink," he slurred.

"Calm down, old Father." Shaking his head, Stama eased Mao away from the door.

Earlier, the old goat had lifted the bottle of whiskey he'd brought back. By the time they were ready to leave the bastard had necked the lot. "That cost me a gold bit you fool," he'd shouted, only for Mao to laugh whiskey breath in his face.

"One gold and Mao is fool, ha." Stama couldn't even argue his case, the old drunk was right. Lucky, found the whole episode hilarious. For Stama, the only thing worse than a decrepit old man laughing at him was Lucky doing the same so he'd ended the conversation there. Knowing Lucky as he did though, Stama knew it wasn't the last he'd hear of it.

Stama heard a bolt slide and the latch moved. With a groan, the door swung open and a rugged, hard-eyed man stood in the entrance. He didn't say anything immediately but stood back indicating they could enter.

Mao was first through and headed without pause for the bar, then Stama. Mercy and Morten followed but the man growled as Nihm stepped up.

"You ain't bringing those in." He motioned at Ash and Snow.

"Keep moving lass," Lucky said from behind, then at the man. "You'd best tell the dogs yourself. They'll not leave the girl."

Nihm took a tentative step forward. The man looked uncertain, his hand resting on the long knife at his hip when Lucky intervened again.

"Wouldn't do that if'n I was you. Only they're a bit testy. Like as to rip ya arm off if you so much as draw an inch of that nose picker you call a knife." Lucky smiled.

Taking an uncertain step back the man let go of his knife. Ash and Snow padded in after Nihm, tongues lolling. As Lucky followed, the door swung shut behind with an ominous boom.

It was dim, the light from several lanterns illuminated the bar but wasn't strong enough to reach much past it and the edges of the room were shrouded in darkness. It made no difference to Nihm; she counted ten men hiding in the shadows. They were silent but alert and several held crossbows. Nihm had a sinking feeling in her gut that things were about to get ugly and what, if anything, could she do or say.

"You said, six people. Didn't say nothin' bout no dogs."

Nihm's gaze swept back to the bar and the large man stood behind it. "The dogs stay."

The barman was pale and rough with a couple of days growth on his face and a red, blotch-like rash on his neck. There was a harsh edge to him. Nihm didn't like the look of him at all.

Stama laughed. "They're dogs, hardly worth a mention now friend," he cajoled.

"We ain't friends and you know jack shit," the barkeep replied. "Could be where we're goin' dogs can't go."

"Could be, huh," Stama muttered. "A gold bit for each, now let's have no more mention of dogs."

"You're free with your mouth. Funny thing is all I see'd so far is one gold bit. How's 'bout we settle business first, eh!"

"Half now, half when we get out," Stama countered.

It was already tense in the room, but Nihm felt it ratchet up even higher. The men on the fringes of the room all shifted and took a step closer to the light, hands-on weapons. Ash and Snow stared into the gloom their hackles rising. Nihm laid a comforting hand on each to still them.

Mercy, Lucky and Morten felt the tension as well, Nihm saw, though she suspected they couldn't see the men in the shadows and didn't know what they faced. Certainly, Morten would have gawped at them if he could, given his antics outside.

The barkeep smiled grimly and shook his head, "Howsa 'bout all now and I don't kill ya."

Nihm was suddenly aware of a small noise which, ordinarily, would have been impossible to hear over the din of the waterfall, but Nihm was quickly learning there was nothing ordinary about her.

<There is another,> Sai intoned. Nihm's eye was drawn to a robed figure stood in a dark recess to the side of the room. He must have entered through the nearby side door that smelt like it led to the kitchens, Nihm extrapolated. One of the shadow men, no doubt set to guard the entrance, sat silent and unmoving on a chair.

Intrigued, Nihm watched covertly as the figure ghosted behind another man hidden by the dark. Concentrating, she heard the faintest of sounds and the man was suddenly limp and lifeless. The mysterious figure caught the body and propped it upright in a chair. The noise Nihm heard earlier made sense now. It was the scuff of feet dragging and the slight scrape of a chair as a body settled into it.

Nihm kept an eye on the robed man, wondering what was happening, whilst at the same time following the scene at the bar.

"Mao, thirsty," the old man grumbled loudly, tapping his hand against the bar top in a frustrated manner. "Drink first, business second."

The barkeep slid a bottle across the counter towards Maohong. He looked amused. "Hey old man, someone sat on your face and fucked you up pretty good." Then, turning to Stama grunted. "Show me gold or you'll look a ton of shit worse than your grandda here."

Mao, chortling like a crazed person, grabbed the bottle and poured its contents into a glass, spilling as much again on the bar top, oblivious to what was going on around him.

Stama held an empty hand out, palm open for all to see. Reaching into his pack, he pulled out a small bag neatly tied. It chinked as he hefted it and again as he dropped it onto the bar top.

Nihm observed that the robed figure had moved around the room and silenced another guard. <*He seems to be taking them out. Is he a rival or helping us do you think?*>

<*There is insufficient data to draw a definitive conclusion. I estimate a 68.452% probability that our party is his target given the available parameters,*> Sai intoned. <*Although, I cannot ascertain if he is here to help us or hinder us or conclude which is more probable.*>

<*Help obviously. Don't you know anything?*> Nihm replied. <*If he wanted us dead all he need do is trigger those guards and they would do it for him. If your target is surrounded by wolves why kill the wolves. You have a lot to learn, Sai.*>

<*Yes, my human logic routines are only 186.5 hours old. Updating routines,*> Sai replied.

With hungry eyes, the barkeep had watched the bag of coins from the moment it left Stama's pack. Eager, he moved to pick it up, suspicion and greed warring across his face. Slipping the tie, he gazed inside and smiled broadly, showing his yellowed teeth. Satisfied, he pinched the bag's neck and retied it before slipping it inside his jerkin. He looked at Stama then, his arms held out as if only now seeing him for the friend he was.

"Thank you. It's been a pleasure doing business with you all. Now, how's about ya show me what else you got in that pack of yours," His grin turned evil. A long knife suddenly appeared in his hand and he twirled it theatrically.

"So, I guess we're doing this the hard way?" Stama queried. Stepping back he tilted his head a little before muttering in Mercy's general direction. "I'm sorry, my Lady, there seems to be some misunderstanding, please give me a moment."

The barkeep sneered. "Hah, that strumpet's your lady? Might be I take her along and the girl here for a bit a fun later. But you, friend, are fucked. As for the lad there, if'n he's a mage then I'm a white priest." He laughed, then abruptly serious, hissed at Stama.

"Thought I was fool enough to fall for that? You insult me." He tapped his chest looking affronted. "I got me twenty-men around this room, so do as I say else I'll be picking over your dead bodies." He waited a moment, but Stama made no move to comply.

"Come now, times pressing, seems them urak are firing the town and murdering everyone, so," leaning forwards, he placed his hand on the bar top, voice raising, "Put your fucking bags on the counter."

Stama struck. Nihm, watching the exchange didn't see where Stama drew his knife from but he thumped the blade through the meat of the barkeep's hand, pinning it in place. Before he had a chance to scream, Stama was spinning away.

Lucky and Mercy were moving the instant Stama struck. Upending a table they took cover behind it. Lucky dragged Morten down beside him but when Mercy turned for Nihm, she was gone.

For Nihm, the moment Stama drew his knife, it was like time slowed. Her senses were instantly elevated and she saw and assessed several things in the space of a heartbeat. She saw Stama's intent the instant before he delivered it. That the robed figure had accounted for seven of the shadow men but that three were still standing, one of which held a crossbow.

Nihm wasn't sure how, but she knew from the crossbows height and angle its bolt would strike Mao and that she was too far away to do anything about it. But she had to try, her body already moving of its own volition.

Snow and Ash immediately leapt, disappearing into the shadows. Nihm let them go, there was no calling them back. They sensed danger and were dealing with it.

With a click-snap-hum, the crossbow released. To Nihm, every action seemed sluggish and drawn out. Amazingly she could see the flight of the bolt as it whipped by. Felt almost as if she could reach out and touch it, but the moment was gone as soon as the thought and she barely had time to turn as it buried itself into Mao's back.

Only it didn't. It missed.

<It didn't miss.>

It was true. Somehow at the last instant, the quarrel seemed to flex and bend, rolling up over Mao's shoulder and burying itself into the barkeep's head with a sickening crunch. The fletching filled the left eye socket as the rest of the bolt sunk into and out of the back of the skull in a sudden spray of bone and bloody brain matter. There was an audible snap as his arm broke when he collapsed, his dead weight held up by the knife that bound his hand to the bar-top.

There was a snarling and tearing amid cries of pain and Nihm spun to see the dogs mauling two of the remaining shadow men. The third crashed to the ground in a loud clatter, his crossbow skittering away across the wooden boards of the floor. The robed figure hadn't bothered catching and lowering him it seemed.

"Lumousim arctum!" shouted Mercy, thrusting her staff up above the table and glancing around its rim as a light burst from the end of her staff. It lit up the room and slightly bemused, Mercy counted seven bodies slumped in chairs as if sleeping.

The screams from the two men being savaged suddenly cut off and a wild ripping, crunching noise was all they could hear as the dogs finished their work.

"Well shit." Stama looked over the counter at the dead barkeep. He gripped his knife handle and waggling it, pried it loose. The hand it pinned slithered away, leaving a trail of blood.

"Ah well, he talked too much anyway," Stama muttered, before smoothly leaping the bar and rummaging through the barkeep's jerkin.

Nihm studied the silent man, they all did. He looked old. His face lined and scarred. His robe was brown, loose-fitting, and cinched at the waist. Considering he'd just accounted for seven men he didn't look dangerous, his stance unassuming and non-threatening.

The dogs, strangely, didn't seem to perceive him as a threat. Nihm whistled and they stopped their grisly business and returned to her side.

"Thank you for the help friend," Mercy said, rising to her feet. "Sorry to be blunt but we've had a hell of a day. Who are you and what do you want?"

The robed man's eyes twinkled it seemed to Nihm and his mouth quirked. "You are most welcome. I am …"

"Master Hiro," Mao slurred. "Mao say Hiro come. No one listen to Mao." He took a swig from the bottle he was holding.

The robed man, Hiro, waved a hand and the bottle shattered. Mercy immediately raised her staff, dropping into a battle stance, Lucky raising his sword. Hiro glanced at them, unconcerned he addressed the old man.

"Mao, you are drunk and with whiskey to boot. What did we agree about drinking whiskey?" Hiro said, approaching. He stopped suddenly and looked quizzically at the old man.

"Oh Mao, what have you done?"

"Not Mao, Red Cloak," Mao replied looking disgruntled.

"I take it you're here for the old man? Well, you're welcome to him," Mercy said.

Hiro pondered his friend for a second or so before turning to Mercy as if only now registering her question. "Actually, I'm here for Mao and the girl." He indicated Nihm.

"The girl's with me and under my protection," Mercy replied, taking a step towards Nihm.

"I'm not a girl, I'm a woman and this woman has a name," Nihm said, put out at being discussed like a piece of baggage.

Hiro bowed at Nihm. "Forgive me, old I maybe but not wise, neh!"

Mercy for her part simply grunted.

Lucky, wandering the room, was inspecting Hiro's handy work. He whistled, nodding his head. "This is some neat work friend, I don't know how you managed it but it's very tidy. However," he looked across at them all, "judging by the sour look on friend Stama's face over there anyone that might have known the way out of this place appears to be dead."

"He knows a way out," Nihm said. "Isn't that so, Master Hiro?"

"Just so," Hiro's mouth curled. "We should go. Urak are near. There will be time for questions later. However, I have one last one before we leave."

"Zoller take Renco, Master," Mao stated, knowing the question.

"Ah," Hiro sighed.

To Nihm he looked deflated all of a sudden and she watched as he crossed to Mao. "Can you walk, old friend, or do you need my arm?"

"Bah, Mao not dead," Mao grunted, dipping his fingers into the spillage on the table before suckling on them.

Nihm couldn't help but notice Mao's mood had soured. Whether at his Master's return, his smashed booty, or maybe, she suddenly intuited, it was the mention of Renco. She wasn't sure. Renco was the young man's name then. At the thought of him, he was suddenly there in her mind. Nihm pictured him as he looked directly at her from atop his horse as the Red Cloaks pulled him away. *<Help him,>* he'd said.

Nihm moved across to Mao, "Let's get out of here, old father." She took his arm and glanced at Hiro. He was lean and wiry and no taller than she.

Hiro nodded his head in thanks before marching over to the side door. There, he picked up a pack and staff before leading them down a corridor and into the kitchens. Opening another door revealed a stairway leading down.

It was musty and cold in the cellars. Several wall braziers were lit providing a tepid light to see by. The cellar was large with lots of barrels, bales and crates littering the place. Taking them to the back of the room, Hiro felt along its far wall until he found what he looked for. With a snick and click a crack appeared in the wall. Hiro pushed and a section of stone suddenly moved revealing an opening.

Nihm was impressed, the hidden door was cunningly disguised and almost impossible to detect from the rest of the wall. The stone door was heavy and Lucky stepped forward to help turn it on its pivot.

The passage beyond was dark and dank. Mercy led the way with her staff, providing ample light for the others to follow.

Ash and Snow whined at the entrance.

"Ya big babies, come on," Nihm chided and reluctantly they followed her into the passage beyond. Lucky was last through and putting his shoulder to the door slammed it shut with a loud crunch.

## Chapter 9: More Questions than Answers

**Kingsholme, The Holme**

*"Hey kid, wake up!"*

Tomas became aware of the hushed voice in his ear. He'd heard it before but where? And why did he feel so groggy? He lay still trying to gather his thoughts. He was warm and comfortable. He lay in a bed with covers that smelt fresh and soft and he had no clothes on. He knew he was in trouble.

*"Kid, come-on. He'll be back soon and I'm burning up here."*

His memory returned, smacking into him like a door slamming. He sat bolt upright the soft covers spilling from his chest. That voice, Bortillo, falling, hitting the ground. Why wasn't he dead? He patted himself feeling his body. It was fine. No not fine, it felt like he'd had the snot kicked out of him but nothing wasn't broken. He was breathing. Tomas moaned, his aching head, seemingly catching up with his sudden motion, decided to throb its protest, and he sunk back down onto the pillow. Pillow, he laughed at the absurdity of it all. Despite the pain, he couldn't help it. It was a real pillow, so soft his head sank into it.

"Agghh, my head," Tomas groaned.

*"Yeah, yeah you're lucky you're alive. And it's all thanks to me. You owe me big time."*

That voice again, it was the ghost. Gritting his teeth, Tomas mumbled. "Who're you? Where am I?"

*"O'si, third level Sháadretarch. Your kind calls us demons… fools. You're in a bed, but right now I need you to open my vessel. I need some serious downtime."*

"Your vessel?" Tomas asked.

*"Yeah, the door's shut so to speak. I need you to open it."* O'si whispered.

Tomas screwed his eyes tight shut, his head pulsed and he felt nauseous. He couldn't focus properly. The ghost was a demon, he could manage that thought. He should be afraid but there wasn't room in his head for it at that moment.

*"Schniétrakor kid, say the word. I'm dyin' here,"* O'si hissed.

Tomas wanted the voice to go away, every sound was like a spike through his brain. Please just go away he willed.

*"You owe me. I saved your hide. Come-on snap out of it. Man up kid! Come on, you can…"*

"Schniétrakor," Tomas muttered.

The air seemed to crackle, then, blessed silence. Tomas lay there, his head seeming to find a balance, the throbbing receding as long as he didn't move. Who knew doing nothing could be so rewarding, Tomas thought. He was thirsty, parched in fact and he needed a piss but he couldn't bear to open his eyes let alone move. He drifted off.

When Tomas awoke it was dark. His head was tender still but on the whole, it felt a lot better. The voice was gone, the one that tormented him. Had he imagined it? As he lay in bed awareness slowly returned to him. He wasn't alone. He knew when a room was empty and this one wasn't.

Not moving, Tomas cracked open his eyelids but the darkness in the room gave little help.

"You must be thirsty? You've been out cold for two days now." A voice in the black.

Tomas considered feigning sleep but discarded the notion. Whoever he was, the man knew he was awake. Tomas opened his eyes, turning to the voice.

"Who are you? And where am I?" Tomas asked, his head ached but it was manageable.

"Ignatituum forus arctum." A flare of light, as a candle suddenly ignited.

It sat on a bedside table next to Tomas and he instinctively leant away from it as it flared, shielding his eyes from the harsh brightness. His mind immediately went to work weighing up what he knew, where he must be. Fear gripped him but Tomas had lived with fear his whole life. It didn't rule him.

"You're a mage," Tomas said. "I'm in the Enclave."

"A mage? In a manner of speaking, yes," the man replied, "but no, we're not in the Enclave." Behind the candle, the man's face was shadowed. He leaned forward into the light.

He's old… thirty or forty was Tomas's first thought. The face was long and narrow and the man wore a neatly trimmed goatee, black but flecked through with a little grey. His lips were thin and his nose aquiline but it was the eyes that commanded attention. They were a grey-green and intelligent, piercing in their intensity. He wore a grey robe, cinched at the waist with a wide band of black cloth. Even under the man's scrutiny, Tomas felt a sense of relief. The man was no mage or at least he dressed like none he'd ever seen.

"Can you sit? Do you need water?" the man asked.

"Need a piss," Tomas responded, looking to see how his words were received. Tomas liked to watch people. He found he could tell a lot about a person from how they reacted to things.

The man looked amused. "There's a piss pot under the bed." He moved back, his face disappearing into shadow.

Tomas sat up, recalled that he was naked, and wondered where his clothes had gone. He glanced at the shadowed figure then shrugged. If the pervert wanted to watch, let him. But if he so much as moved to touch him he'd bury the candle in his eye.

Slipping gingerly out of bed, Tomas hooked the piss pot out with his foot. It was enamelled ceramic and looked expensive. He snorted, the things people wasted money on never failed to amaze him but really, this was taking the piss. His observation made him chuckle and his head repaid his humour with a dull throb.

Tomas winced then scowled, he'd not had cause to use a piss pot before and wasn't sure how. Did you lift it up or squat down. Ah well, shrugging his shoulders, Tomas took aim and let fly with a steady stream that he found highly satisfying. He splashed a bit at the start but once he got his aim in it was oddly rewarding.

It took him a while to empty his bladder; about midway through he wondered if the pot would be big enough. Finding it funny, Tomas fought to stop himself from laughing. If he laughed he'd miss his aim. The thought made him want to laugh all the more and he had to bite his lip to control himself. Finally done, Tomas shook himself before hopping back to the bed and the safety of his covers.

The man leaned forward again still looking amused. Tomas wasn't sure what it told him, not yet.

The man indicated a wooden cup next to the candle. "Please, you must be thirsty."

He was, Tomas reached for the cup and took a sniff. Nothing, just water, he took a sip, then a gulp until he'd finished it. He placed it back down. "Thanks, errmm, who are you exactly and where are my clothes?"

"I threw them out," the man replied. "My name's Renix and yours is?"

"Bort," Tomas lied. "Why did you throw my clothes away? I kinda need them."

"Bort," Renix said as if tasting the name. His mouth curled.

"I didn't see you fall, just heard you land," he said by way of explanation. "You must be the luckiest thief alive. Fell forty feet or more into a pile of refuse. You stank so bad I'm afraid the clothes had to go. There's more in the dresser over there. My son's, you look of a size."

"I'm no thief," Tomas said.

"You're a thief and a liar and apparently not much good at either," Renix said. He hefted something heavy onto the bed.

It was the tome. Tomas recognised it instantly, Sházáik Douné Táak, the Book of Demons. The last time he'd seen it was as he placed it in his pack.

"Damn near killed by a book. What an epitaph that would have made, eh," Renix mused.

"It was in your pack, made a hell of a thud when it landed. Missed me by no more than an arm's length and damn near frightened me to death," Renix continued. He rummaged at his feet and threw Tomas's pack on the bed. "Now, no more lies. I've met the most famous thief ever lived, so I know one when I see one."

"You know Bortillo Targus?" Tomas couldn't help himself; Bortillo had tried to kill him. Did the man know Bortillo? Instantly Tomas was on edge and he looked about for anything that might be of use, a weapon or better yet a way out; but the room was big and the candle small. There was nothing he could discern.

"Bortillo Targus?" Renix laughed. "In a manner, but no, I don't speak of your master, Bort." He emphasized the name.

Tomas chided himself, what a fool. He said nothing more. Sure that whatever he did say would only get him deeper in trouble than he already was. The man Renix was silent, no doubt weighing up his next question before asking it.

"You interest me whoever you are. The book has the stench of the Enclave on it but I can find no sign of the mages taint on you. Which is most interesting."

"What's the taint?" Tomas asked.

"It's like a mark. For those not permitted entry to the Enclave it clings to them, makes them easy for the council to find. The book I am in no doubt came from the Enclave, yet somehow you do not carry the taint. Which is both intriguing and lucky, I couldn't afford to help you if you had it. Now, if you do want my help you need to start talking the truth. I'll know it if I hear it, trust me."

"You're no mage," Tomas stated.

"I am not of the Enclave," Renix qualified. "Now tell me. Why did you steal the book? Do you know what it is?"

"It wasn't part of the job. I just saw it and took it. I like books," Tomas said, miffed at Renix's raised eyebrow. "I can read ya know."

"Can you now? A ten-year-old street thief can read?" Renix sounded sceptical.

"Of course," Tomas said, then feeling the need to prove his point, "It's the Book of Demons and I'm not ten I'm twelve… I think."

Renix's eyebrows rose even further at this. "Now that is interesting, a young street hustler who can read archiárcik script," Renix muttered. He gazed intently at Tomas.

"Tell me, thief, who is not a thief and Bort, who is not Bort. What does Bortillo Targus want with you? Nothing good I surmise. He looked furious; scared too when he found you gone. Why would that be?"

"I don't know nothin' about no archursik, whatever you called it. They're just words, that's all," Tomas replied. "And I don't know nothin' about Bortillo neither," which was true. He didn't know why Bortillo had tried to kill him. He'd stolen the relics. Did the king of thieves think he'd stiff him?

Guiltily, Tomas felt for the bracer on his wrist and twisted the ring on his finger. They were the only things of value he had on him, although to be fair they were the only things he had on him, he grinned. It made him wonder though, why hadn't Renix taken them? His grin faded, he had more questions than answers and didn't seem close to solving any of them.

"You've given me much to think on. Rest up, I'll be back later. Maybe we can start again from the beginning, truth this time, eh!" Renix stood. "You will find food on the table. Help yourself."

"I'm a prisoner then?" Tomas asked accusingly.

"No, I bind no man or woman. You're free to go, but you're safer here," Renix said. "If you do decide to leave though, I should warn you, my contacts tell me Bortillo is looking for a boy named Tomas the Mouse. His description is a fair likeness to your own. You have a big bounty on your head for one so small. You must have crossed him badly, Tomas."

"I didn't cross no one, least of all Bortillo. He crossed me," Tomas said.

Renix nodded his understanding. "Stay safe." He sunk into the shadows and seconds later a door open and closed.

Tomas listened for the lock turning but there was nothing. Just the soft sound of Renix as he walked away. With a scowl, Tomas realised he had answered to his name and admitted his involvement with Bortillo Targus.

## Chapter 10: The Roaring Cave

**Fallston, The Rivers**

The hidden passageway in the Loud Water Inn fed into a large cave system, one that was well used. They wandered for twenty minutes with Hiro guiding them, down narrow rock-hewn corridors and small caves containing crates and bales of produce both legal and illegal.

Finally, they entered a large central cavern that seemed to be the main storage and living area. The cavern had clearly been in use for a long time. It was almost comfortable, after a fashion, with torches and braziers providing a dull light to see by.

There were five cots arrayed about the place along with a couple of tables and chairs. The air was chilled, no real light ever penetrated here and it was left to the braziers to provide what little warmth there was.

Snow and Ash were agitated and led Nihm to some crates stacked near the back of the cavern where she discovered two bodies. Unassuming and old the monk might be, thought Nihm, but he was dangerous. That was nine bodies he'd accounted for and he didn't have so much as a mark on him to show for it.

Hiro directed Stama and Lucky in the disposal of the bodies and they dragged them through a small passage that opened up into a cave filled with the loud rumble of the falls.

Curious and keen to explore, Nihm followed and was forced to cover her ears as she stepped into the cave. The sound of the water was so loud it was oppressive making it hard to hear even her own thoughts. Her ears seemed to adjust, the air shifting and thickening until the intensity of the sound became muted and bearable.

Nihm found the cave fascinating and the reason for the noise obvious. The far end of the hollow was open and the falling water of the Oust roared by, the rocks near its maw slick and treacherous. Water seeped from cracks and holes in the walls and ceiling in a constant patter of rain that filled the myriad of shallow pools littering the cave floor. The pools were all interconnected and the water they collected dribbled lazily back through the opening to re-join the river.

Lucky and Stama hefted the bodies one at a time, swinging them out and into the crushing force of the water where they were snatched away in the blink of an eye. Job done, Hiro led them back into the main cavern where Mercy was waiting for them.

"We need to talk," Mercy said, as Hiro emerged from the roaring cave.

"We wait," Hiro answered.

"I take it there's another way out, one that leads us away from Fallston?" Mercy insisted.

"Yes, but it would be unwise to take it now," Hiro said.

"Why? It's night. We could be leagues away come sun up." Mercy said.

"Where is it you go?" Hiro asked.

"Away, then, when we can, south to safety."

"To the south lies the Grim Marsh and beyond that the Wolds. Both are treacherous and dangerous to navigate, though for different reasons." Hiro gestured Mercy to take a seat. For himself, he folded down onto his legs. "To run is instinctive but to do so blindly without thought is foolish."

Nihm saw Mercy stiffen at the old monk's tone. The mage was tense and tired. The last few days had taken a toll. When she spoke though it was considered and calm.

"You're right. We need a plan and I admit my knowledge of the Rivers is limited, as are our options. I will listen to your counsel, but first I need some answers."

"Good, knowledge is the start of understanding, understanding the start of wisdom," Hiro said. "We have plenty of time. We will be here a while. Time enough for talking and planning. First, some introductions I think."

"What do you mean we'll be here a while," Lucky said. "We're at the front of this urak invasion. We hang about any longer we'll be in the middle of it."

Hiro looked up at the large towering man, considering his words before replying.

"We are hunted. Or rather, it is Nihm they hunt. I think you were caught before just north of Fallston. That was a Taken you fought." Hiro saw the furtive looks they gave each other, confirmation of what he said. "There's another Taken in Fallston, I felt his disturbance in the Inn, and so he must be close. Here underground, I cannot sense the Taken nor the Taken, I suspect, Nihm. So to run would be a mistake, like a deer startled from the bush. No, we will stay awhile."

Stama joined his friend, shaking his head in disbelief. "You tell us children's tales. The Taken are from an age long past, they died an aeon ago. Now you're saying they've returned."

"Time is a harsh master and we a fickle race. The urakakule are monsters spoken of in tales around campfires and in taverns. Tales told but never really believed. Well, they are neither a tale nor monsters and they are here, now. Claiming what they believe is their own," Hiro said, looking at each in turn as he spoke. "People believe in them now. You believe in them because you have seen them. So why do you find it so hard to believe in the Taken? After all, you fought one."

They were silent at that, thoughtful. Their faces worried as the implications of what Hiro said sunk in. Nihm was first to speak, her worries different than the others, more immediate.

"Why me?" Nihm asked.

"Child, you are so bright can you not see?" Hiro replied. "If Keeper knew, you would have been kept close. Safe, neh! Your essence, your self is so strong it is like a light in the darkness when I look for it. The Morhudrim too looks for the light in the dark. I think they see you and are afraid. That which they fear they hunt."

A lot of thoughts flitted through Nihm's mind then. A memory surfaced, similar to the one she'd had earlier that day, from when she was little more than a babe. She saw Master Hiro leaning over her, much as Maohong had in her earlier memory, only Hiro didn't coo and cluck over her like Mao. He held an arm out in front of him, two fingers raised, his eyes shut tight, his face a mask of concentration. Eventually, his eyes opened; the same dark eyes that regarded her now. "She has ability but it's blocked and limited much like your own, Marron."

Her mother appeared over Hiro's shoulder, looking down at her. She looked relieved at his words. "Good, what will you tell Keeper?"

"The truth, she's not suitable," Hiro said. Her father came into view. Where her Ma looked pleased with Hiro's announcement her Da looked… disappointed? Upset? "I'm sorry." Hiro laid a hand in comfort on her father's arm before moving away. The memory faded.

Hiro watched her, silent.

<*He was sent to assess you.*>

<*Yes,*> Replied Nihm <*But for what?*> She turned away, not sure she wanted to know. The image of her parents was all she could think about. So clearly had she recalled them that it left her feeling unsettled. Tears sprang, unbidden and she walked away; she didn't want anyone to see. The last thing she wanted was sympathy or to be someone they made allowance for. What she wanted was to be left alone.

But she was never alone, not now. The soft patter of paws sounded as Snow and Ash moved alongside, noses nuzzling her hands as they sensed her distress. No one else followed or called out.

Nihm found herself at the entrance to the passage leading to the roaring cave. The noise was too loud for the dogs' comfort. She commanded them to wait and they sat obediently, watching silently as Nihm disappeared into the cavern.

There was no light in the roaring cave but Nihm's eyes compensated enough that she could navigate. Surefooted, she moved to the opening where the noise was loudest. Her hearing adjusted, dampening down like it had before and the sound became muffled and tolerable. Finding a rock she sat, no more than a pace from the crushing wall of water.

Here, Nihm didn't have to think, she could just be; absorbing everything and nothing.

The sound of the water drowned out all thought. The vibration in the rocks matched her body as it shook. The moisture in the air and on her skin mixed with her tears until there were none left. For the first time Nihm could remember, she felt nothing. No thoughts, no feelings. She could stay here; there was no pain, just peace and serenity. She felt at rest; at one with the world yet blessedly alone.

<*Your core body temperature is dropping. Your systems are starting to shut down with the cold and you are burning a lot of energy reserves to compensate. You need to move*

away now and change out of your wet coverings. I do not understand your function here?> Sai intoned.

But she was never alone, not now. Now, she had Sai. The thought was there, the same one she'd had earlier.

<Earlier was one hour and twelve minutes ago,> Sai said.

<Go away.>

<Negative. Please comply,> Sai responded.

Nihm was suddenly annoyed. She'd told Sai to say 'no' not 'negative'. It irritated her, why couldn't he talk normally like she asked? She shivered violently, her teeth chattering. She was cold she realised, her head ached with it.

Whatever was she thinking? What was she doing here? She had to get back, get warm. Her Ma and Da would be upset and disappointed to see her so. The thought was a crushing revelation. It was true and enough to jar her out of her lethargy.

Standing abruptly, Nihm turned to head back to the others and slipped. Time dilated. Her muscles, cramped with languor and cold, failed, her earlier surefootedness gone in a moment. Her hand extended wildly; latching onto the rock she'd been sat upon.

It was a desperate lunge and Nihm felt a nail rip from her finger at the effort. It wouldn't be enough; she knew it the moment she made the grab. The rock had been worn smooth over the millennia by water, smooth enough that she could find no purchase. At that same instant, as she stumbled inches from the wall of water and death, she was aware of the old monk, Hiro. He stood not two feet away. His hand moved. So quickly, even as everything around her seemed to slow, and clasped her arm. His grip was firm. It was enough to steady her.

Recovering her balance, Nihm pulled herself over the rock-seat to safety. Shaking violently at the cold in her bones and at how close she had come to death.

Her body had adjusted well this day, to the point where walking and moving was not something that required her conscious thought. Everything had snapped into place almost seamlessly on the walk into the Hang earlier. It made what she had done all the more idiotic. Like her body, her mind had acted without thought. Nihm felt Sai's disapproval at the abuse she had visited upon herself. She had been careless.

<Reckless.>

Yes, she had been reckless.

The old monk released her arm and turning, headed back the way he'd come. He paused at the entranceway to stare back at her and impatiently signed that she should follow before disappearing into the passageway beyond.

It occurred to Nihm that Hiro had brought no torch with him and yet appeared to see her as clearly as she saw him. Feeling strangely connected, Nihm followed. Her muscles ached where they'd cramped but it felt good as she stretched them out, her steps once again becoming light and sure.

Back in the large cavern, Nihm found everyone gathered. They shared a mix of concerned looks. Stama and Lucky shook their heads, no doubt at her foolishness. Mercy scolded her whilst at the same time whipping her cloak off and throwing it about her shoulders. Morten looked relieved.

"I thought you in trouble, Nihm." He rushed up. "But Snow and Ash wouldn't let me through. Not any of us 'cepting him." He indicated Hiro, accusingly.

"It's alright; I'm fine, just having a fool moment. I'm sorry I worried you all," Nihm muttered, embarrassed at the concern they showed.

Hiro for his part moved over to a table as if the event was of no moment. Food had been found and laid out and he helped himself to it with gusto.

Nihm searched for Mao and spied him at rest in one of the cots, snoring gently. She smiled, he was the only one it seemed not worried for her. Nihm let out a breath of relief. She'd felt responsible for Mao ever since Renco bid her help him and felt guilty that she'd just walked off and left him. He was old and injured still.

<You are wet and need sustenance,> Sai prompted. As if reading Sai's thoughts, Mercy slipped an arm around Nihm's shoulders and steered her towards the cots.

"Come on, let's get you dry, then some food," Mercy said.

Nihm followed willingly enough. She wasn't shy about getting changed but Mercy held a blanket up whilst she stripped out of her wet clothes and undergarments.

"You were gone an age in that cave. I don't know what possessed you, Nihm. Promise me you won't just wander off again like that," Mercy said.

"You're not my mother," Nihm snapped, wishing instantly she could take it back. Mercy flinched like she'd been slapped and her face reddened, in anger or embarrassment, Nihm wasn't sure.

"I'm just looking out for you, Nihm. That's all. I'm not looking to replace Marron," Mercy whispered, looking around to see if any had heard.

Nihm thought Mercy wanted to say something more but instead closed her mouth and held her peace.

"Sorry, that was cruel of me," Nihm said, meaning it as she removed the last of her wet clothes.

Mercy didn't speak for a moment and when she did it was brusque and business-like. "Found some crates with clothing and such like in. I had Lucky drag them over here." Mercy nodded her head, indicating behind Nihm. "Should find something to fit, take your time, I got all night."

<Mercy's disposition seems angry,> Sai questioned.

<No shit,> Nihm responded feeling shamed. She dried herself, the blanket she used prickly and rough against her skin. It was oddly comforting, suiting her mood whilst at the same time irritating her skin and rubbing feeling back into her bones.

Rummaging through the boxes of clothing, Nihm picked out leather trousers that fit uncommonly well, some strapping, a wool vest, linen shirt and leather jerkin. She dressed quickly, and silently. Mercy nodded approval but said nothing, moving away once Nihm was done without saying another word.

<I'm gonna have to do some serious kiss-ass to get back in her good books.>

<What is kiss-ass?> Sai asked.

<You'll see,> Nihm promised, moving to the food table. She took her fill, encouraged by Sai who had the annoying habit of telling her what to eat. Finally

sated, Nihm moved to one of the cots. She wasn't sure what had been discussed and agreed in her absence but it was clear that they weren't going anywhere.

Nihm settled into the cot next to Maohong. She had thought him asleep but when she glanced over at him, he stared at her, eyes alert. He smiled his crooked grin and winked before turning onto his back. Moments later he was snoring loudly.

Maybe this cot wasn't the best idea, thought Nihm but she didn't move. Instead, slipping into an easy sleep, where she dreamt of the roaring cave and the peace it offered.

## Chapter 11: Grim Times

**North of Fallston, The Rivers**

They found the woman on a shale bank half a league down from the burnt man, half-drowned and so pale, Tom thought her dead at first.

The burnt man they'd left to die. Black Jack had no use for him. He was of no value and was clearly knocking at death's door. Black Jack hadn't even the decency to slip a knife in his heart to ease him on his way and Tom felt bad about that. And guilty that he'd not done it himself, but he knew better than to cross Black Jack.

A lone wolf, grizzled and vicious, attracted their attention, howling defiance at them else they'd never have found her. Curious, they had chased it off to see what it guarded; the hope being it was another body to plunder. It was. That the woman still lived was a miracle. She was old enough to be his mother, Tom judged and would have been pretty, all things considered, if not for the tattoo of black bruising her eyes and mouth, as if, like stale fruit, she had started to turn and go rotten.

Finding her was more than chance. The tri gods must have been looking over her, for she'd have died if they hadn't found her. It was still likely looking at the knife sticking out of her chest and if that didn't finish her then the wolf surely would have.

Black Jack asked for no volunteers and searched her himself, hands roughly groping her body, breasts and thighs. Happily declaring she had all her teeth, he came away with a purse heavy with coin and lust in his eyes.

Tom and Hissings were ordered to construct a stretcher out of the long poles and bedding and they carried her south, down the embankment, a tricky endeavour, then onto a skiff, which they'd hidden in the reeds on the edges of the Grim Marsh.

The lone wolf tailed them the whole way, sour at losing its easy meal and Tom watched in fascination as it moped, agitated on the bank as they paddled away. He'd heard and seen plenty of wolves roaming the plains north, they moved in packs but he'd never seen one this close up before. It was a big, mean-looking cur.

The Grim Marsh was dangerous, its channels and waterways constantly shifting and changing but they knew its secrets as well as any creature living, and the lodestone Black Jack carried, drew them unfailingly on to the Grimhold.

Two days they paddled through the Grim's treacherous waterways and fetid mud pools. Tom managed at least to fend off the bugs and insects, a simple barrier spell enough to keep them out. The larger denizens were more troublesome and the long poles were called on to encourage them to look elsewhere for a meal.

Somehow, the woman managed to live through it all. Her skin was sallow, and together with her blackened eyes and lips, gave her a ghastly, moribund appearance. Thankfully, she never awakened; something Black Jack took full advantage of on the few occasions they found ground firm enough to make camp on. His heavy grunting into the night was loud and disturbing. Tom hated the man but never so much as he did then.

The end of the second day saw them to the Grimhold. It sat on a large island in the marsh. The hold was little more than a dilapidated tower with broken walls, inside of which was a town of sorts. It was by no means the only hold in the Grim, nor even the only one named the Grimhold but it was theirs. Its location provided better protection than any castle wall. It was home and Tom loathed it.

Black Jack called for the physiker, an ugly old woman named Hettingly. Brusque and surly, she ordered the woman to be taken to the shack next to her cottage which she used as her apothecary.

As ever, Tom was curious whenever Hett worked. His own magic was rudimentary at best and self-taught. No one knew of course. Tom hadn't even entrusted his mother with the knowledge, knowing she would talk, and there was no one else to tell, not anymore.

It was by accident, Tom found, that if he was close enough when Hett shaped her magic he could feel it, even if he didn't understand how or what she did. Tantalisingly, he could almost sense how the old witch manipulated her magic but it never stuck, eluding him whenever he tried it himself. It felt so alien, Tom was sure he did something wrong. If the witch wasn't so cantankerous and vicious with it, he might have asked for her help. It was hard trying to work things out by himself, mistakes happened.

Once, he set flame to Torgrid's house trying to ignite his own fire. Tom smiled at the memory. It hadn't really been his fault. Torgrid was having a stand-up row with Jessop at the time and it had turned nasty. It distracted him, his attention shifting momentarily from his stacked woodpile to the ensuing fight; knives had been drawn, blood would be spilt. Instead of gutting each other though, Torgrid's house thatch suddenly burst into flame and the fight was forgotten. So some good had come of it at least. Lucky for him, Torgrid took the blame for it; evil shit that he was it was well deserved.

Tom sat discretely with his back to the apothecary's sidewall, learning what he could, as Hett drew on her magic. He heard the heavy tramp of feet on the path. He knew the tread and stride and sat still and silent. There was a loud banging.

"Hetty, you hag. Open up." It was Black Jack, his coarse voice instantly recognisable. Tom felt the moment Hett's weaving vanished.

"I'm working, come back later," Hett bellowed back.

Black Jack tried the door but it was barred from the inside.

"I said open up, you dry old cunt." Black Jack smacked his fist against the door.

"Knock that door again, Jackson and it'll not be me helpin' you next time you get the black shits," Hett shouted back.

The banging stopped. Tom didn't blame him, the black shits were bad. People died from it and not quietly in their beds neither. A lot less would survive it if not for old Hett. She was the most valued person in the holdstead, though not necessarily the most liked.

Tom heard the bar slide and the door open. He imagined the squat shape of Hett filling the entrance.

"Afore ya ask, I don't know Jack. She'll likely die despite my efforts but she'll surely die if you keep bangin' on my door, draggin' me away from my work." There was a snap of fingers clicking. "Stop ogling the woman, you seen a naked woman afore ain't ya."

"Anything you need Hett, I'll get it you. I want her alive," Black Jack muttered, his voice low, almost pleading. Tom hadn't ever heard him talk so before.

"Yeah, I know what you want 'er for an all. Fucking men! Piss off and let me be, that's all I need from you," Hett cursed, before slamming the door shut.

Tom expected Black Jack to walk away but he didn't, not immediately, he just stood there still as a post. Tom sat unmoving, scared hardly to breathe, wondering what he was doing. Eventually, Black Jack turned and shuffled away, bellowing at someone he'd seen, just like normal.

Breathing a sigh of relief, Tom startled when the shutters above his head rattled. They swung wide in an instant and Hett's large round face appeared over the sill peering down at him. It was a fat face, her jowls loose, the skin saggy and blotchy in places. She was, without doubt, the ugliest woman he knew. Hett's eyes narrowed and before he could move she latched a meaty paw on his hair and pulled him upright.

"Little shit. What've I told ya about sittin' outside spyin' on old Hett?"

Tom cried out, she was none to gentle with his hair. "Ouch, sorry Hett."

"That's all ya gotta say, eh. Sorry," Hett growled, "You perving like Jackson? Want an eye full do ya?"

"No, Hett it ain't like that, I swear it," Tom gasped. Mercifully, Hett let go of him and he rubbed a hand over his scalp half expecting it to come away wet and bloody. The witch had about pulled his hair out.

Hett watched him. Her bright blue eyes, the only pretty thing about her, stared intently. She sniffed and Tom realised he must stink; he hadn't bathed in days.

"Well, don't stand gawping, get in here. As it happens I could use some help."

Even as she said it, Tom's eyes were drawn past Hett's glowering face to the table in the middle of the room. The woman they'd saved was laid upon it completely naked and looking peaceful as if she was at rest. Hett pulled the shutters closed with a loud crash making Tom swerve his head back to avoid contact. He could see the naked woman still in his mind. Guilt washed over him. He felt dirty that he'd looked but also strangely excited.

"Don't keep me waiting boy," Hett grumped from around the front, where she'd unbarred and opened the door. Tom shook himself, he must have been stood there longer than he realised. He ambled around to the front of the hut and, taking an anxious breath, stepped inside.

The interior was ill-lit, but good enough to see that the room was busy. A table lay against the far wall with cupboards and shelving lining every space with all

© 2020 A D Green

manner of things. He saw blankets, stripped cloths, vials, bottles, and boxes along with an oddment of books and other paraphernalia. Rows of plants of all sorts hung suspended on hooks drying. They gave the room a pleasant, fragrant smell.

The far table held an assortment of bottles, containing who knew what and something that looked like a still. At least it bore a passing resemblance to the still Odd-John used for brewing his whiskey mash. The table also had a knife block and even a little bone saw that sat glinting on a rung above.

In the centre of the room lay the woman. Hett had taken the time to drape a cover over her and Tom was thankful for it. Outside looking in, Tom had thought her peaceful and at rest but up close he saw that wasn't the case. She looked pallid and ill. The black around her eyes and mouth had spread like tendrils across her face.

He'd seen Len Chadst die to poisonblood in the space of a few hours, a dark black line from the cut on his arm spreading to his heart. He wondered if this was the same thing although he could see no cuts on her face.

"She looks bad. She gonna die?" Tom said, then cried out as Hett slapped the back of his head. "What was that for?"

"You're smart, cleverer than most folk," Hett growled. "That was for bein' stupid."

Tom rubbed the back of his head; his scalp still ached where she'd grabbed his hair. He was sore, tired, hungry, and he stank. What did she expect? He grumbled to himself.

"And don't mutter. It's rude," Hett snapped. "Now pull that chair over here by the table and sit."

Tom complied, scraping the legs along the floorboards until the glare from the hag convinced him to lift it. He sat on the side near the woman's head, his eyes fascinated by the dark traces across her face. He was drawn to the knife still sticking out of her chest. It would have to come out; maybe Hett needed his help with that. The witch prowled the other side of the table looking vexed.

"So what do you want me to do?" Tom asked, grateful at least that he was out of arm's reach.

"The woman's dead, Tom," Hett said with no preamble.

Tom looked at the woman lying still on the table. Still enough to be dead but there was the faintest rise and fall of the covers. She was breathing. Hett was wrong. He looked at the physiker puzzled, only to see her smiling grimly back.

"I see it too, boy. She's breathin' and there's a warmth to her skin that tells me she's not dead. Only, she ain't alive either."

"I don't understand," Tom said.

"I'm a physiker, Tom. I mend people and I manipulate their essence to do it. It's delicate and tricky messing with people's essence. There's a natural resistance to it that makes working it difficult," Hett explained. "I know about essence, the shape, and structure, the radiance and taste of it. It's all very familiar, there's a sameness about it. Don't get me wrong, everyone's different, unique even, but similar enough."

"And why are you telling me this?" Tom asked he'd never seen Hett ramble on so, it was disconcerting.

"Because she ain't got none, boy, not like it awt ta be." Agitated, Hett clenched her chubby hands together and wandered around the table.

Tom was worried. What did she expect from him? "I don't know nothin' bout essence, Hett."

Hett clipped him hard around the ear. "Ow, what was that for?"

"That was for bein' stupid, and for thinkin' me a fool," Hett repeated. "Sit outside my window, set fire to things, and countless other little acts of vandalism and think I don't know it. You wield the art boy, not well it has to be said, but you're a practitioner."

Tom was agog. "You know? Why haven't you helped me?"

Hett wandered over to the table set against the far wall whilst she considered his question.

"Three reasons. First off, I'm a physiker. I work with the essence in things, I don't draw it or use it, can't. Trust me, tried plenty a times when I was young. You draw essence and use it. Different altogether," Hett stated.

"Second, if I helped you others would notice. They would talk and assume things, wrongly, cos they're all fuckheads but you would have value to them. They would use you and I'll not be a party to that." Hett moved back to the woman and bent to examine the knife wound.

"And the third?" Tom asked.

"Eh?" Hett sniffed the flesh around the knife. It looked red and angry.

"You said three reasons," Tom prompted.

Hett never looked up from her examination. "You never asked."

Tom thought about it. She was right on the last two counts, the first he didn't understand well enough. He knew one thing though. If she needed his help it wasn't for holding bandages and the like. She would've called Lizzy or one of the other women in.

"I don't know how to use it. I mean, it's all trial and error, Hett. I can feel this energy all around me but I don't know what it is, just that I can draw on it sometimes."

Hett stood and stared at Tom, considering. "Okay, well I want you to do that now."

"What?" Tom was taken aback. He didn't know if he could. He usually just did it without thinking; little things like the barrier spell or blocking smell from his nose, both useful things he'd done a hundred times or more. Thinking about it was when things went wrong.

"I want you to try and draw some essence, hold it in your hand if you can then lay your hand over the woman." She watched Tom carefully, "Now, Tom."

Tom was nervous all of a sudden. He didn't like being put on the spot. One look at the Hag's face though was enough to convince him to try. He held his hand out over the woman. Then, trying to ignore her, he closed his eyes.

It took him a while to centre himself, to reach out. He could feel it all about him. The essence, Hett called it; the marsh was rife with it. He reached for it and tried to draw it in but it was intangible, like clutching at smoke.

"Hope you fuck better than you magic," Hett interrupted, breaking Tom's concentration. He glared at her and she glared right back.

"You're not helpin' any," Tom said finally.

"Try not to snatch at it. When you want water out a river ya don't batter your fists at it do you? No," she answered herself, "You cup your hands, dip it in gentle like and hold it. You need to be more subtle boy, more delicate. At least that works for me."

Tom stared. Subtle and delicate and Hett just didn't seem to fit. Her words made sense though.

"Okay," he said, grudgingly.

Tom concentrated again. He wasn't sure how to cup something using his senses but he held the image in his mind as he felt the essence surrounding him, imagined stroking at it, coaxing it, and was amazed when it seemed to respond. Oh, not well to be sure, but it did seem to eddy and coalesce, thickening around his hands.

Mindful of Hett's river analogy he moved his hands together, agitating them, imagining the energy pooling in them. It was working. He could see energy balling and swirling. He was doing it. Amazed at his sudden progress, Tom grinned. Then, with a sudden crackle and hiss, at least in his mind, the ball of energy disappeared.

Tom sat back blinking wondering what had just happened. He was so close. He'd held the energy literally in the palms of his hands. What had he done wrong? He looked up apologetically.

"Sorry, want me to try again? Hett…."

Hett looked entranced, her eyes glazed over as she stared avidly at the woman. She shivered suddenly, her head shaking and sending little ripples through the fleshy folds of skin on her neck. "Interesting…."

She looked at Tom. "That was well done. Did you see it?"

"I'm not sure. I had it," Tom laughed, nervous uncertain. "I mean I had it in my hands and then it was gone. I don't know what I did wrong."

Hett made a noise, something between a cough and a bark. It took Tom a moment to realise she was laughing. His cheeks coloured. He'd tried damn her, his euphoria instantly vanishing. He stood and turned for the door.

"You did nothing wrong, Trickle. Sit down," Hett commanded, all humour suddenly gone.

Tom looked back, surprised and more than a little puzzled. The door was damn inviting. It was only a few paces away. But Hett had an answer to what had happened. Ah, fuck it. He sat heavily in the chair and stared at her, expectant. Damned if she didn't look a little grateful.

"I was watching. She took it." Hett stated, "Swallowed it up in the blink of an eye. All that pooled essence, like a leech sucking blood."

Tom's eyes dropped to the woman. She looked no different than before as far as he could tell. "What does it mean?"

He flinched when Hett moved. She was quicker than she looked as he'd already discovered.

"A good question, finally. One I don't have the answer to, yet. But I know this much." Hett paused.

"Yes?" Tom prompted.

Hett scowled crookedly. "Whoever this woman was, she's dead, been dead a while at a guess. Whatever is in her, it ain't human, ain't like any living thing I ever seen before."

"You're not making any sense. She's breathing, Hett," Tom said.

"There is a trace of water in her lungs, I can sense that much. I'd say she drowned and something moved in whilst she moved out."

Tom thought on that a while. It was incredible and creepy at the same time. Living in the Grim, stories abounded of ghosts and wights, demons and the like. All told to scare the littles and discarded when they got old enough to know better. But somewhere in the recesses of his mind, the stories held sway still. Those dark nights out on his own in the marsh, he'd hear things. Things he couldn't explain, sense things that made his spine crawl, hiding just out of sight.

"You think she's possessed? Like, by a demon or something?"

"Don't know, do I look like a fucking oracle?" Hett barked. "Need to decide what to do."

That Hett looked worried alarmed Tom more than he wanted to admit.

© 2020 A D Green

"Is she dangerous? Ya think maybe we should just, you know…." Tom drew a finger across his throat just in case Hett didn't take his meaning.

"Ai maybe, but I'd like to study her first. See how this thing develops, but Tom," Hett said.

"Yeah."

"Only you and I will know of this. Don't tell anyone what we seen and talked about, especially that cockshitter, Jackson. I hear it talked about I know who to come looking for," Hett warned.

"No need for that," Tom said. "But Black Jack, he ain't gonna be pleased if ought happens to her. I heard him."

"Fuck him. Whatever this is," Hett waved at the woman. "If it's a danger, I'll end it. If anything happens to me Tom, you'll have to do it. Swear it."

"Just do it now," Tom said, uncomfortable at the sudden turn of events. Hett stared back, her gaze unflinching.

Finally, relenting and feeling emboldened, Tom nodded. "Ai, Hett, I'll take care of it but only if'n you help me. I need to understand how to use this magic."

"I'm a physiker. You're a practitioner, a mage Tom, although that's stretchin' things," Hett mumbled.

"I did something today I ain't never done. You showed me that. I know you can help me." Tom bit back on the please. Please never got you nowhere in the Grim.

Hett didn't take more than a moment before she nodded her head. "Agreed, now fetch Lizzy for me. She can help me with this knife wound."

"You think that's a good idea? Maybe I'd be better doing it. Less people that know and all that," Tom said.

"Lizzy will do. By sundown, everyone will hear the woman's near-death unless I miss my guess and that will suit just fine for now."

"What about my training," Tom asked.

"Bah, don't vex me, boy… I said I'd help. Didn't say nothin' bout training you," Hett hissed. Then, as Tom stood and walked to the door, she relented.

"I'll think on it. Need a plausible reason else everyone will wonder what we're up to and I got my virtue and reputation to think of." She cackled at her own humour.

As Tom opened the door, he glanced back. Hett looked and sounded every bit the witch. Relieved to be gone, he stepped outside.

## Chapter 12: Greentower

**Greentower, The Rivers**

"Why don't they call it the Blacktower?" James Encoma asked.

Darion ignored the lad. It had been difficult between them and Darion wasn't entirely sure why but right now he couldn't care less. It was Kronke he'd asked in any case. He noticed the lad never seemed to stray far from the burly sergeant.

"Aye, it looks black right enough, guess that's what time and weathering does," Kronke said, agreeably.

"Bird shit, more like," Pieterzon retorted, sparking off a fierce debate.

"Ain't bird shit, dumbass." Jess Crawley laughed as the argument was joined.

The tall tower under discussion dominated the horizon and the town it overlooked. Greentower was set in rolling hills and the tower sat atop one of them with the town nestling in the valleys below like a quilted blanket.

The decision to head for Greentower was not made by Darion, who had fallen inextricably ill. It had only been moments after leaving the hills overlooking Thorsten that Darion suddenly went into apoplexy, his body spasming violently before rolling forwards and out of his saddle.

When Darion regained consciousness he found himself tied to his horse with M'rika sat behind holding him steady, her grip on him, firm. He'd no recollection of the incident, just a dull ache in his chest and a searing pain on his left hand, his ring finger, to remind him of it.

Darion had lost a day to oblivion and on waking found they were on the plains southwest of Thorsten, Kronke having led them on the road to Greentower. Their path took Darion away from Marron and Nihm and he was apoplectic with rage. He'd never felt anger take him so before. He became unreasoning and not even M'rika's calm logic explaining that the bridge across the Oust was taken and that urak prowled both east and west banks would calm him. Bindu became agitated, not understanding why her master was so angry and snapped at any that came too near.

In the end, it was grief that stilled Darion. His heart ring was cold, icy cold on his finger, burning like a brand. His heart made the connection before his head, the reality hitting him a moment later. She was gone. His rage instantly evaporated and Darion clutched his hand to his chest, twisting his ring, trying to coax something, anything out of it. But the ring was lifeless and cold. Marron was gone and so too, Nihm. Marr would give her life before letting anything happen to their daughter.

After that, Darion followed, morose and introverted, his mind a fugue. Bindu pattered along behind Darion, her head low mirroring her master's mood.

They spent another day crossing the plains that sat between Thorsten and the Greentower foothills. The road allowed them to travel quickly until they caught up with people fleeing south. Their party brought many stares and not all of them friendly when the ilfanum were seen. Most weren't sure what the ilf were, none had ever seen one before and they wondered fearfully if maybe they were urak.

"Horsemen approach," R'ell stated. The road ahead snaked downhill and small pockets of people dotted the approach to Greentower. The horsemen, R'ell indicated, were half a league distant and riding against the tide. They walked on, their horses were weary and badly in need of food and rest.

As the riders approached, Darion could make out the flag the bearer carried, a green tower between twining rivers. Darion lived on the fringes of the Rivers, as far north and east as it was possible in any of the Nine Kingdoms. Far enough away that he didn't ordinarily bother with the politics and machinations of the Kingdoms, which held no interest to him. That though didn't mean he was ignorant of them. Duke Winston Brant was Lord of Greentower. Duke, since he was cousin to High Lord Trenton Twyford who thought himself King of the Rivers not merely its High Lord. At least that was Keeper's take on things. So Greentower was no safe-haven, his association with the Order, should it be known, would be enough to see him imprisoned or worse. That the ilfanum rode with them meant he'd need to hide in plain sight; there could be no disguising them.

"I'll see no welcome here," Darion told Kronke.

The big sergeant understood his meaning. "They've seen us. If you run they'll give chase and the horses are tired. Best ta blag it out." It was still strained between them, they'd argued fiercely over their route after his illness and the aftermath of it was still felt by both men.

"They'll not hear anything from us," Kronke said. He stared in turn at Jess, Morpete then Pieterzon, the remnants of his command, waiting until each acknowledged his words. They all knew that if not for the woodsman and the ilf they'd have died in the homestead that night. A debt was owed.

Darion measured each of them as they answered Kronke. He felt uneasy. He didn't know any of them and felt little trust, especially for Pieterzon. The one-eyed man looked like he'd sell his mother for a pint of ale given half a chance and had already proven himself a craven.

The ilf were another problem, they were high stakes. The Duke would insist on seeing them but what would he do? Contact with the ilfanum was unheard of in longer than anyone could rightly remember. Darion signed to M'rika and R'ell and they waited whilst he manoeuvred Marigold next to their horses.

"We've discussed 'afore bout Keeper and the Order bein' outlawed in this land."

M'rika and R'ell made no reply. R'ell, in particular, found the need of humans to repeat things already spoken of an annoyance. They waited.

"I'd have you say you're emissaries to High King Edward Blackstar. Probably best not ta mention Keeper at all," Darion said.

"You would have us lie?" R'ell asked. "Like a human."

M'rika gestured and R'ell fell silent. "You think the Lord here will detain us if we state our true purpose?"

"Yes," Darion replied, grateful that M'rika grasped his meaning without having to explain further.

"I see." M'rika paused. "It is unnatural for us to tell untruth but I understand your need. For expediency," M'rika finished.

"Yes. For expediency," Darion confirmed.

"Then you will speak for us," M'rika stated.

Darion caught James Encoma watching his exchange with the ilf but he turned away as Darion swung his steel-grey eyes onto him. "There could be trouble ahead lad. If you slip away now you'll not get caught up in it."

"Where would you have me go?" James replied. "I've got nothing left."

"Lotta folk got nothing, me included," Darion said, pained at saying it. "You've got your life. That's someat. Head south and keep heading till ya don't have to worry none about urak and death. Save your grieving for then."

"That what you gonna do, run south and hide?"

Darion detected a tremor in James' voice as he spoke, "Would if I could," Darion murmured, knowing it for a lie as soon as he uttered it.

The clatter of hooves on the road ended any further discussion. The troop of riders was a score strong and neatly attired in light armour and green tunics bearing a tower emblem. As they drew close, the leader signalled and the column drew to an orderly halt.

"Hail. You're Crows, I see. What brings you to Greentower and what in the Trinity are they?" The leader, a sergeant from the armband on his sleeve, addressed Kronke. The man was tall and clean, his blonde beard neatly trimmed.

Kronke stiffened. There was little love lost between his Lord and Greentower. Black Crow was an affectation of his Lord, given by his people. In Greentower though, Crow was meant as an insult and used in scorn. That he had to bear it riled him somewhat.

"They're ilfanum from the great forest," Kronke said.

"And what are they doing with you? What are you, a sergeant?"

"Ai, Kronke's the name and you'd do well to mind your tongue," Kronke growled. "Sir Anders Forstandt lies dead in the north. This is all that's left of his company. The rest is for your Lord's ears, not his lackey's."

The man's eyes hardened. He looked at Kronke critically, a big man and dirty, his beard rough and unkempt, as if he'd been in the field a month. He looked weary as well, too long in the saddle judging by the state of his horse. The man gestured and ten of his riders peeled off, forming up behind the Black Crows and the ilf.

"I'm Witter. You'll follow me," he commanded.

Witter gave a final, intrigued look at the ilf. Seeing them up close, their green-skinned bodies appeared to be covered in tiny scales; they were perfectly humanoid in form and all the more alien for it. Uneasy, he turned his horse about and fired off a final barb as they set off.

"The walls at Thorsten have fallen and urak raid the town at will. Word is the keep still stands but it's only a matter of time before it's breached."

It was a bitter revelation. Kronke made no reply but his heart broke at the news. His wife was there; she'd refused to leave without him. Kronke heard shocked gasps from behind from Jess and Morpete. His mind railed, had Thorsten really fallen in little more than a day? How was it possible? The teaming hordes of urak as they swarmed the plains outside of town swirled in his head like a bad dream. They were legion but still, to have breached the walls so quickly?

The journey to Greentower proved uneventful. The road cleared ahead of them, the people on it parting as the riders approached. The town had a small curtain wall but it was nothing compared with Thorsten's own, Darion observed. It would do little to stop any attacker, let alone urak.

The town encompassed by the wall was neat and tidy. The streets were clean and wide and busy with people, most of whom were leaving and heading south, the carts and wagons all moving in the same direction. Clusters of soldiers, all wearing green livery, sat at each junction organising and directing people through the town.

Darion expected them to turn for the road leading up to the tower and was surprised when instead they were taken through a maze of streets and thoroughfares before ascending another hill. Looking back he could see the town laid out as it wrapped itself around the valley.

Here, the houses were mansions. Big and well-spaced with large gardens surrounded by walls and with guards at their gates. It was to the largest of these they headed.

The gates swung wide at their approach and they were waved through, hooves clattering, onto a large courtyard that teemed with soldiers and servants. There were half a dozen large covered wagons and Darion observed as men and women shuffled back and forth from the mansion with all manner of valuables, from paintings and bronze statues to chests and even armour, rich and ornately cast.

Grooms rushed to take their horses as they dismounted and the fellowship watched with unease as their mounts were led away around the side of the building. They'd pushed them hard over the last ten days; it felt strange to part with them without so much as a word and in a town strange to most of them.

"Better look after her fuckhead," Jess Crawley groused at a groom, little more than a boy. "I'll be back for her and she better be fed and rubbed down," she warned.

They followed Witter through large double fronted doors leading into an entrance hall, the ilfanum drawing many looks and whispered exclamations. Directing them to a reception room just off the hallway, Witter posted guards outside before disappearing. Wherever he went they didn't have long to wait. A well-dressed man soon entered, his eyes growing large as they took in the ilfanum and the wolfdog.

"I am Nesbitt, chamberlain to Duke Winston Brant. Please leave your weapons. Your wolf will have to stay as well. He'll be quite safe, I assure you. Now please follow me, the Duke is waiting."

"He is a she," Darion said pointedly of Bindu as he set his ilf bow down on a bench.

"And she'll be fine, so long as none enter in my absence. Bindu stay," Darion commanded. Unbuckling his sword, he laid it alongside his bow and did the same with his knife.

The rest, following his lead, reluctantly disarmed as well. Then they followed Nesbitt to a large crowded room that fell silent as they entered. Darion spotted Witter in the midst of a large knot of men. At their approach, Witter whispered to the man standing beside him.

The man was lavishly dressed, his clothes heavy and expensively embroidered. Darion thought him tall and regal apart from the slight paunch around his middle. His dark hair was oiled, his beard a neatly trimmed goatee with a fleck of grey in it. Duke Winston Brant, Darion surmised.

Confirming his thoughts, the man clapped his hands and, in a loud voice, bid everyone leave. Silence broken, the hubbub of voices resumed. People gawped openly at the ilf as they filed past and out of the room until it was empty of all but the guards and a group of men, counsellors by their look, clustered near the Duke.

"I am Duke Winston Brant, welcome to my home." The Duke's eyes lingered on the ilfanum, sparing the rest hardly a glance. His greeting was met with stony silence and the Duke's neck reddened as it became pronounced.

Kronke and the others shifted uncomfortably as it stretched on.

"What's wrong with them, do they understand me?" Brant asked, turning to Witter.

"I've not heard them speak, my Lord." Witter offered.

Taking a deep breath, Darion stepped forward. He bowed his head a little at the Duke. It had been a while since he'd bowed to any man and it felt stiff and unnatural. He felt the Duke's eyes swivel to him along with everyone else's in the room.

The Duke assessed Darion with an averse look. The man was big and rough, his hair knotted. It looked and smelt like he hadn't bathed in a ten-day or more. Brant wafted a perfumed handkerchief under his nose.

"You have something to say?"

Darion heard the challenge in the question. Better make this good, he told himself.

"My name is Darion Castell and I speak for the ilfanum."

"You speak for the ilfanum?" Brant repeated, "How so?"

"It's a long story, Duke Brant. Sparing the long, the short of it is, I strayed on to ilfanum lands, and a debt was owed, me to them and them to me. After a fashion," Darion qualified. "These ilf have been sent as emissaries to the High King and I have been charged with taking them."

Brant laughed. "You jest? Am I to have you taken outside and beaten? The only thing you look fit to be charged with is poaching." He smiled at his joke and looked about his council to see it had been well received.

"Forgive me, Your Grace; I'm no poacher but a woodsman," Darion replied.

"A woodsman with manners," Brant chewed with distaste. "Tell me then, why do they not speak for themselves or answer when I address them?"

"Their ways are as strange to us as ours are to them, Your Grace," Darion fudged. "May I introduce them to you?"

Annoyed but intrigued despite this, Brant grudgingly nodded his assent.

"Duke Brant, this is M'rika dul Da'Mari, she is Visok and K'raal and this is R'ell del Da'Mari, Visok and Umphathi." Darion indicated first M'rika and then R'ell. Both inclined their heads a fraction but otherwise remained unmoved.

"What does that all mean? What is a Visok and K'raal and Umphathi?" Brant asked, badly mangling the pronunciations.

"Your Grace, there are many sorts of ilfanum. As I understand it Visok is a type that is most like us, in appearance at least. Umphathi means warden or guardian, whilst K'raal is harder to explain. I guess it's simplest to compare them to a Lord or Lady but that's not entirely accurate. As I said, it's hard to explain and I'm not sure I fully understand it myself. And yes, they speak and can understand everything you say."

Looking at the ilf, Brant thought there was nothing human-like about them. They seemed alien. Their black eyes showed no white and were unfathomable. Their skin or scales or whatever the seven hells it was that covered them were green and mottled.

His ire was raised. If they could understand him why did they insult him by not speaking? He snorted, the ilf were unknown, may even be dangerous. He beckoned to a black-robed man and waited whilst he moved close.

"Mariusz, you're learned in these things. Correct me if I'm wrong."

"Yes, my Duke." The mage was tall and thin, his hair receding.

"The ilfanum," Brant said with disdain. "We are not welcome in their lands on pain of death. Any that enter their great forest never return." He glanced at Mariusz, who said nothing.

Brant moved over to a large table and gazed down at the map and the markers upon it. "The urak have taken Thorsten. Thorsten, with its tall walls and the Black Crow to defend them and it fell in little more than a day. Now the urak turn their eyes south, to my lands."

Brant circled the table, his eyes lifting to all in the room. Darion could see the worry etched and lined in his face. He looked tired and irritable, his voice resigned.

"If Thorsten's walls and the Crow couldn't turn them back then what hope I? Greentower is not so easily defensible," Brant said.

He raised his voice, his tone hardening. "And into this come two ilf, unheard of and unbidden, to my land. With them a disparate mix of malcontents that somehow, miraculously escaped Thorsten's demise, to arrive at my doorstep. The ilf have shown themselves no friends of ours. Is it coincidence that they ride at the forefront of this urak invasion? I think not. Then to ignore me, Lord of Greentower, in my own home. The temerity…." Brant was in full flow when Darion interrupted.

"Duke Brant…," Darion was forestalled as the Duke held his hand up for silence.

"You speak when I bid you speak, else that tongue will be removed. Understood?" Brant rasped.

Nodding assent, Darion stepped back into the group as Brant turned to address the ilf.

"Emissaries to the High King? Maybe so or maybe not. I need time to think on it. But I am Lord of this demesne and make no mistake. When next we speak you will address me directly."

The ilf stared back, unmoved.

"Witter, take them away," Brant ordered. "See they are safe and comfortable."

"Shall I place them in the dungeon, my Lord Duke?" Witter asked.

"Don't be absurd. They are guests for the moment. Put them in the Town Hall," Brant snapped.

"Yes, Your Grace, and the Black Crow's men?"

"Do not try my patience, Witter. All of them!" Brant raged.

Stepping forwards, Kronke dropped to a knee waiting to be acknowledged.

Impatient, Brant growled. "Yes?"

"Duke Brant, the boy we picked up on the road. He ain't nowt to do with any of this. His entire holdstead was killed by urak, he's all that survived. The boy's lost everything but what he's standing in," Kronke said.

Brant's harsh eyes looked over the young man as if seeing him for the first time. Poor, his clothes were the rustic hardy type worn by farmers and holdsteaders alike. Seriously, didn't the big oaf see everything he had to deal with and he bothered him with this.

Kronke had misjudged, he could see it in the Duke's face and in the way he stood. Just as he feared he'd misspoken, a white-robed man stepped out from behind the group of counsellors, a Holy Father, a white priest.

"Duke Brant, I could use the young man. There are many come from the north and our church is struggling to cope," the priest said.

The Duke's attention shifted abruptly.

Darion watched the interplay with interest. The Duke seemed volatile as a range of emotions flittered across his face. The priest for his part stood calmly, waiting. He was an older man, bald apart from a scruff of white hair around his ears and a long white beard, neatly plaited.

Forcing a smile to his face, Brant slowly touched his right hand to his forehead, acknowledging Nihmrodel, the White Lady. "Sorry Father, I didn't realise you were still here. Of course, if the church has need and the boy is willing?"

"Then by your leave, Your Grace," the priest waited for the Duke to nod assent before walking across to the young holdsteader.

"Please, come with me." Not waiting for an answer the priest headed for the door.

James looked uncertainly at Kronke and the others. Darion gave a small nod of encouragement and, with a reluctance he didn't understand, James followed after the priest.

Once the priest and the farmer's boy had gone, Brant turned his gaze back to his sergeant. "Keep them secure, Witter until I call for them. Time's pressing and it's a commodity I have little enough of."

The sergeant bowed to his increasingly agitated Duke. Gathering his men, he ushered the Black Crows, the woodsman, and the ilf out of the room.

## Chapter 13: Your Will, Father

**Greenholme, The Rivers**

Three days out from Fallston and Father Henrik Zoller was pleased. They'd made good progress despite the mass of people sharing the road. They at least all moved in the same direction, with his Red Cloaks bullying a path past any too slow.

Fallston had been a close call. Too close. That he'd escaped just ahead of the urak was the Red God's doing, bringing him to Lord Menzies just as word arrived of the fast-approaching urak.

Then there was the young woman, Lett, sent by Kildare to deliver an old adversary right into his hands. The monk, Hiro, was of the Order and had clashed with him a decade past, interfering in church business, taking something he'd no right to take. Harbouring a deep animosity, Zoller had hunted Hiro only for his trail to grow cold. That was years past, Hiro seemingly vanishing, either to another Kingdom or possibly leaving the Nine Kingdoms altogether.

So, when he'd heard of the monk's reappearance, he'd tried for him, how could he not. That the fates conspired and Hiro slipped his grasp yet again frustrated him no end. Still, he was consoled. If the monk lived through Fallston and the north he would come for the boy, he was sure of it. All was not lost.

Thinking on it now, Zoller berated himself. Conceded, grudgingly, that his resentment led to a miscalculation. It clouded his reasoning and almost trapped him in Fallston. In the end, it had been a close-run thing, escaping by an hour at most. He'd heard the drums and seen the smoke. Lord Menzies' men at the rear of their column had even tussled with some outlying urak. There were only a hand of them and Menzies men were mounted but even so, it cost six of his twenty guards and crippled three others. Not waiting, Zoller had ridden on, leaving Menzies to catch up.

Looking back now, Zoller hardly dared think about what fate would have brought if he'd tarried longer. Touching a fist to his stomach, Zoller dipped his head, acknowledging the Red God and his clear interventions.

At Longstretch he'd been unable to secure a barge. The lake town was a buzz of panicked activity, word reaching ahead that Fallston had fallen. They were next, was the general consensus, and people left by any means they could find. So by the time he arrived in the dark of late evening, no boats remained to bear his entourage south.

Paranoid at any delay, he pushed on through the night leaving Menzies and his men behind. The urak moved so quickly, Zoller reasoned, they might reach the town on the morrow and he couldn't risk that. Besides, Longstretch would surely slow the urak down long enough to see him to safety.

That Holt and Tuco offered no argument was, in its way, an endorsement. So they'd eaten, rested a few hours then left travelling through the night, the moons of Kildare and Nihmrodel providing enough light in the dark to follow the road.

Travel thereafter had been slow; the horses needed frequent resting according to Holt and Tuco, one of the few times they'd agreed about anything, so grudgingly he had acceded.

And when Tuco announced they had rounded the elbow, where the Oust turned due south, he felt a sense of relief. They were halfway to Rivercross.

The following day and night saw them to Greenholme with little incident. The market town was full of people and food and supplies were hard to come by. Room as well was at a premium and tired, Zoller was forced to secure accommodation at the church rather than the comfort of an inn.

The church served the Trinity and was full of refugees from the north. Using his authority, Zoller evicted two families and appropriated their room. The priests of Nihmrodel and Ankor were unimpressed and said as much but Zoller paid them no heed. They were nothing to him; wearing their piousness and mercy like masks. Their need to be beloved by the people a thin veneer he had no tolerance for.

Now, at rest in his room, Zoller's mood was surly; his backside ached from sitting hours on end in a cushioned carriage seat. The bumpy roads and his anxiety had made it nigh on impossible to relax and meditate, and he had much to meditate on. The urak were a worry to be sure but since their immediate threat lay behind he turned his mind instead to other matters. Chief amongst these were Cardinal Tortuga and the church hierarchy, all of whom would demand answers. He needed answers of his own but found he couldn't concentrate on the plans he'd formulated. Instead, his mind drifted, contemplating his journey from Fallston.

That first day out the woman Lett rode with him in the carriage and had been a distraction, just not the good sort he'd hoped and anticipated for. Red-eyed and teary she refused to talk, frequently bursting into wracking sobs. It had proven unbearable and by midday he'd had enough and made her ride up front with the carriage driver.

The girl's mood hadn't improved subsequently either. Sullen, speaking only when required, he often caught her staring at him with venom. He tolerated it given her grief but his patience with her was running thin.

He'd brought her, trouble as she was, because of Renco, to use as leverage against the boy. Zoller wanted to question him when time permitted, though his interest had waned somewhat. Intuition told him the boy knew little and this, added to his own doubts about the lad, fed his disinterest.

Renco for his part hadn't spoken a word the entire journey and Zoller knew his Red Cloaks thought him a mute and simple in the head. He knew differently though, had seen the violence in his eyes that day outside Fallston. The boy had been within a breath of it but somehow held it in check, submitting in the end, meek as a lamb.

Now Zoller's thoughts coalesced to tell him the boy's best use was as bait for his master. As for the girl, she was proving surplus. Zoller had kept her apart from Renco but observed the two trading looks. The lad hid his feelings well but Zoller sensed anger and something else he couldn't quite read in his expression, resentment? Understandable, the girl had betrayed him.

Lett, on the other hand, didn't attempt to hide her feelings. The hate and loathing in the girl was obvious, he'd seen its face many times and knew it well. They're young lovers no more, Zoller mused, finding the thought vaguely amusing.

So, how useful a tool could she be? Zoller questioned. If not love then hate and if hate then what leverage the girl for the boy. Still, he disliked waste, maybe there was some use for her he hadn't considered. Both were young, their emotions little better than a child's. Did they really detest each other, hate each other? He would have to test them to be sure. He was pondering the problem when there was a knock at the door.

"Enter."

With a squeal of hinge, the door opened and the big frame of Holt appeared.

"I've brought food, Father. 'Fraid there ain't much," Holt mumbled. A wooden platter was clutched in one hand. Looking about the cluttered room at where to set it down, Holt opted for a desk covered with scrolls and parchments, inkpots, and papers. There didn't seem to be anywhere else.

"Holt, you've laid that on a very expensive treatise on the White Lady," Zoller chided. He waved Holt away as the brute, alarmed, went to pick the plate up again.

"It's of no matter, tis only the Lady and she'd no doubt welcome the opportunity to help any of her children, even if it's only as a placemat."

Holt looked uncertain, not sure if the Father jested or not, before deciding the simplest thing was to do as instructed. He stood and waited.

Zoller spared a glance at the food; a mouldy lump of cheese, an apple that looked like it had been picked too early, and a hunk of bread. It was more than his men had, he was sure, Holt would have seen to that.

"That matter you asked me to look into, Father. Tuco has him out back where we're camped with the other Cloaks," Holt said.

"Ah, very good. You've done well, Holt. Kildare's blessing upon you," Zoller intoned, smiling as the giant puffed his chest out at the praise. Like a faithful dog, Zoller thought; his dog.

"I'll be out to see to things directly once I've taken my victuals," Zoller said. "Do the men have enough to eat and drink?" he asked, his mind already drifting elsewhere. He knew Holt's answer in any case before he uttered it. But this was an important ritual. Asking the question was enough to intimate concern for his men's wellbeing. Holt would tell them all that the good Father had asked after them before eating, this he knew.

"The men are fine Father, eager to do your bidding. Will you bless their food before they eat?"

"Of course, I'll be there momentarily," Zoller said. Then, as Holt departed, the priest called out one last instruction.

"Oh, and when I come for the blessing, move the girl next to the boy. It will be easier to keep an eye on the pair whilst we attend to business, yes."

"Your will, Father." Opening the door, Holt ducked his head and departed.

Zoller picked at his food. He removed the mould from the cheese finding evidence of weevils. Famished, he ignored it. The bread too was hard and stale but bearable with the cheese and washed down with watered wine. The apple looked tart and he fancied it not at all, resolving to save it for later he slipped it into his pocket.

Thoughts turning to matters at hand, Zoller left his room. There was no lock to secure it but Holt had placed a Red Cloak outside its door. Brother Thomas Perrick he recalled. Zoller offered the guard a quiet word of thanks for his dedication and promised to have food sent.

"Thank you, Father." Brother Thomas dropped to a knee grimacing briefly in pain, before bowing his head.

Placing a hand on the man's shoulder, Zoller offered a blessing before making his way outside.

The Red Cloaks were camped behind the church between its stable block and storeroom. A small fire was burning at the centre of the camp with most of his men gathered around it.

Zoller saw that Renco had been tied to the stable block, bound to one of several iron rungs. Feeling the weight of his gaze, Renco's head rose and they locked eyes briefly, as he crossed the yard.

At Zoller's approach, the Red Cloaks all got to their feet facing him, whilst Holt made a grab for the woman sitting by the fire and dragged her upright.

"Don't touch me, ow." Pulled harshly towards the stables, Lett became fearful and struggled, crying out. Her arm ached where the brute gripped it.

Holt slapped her. "Quit your mewling."

Wild, Lett fought back. A swinging hand clipped the side of Holt's head and her nail scored his cheek drawing blood.

Angry, Holt jabbed a short sharp punch to the side of her head. Releasing Lett's arm he grabbed a fistful of dirt blonde hair and dragged her, screaming to the stable block. He threw her the last few feet to slam against the wall. Taking a leather thong from his belt, Holt swiftly and expertly bound her hands above her head and to an iron ring.

Feeling eyes on him, Holt turned to the mute tied no more than a pace away. The boy regarded him impassively, his brown eyes dark and unwavering. He ain't all there, Holt thought with a grin, his hand curling into a fist. He resisted, reining in his desire to crush the boy's face. One blow would do it, 'cepting the Holy Father ordered otherwise.

Unclenching his hand, Holt patted the girl's cheek before standing and looking down at her. A pretty little thing, her arms bound high accentuated her lithe body. Too scrawny, not enough meat on her bones for his liking, but still, the Holy Father had made no such concessions about her wellbeing.

A glance at Father Zoller showed he was watching matters even as he finished praying for the men and their food, such as it was.

"Brother Holt, where is he?" Zoller asked once the blessing was complete.

"In there, Father." Holt indicated the stable door next to the mute, the rest of the stalls housed their horses. Striding past the hate-filled eyes of the girl and the impassive ones of the boy, he pulled open the stall door.

Father Zoller signalled Tuco to join him before walking over and peering inside the stable. A man lay in the straw, face bruised with one eye blackened and puffy and his lips swollen and bloody.

"I understand you're the blacksmith at Greenholme?"

The man glared back. "One of 'em, why am I bound and beaten like a criminal?" he cried. His teeth felt loose and he ran his tongue over them wincing as he spoke.

Zoller looked questioningly over his shoulder at Tuco who stood quietly by.

"He's the right one Father, names John Carterson," Tuco stated.

"You made repair to my carriage a while back?" Zoller said to the blacksmith.

"Ai, I remember, broken rear axle. Needed replacing, told your man it'd take a day." He nodded vaguely at Holt. "He ordered me to fix it overnight good enough to get you to Thorsten, so I fit an iron sleeve. It should've got you there but I told 'im it would need proper repair in Thorsten."

Zoller mulled this over; it wasn't quite the story he expected. He, himself, told Holt he would brook no delay, and Holt, ever faithful, was simply carrying out his instruction. Zoller spared his men a glance. Holt looked anywhere but at him, confirmation enough if any was needed that the smith was telling the truth.

Tuco, with a glint in his eye, couldn't resist a dig. "Maybe the good Father is looking to punish the wrong man."

The glare Holt returned only served to broaden the jeer Tuco wore.

"Enough," Zoller admonished, turning back to the Blacksmith.

"Your shoddy workmanship almost cost my life. A price must be paid. You need to atone. Are you a believer my son?"

"Yes Father, I'm a man of faith. I follow the Trinity," John Carterson implored, hope and fear vying in him.

"Very well, ten lashes will be penance enough," Zoller said. The blacksmith's eyes bulged in shock, stunned to silence.

"I'll see to it," Holt said, flexing his shoulders.

"No, you won't. You'll not even bear witness. You may relieve Brother Thomas," Zoller admonished. He gave a nod to Tuco. "You see to it."

"Ai Father, my pleasure," Tuco said, grinning at Holt.

"Forgive me, Father." Shamed, Holt ducked outside.

Ignoring the big Red Cloak, Zoller followed him out, leaving Tuco to his task. He'd ordered and witnessed many whippings and had no morbid desire to watch another, his interest lay elsewhere. Taking a seat by the fire where he could observe the young man and woman, he watched and waited.

It proved a tame affair to start with; each ignored the other it seemed. Still, patience was a virtue and he had plenty of that.

His eyes followed Tuco as he left the stable and returned moments later with two other Red Cloaks. It wasn't until the first crack of the whip fell and the blacksmith gave a muffled cry of agony that things got interesting.

At the snap of the whip, Lett flinched and looked at the stable door, her eyes flicking furtively across to Renco. There wasn't a ripple of movement from him. He's a cool one, Zoller thought.

The whip-crack sounded three more times. Each time the cries from inside grew louder and more pained than the last. Lett was frightened and tears tracked down her cheeks. She looks wretched, Zoller observed. Bound, dirty, her face puffy from crying, she didn't look so pretty anymore.

At the fifth stroke, Renco moved, little more than a fidget. Lett had said something but though he watched carefully, Zoller couldn't quite make out what. She was trembling so much it was difficult to read her lips.

Whatever it was, Renco turned to face her, his movements sudden and precise. Not much, his bindings gave little slack, but enough he could kneel with his hands held in front of him.

He doesn't look impassive now. Just sad, Zoller reflected, intrigued.

Clasping his hands together, Renco bumped them against his chest then out, moving his hands apart, as far at least as his bonds allowed.

The result was interesting. Lett looked deflated, she shook her head. "I'm so sorry." Zoller read, this time finding it easy to interpret her words.

With a sad frown, Renco moved. With a grace that belied the fact he was shackled to a wall he sat back down, cross-legged then closed his eyes. He looked almost serene.

Zoller was surprised to find that Renco enthralled him. There was something engrossing about him and familiar that tantalised his memory. The girl regarded Renco as intently as he and looked utterly dejected, or at least more so than usual, Zoller mused. The whole exchange was fascinating and cast a new light on them both. The girl might have a use yet. He would have to test it.

With a loud crack, the last of the lashes landed. Zoller could still hear the muffled sobs from the man within but they were muted, his cries little more than a whimper.

Tuco appeared at the stable door looking pleased. A thin line of blood ran across his face, clearly not his own.

So engrossed was he with the scene playing out in front of him, that Zoller startled when he realised someone stood by his side. Turning, he found Brother Thomas.

"Yes?" Zoller snapped.

"I wanted to thank you, Father." Then, at Zoller's querying look. "You saw my discomfort. My knee is pained and you sent Brother Holt to take my watch."

Zoller looked at the man. He was ordinary. Could have been a farmer or carpenter as easily as a Red Cloak. "Are you married, Brother?" Zoller asked.

"No, Father," Thomas replied.

"Good," Zoller said. "There's a man in those stalls." Zoller indicated the stable where the blacksmith lay beaten. "See he gets home safely."

"Yes, Father," Thomas walked past to attend to his duty but Zoller wasn't finished.

"Brother Thomas," Zoller called, loud enough that all would hear. "On your return, take the girl to the stall. Stay with her, see she remains unharmed."

"Father?" Thomas asked.

"Was there something I said that was unclear?" Zoller said. The Red Cloak shook his head no but was clearly uncertain of his meaning.

Zoller's lip curled. "Good, then see to it."

"Your will, Father," Thomas intoned, turning back for the stable.

In his periphery, Zoller watched. Both must have heard his conversation with Brother Thomas. The young man was unmoved, not even opening his eyes, but not so the young woman. She looked afraid, crestfallen even.

Brother Thomas might be uncertain of his meaning but Lett, it appeared, was under no illusion. It would be interesting to see if Renco's demeanour changed any after tonight.

## Chapter 14: The Essence of Things

**Fallston, The Rivers**

Nihm was a revelation. She was a prodigy. So like her mother, it was painful to look at her knowing that Marron was gone. *Dead she may be but her daughter lives*, Hiro told himself, *I must look after her*.

Hiro was no stranger to death. To have lived so long and survived so much it was impossible not to be on knowing terms. It was never easy when people he cared about died but there was honesty in it too; after all, death came to all things eventually. It allowed him to acknowledge the likelihood that Darion was gone too. That he'd not turned up at Thorsten or caught up with Marron or Nihm on the road boded ill. Hiro shook his head at his morbid turn. If any could survive the north and the urak it was Darion. He'd not give up on him just yet.

He watched as Nihm moved gracefully through the forms he'd taught her, hands and feet gliding smoothly and unerringly, weaving and creating shapes and patterns in the air. Moves he'd only needed to demonstrate once. It would only take Nihm a few slow passes at each for them to take.

Renco was the best student he'd ever trained but even now had need of the occasional correction. His posture might be marginally out and Hiro would tap arm or leg, hand or foot, correcting until Renco got it right. With Nihm there was no need, every action was perfectly formed and precise. The girl was a marvel, different from anyone he'd met and he knew why. Or at least he knew part of the reason, he conceded.

With a little prompting, Hiro had garnered the story of what had happened in Thorsten from Mercy and the others. None, however, knew what had saved Nihm's life, not even Nihm herself. Deeproot was lethal. He'd used it on occasion himself in a previous life and there was no walking away from it.

It was clear Nihm should have died that night but Marron had done something extraordinary. Hiro did not believe in the One God or the Trinity or the hundreds of other deities humanity worshipped in one form or another. But if he did, well, then he would have deemed Marron's actions miraculous and godly. But he didn't and being so long-lived he'd seen much that defied explanation.

'Everything is a mystery until it is understood,' Keeper had told him once and it was true.

Having thought on Nihm's 'miracle', Hiro suspected what must have happened but the result was so much more than expected. Marron's actions should have killed her weakened and untrained daughter. Instead, it had created something… new. It fascinated him beyond measure.

So he tested and pushed Nihm hard. But whatever he threw at her she handled, relished in fact. It didn't mean she was perfect, Hiro acknowledged. Her stance and posture might be correct but her muscles were still weak, not honed the way they would be from countless exercise. And her reactions, whilst quick, lacked strength and anticipation. Like pieces on a Shojek board, Nihm needed to intuit moves before they happened, calculate possibilities in an instant, and counter. That would come through training and practical experience, Hiro knew. He shook his head, to think, just a few days ago she could barely walk.

She enjoyed their sessions together, he could tell and Hiro grudgingly admitted he looked forward to them as well. How could he not?

They trained morning and night in the roaring cave. It was dark, noisy, and damp. It brought them privacy. Hiro knew Nihm was like him, in that she had no trouble seeing in the darkness and could block out the noise of the waterfall to the point where it wasn't a painful distraction. They couldn't easily talk and so never bothered. Hiro would demonstrate and Nihm would watch and do. And so it went.

With today's training session finished, Hiro wandered back through to the central cavern, leaving Nihm to follow when she was ready. He passed the two wolf dogs, Snow and Ash, who stood guard at the entrance as they always did and ruffled their coats as he went by. He found Mercy waiting for him. Stama and the big fellow Lucky stood just behind.

"When do we move? We can't stay here forever, Hiro," Mercy said. They were into their third day in the caverns and still, the old monk had given no sign it was time to leave. Apart from Nihm and Hiro, time was hard to judge for the rest. The lack of a day-night cycle made it feel like time was stretched and longer than it was. Three days, felt more like seven.

"You said we'd go when you deemed it safe and Mao well enough to travel. I judge him so," Mercy persisted. It was true; the old man was healing remarkably quickly considering his age and the beating he took.

"I have one thing more to teach Nihm. When she has mastered it, we will go," Hiro said.

"What exactly are you teaching her in there? The waterfall cave is too dark and noisy to see or hear in and you take no torches with you," Mercy asked. It was a curiosity that had intrigued her for days now.

"Not all lessons are spoken and not all darkness is absolute," Hiro replied cryptically.

"Fine, keep it to yourself. But we need to prepare for the road ahead and since you seem to know where that lies some idea where and when wouldn't go amiss," Mercy snapped.

"We'll travel the fringes of the Grim Marsh and make for Hilden. It's morning now. I expect, provided Nihm is ready, we can leave tonight under cover of darkness," Hiro said. "I will help prepare, we must pack wisely, for we travel light and fast."

Mercy returned a piercing look but bit back the first retort that sprang to her lips, chewing it over but not spitting it out. Instead, she settled on, "Ai, fast and light, shoulda thought of that."

Hiro nodded as if it were the wisest thing Mercy could have said and moved past, spotting Morten lying on his cot. The young man had been despondent and Hiro sensed he was conflicted. He'd watched him train with Lucky on occasion. The weapon of choice was the staff. He thought Lucky a good instructor but saw Morten's mind was not fully engaged in the task. He observed too that the lad was on edge whenever Nihm was near. At first, he put it down to infatuation and awkwardness since Nihm also appeared uncomfortable but watching them both over the last few days he'd concluded there was more to it than unrequited feelings. Well, it wouldn't do if they were to travel together.

"You boy, come with me," Hiro said, standing over Morten's cot.

Morten cracked an eye open. "I'm sleeping. What do you want?" But he spoke to the old monk's back. Hiro had turned away towards a cave passage at the back of the cavern.

Groaning in frustration, Morten threw back the blanket and rolled out of bed. Slipping his boots on Morten had to jog to catch up with the monk who had already disappeared from view.

The passage was rough and the roof, close, forcing Morten to duck his head as he entered. He found Hiro in the adjoining cavern. It was smaller than the one they camped in but still large and used as a storeroom. They had discovered it when first exploring the cave system. A single sconce was lit and Hiro took a torch from a half-barrel on the floor and held it to the flame. It was a familiar routine to Morten, one of his assigned chores was keeping the braziers and torches lit in the main cavern.

"What are we doing here?" Morten asked.

"Looking," Hiro replied.

"For supplies right, we're moving on?"

"So, a boy was not sleeping but listening," Hiro said turning and arching an eyebrow.

"Why do you call me boy all the time?" Morten retorted. "I'm a man grown."

Hiro wandered deeper into the cave and started lifting covers looking for something. Morten was forced to light a torch and follow.

"You are a man but mope like a child. Why?" Hiro asked.

Morten felt his anger flare. He was about to snap a reply when Hiro spoke again.

"There is sadness in you. Maybe you have family in Thorsten, neh?" Hiro said. "It's difficult when you fear for loved ones but I sense more than that. You seem lost. Are you lost, Morten?"

Morten's retort died on his lips, his temper fizzling out as Hiro's question sunk in. He was lost, he realised. What was he doing here? He was no use to anyone. He ran a tavern with his parents. What possible use could he be? He should be home with them. If they still lived, he thought, guilt-wracked. He sat suddenly on a crate too tired to think clearly.

Hiro carried on rummaging behind him.

"You're right. I am lost. I thought this'd be a grand adventure. Take me out of my humdrum life," Morten said, not thinking, letting his mind and mouth ramble. "Now I find myself longing ta pour a pint and wipe a table."

"Why did you come?" Hiro asked.

"I thought it'd be exciting. I'd travel ta Rivercross with Nihm; show her I'm more than just a taverner's son." Morten didn't know why he was opening up and to a stranger. Maybe it was because the old man always seemed so calm and centred. Even back at the Loud Water, Hiro seemed at ease, despite having taken out a roomful of men he'd have crossed a street to avoid. Maybe that was it.

"I'm not cut out for this. I'm a town boy." He flinched when he realised he'd said the word boy. "I can't fight; seven hells I can't even swim. I couldn't have saved Marron even if I'd had the chance. Don't know what I'm doing here. I'm a coward."

A tear leaked from his eye and he brushed it away angrily with his sleeve. "Look at me, blubbing like a baby. You're right; I'm a boy pretending to be a man."

There was a loud bang then clatter and Morten jerked in shock. A long pole rolled up against his boot. It was a staff, with metal caps on each end. Morten reached down and picked it up. It was heavy, felt solid, and sturdy. Much more so than the one he practised with.

Hiro stood alongside Morten and crouched, staring up at him. "It is good to say things out loud I find. Clears the mind, helps it to focus on what's important," Hiro said.

"And what's that then?" Morten muttered.

"What you do next. It is all that matters. What happened in the past cannot be changed, nor should it. It's what brought you here, made you who you are. So you see, it's really quite simple," Hiro said.

"Simple. Maybe for you, you can take care of yourself. You can fight and do things I can only dream of. You know they're all a little scared of you right." Morten sniffed, trying to keep the bitterness from his voice.

"That's because they're smart, neh!" Hiro's eyes crinkled as he spoke. "But come, you confuse matters and miss the point. Fighting is a product, an art if you like. As there is an art in pouring good ale, yes?"

"Now you're making fun," Morten said.

"Maybe a little but my point is valid. To do something well requires work and dedication. Practise it with the whole of your mind and body. Then you learn. The more you learn the better you become. We cannot control the world around us, only ourselves," Hiro stated.

Then, seeing Morten looked unconvinced still, "I was once like those men I killed. That was my past and could have been my future. To be like them; to take what others had with no thought of consequence."

Hiro's brows furrowed as he quipped. "So really you've no cause for complaint. You start from a much better place than I ever did."

"Really? You were a cutthroat?" Morten asked, intrigued enough to forget his self-pity and miss the sad tone in Hiro's voice.

"Once. In another life," Hiro said, then, reflectively, "I haven't told anyone that in a long time."

He stared at Morten. "I have learnt much in my life, mostly through my own folly and mistakes. Cherish them, Morten. How you deal with them and the adversity in life shapes you, teaches you who you are."

Hiro stood, he had spoken too much and too long. He'd always been a soft touch. He couldn't resist one final piece of advice, however.

"No one is ever the best of a thing, Morten. There is always more to learn or those that know more of a thing than you. All you can do is your best and hope it's enough. So again I say to you, what you do next is important. Whether that's running a tavern or swinging a blade and to anything and everything in between, it's up to you."

Hiro sensed they were being watched from the darkness of the passageway. The airflow had changed some minutes past, the faintest traces of smell told him it was Nihm. He patted the young man on his shoulder. Hopefully, he would ask himself those questions that needed asking and have an answer.

"Would you teach me?" Morten asked, suddenly emboldened.

Hiro turned in surprise. Morten held the staff in his hand, hope in his eyes. Hiro scowled and turned away. "No."

"No." Morten's hopes came crashing down. "You're training Nihm aren't you? That's what you do in that cave all day isn't it?"

"Yes."

"Why Nihm? Why not me?" Morten asked, suddenly angry. He thought the old man cared.

"You have an instructor in Master Lucson. He is very capable and you are fortunate to have him. You do him a disservice," Hiro said. "As for Nihm, that is not your question to ask."

Morten stood feeling a little awkward. The monk had helped, he wasn't quite sure how but he had.

"Thank you," Morten said, feeling the words were inadequate but not knowing what else to say.

The old monk grunted in response.

Gripping his new staff in one hand, Morten moved towards the passageway. He had a lot to think on but found he felt better than he had in days, his mood lighter.

"Ask Nihm to come see me."

Morten turned and glanced back. Hiro sat cross-legged on the floor, hands in his lap looking composed and relaxed. "Ai." Ducking his head, Morten disappeared into the passage.

Hiro sensed Nihm's approach minutes later, no stealth this time he noted. Her dogs were with her. They were young, eager to please, and took their cues from their Mistress who signed with her hands. They trotted off, sniffing and exploring the cave, leaving Nihm alone in front of him.

"You wanted to see me."

Hiro looked up from where he sat, one eyebrow arched in question, but saw it was no use. The girl looked puzzled and didn't understand. "Students normally address their instructors as Master," he prompted.

"Didn't know I was your student. Thought you were just showing me things," Nihm said.

Hiro considered her response. It was true, they had formalised nothing. Besides, he had a student in Renco and he never took more than one.

"Please sit." Hiro indicated the floor opposite him.

Nihm sat, crossing her legs. The ground was cold, the chill seeping through her leathers. She waited. Ash came over to investigate and she shooed him off with a friendly pat on his flank.

Hiro shifted into the flow. The gloomy half-light of the cavern was instantly gone, replaced by the bright flare of life before him. Her tae'al, her essence, swirled in a myriad of colours, mostly white with hints of green and brown threading through it but there were other colours as well, faint tints of blue and red. It was so bright it was hard to comprehend that it was all contained in the vessel that was Nihm. Hiro phased back to find brown eyes staring unblinkingly at him.

"We leave tonight. Before then you must learn to shield yourself, else it will make evading the enemy nigh on impossible," Hiro said.

"I don't understand," Nihm replied.

Hiro nodded sagely. "I will explain and teach if you are willing."

"That mean I have to call you Master?"

Hiro smiled and shook his head. "You reminded me, I have a student already, so no. This I teach because it needs to be learned. Are you ready?"

"Affirmative," Nihm said, the ghost of a smile flitting across her face.

Hiro looked at her strangely for a few seconds, before settling himself and beginning.

"Everything in this world has an essence, a life energy if you will, that binds it; from a lowly pebble lying on the ground to a soaring eagle in the sky. If you have the gift and know-how, you can sense it as easily as looking or smelling," Hiro said.

"The ancients call this essence, tae'al. Loosely translated it means all of a thing or all of everything. It is called by some the allthing and by others aether although those that do generally lack full understanding. Magi for example call it aether and perceive it as magic, which I guess if you look at it a certain way, it is."

"A pebble has life? But it's just a stone," Nihm interrupted.

"There's fierce debate even now by those more learned than I over such a thing," Hiro said, eyes twinkling. "Some say no, others yes but that the stone's essence is so infinitesimally small that it makes no difference. For this discussion it is unimportant."

"Okay." Nihm was intrigued.

"The tae'al of every living thing is unique and different. Those with the ability can read this essence. In the same way that you see a wolf and know it for a wolf, so you can do by sensing their tae'al."

"To what end? If I can see a wolf why would I need to read its tae'al to know it for a wolf? My eyes have already told me," Nihm said.

"Just so. But if that wolf was hiding in a forest your eyes might deceive you. You may not see past the trees and undergrowth to the wolf." Hiro waited. Nihm's face was impassive as she digested what was said.

"Trees and undergrowth have an essence? Surely it would hide the wolf just as effectively," Nihm argued.

"When you sense, you sense all things, all essence. But it is not like looking at something. Think of tae'al as being opaque, you can sense through one essence to those beyond. Tae'al is different for every living thing. Some, like your own, are bright and distinctive. Whilst others, like the aforementioned pebble, dull and clear," Hiro explained. "If you have the ability, then with training, you can shift and filter, reading what you sense. The deeper you go though, the harder it becomes and the cloudier the less clear things become."

"I think I understand, but what has this to do with me?" Nihm asked. "Why not Mercy? She's a mage."

Hiro was surprised but pleased. "Sensing tae'al is one thing, reading it another entirely. There's so much of it in places that it is like the roaring cave, loud. So loud it's hard to hear, neh," Hiro said, "But your essence is so very strong. It will be easy to sense against the background of life. A light from a window is easy to see in the darkness."

"Why is my essence so strong?" Nihm asked.

"A good question and one to examine another time," Hiro said.

Nihm nodded. "The other day you said, 'The Morhudrim look for the light in the dark. I think they see you and are afraid. That which they fear they hunt.'"

"I did," Hiro said.

"So if they can sense me, what can I do?"

"It is harder to see a light when the sun is high, neh. And at night you close a shutter, so the light is hidden." Hiro replied.

"Show me."

"Good." Hiro was pleased. "Now, concentrate and listen to my instruction."

The next several hours proved difficult for Nihm. Hiro instructed her in closing off all of her senses. Her touch, taste, and smell were difficult at first but Sai helped her, switching off receptors in her head. Her hearing was easier to manage. A few days in the roaring cave and she hardly need think about it and her hearing would adjust. Her sight too was simple, she simply closed her apertures as Sai liked to call them. It was peaceful and scary, devoid of her senses, like floating in the darkness, with no sensations from mind or body.

<*We are blind. We have no outward stimulus. We are defenceless,*> Sai intoned.

<*Ash and Snow will look after that. Now quiet, or better yet go, hide yourself away,*> Nihm ordered.

Sai didn't respond. His absence was strange. Feeling truly alone, Nihm's mind wandered. If time passed she was not aware of it, it had no meaning here. There was nothing, just her consciousness floating in a black void. After an eternity of no time, she became aware of something. A faint pinprick of light in the dark, subtle at first but as she focused on it, it brightened growing closer, larger. So bright, if she had eyes she would have closed them.

<*Can you sense me?*>

<Sai…> It was not Sai. Her mind felt sluggish, but she knew instinctively it was not Sai. <Hiro…?>

<Who is Sai?>

Nihm didn't know why but she didn't want to say. She felt Hiro's curiosity but he made no further comment.

She found herself transfixed by his essence, it was so beautiful. At least that's what it must be, she concluded. It was so bright, predominately white with a swirl of greens and browns complicating its pattern. In her mind, it resolved into a man shape though with no defining edges.

<This is my essence, my tae'al. Now that we have touched minds we can talk so, as long as we can sense each other and both will it. Do you understand?>

<Yes.>

<Good. That was very quick for your first time; many lose focus at this point. You have done well.>

<The ancients call this ki'tae. With practise, you will be able to enter and leave this state at will, although it can be disorienting for a moment. In time, you will learn to overlay ki'tae with your sight. There are other benefits as well, heightened awareness, increased thought, and body control and movement. That, however, takes much time to master. For now, we will just work on expanding your sense of tae'al.>

<You're so bright. It's as if my eyes are open and staring at the sun but they aren't, are they?>

<No, you're not seeing with your eyes now. You are using ki'tae, your hidden sense. One that all have but few are aware of and fewer still can control. You are one of the few,> Hiro said.

<Do I look like you?> Nihm asked, curious.

<Yes and no. As I said before, all things are different. Your essence is as alike to me as our looks. You are more than I,> Hiro said, Nihm felt awe and wonderment but it was a strange mix, as much his feeling as hers.

<The Taken, they can use this sense. They can see me?>

&lt;The Morhudrim possess the Taken. It is thought that it is they who can 'see' essence as we do but we do not really know. That is why we are here,&gt; Hiro replied. &lt;Underground we are hard to sense; the river, earth, and rock distort things. Their tae'al is weak but there is so much of it. Like looking into a deep lake, you cannot see the bottom. Once we leave here though they may sense you if they are close enough.&gt;

&lt;So what do I have to do?&gt;

&lt;I was aware of you from the moment I shifted into ki'tae but you did not see me immediately. Partially it was because you didn't know how to sense me, but mostly it was because I hid my tae'al. That is what you must learn to do.&gt;

&lt;Like closing a shutter,&gt; Nihm said, remembering his earlier analogy.

&lt;Just so. Now concentrate. This is easy to explain but hard to master,&gt; Hiro said, &lt;Your tae'al can be moulded and turned to reflect inward. Like a lantern with blacked-out glass, the light is held and contained.&gt;

Nihm nodded her understanding but was still unsure what to do. Hiro demonstrated with his own essence, his own tae'al. Showing her how to turn and bend it in upon itself. It seemed natural and easy when Hiro did it but when Nihm tried it was hard, her tae'al kept slipping and flowing around her as she grasped at it with her mind.

&lt;You are squeezing when you should be caressing,&gt; Hiro intoned. &lt;You lack a deftness of touch. Keep trying.&gt;

If Nihm could glare at him she would have but he was just a bright glob of essence.

&lt;Maintain calm. Anger and frustration will not aid you in this,&gt; Hiro said. &lt;I will leave you to practise. But I will be watching.&gt;

Hiro's essence shifted, moving away from her. It was infuriating watching the ease and control the old monk showed. Calming her mind she tried again, experimenting, stroking, and shaping a part of her essence. It seemed to magnify, shining brighter at her. What was she doing wrong?

Then understanding dawned. Of course, her essence would appear bright to her if she turned it inward. Encouraged she renewed her efforts.

Hiro watched from the cave's passage, impressed. She was so quick to pick things up. He remembered the first time Renco had shifted. The boy was so surprised he'd fallen off his log losing his focus. It had taken him more than two cycles of Nihmrodel to master the technique enough that he could control his ki'tae sufficiently well. Nihm had managed it in a half-day.

He turned away. The others would be impatient to go and his promise at helping them pack for the journey lay broken. He would check on Maohong, see how his friend was doing and make sure he was prepared for the road ahead. It would be tiring and dangerous, urak, or no.

## Chapter 15: The Ugliest Children

**Greentower, The Rivers**

As jails go it was a pretty nice one, Darion thought.

They'd been given several rooms on the third floor of the town hall. They must have served as storage rooms to keep records, coin, and other items of value judging from the half-full bookcases and bare shelving. The rooms were otherwise empty but Darion could tell where chests and caskets had lain from the indents in the rugs and discolouration on the floorboards. Thinking back to Brant's mansion and the wagon's being loaded it was safe to assume that the Duke was leaving and taking everything of value that he could.

The rooms were all shuttered and barred and the short corridor leading in and out had a stout wooden door at the end that was both guarded and bolted from the outside. Witter had left them with camp beds, water, and food but little else.

"I'll have fresh water buckets delivered so you can clean yourselves up. You look a disgrace," Witter uttered in a snide dig at Kronke. That had been hours past. They had long since washed and cleaned as best they could. Now, with nothing to do but wait, Crawley, Morpeth and Pieterzon took the chance to sleep. But Darion couldn't. Every time he laid his head down his mind turned to Marron and Nihm, his fingers twisting the cold lump of metal on his finger. It hurt to think about it, his emotions too raw and open still. It was far easier not to. Better to keep busy.

Darion had Bindu wait on a blanket. At least she could get some rest, he thought as he moved to a window. Witter had tried to separate Bindu earlier seeking to cage her, but Darion had refused to be parted from her. It was only M'rika's intervention that ended their stalemate. Witter had been forced to concede, unsure as he was of the ilf's status with his Lord Duke.

Opening the shutters, Darion looked out through the bars. The town hall was the largest building hereabouts and the view, obstructed as it was, allowed him to see one end of the town square. He watched as throngs of people came and went, all it seemed taking the south road to Kroy, carrying what they could, many pulling hand carts or riding small wagons loaded with their possessions.

As the afternoon deepened this changed, as slowly but increasingly, the square was taken over by guardsmen and teamsters riding wagons. It soon became a staging area where wagons were loaded up and organised then moved off in orderly convoys, escorted by scores of guardsmen.

Darion felt Kronke move up alongside him.

"Brant's leaving it seems and taking what he can with him," Kronke said, glancing through the bars at the gathering below.

"We saw that at his mansion. What's on your mind?" Darion asked.

Kronke sighed heavily. "Don't know truth be told. Might be I'm all that's left of the Black Crows. If Thorsten is gone then maybe Lord Richard is too. What do I do now? Where do I go?"

Darion looked at Kronke. He'd not given the sergeant much thought up till then. He saw the binding ring on Kronke's hand, not dissimilar to his own. "You have a wife, a family?"

"A wife, Marg, in Thorsten. Never managed no children, though we wanted them bad enough," Kronke said. "She's likely dead unless the castle still stands."

"I'm sorry." Darion laid a comforting hand on Kronke's massive shoulder. "I didn't know."

"Why would you?" Kronke turned and looked at his three charges laid out on their bedrolls. "Guess they're my family now." He smiled at Darion, his eyes full of grief. "I coulda done better, eh! The ugliest children ya could imagine."

Darion returned his smile but it was shallow, a gesture that didn't reflect the sadness and guilt he suddenly felt inside. "You take what you're given I guess. You've done well by them, brought them to safety at least."

There was a loud crack then a crash from outside. Looking out they saw a crate smashed on the cobbles next to a wagon. Guards and people milled around it. There was a lot of shouting and swearing. It was enough to break their dour mood.

The big sergeant laughed. "Ai, we're real safe, locked on the third floor of a building in a town being abandoned, whilst Brant packs his wealth up and runs south."

"I think he'll take us with him. The ilf will guarantee that at least."

"The ilf, maybe you, but Brant has no need fer the rest of us."

"Ai, you may have the truth of it there." Darion conceded, he hadn't given it any thought but it made sense. It brought Darion neatly back to Kronke's initial question. What to do and where to go?

"This thing we face is bigger than lords and realms. We've grown weak and fractured as a nation, Kronke. Something is coming and I don't just mean urak. This is a fight to survive the likes of which we've not faced since the Taken Wars. We'll all have to play our part if we're to have any chance."

"The Taken, eh?" Despite all that had happened and all he'd seen, Kronke was dubious still. "What would you have me do?"

"Me? Nothing, that's for you to decide. If Lord Richard is gone then you need to find another Lord to fight for or head south. Maybe join up with the Kingsguard."

"And you're taking the ilf to see this Keeper of yours. What then?" Kronke asked.

"Marron is gone but it might be that my daughter, Nihm still lives. I'll look for her. After that… I don't know. What I must I suppose. Keeper will know. This is what the Order was made for," Darion finished. It was a lame answer and he knew it but he had no other. Not wanting to talk, he patted Kronke on the shoulder and walked away.

* * *

Night had fallen and the activity in the town centre continued unabated. They saw no sign of Witter but the guard that brought them food that evening had been talkative enough. Jess Crawley spoke to him like they were old comrades and soon gleaned from him that Duke Brant was leaving on the morrow. Nothing about whether they would be going or not. The guard had left, Jess walking him out, her hand on his arm and head leant to the side, listening as he chatted amiably to her.

"Why is ya fawning all over that Greentower fuck? You got you a good Crow's man here if you're feeling horny." Pieterzon grabbed his crotch, "This is the only tower you'll need, girl."

Jess laughed, "Only thing ya got down there Zon is lice. You can keep'em." She turned to Kronke. His frown reflected her feelings. "We need to get out. Tonight, Sarge."

"Think we'll be on our way in the morning, Brant's leaving. You heard." Kronke rumbled.

"Ai, they might but you think they'll let us out, leave us our horses and give us our gear back?" Jess growled. "He'll take the ilf and Darion maybe but Brant don't give two shits about us. Probably already forgot we're here."

"No fucking way man. I ain't walking. You think those urak are walking?" Pieterzon shouted.

"Keep your voice down. Are you simple in the head you fuckwit?" Jess snapped.

"Jess is right. We need to go now, tonight, whilst we can." Darion interjected suddenly.

Kronke and the others turned. "Why?" Kronke asked.

"As I said, Jess is right."

"No, I mean why you? Why the Ilf? Brant will likely take you out of here. Ilf are too big a deal not to."

"I have no trust in Brant. He packs his gold and wealth. Abandon's his people to fend on their own when they need him most. Brant plays his own game with the ilf; he'll use them to advance his position. For that, he'll not need me. He may take me with the ilf but I wouldn't count on seeing Rivercross." Darion looked at each of them in turn. "And frankly I don't have the time to waste. We've seen how fast the urak move. Brant's wagons will be heavy and slow."

"What do the ilf say to all this." Kronke turned to M'rika.

Both ilf had been quiet since they'd arrived. Sitting meditating, eating none of the food, drinking none of the water, keeping more or less to themselves. R'ell's raven, Bezal made an occasional appearance but never stayed more than a few minutes.

"We follow Darion's lead," M'rika replied.

"Shit." Kronke rubbed his fingers over his moustache, tweaking the ends. He thought briefly of Anders and wished he was there to make the decision. It wasn't an easy thing to do. But he wasn't here; it was on him.

He glanced at his charges. Morpeth, barely a man, beard little more than peach fluff, looked trustingly at him. Jess on the other hand seemed angry and was finding it hard to sit still. Kronke knew her well enough to know it was because they were locked in. As for Pieterzon, he was as weasel-like as ever. Kronke could tell Zon was nervous by how his one good eye constantly roved around. It gave him a slightly manic look. They might be all that was left of his command but they were his. Ugly children indeed, he grinned.

"Okay, let's do this?"

\* \* \*

"I need to piss, John, please." Jess pleaded through the door.

"I can't, no one's to leave and Sergeant Witter ain't here to clear it with." A muffled voice replied. "Use the bucket."

"I can't, not in front of everyone. You can bolt the door soon as I'm through and show me where to go," Jess begged. Her tone turned sultry, "I'd really appreciate it."

There was a pause and Jess knew she had him. "Look, I'm unarmed and you've got a sword if you need to use it."

There was a rasp as a little hatch opened and the guard peeked through it. He saw Jess stood alone in the corridor. A couple of buttons on her shirt had worked loose showing a hint of cleavage that drew his eye. He stared into it and subconsciously wet his lips, before glancing once more down the corridor. The hatch shut with a thud.

Jess heard the bolt being removed and then a clunk as the lever bar was twisted up. The door swung open and Jess slipped through the small gap before it slammed shut again with a bang.

Kronke and Darion moved into the corridor and strained to listen through the door. They were in time to hear a groan and a thump, then moments later several more thumps. Kronke smacked his hand against the door. "Don't kill 'im, Jess."

The thumping stopped. Moments later the bar slide free and the door cracked open. Jess's head popped into view. "Easy see."

They found the guard lying on the floor in the foetal position, clutching his groin with one hand and his stomach with the other. One eye was swollen shut and his nose and mouth bled where Jess had kicked him. He was groaning softly as if even that small effort hurt.

Jess had disarmed the guard and held his sword out for Kronke who took it, noting as he did that Jess had slipped the guard's long knife into her belt.

"Seven hells, you're a piece of work girl," Kronke growled, impressed and wincing at the same time.

"What?" Jess shrugged, misunderstanding. "Fucker groped my tits."

Grabbing the guard non to gently, Darion and Kronke dragged him unceremoniously down the corridor and into one of the rooms. R'ell watched them, shaking his head in disgust at how easily the guard had succumbed.

Kronke bound the guard with his own shirt, tearing it into strips to do so. "How many downstairs?"

The guard moaned, his head flopping down onto his chest.

"Come on now lad, don't make me ask again." Kronke grabbed a handful of hair pulling his head up.

"Don't kill me. I gotta wife and kid."

Jess, standing nearby hoicked and spat a wad of phlegm onto the floor near his boot.

"No one's killing no one. We need out, quiet and easy like." Kronke patted the man's knee. "Tell me what I need to know. That'll be easiest for everyone, especially you."

Bezal chose that moment to appear, flapping onto a window sill before taking a short hop onto R'ell's proffered arm. The ilf cocked his head to one side then closed his eyes briefly. When he opened them again he addressed them all.

"Urakakule are on the plains before the green hills. They will be here in half a turn."

Kronke tapped the guard's cheek with his hand to get his attention. The guard's head snapped up. "Four. There's four downstairs."

Kronke nodded his head agreeably. A hand sounded about right, Brant must be stretched thin looking at all the activity in the town's square. He wadded some cloth and shoved it into the guard's mouth before binding it with a strip.

\* \* \*

"Caw"

Janes turned at the sound. "Would you look at that? Bold as brass."

A raven sat on the table pecking at the stale remains of the loaf they'd broken earlier. The three other men looked up from where they rolled dice watching as Janes rose and shooed the bird off, only to see it flap and glide through the door and into the corridor.

"Cheeky bugger," Janes grinned following it. The others turned back to their dice. It was a minute before anyone noted he hadn't returned.

"Where's Janes?" one of the guards posed.

"Leave it, Sagan, Janes has likely gone fer a piss. Now roll."

But Sagan didn't leave it. Something was off and he left the dice sitting untouched in front of him. Ignoring the moaning complaints of his companions, he stood. His sword was on the peg along with the others, the thing was too damn heavy and cumbersome to wear playing dice. Just as he stepped towards it, a large man appeared in the doorway. It wasn't Janes.

There was a sudden rush and the room was filled. Sagan had time to wonder what in the seven hells they were doing out of the rooms above when a crunching blow connected with the side of his head and he thought no more.

The other guards had no chance. The ilf moved so quickly they'd barely stood from their game when they were set upon. One managed to get a grip on R'ell's arm before crying out in pain and snatching his hand back. It was lacerated and bleeding deeply.

Darion saw it happen in his periphery. The leaf scale on the ilfs arm had risen up like razors, although flattened almost immediately after, smoothing back to the contours of his arm even as Darion watched. The bloodstain on R'ell's arm the only sign the man had laid his hand upon the ilf.

The guards were bound and questioned before being gagged. Their confiscated weapons and belongings were locked away in an adjoining storage room. The guards professed not to have the keys for it but as they were searched it turned out they had no need of them.

Pieterzon had already moved to the lock on the door and taking a thin bit of metal he had stashed somewhere about him, proceeded to pick the lock. Pieterzon felt eyes on him as he worked but ignored them. The lock was big and solid but simple. With a few deft twists and turns of his pick, the lock clicked and popped open. He stood back, pleased with himself then turned back to find he was the focus of attention.

"What?" He shrugged his shoulders. "I had a troubled childhood."

They rearmed themselves. The ilf donned cloaks and hoods to mask their appearance as much as possible. In the darkness, it would have to do.

Stealing out of a side door, away from the torch-lit square and the mass of people gathered there, they moved into an alley and the protective shroud its darkness offered. The wind suddenly rose and the first light patter of rain fell.

They found no sign of their horses, they had gone. Appropriated, Darion presumed and they'd no time to waste looking further for them. Their path was set, discussed earlier, and agreed, dictated in part by Duke Brant. The road to Kroy was too dangerous and troublesome to take with Brant riding it. So it was Merik to the southwest or Hilden almost due east. Hilden was a risk too far; there was every chance the urak had already reached it. So, in the end, all they could do was run before the storm. Merik it was.

"Wait here and give me twenty minutes," Kronke rumbled. There was an anxious complaint in the dark at this and the ilf looked perturbed. Only Darion understood his meaning.

"Be quick, if the lad doesn't want to come don't argue it with him. We've little time and we all make our own choices in life." Darion clapped the sergeant on the shoulder. With a nod of agreement, Kronke turned and disappeared into the night.

The light rain turned heavier as they waited for Kronke's return, uncomfortably aware of how close they were still to the town hall. Pieterzon complained until Darion moved next to him, Bindu at his heels. Darion didn't say anything, didn't need to.

Bindu suddenly stood looking back down the alley. "He comes but not alone," M'rika announced her eyes and ears picking out what the humans could not.

Staring intently, Darion made out the grainy bulk of a man approaching, unresolved in the darkness, and then a smaller figure next to it.

"You still here?" Kronke's voice was raised against the wind and rain.

"Ai, let's go," Darion declared.

"I've Jacob and Father Melbroth, the white priest, with me. He's insisting on coming," Kronke said, as another shape materialised, moving closer to them.

"My brethren left for Kroy a short time ago. My path is not with them."

"Sorry Father, with no horse we'll have to move quickly. I don't think you'll be able to keep pace," Darion said.

"About that," Kronke interjected.

"We have a small chapter house on the outskirts of town. Your horses are in a barn awaiting us. Follow me," Melbroth said without preamble. The priest edged past Darion, moving deeper into the alley.

Perturbed by the sudden change in events, Darion scowled at Kronke, who shrugged.

"He's a good man," Jacob Encoma said from the darkness. "I've seen it."

"Best hurry before your absence is discovered," Melbroth called back.

Darion gave a short sharp whistle, and Bindu bounded ahead before he turned and followed the priest into the night.

## Chapter 16: The Lake to Longstretch

**The Reach, The Rivers**

"You're crazy. I already told you what happened on the lake," Mercy argued.

"Fallston has been fired, the urak have gone and a storm has come." Hiro bent and dropped his backpack into the canoe as if his response was final, but Mercy wasn't finished.

"You said we were going to Hilden."

Hiro grunted. "We go to Rivercross. This morning the best way was Hilden, tonight it is Longstretch." He glanced at Nihm and signed for her to pick up the other end of the boat.

Nihm looked at Mercy then back to Hiro. The monk had been outside not an hour past and returned wet but smiling. Deciding, Nihm threw her pack into the boat before grasping the rim and lifting it.

There were four canoes, looking old and battered, all neatly stacked in an alcove near the cave exit. The cave system, Nihm discovered was extensive, extending like hollowed tree roots into the bluff above Fallston. They stretched from the Hang to beneath the River Oust and the falls, then south another five hundred paces. It probably extended further Nihm supposed but the little cave they were in was the exit used by the black marketers of the Hang and she had no reason to look further.

Mercy's scar twisted as she scowled. Reluctant, she placed her staff and belongings into another of the boats. Morten, following Mercy's lead, dropped his own in then they each grabbed an end and raising the canoe trudged after Hiro and Nihm.

The cave's entrance was low forcing them all to crouch as they manoeuvred three of the boats outside. They found themselves in a small clearing surrounded by a dense thicket of needle bush and ferns. The wind howled through the branches and the rain managed to find its way through the leafy canopy above. Lucky swore as he clipped his head on the low overhang; he and Stama were the last out.

Nihm heard Snow and Ash rummaging in the undergrowth. The dogs had beaten them all outside, unable to restrain themselves once they got the scent of fresh air. Nihm couldn't blame them. Underground, in the dank and dark, she'd found the air sluggish and oppressive. It was good to be out in the open again and feel the wind on her face. Even the gentle patter of rain on her head felt good.

Her eyes sought out Maohong. His face looked battered. Dark purple and yellow bruising marked both eyes and the bridge of his nose. The stitched cut above his right eye had looked red and angry before Mercy hid it behind a dark bandage.

That first night, Hiro had reset Mao's broken nose and the old man had barely cried out. Then, as he convalesced, Mao had become increasingly more remote and distant. Hiro never gave much away but it was Nihm's impression that he worried for his friend. He'd spent little enough time with Mao but Nihm often caught him watching the old man. She wondered perhaps if their change in route was as much about Mao as it was circumstance. A day or two in a boat would offer more time for his recuperation than trudging the edge of the Grim Marsh to Hilden.

Hiro led them through a subtle break in the needle bush and through the thicket until finally, they stood on a bank overlooking the Reach. Away to the right the Grim Marsh stretched, water reeds and mud banks giving barely a hint of the dangers that lay within. Out of shelter, the wind was brisk, whipping their cloaks about their bodies and driving the rain into their faces.

"Soon be dark. Hardly see the nose on me face then. Don't much fancy paddling about in this," Lucky groused.

Nihm paid him no mind. Her eyes drifted instead across the lake to the distant town. It was all but invisible through the murk and rain, even to Nihm's enhanced sight but curious and intrigued at her newfound ability she decided to try it out.

Closing her eyes and concentrating, Nihm made the shift. Aether ebbed and flowed all around her in its myriad of hues and patterns. At first, she was not sure what she looked at or how to interpret it. The sense of aether was fuzzy and complicated, in constant flux. Her mind discerned the shaped radiances that must be her companion's, their essences similar in form but subtly different.

Nihm's mind smoothly slipped past them and across the pale pink glow that could only be the lake. It was beautiful, even the air seemed to shimmer with aether. As she stretched her ki'tae sense out towards Fallston her focus shifted, sliding through the strands of colour.

<*Stop that.*> Irritation and annoyance were conveyed in Hiro's silent command. The intervention was unexpected and Nihm stumbled, disoriented as she snapped back.

<*Sorry.*> Nihm felt guilty at being caught followed immediately by a flare of annoyance.

Ignoring Nihm, Hiro instead addressed the group. "We'll raft the canoes together. Lucky is right, it's dark, too easy in this storm to get separated or worse, overturned."

Explaining what he wanted, they soon had the three canoes lashed together using two of the paddles stretched across the hulls. Together with the aft and bow painters tied the raft was surprisingly stable. Nihm and Morten took one side with the two dogs coaxed in with them. Hiro, Lucky, and Stama took the other leaving Mercy and Mao in the middle.

"Just in case we need that staff of yours," Hiro explained at the frown on Mercy's face.

As they paddled east, the faintest of glows creased the dark sky to the north, evidence that some fires burned still in Fallston despite the rain. No arrows of flame or balls of fire assailed them as they slipped by, Hiro steering them unerringly and the tell-tale of Fallston soon fell away behind them.

The storm hid what little noise they made as they skirted the southern edges of the Reach where it melded into the waterways and reed banks of the Grim Marsh. Soaked to the skin by the rain and chilled by the icy wind, it was a thoroughly miserable escape.

* * *

Morning brought a muted light as they paddled eastward. It was their only respite, as the rain continued to fall, the northern shore of the lake barely discernible through its veil. They saw no sign of life and Hiro sensed no human or urak presence.

Late morning, Hiro steered the raft to a small maple wood nestling against the lake's north bank. There they rested and took food. Hiro had them break the raft up and empty the water that had collected in the bottom of the boats as he contemplated their journey so far.

© 2020 A D Green

It had been slow going, the canoe raft was stable but paddling against a headwind had been hard work. Reluctantly, Hiro directed that the canoes be bound back together. As tempting as it was not to do so, none of their little band was proficient on the water and Morten couldn't swim. He worried as well that the dogs might affect the stability of a canoe, at least rafted together there was little chance of capsizing.

"I'm sick of this weather, wish this rain would clear at least." Morten stared ruefully at the sky. He was shivering, his hair plastered over his scalp despite the hood he wore.

"Careful what ya wish for, Red. This rain's the best cover we got." Lucky clapped a big hand on Morten's shoulder. He pointed at Maohong sitting silent, back against a maple tree. "Ya don't see ancient father there moaning none."

Nihm, overhearing the conversation, turned to look. Mao seemed okay all things considered. At least his eyes were bright and alert. There was something off about him however that she couldn't place. Sai had no insight either as to what it might be <*Maohong appears functional,*> being his only offering. Functional maybe, but Mao had uttered barely a word since entering the caves. Resolved, Nihm rose and wandered over to sit with him.

"You've been quiet. How are you holding up?" she asked placing a hand on Mao's knee. She felt guilty. In the caves, she'd been so focused on herself and Master Hiro's lessons she'd thought little on her patient. So it was that Mercy, without word or discussion, had taken over his care.

The old man glanced at Nihm's hand where it rested before his eyes turned to regard her. His look was intense. Just as Nihm started to feel uncomfortable, he answered. "Mao is better than he was."

<*Leave Mao be,*> Hiro interrupted her thoughts.

<*He seems different than before. Not the same.*> Nihm knew this to be true, though she couldn't explain how or why it was so. After all, she barely knew him. Maybe it was Mao's words. He'd not spoken in that sing-song, halfway of talking that she liked or expected.

<*Mao is in a difficult place. I will deal with him when time permits. Until then stay away from him.*>

Nihm stared across to where Hiro was tying the canoe painters tight. He hadn't stopped his work whilst they communicated. Before Nihm could ask what he meant the link was terminated. Frowning in annoyance, Nihm stood and wandered away, aware of Mao's eyes following her as she left.

They set off again shortly after, paddling out to the far side of the lake, before turning east again towards Longstretch. There was little talk, the mood on the boats matching the weather.

As the day grew long, the wind gradually abated and the rain became sporadic. It was a nervous time, for in between rain squalls they could see the lakeshore to the north and it left them feeling exposed. They would be easy to spot if any cared to look.

Only Hiro and Mao appeared unconcerned. Nihm suspected Hiro used his hidden sight, as she had come to think of it. Mao for his part was indifferent altogether to their plight, lost in his mind it seemed.

Nihm glanced up at the slate grey sky. It was late autumn with winter not far off and the days were shortening rapidly. That and the heavy cloud meant night would creep in early. She gazed across the water and noticed that the lake had started to narrow. In the far distance, she could make out the hunched shape of a town, Longstretch.

Paddling was easier now, the headwind had dropped considerably and the faintest of currents helped pull them along. After a time, Morten sat upright in the front of the raft and called out, "Longstretch."

Mercy eased herself up from where she was laid slumped against the gunnels and stared ahead, as did Lucky and Stama. They could see the town and could discern a faint black smoke trail against the leaden horizon.

"I see it." Mercy turned to Hiro, "Probably not a good idea to just blunder in there."

Hiro glanced at the lowering sky. "It will be dark soon and we must pass, neh?"

"Even so, care is needed. That smoke bodes ill," Mercy pointed out the dark plume, more evident now they'd seen it.

"Let me go take a look and scout it out," Stama offered. "No point all of us walking into danger."

"I'll go too," Lucky said agreeably.

"No," Stama said. "Quicker I go alone. No offence Luck but you lack a certain subtlety."

Nihm and Morten watched the exchange in silence, excluded from the discussion.

"I will also go," Hiro stated. "Mr Lucson, get out of the boat."

"You what?" Lucky glared, perturbed at the sudden direction things had taken.

"Out, out," Hiro shooed with his hands. Mercy nodded her agreement at Lucky.

Feeling outnumbered, Lucky huffed. "I can be subtle." But, resigned to his lot, he reached out grabbing the side of the middle canoe. The next few moments proved awkward, the makeshift raft rocking alarmingly as Lucky half crawled, half rolled into the other boat. Stama laughed, Mercy swore and Ash barked as the raft bobbed and rolled wildly. Nihm stilled Ash with a word and a hand on his ruff.

"Sound travels far over water," Hiro admonished, unimpressed by their antics. He sniffed, disgruntled, and began untying the hitch knots in the aft painter. Stama reciprocated with the bow rope.

Hiro moved to the paddles that bound it to the raft, fingers working. "I will signal three times if all is well."

Without another word, Hiro edged his boat away from the others before he and Stama paddled softly into the gloom and the wisp of mist that had started to form over the lake.

\* \* \*

Longstretch was deserted. The town had been sacked and bore the scars. Doors and shutters lay broken or hung loosely from their bindings. The houses they ventured into were trashed, furniture smashed and overturned.

"No people, dead or otherwise. I hope they all fled south," Stama said. "No food to be found neither." He let the cupboard door he held swing back, limp in its frame.

"There's no metal either," Hiro observed. Moving back outside, he bent suddenly under the eaves of the building and pressed his fingers into the ground where it was stained. He raised his hand to his nose, blood!

Rising, Hiro surveyed the town knowing it was empty; the largest signs of life he sensed were birds and rats. No one was here, urak or human. He said as much to Stama and although Stama didn't question him, the raised eyebrow was enough to tell Hiro his companion's interest was piqued.

Despite his assertion, Stama moved with care and craft as they explored further. It pleased Hiro. Precaution over presumption; he approved.

They traced the source of the smoke to a large bonfire in the town square. Its flames were a dull glow, its anger having burnt out, but the embers were still hot enough to send smoke plumes spiralling into the sky. On the far side of the pyre, they found a man. Dead of course, else Hiro would have sensed him. He was staked before the fire.

"Poor bastard. Wonder who he was?" Stama grimaced moving closer. A sign was hung about the man's neck but he couldn't read it, the language strange. The heat was uncomfortable as it washed over him. After a time it became unbearable and Stama was forced to step away.

"That's an evil way ta go."

Hiro agreed. The man had been stripped naked and lashed to the stake only a few paces from the pyre, facing away from it. The man's features were easily discernible. His face contorted in a rictus of pain. He had died in agony. Hiro knew the man's back, should he care to look, would be suppurated and red where he'd been roasted.

Hiro stepped closer to the fire. The charcoal smell of cooked meat assailed him, mixing with the sulphurous scent of burnt hair. The sign the dead man wore was a combination of pictograms and harsh bold strokes, "Urakakule."

"I kinda figured that bit out," Stama said. "Don't s'pose you can read it?"

Hiro spared a brief glance before turning back to examine the sign. "A little, the message is to the White Hand I think. It's an offering or warning, I'm not sure with any certainty which. This symbol here," Hiro pointed, "is a name, though I cannot decipher it."

"If it's an offering does that make this White Hand one of their gods or an urak?" Stama asked.

"Neither, it's a clan, a gathering of tribes. It gives me much to think on," Hiro said, thoughtful as he read the sign again, consigning it to memory for later consideration. Keeper would know.

"It tells us at least two of the five clans are involved and, just in case you were in any doubt, proves this is more than just a border skirmish."

Stama looked nervously around the square. "I got an itchy feeling between ma shoulder blades. If you're sure the town's dead I say we signal the others. The sooner we're gone from here the better."

"I am and I agree." Hiro gathered himself. Tearing his eyes from the sign and the cooked man he stepped away.

By the time they reached the lakeside, darkness had settled. Clouds shrouded any light offered by the moons and hid any sign of their companions out on the water. A pity, Hiro thought, if he could see Nihm he could have mind linked to her. As it was he didn't wish to use the art, not when he had no clear knowledge of where the enemy might be. Crouching down he slung his pack onto the ground.

"Here let me," Stama offered, rummaging in his bag and emerging with a small wooden box. "I need the practise."

Stama moved to the building nearest them and pulled a log from the woodpile that had escaped the earlier rain. From his box, he removed a flint, a small strip of cloth, and a fat candle and laid them on the log end. Hiro watched with interest. The cloth was covered in runes.

In short order, Stama struck a spark. The cloth strip ignited instantly, flaming brightly. Taking the candle Stama lit it and, rising, handed it to Hiro with a grin.

"Clever. Did you infuse the cloth yourself?" Hiro took the candle, shielding it with his body and hand from the wind.

"Let's just say it's one of the perks of having a mage along," Stama smirked.

Hiro walked to the edge of the dock. He could sense where the company waited on the raft and directed the candle at them then shielded its light. He repeated this twice more, then blew the candle out and handed it back to Stama.

They waited.

"You think they saw the signal? Candle don't give off much light. Thought you was gonna use a torch," Stama said. Hiro looked at Stama but passed no comment before staring out again across the water.

A short time later they both heard the soft stroke of paddles and through the dark and mist, the canoe raft emerged. Stama grabbed the rope Morten threw him and deftly pulled them in, tying it off to a wooden bollard.

The dogs, unable to wait, leapt ashore and raced off amongst the houses. Nihm let them go.

"Eat and take what rest you can. At midnight we'll ride the river south as far as we're able," Hiro told them.

"What of Longstretch?" Mercy asked.

"Dead, its people are gone."

## Chapter 17: Reflections On The Road

**South of Appleby, The Rivers**

Zoller and his Red Cloaks left Appleby behind them. It was the afternoon of their second day out from Greenholme and travel had been frustratingly slow. It seemed every little path or road spat more people out in front of them and whilst all moved aside making way there was a surly indifference in most as they did.

Renco, watching from atop Luke Goodwill's mare, observed it all in silence. The creak of harness on leather and clatter and tramp of people as they moved south was occasionally punctuated by the crying of a babe. Dogs barked in warning and men called out asking for news from the north only to be ignored. The Red Cloaks had tired a day past of answering that question.

Most people walked. If they had a horse or mule it was invariably loaded down with whatever they had of value. And their fear was pervasive. Scared of what they ran from and of the future and what it might bring. Renco saw anger and resentment on many faces at having to make way for the Red Priest and his escort. Zoller's gilded carriage looked opulent and, together with the armed guards, provided a sense of protection that the people yearned for but couldn't have. They were on their own in their desperate plight.

The Red Cloaks for their part were indifferent to the travails of those around them. Their only concern was getting past with their charge as quickly as possible.

Brother Thomas Perrick led Renco's horse. Holt, the giant Red Cloak that had beaten Maohong so badly, had baited him continuously when they'd first left Fallston. But Renco had had little regard for the taunts and knocks that came his way. It was really quite predictable and he'd had worse over the years from Mao. Tiring of his sport, Holt had moved to the front of the column to better harangue people off the road.

Mao. Renco's concern for his friend suddenly bubbled to the forefront of his mind. Mao was old and the beating he'd taken had been vicious. If Fallston had fallen to the urak horde and his friend survived it, where was he now? If he lived, Master Hiro would find him. There was much about Master that was a mystery to him still, despite being his student all this time, but of that he was sure.

His mind switched to the dog girl who burned so brightly and with whom he'd felt an instant connection with. She was different; he knew it instantly he'd seen her in the aether, looking like an angel from the heavens with wisps of liquid energy swirling about her. He'd mind linked her, not sure why he tried. On some primal level, they had touched, but Renco didn't understand how or why no matter how much he turned it over in his head.

In quiet moments his thoughts often turned to her. She wasn't pretty in the way Lett was, her features weren't delicate and soft like that, more robust. Hair black, eyes brown and intense, she was dark to Lett's fair in many ways.

Renco turned his gaze to the carriage in front and to Lett who sat perched next to the driver. Her blonde hair was bound back into a ponytail but several strands had escaped in the breeze. He felt conflicted. She confused him beyond measure. He thought he loved her but knew he shouldn't. He should hate her and he had at the moment of her betrayal. But since then he'd had plenty of time to think and reflect.

Hate is a powerful emotion, Master Hiro had told him once. It can lend strength when it is needed but ultimately it takes more from you than it ever gives. Blind hatred doubly so, unreasoned and uncontrolled, it taints every action. Renco recalled the lesson clearly; even the little 'Neh' Master punctuated his statements with.

Lett thought she was saving him. She'd been suspicious of Master Hiro and said as much to him. Her actions had triggered a series of events that led to the murder of her father and clearly, that wasn't her intent. She'd lost everything as a result, far more than he. Guilt and self-pity wracked her.

She'd barely spoken to him since that day. Opportunities had been few, but her misery was clear to see. He'd felt love vie with hate but that had ebbed and waned to be replaced; now he just felt sad. For what she'd done and for what had happened.

When Lett was bound next to him at Greenholme, Renco was surprised to find he felt protective of her. It had been especially hard that night. Brother Thomas had taken Lett into the stall where the blacksmith had been whipped. Chained as he was, Renco heard it all. It hadn't been violent, at least not in that way. Lett hadn't struggled, remaining silent throughout her ordeal. Not a cry or whimper, her own, personal form of defiance. But the grunts and moans from Brother Thomas left no doubt what had occurred.

Renco had closed his eyes even as he bore witness, calming his mind with a mantra, Master Hiro had taught him. All the while he'd watched Zoller through hooded eyes.

The priest sat on the far side of the fire, hidden in the dark, thinking himself unseen. It was afterwards when the camp was still and silent and he heard Lett quietly sobbing, that he made his vow. It was the same vow he'd made as a child after the priest had murdered his parents. After Master Hiro had saved him and nursed his battered body and broken mind back to life. This vow was different though. It wasn't driven by hate like his first. It was simply a redressing, a balancing. The priest would die.

A commotion sounded up ahead, cheering. Thomas Perrick rose in his saddle to see what was happening. Renco followed suit, balancing easily in his stirrups despite having his hands tied. The Red Cloak glanced at him briefly but passed no comment.

Renco's eyesight was exceptional and he could make out a column of horsemen in the distance. As the riders drew closer he counted twenty hands riding two abreast in a neat orderly file. The noise grew as people scattered from the road ahead, clapping and cheering.

"High Lord's come," was shouted out and taken up.

"King Twyford," yelled a few bolder voices, which was treasonous but none cared, all here were River's folk and a sudden hope had kindled at the sight of the armed horsemen.

Father Zoller called out and the carriage drew to a slow stop. The driver clambered down, murmured an answer through a crack in the window before opening the door and standing back. Zoller stepped out, his red cassock immaculate, blinking his eyes in the full light outside. He clambered up onto the carriage seat hardly sparing a glance at Lett, who instinctively edged as far away as she was able.

The road ahead cleared as the troupe of riders approached. Holt, sitting impassively on his big destrier, waited as they reined in.

The horsemen were neatly attired in leathers and light armour wearing a brown crest. The crest was embossed with a flaming cross over two rivers twined together.

Their leader removed his helm, shaking damp hair loose. His eyes slid over the hulking form of Holt on his warhorse, before settling on the red priest.

"Well met, Father. I'm Sir Aric Nesto of Charncross."

"Father Henrik Zoller. Kildare's blessing to you, Sir Aric," Zoller replied.

"What news from the north?" Aric asked.

Zoller looked around. The land was flat hereabouts the road running straight, more or less, through a field of meadow grass and accacha bushes that were dotted here and there with purple clumps of idris flowers. To the west, a hundred paces or so was the River Oust.

"I could stretch my legs," Zoller said. "Might I suggest we take our rest in the field and share a cold tea? Then we can exchange news."

"Very well, Father," Aric said, agreeably. They'd ridden since first light, his horse and riders were due a rest. Turning his head slightly, he issued orders to his sergeant at arms.

They made an impromptu camp in the field adjoining the river. Zoller thought them well organised, each rider knowing their duties. Horses were led to the river to drink their fill and then staked to graze on the meadow grass. Sentries were posted around the perimeter, whilst those remaining took food and drink or inspected weapons and harness.

Zoller left his carriage on the road under guard. It meant people had to move around it to get by, much to their ire. Zoller didn't care, after the trouble experienced already with the carriage he wouldn't risk it to the unknown rigours of the field.

He had Brother Thomas and two of his red cloaks stand watch over Renco and Lett, sitting them inside the circle of the camp. The boy had shown no signs of trying to escape but that didn't make Zoller complacent, far from it. He would've preferred Tuco or Holt watch over them but Tuco had disappeared and Holt he wanted with him.

Zoller proffered a cup to Sir Aric; the tea was cold but freshly brewed that morning.

Aric took it with thanks and sipped from it, considering the Father as he did so. The priest was important to command a dozen Red Cloaks.

"May I ask where you have travelled from, Father?"

"Thorsten, Sir Aric. I travel from Thorsten and escaped just in time or so I believe."

"Indeed, the town walls fell ten days past; though it is said, the keep still stands." Aric's statement was matter-of-fact. "The High Lord got word just as I left."

It was a shock; one Zoller gave no sign of as he sat sipping his tea. The Black Crow was a renowned field commander and had ten thousand men to guard the town walls, maybe more. How could it have fallen so fast? His mind turned briefly to Father Mortim; at least that fool was gone. He was surprised to find the thought not as satisfying as anticipated.

"Fallen you say," Zoller repeated. "I escaped Fallston eight days ago, just ahead of the urak." This was troubling. How could the urak sack Thorsten and Fallston, it was several days travel between them? The implications needed thought but it suggested that the scale of the invasion was bigger than he'd supposed.

Sir Aric digested Zoller's announcement. He was young, having only seen twenty-three summers, but was a soldier, a knight. He understood his craft and reached a similar conclusion.

"I'll send a rider back with your news. High Lord Twyford will be at the Defile a day north of Rivercross if he left as planned."

"He's only just leaving?" Zoller exclaimed, perturbed. The Defile was a hill east of the River Oust and a day north of Rivercross. It had steep bluffs and a plateau that held an ancient fortification that shared its name. The fortress overlooked the river and the north road and occupied a perfect, defensive position. It had seen little use however, its upkeep deemed expensive and unnecessary with Rivercross only a day away.

"He's an army of twenty-five thousand to move, with little time to prepare them for travel, Father," Aric said, "You're a priest, not a soldier. I'd not expect you to understand the logistics."

Insolent pup, Zoller riled but bit back on his immediate response. "What are your orders, Sir Aric?"

"My orders are between me and the High Lord," Aric said. "I suggest you attend to your own business, Father Zoller."

Holt rumbled forward glowering at the young knight. Zoller held his palm out flat signing for him to wait, not needing to look to know his giant protector had risen.

Aric's eyes narrowed. The man was massive and ugly and promised violence. Several of his men had seen it too and gathered behind him, hands-on sword hilts.

"Forgive Brother Holt, he can't abide rudeness," Zoller said, rising from his seat to better defuse the situation. Turning to Holt, he jerked his head at him.

Holt, staring intently, took a step back and slowly removed his hand from his sword hilt.

"Your dog's well trained, Father," Aric said, drawing a laugh from his men. Relenting, he held his hands up. "No offence was intended, Father. It's no secret I ride the north road. As to my purpose, I'm sure you can work that out without me breaking an oath. Please sit, take your ease, and tell me about your journey."

Zoller let the young man cajole him and sitting quietly they exchanged news whilst drinking their tea.

"The Bouchemeaxs were never popular in court. They always thought themselves hard done by and overlooked out on the borders," Aric said at one point. "But my father respects the Black Crow. Says he's never met a cannier general on the battlefield. Coming from my father, that is high praise."

Zoller sipped his cold tea, listening.

"I was in court when the first bird arrived from Thorsten. High Lord Twyford was livid, thought it a ploy to avoid the Westland's campaign. Rumour has it the Black Crow wasn't enamoured of it. The High Lord thought Bouchemeax was going soft, losing his appetite for battle."

"Lord Richard seemed highly competent when I met him, shrewd and hard in a way that is lacking in court," Zoller offered, enjoying the indignant look on the young popinjay's face. "All the more concern the town fell so quickly. Please continue."

"The second bird arrived a day later. Lord Bouchemeax reported Redford had gone, his brother and family thought lost. Then Trudoc, that's Lord Twyford's mage," Aric elaborated, "advised that the Council of Mages had received a report of urak in the north and confirmed Redford's fall."

"Did Trudoc say what the council proposes?" Zoller asked, interested.

"They're sending a hand of mages from Kingsholme to look into matters. The High Lord didn't want to wait for them and so mobilised north."

Indeed, thought Zoller. It would take three weeks or more for the mages to make the journey from Kingsholme. In that time, Twyford would lose half the Rivers to the urak the way things were going.

"What of the High King?" Zoller asked.

"Not heard." Aric shrugged, indifferent it seemed.

They parted soon after, both men thoughtful and reflective. Aric's riders were well drilled and pulled out in short order leaving Zoller and his Red Cloaks behind. Tuco appeared immediately after they'd gone.

"What happened to you?" Zoller asked, one eyebrow rising in question.

"Best the young Lord not see me," Tuco muttered.

Zoller decided he didn't want to know. "What did you find out?"

"Not much, they're scouting north but we already knew that," Tuco said. "Word is Twyford has sent messengers to Midshire, Cumbrenan, and Norderland asking for support."

"What of Westlands and the High King?"

"Bad blood with Westlands, Twyford will not entertain inviting them into the Rivers. Nought about Blackstar, acceptin' the usual rumours and none of them reliable."

"Tell me," Zoller ordered.

"The High King's sick. That he's paranoid, worried of treachery. That Great Olme in the south will war to break free of the Kingdoms; or just that he don't give two shits bout the North and will leave 'em ta rot. Like I said, the usual." Tuco rubbed an apple against his tunic that he'd appropriated from somewhere, then took a bite.

Zoller was thoughtful. A lot of rumours abounded about the High King in recent years. Some he knew were planted by Cardinal Tortuga, or at least orchestrated by him. A risky game to play in the Rivers; in Kingsholme, where the Cardinal was now, it would be downright dangerous. The rumours were designed to marginalise the Order and raise the Red Church's standing in the Kingdoms. If mishandled or discovered it would cause much trouble for the church. What did Tortuga know of the High King and what was he about? Zoller wondered.

He'd not thought much on the Cardinal since his flight from Thorsten. Now that Rivercross lay only a few days south he'd have to turn his intellect back to more important matters, namely the church and his former mentor. Zoller sighed, taking a weary breath.

"Very well, let's be off. The sooner we're gone the better."

## Chapter 18: Into the Storm

**Thorsten, The Rivers**

High in the castle's keep, Amos looked out over the walls at the surrounding town. Thorsten held an eerie stillness. The background sounds of a large town he'd barely heeded before were evident now by their absence. No hustle and bustle of people going about their business. No hammer on anvil as the blacksmith plied his trade. No sound of the carpenter working. No cries from street hawkers plying their wares and a thousand other snippets of life taken for granted and that gave a heartbeat to the town.

The heart still beat in Thorsten, but barely. The vibrant sounds replaced instead with the muted cries of the townsfolk below. Thousands of them crammed the market square in makeshift camps, trapped. No room in the keep for them and no hope of escaping the urak that occupied the plains outside the town walls.

Smoke dribbled lazily into the sky from a score of campfires and following it, the stench of humanity. There was no dignity in what Amos saw. The people endured but barely and there were fewer of them every day.

Some, the fit and able, escaped into the night preferring to take fate into their own hands it seemed rather than sit and wait for the urak and death. Whether any made it through, Amos didn't know. The hordes of urak had thinned so maybe some had, he hoped.

The urak themselves were content it seemed to camp in the plains surrounding Thorsten, shunning the town and the shelter it offered. The urak numbers may have diminished but they were still impressive, Amos thought. Many had moved off in the preceding days in warbands large and small heading south and east whilst more arrived from the north.

The town's remnants huddled as close to the castle walls as they could for the protection it offered. Last night, for the first time since the town was cut off, urak had attacked under the cover of darkness, aided by the lowering cloud that blocked the light of the tri moons.

The defenders on the castle walls could only listen as the camps below were raided. Come the morning over a hundred were missing, taken. Amos knew this because there were no bodies to show for it, just trashed camps. The collapsed canvases of lean-tos and tents looking ominously like bloodstains from the heights of the keep.

It was a desperate situation and guilt sat heavily upon him, that he should sit safely behind castle walls whilst watching the slow death of those below. He heard footsteps behind but didn't turn. He wasn't much for talking right then.

Lord Richard Bouchemeaux, the Black Crow, leaned against the wall and peered out over his town, his hands resting on the solid stonework, taking strength from its enduring permanence.

Sensing another behind him, Amos instinctively turned his head and saw Bartsven in his periphery. Lord Richard's firstsword stood guardedly several paces back.

Amos glanced across at the Black Crow. He looked worn, dark circles evident under his eyes and a worried frown marring his features. Pale blue eyes, piercing in their intensity flickered to Amos before returning to consider his town and his people.

"Do you read, Amos?" The Black Crow's gaze never wavered from its observations below.

"Of course," Amos wondered at the question.

"That's not what I'm asking. I meant, do you read just for the sake of it; for the pleasure of the writing and the words?" Richard didn't wait for a reply. "I do, I have a small library here. I must have read every book it contains at one time or another. At least it feels that way. I love history, you see. You can learn a lot from the past if you study it. You know what I've learnt most?"

"No."

"That despite our books and our learning we're ignorant. Doomed to repeat the same mistakes our forebears made."

"And what are those?" Unease lay upon Amos.

The Black Crow ignored the question. "I have spoken to Lutico and reread the books of old I'd long forgotten. Fanciful books, telling of war and the Taken, to me they were brutal but heroic. I recall with the conceit of youth that I wished I had been born in such times so that I would be written about in history books and so that I would be remembered."

"We all have dreams like that as boys," Amos offered, but it was as if Richard never heard him.

"Thorsten was known as Tors Step back then. Do you know who the Lord of Tors Step was in those times?" Richard saw the slight shake of the head from Amos. "Well neither did I. Lord Justin Garthford it is written. Written but still forgotten just like the lessons of old."

Amos was at a loss at what to say but Richard wasn't finished.

"The first we knew of the Taken back then according to my history books was urak invading our borders. They conquered all of our northern lands, kingdoms as they were in those days, and in only a few short years. Hundreds of thousands died, slaughtered." Richard laughed the sound incongruous given the dour mood that lay upon him.

"The irony is not lost upon me now. That I do live in those times and oh how I wish it were not so." He paused regarding again his people below. "They are dying and I can do nothing to save them and nothing to save us. All I can do is delay and buy time."

"That bad? Is all hope lost then?" Amos said.

Richard screwed his eyes tight shut and shook his head no. He turned then to Amos. "Look at them all." He indicated the urak out on the distant plains surrounding the town. "They are so many. Too many for High Lord Twyford even were he to gather all the armed might of the Rivers. Our one advantage should have been our magi but it seems they have their own."

"So what is the answer? What do we do?" Amos asked, the knot of fear in his belly had been there since Eagles Watch but now it uncoiled like a lead weight in his gut.

"We endure however we can. Save whatever we can and hope that in a thousand years there are people still that will not recall my name or know who I was." He clapped a hand on Amos's shoulder. "I have a mission for you if you will take it."

\* \* \*

"Preposterous father, we'll never survive it. I won't abandon you or our people here," Jacob Bouchemeax exclaimed.

"Do not raise your voice to me. You will and you must." Richard replied.

Jacob took a breath, biting back his retort. Richard waited patiently until finally, Jacob relented, "How then?"

Richard waved a hand at Lutico and the mage stood forward. "There is a storm coming from the east, I have sensed it, and it will be upon us by nightfall. You will leave through the tunnels to the docks at Oust Bridge then take a boat downriver as far as you can. The storm should mask your passage. If Fallston still stands you can take a horse or boat to Rivercross. If it has fallen you will have to cross into the Grim and make your way as best you can."

Jacob looked at his father. "Why? I don't wish to go or to leave you. It's not honourable, father. Not when our people are dying outside."

"Honour be damned, Jacob. You will take your sister and you will endure. You must. There will be no help for our people, no help for any of us here. The urak are too many. The High Lord doesn't have the numbers to defeat them even with the raising of the banners. We will see no relief." Richard didn't state the obvious and Jacob understood his meaning.

"Then come with us, father. Let us escape together or at least die together."

"I am Lord here. Not you. I stay with my people until the end," Richard said. "You must survive, Jacob. Keep your sister safe and remember us, remember all of us. To you will fall the task of taking back our lands and rebuilding."

"How and with what? It's not right." Jacob despaired at his father's words.

"Enough." Richard clasped his son to him and held him. "Life's not fair, not for most folk."

He stepped back, laying a hand briefly on Jacob's cheek as he did so, eyes sad. "You must be strong, son; hard decisions must be made - never shy from making them. Now, I've made arrangements as best I can. Amos and his men will lead you. He has offered refuge for Constance and yourself on behalf of the Duncan and I have accepted it."

Jacob turned towards Amos who had watched the exchange silently, his two men stood a pace further back. They were solid, dependable. He recalled them from the plains of Northfield when he'd ridden out to save them. The dark-haired one with a moustache curling around his mouth nodded his head at Jacob in acknowledgement, a cocky half-grin on his face. Jacob nodded back sombrely.

"Five of us then," Jacob said.

"Ten," Richard replied. "Captain Stenson suggested Thornhill and Mahan attend you and to I thought you may have need of some mage craft."

Jacob looked sceptically across at Lutico. "No offence but you're hardly a spring lamb. You up for this old man?"

"Thanks for the kind words but my place is with Lord Richard," Lutico scowled. "Junip will go in my stead."

Seeing the dismissive look in Jacob's eyes he snorted. "She is very competent I'll have you know. You're lucky to have her."

Jacob made no comment, turning instead back to his father. "That's only eight."

"Ned Wynter. He's a ranger and the best bowman and tracker I have. He knows the Grim better than anyone." Richard replied. He looked across at Amos. "And err, Annabelle."

"Who's she then?" Jacob asked.

"Me," A little voice pipped from behind Amos and his men. A small head popped out to peek at Jacob. A young girl, her face smudged.

"What, an eight-year-old?" Jacob shook his head, incredulous.

"I'm ten." She stuck her tongue out whilst the blonde man she hid behind placed a quieting hand on her head.

"Hush, Belle," he admonished, unable to hide the small curl of his lip showing his amusement.

Jacob wasn't impressed. "It's too risky."

"For you or her?" Amos retorted.

"For all of us, she's a child," Jacob snapped.

"Constance is eleven I understand, practically the same age," Amos said. "She's my ward and she comes."

Jacob gritted his teeth. That his father said nothing in support meant this had already been agreed upon. The thought of his sister calmed him. Amos was right, she was eleven, no older really, and probably not as street smart as Amos's little brat. Conceding defeat he looked to his father.

"We go tonight?"

"Yes. You have a few hours to pack and bid your mother goodbye." Richard said.

\* \* \*

The storm hit as Lutico predicted, the rising wind howling over the castle. Rain lashed down in diagonal sheets drenching everything. The encampment in the market square escaped the brunt of the onslaught sheltered by the bulk of the keep and its curtain wall but not completely. Campfires hissed and died in the sudden downpour and shelters strained, canvas flapping wildly in the wind.

None of this was heard or felt by the men and women deep below the castle. The tunnel was hidden in one of the larger cellars behind an immense wooden barrel that lay on its side on wooden chocks. It took ten men to move it, revealing as they did so, a large cast-iron door bolted and locked.

The room was dank and cold and the door had long since seized. It took a blacksmith to work the lock and hinges until finally, with two men straining on it, the door slowly grated open. Groaning its protest it revealed a large wide passage.

The air inside was dead and dry. Looking into its dark maw, Amos's felt a hint of trepidation and wasn't the only one to feel so.

"I don't want to go in there. Father, don't make me go. I want to stay with you and mam." A child's voice, high pitched, and shrill.

"You must, Conn, we spoke about this, we agreed. Besides, your brother needs you, so be brave now." Richard knelt holding his daughter at arm's length. "Now what are we?"

"We're Bouchemeaxs." The little girl sighed.

"And..." Richard smiled as they spoke together.

"We do what needs to be done." They hugged.

When they parted the girl wiped the tears from her eyes but made no further complaint. With a determined look, she reached out and slipped her hand into her brother's. "I'm ready, Jacob."

Jobe and Jerkze lit torches from a sconce on the wall. "Let's get this done." Jobe stepped through the door, Jerkze following a few paces behind.

Amos felt a tug on his sleeve and looked down to see Annabelle smiling nervously up at him. She grabbed a calloused hand in her little one. "I'm brave too, like Nihm."

"Come then little soldier," Amos grinned. They stepped through the portal following the torchlight.

In all, twenty-one went into the tunnels; the blacksmith with his tools and ten men carrying supplies which included two long narrowboats for Amos's party. Amos was sceptical they would be able to manoeuvre the boats through a tunnel but after only a few steps into the passage that worry vanished. The tunnel was wide and well-crafted, a long, endless corridor rather than the rough-hewn hole he'd imagined.

It gently descended in a straight line, the floor smooth and the walls lined with brick. There were a few places that were in disrepair, the brickwork crumbling and broken. Here, dark stains marred the walls where water had found ingress and debris cluttered the ground but it was never enough to hinder their passage.

"How old is this and however did you build it?" Amos asked Jacob as they walked.

"I'd forgotten it was here. It's the first time I've seen it, let alone walked its way," Jacob replied. "Father says it's as old as the Black Keep, which makes it older than the rest of the town. He says that the keep and tunnel were built with the aid of the ilfanum. The Keep's gates are just as old if you believe the stories. Hardwood, gifted from the Great Forest."

"The ilfanum, eh," Amos said.

"Yeah, back in ancient times, we were on good terms with them. I thought them old tales a father told a young boy with too much imagination, but now I think they were true. He likes to read," Jacob said, by way of explanation.

"Bit like those made-up tales of urak and the Taken," Amos said. "Guess they're not tales anymore."

Constance pulled her hand free of her brother's, tired of the men's conversation. It was pretty dull. Having lost her initial fear of the tunnel and surrounded by grown-ups all looking very serious, her attention was drawn to the girl ahead, Annabelle she recalled. She was a skinny thing with mousy brown hair tied back in a single ponytail. She was dressed in plain rustic clothes that looked to have been patched at one knee and an arm.

Curious, Constance moved up alongside and introduced herself. A minute later the two of them were racing ahead toward Jobe and Jerkze laughing.

*  *  *

The journey through the passage seemed long. At various junctures, there were larger areas carved out but they never rested, it was late and time was pressing.

The passageway started to level off and after another hundred paces, it came to an end. Jobe and Jerkze were the first to reach it and holding their torches high examined the wall. There was no door they could discern. Jerkze pulled and pushed on a wall sconce thinking it a lever but to no avail. The two men turned as Amos and Jacob arrived.

"Can't see no door, any ideas?" Jerkze asked.

Jacob stepped up and placed his hands flat against the wall. "Let's see if father's instruction is right or whether we've taken a long walk for nothing." He muttered loudly. Counting brick's down from the sconce he stopped at the third one and pressed his palm against it. Pushing in hard there was a dull crack and the wall shivered. Jacob strained but the wall didn't budge.

"Lend a shoulder," Jacob ordered. There was room for three to lean against the wall and Jerkze and Jobe obliged. As Jacob pressed in on the brick once more there was a grating sound and then suddenly the wall moved. It was not much but it was something. Straining again, Jacob felt a subtle shift through the rock, and with a sudden squeal and groan the wall pushed in a foot and then, on some hinge or other, swung wide to reveal a small room.

Jobe was first into the space beyond, picking his torch up from where he'd laid it and stepping through. It was a storeroom, short but wide. Several crates had been pushed back where they had rested against the false wall. On the far side of the room, a battered iron door stood ajar where it had been forced open.

Looking at the various crates and barrels lying in disorder, Jobe surmised the urak had already discovered and pillaged the stores it held.

The room was cold and draughty through the doorway. The sound of wind and rain loud as the storm raged outside. Jobe handed his torch to Jerkze and, moving to the entrance, peered out.

It was pitch black. Inching and sliding his feet forward, his hands feeling the stone, Jobe stepped through the doorway. Pillars of stone guarded each side arching up and out of reach. Beneath the howl of wind and peal of rain, Jobe detected something else. It was the river, the murmur of the Oust as it flowed by.

In sudden realisation, Jobe knew they were under the Oust Bridge. The pillars at his side, supporting the stone road above. Tapping his foot, he felt into the inky black until the stone ground suddenly dropped away. Lowering himself onto his belly, Jobe found the edge and stretched his arm down plunging it into cold, fast-moving water. Snatching his hand back he inched away. Rising, he returned to the storeroom, pulling the battered iron door closed behind.

The rest of their party had gathered and Jobe explained where they were. Amos and Jacob nodded their understanding. It would be a tricky proposition getting the boats in the river and boarded in the dark whilst a storm raged but the bridge would offer some shelter at least.

The guards and blacksmith sent with them, left their supplies in the room then moved back into the passageway. Mahan, Thornhill, and Jacob lent against the false wall and found it slid closed easier than it had opened; the crates and barrels offering no hindrance this time. With a solid clunk, it shut. Piling empty crates up against it they disguised it as best they could.

In the end, boarding the canoes proved easier than expected. Junip, who had been quiet and pensive the entire journey, seemed happier now she was out of the passage. With a small casting, a soft muted light emitted from the end of her staff, weak but enough to see by at least. "Any brighter and it may be seen," she explained.

They extinguished their torches in the storeroom and let their eyes adjust to the staff's weak light. Moving outside they found themselves in a small alcove beneath the sweeping expanse of the bridge. It was just wide enough for both boats to moor in. Ned Wynter and Thornhill held the aft and bow lines whilst Jacob, Constance and Mahan boarded. Jobe and Jerkze did the same in the other for Junip, Annabelle, and Amos. Then they softly pushed out, steering the boats into the main channel of water and letting the current sweep them along.

The full might of the storm struck as they left the shelter of the bridge. The rain was fierce and the wind raged over the water, tossing the boats about like so much flotsam. In moments, they were all soaked despite their oiled skins but they had no time to worry about it. Unable to see where they were going or what lay ahead, they had no choice but to hold to the gunwales and pray as the current swept them downriver and into the storm.

## Chapter 19: Red Cloth

**Kingsholme, The Holme**

Tomas awoke. He was in the same bed and room as before. His head felt much better. Relieving himself in the chamber pot, he noted with a frown, that it had been emptied. He was unaware anyone had entered the room to do it. He was a light sleeper, had to be. Places he slept, he'd find himself robbed, beaten, or worse if he didn't keep a half-eye open all the time.

A candle burned on a stand on the far side of the room casting an eerie light. He stood, naked and walked stiffly to the wall curtains and drew them back revealing a small shuttered window. He undid the binding, lifted the latch, and opened it, letting light and air into the room. The window was narrow and leaning out gave a view of the street below. It wasn't like the streets he was used to. These were clean and uncluttered and the people well-dressed and purposeful. He was in the Nobles.

He moved to the dresser. On top was a large bowl of water with a soap block and a drying cloth next to it. He ignored them, opening instead the drawers to find they were full of clothes as Renix promised. Emptying them, Tomas tossed the contents onto the bed before sifting through the assortment. They were well made and, judging from the material and cut, expensive.

"Pointless dressing like a prince and stinking like a Garumbat," growled a voice.

Startled, Tomas leapt and rolled over the bed, putting its bulk between him and the voice. He crouched low, uncomfortably aware of his nakedness.

A whoosh of fire burst into life in the corner of the room and, in its flames stood a demon, its horned head almost touching the ceiling. Its feet were cloven and its squat snout filled with razor-like teeth.

Tomas screamed, nakedness forgotten. Even in terror though, somewhere in the back of his mind, a part of him observed there was no heat to the flame.

Abruptly the fire died. The demon's form shifted, blurred, and was suddenly a woman, brown-skinned, scantily clad, and voluptuous. "My bad – was just having some fun." The woman held her hands out placatingly. The effect though was ruined by the deep masculine voice she spoke in.

Fear shivered down Tomas's spine. "You're real. You're a demon?"

"Well, strictly speaking, I'm a Sháadretarch but humans seem to struggle with that." The woman smiled.

"Are you going to eat me?" Tomas stuttered. He couldn't help it. Before, all he'd heard was a ghost whisper in his ear. That, he could put down to his imagination. Not now. All the fears and terrors of a young boy broke loose as the demon, O'si he recalled its name, stood before him dressed in a woman's skin.

"That depends. You owe a debt. I gave you a warning when I had no need and saved your life when you fell. Will you pay the debt?" the woman asked in her man voice.

Adrenaline thrummed through his veins but Tomas's initial terror started to fade. He was petrified still but now his survival instincts took over. The thing talked to him and made no overt physical threat.

"How did you do that? Change shape I mean."

"I manifest how I wish and to whom I wish. Now answer my question. You're trying my patience."

"How can I repay a debt if you will not name it?" Tomas argued, then distracted by bared breast and pert nipple asked. "Can you change into something less weird whilst we're negotiating?"

The demon laughed, cupped the breasts enticingly, and pouted at him. Then in the same instant shimmered and morphed into Renix.

"What the hells!" Tomas was unsettled. Renix was the demon? He shook his head in confusion. No, he couldn't be. Renix was real, how he spoke, how he sat, what he said. This was a game the demon played.

"The debt is whatever I ask. That, or I kill you now."

It was a mistake.

Tomas feared for his life, but he was used to that; had lived with fear as long as he could recall. As well, Bortillo Targus wanted him dead or worse and his chances of eluding Bortillo in his own city were slim to none.

So long as Tomas could remember, his existence every day had been a quest, first and foremost, to live. He might be twelve but he was a veteran at surviving. The demon, O'si, needed him. Threatening to get what it wanted was nothing new to Tomas. Even so, it was a demon.

"No." Tomas sounded braver than he felt.

Renix blinked at him and twisted his head to the side puzzled. "No? You want to die?"

Tomas closed his eyes briefly and cheered inside. He was right else he would be demon fodder right now, he was sure of it.

"Yep, kill me. Really. You'd be doing me a favour. See Bortillo will hunt me down. There's no escaping the thief king if he wants you."

Renix blinked again opened his mouth then closed it.

"I don't think you want to kill me," Tomas pushed. "I think you need me, more than I need you, else I'd be dead already, right?"

"I could kill you before you draw breath. Turn your blood to sand and rupture your eyeballs. Leave nothing but a bloody pulp. In the end, you would beg me to kill you," the demon growled.

Tomas shook but remained silent; he very much needed to use the pisspot again.

"I can help with this thief king you speak of," O'si conceded finally, then with a glint of malevolence. "But I'll have your oath in exchange. And just so we're clear, if you don't help me, I will live still. If I don't help you this Bortillo kills you, else I will. I refer you to my earlier comment vis-á-vis your eyeballs. So for the record, you need me more than I need you. I saved your life. A blood debt is owed and must be paid."

Tomas felt an urge to laugh. The demon was an amateur. "Yeah sure, I always pay my debts." Tomas smiled affably. "But tell me, what it is you need me to do."

"You're a Vox Léchtar Fai-ber. You will open a way to my realm."

"What? What's a Vax Lecher Fairbear?"

"Vox Léchtar Fai-ber, a reader, a wordsmith. The first I have encountered in your world in two hundred and forty-three years," O'si stated.

"I don't know what that is or how to open a way. A door or lock maybe, that I can do," Tomas said. The demon spouted nonsense but his immediate concern was saving his skin from Bortillo. If he had to use the demon to that end then he would. "Still, if you help me out I'll do what I can."

"We're in accord then. The details we can work out later." Renix, who was not Renix stepped forward and held its hand out.

Tomas smiled and spat in his hand. "This is how we seal a deal in my world," he explained, grasping the proffered hand.

The demon held his hand firm, bringing its other hand over the top just as Tomas's grin faltered. A searing pinprick of heat burned the back of his hand, the pain sharp and intense. It expanded and Tomas struggled, trying to pull his hand back but the demon held it fast.

"This is how we seal a deal in mine." O'si laughed as Tomas squirmed, his face contorting in pain.

And then it was gone and Tomas's hand released. Snatching it back, Tomas rubbed it. There was a faint mark, a rune of some kind on the back but before his eyes, it faded then disappeared leaving no trace it had ever been. Worriedly he looked at the demon.

"What was that?"

"It's a seal, for our bargain. Now I suggest you wash. Thoroughly mind you, you have an air about you that is not pleasing to the nostrils. Then choose your attire."

"My what?"

The demon sighed, shaking its head, "Your clothes my young, uneducated friend."

Tomas moved out from around the bed, edging warily past the demon and back to the bowl of water. Wetting the soap block he worked it into a lather. He wouldn't admit it but this was a luxury for him, proper soap.

"What's a Garringbat?" Tomas asked as he washed, aware the demon observed with a critical eye as if to check he didn't miss anywhere.

"Garumbat," the demon corrected, "a small creature that feeds off the excrement of others."

"Charming, is O'si your real name?" Tomas fired back, shivering; the water was cold.

"No, but it's what you may call me."

\* \* \*

Tomas felt conspicuous as he left Renix's apartment. The entrance door was locked but there was a key on the wall which opened it. Locking it behind him, Tomas pocketed the key and descended the stairs. He was anxious, half expecting someone to appear and order him back inside or worse, stick a knife in him and take his head to Bortillo. But nothing happened and he soon reached an archway that led out onto a wide street that bordered a small square.

Standing in the shadow of the arch, Tomas surveyed the surroundings. There were few people about and those he saw looked richly attired. The square itself was fringed by fancy looking shops and expensive house fronts. All were immaculately clean.

Directly opposite was a shop, its sign declaring 'Marn Fabrics'. A woman was outside laying out her wares on a stand. Her face was plain and she had brown hair and Tomas guessed her to be thirty. It felt oddly normal watching her work and he wondered idly if she was the proprietor.

Job done, the woman turned and stopped. She seemed to spy him hidden in the shadows for she stared right at him, her eyebrows pinching together. Tomas's heart thumped loudly as he froze and waited to see what she would do. Nothing it seemed. Dismissive, she spun about and disappeared back inside her shop.

Reassured, Tomas stepped out onto the cobbles and oriented himself before heading for the Trades.

Self-conscious, feeling more like a thief's mark than the thief he was, Tomas feared everyone looked at him as he walked the streets of Kingsholme.

He was clean, well-fed, and dressed in dark woollen hose and breeches with a white shirt and embroidered jacket that was the fashion among the nobles and well to do. The quality of the jacket alone was enough to house and feed him for a year in Gloamingate.

That Renix offered it and let him walk out unchallenged made Tomas both nervous and suspicious. But he had and now he was outside Tomas was free to go where he wanted. He could disappear and Renix would never find him.

"Stop looking about. You're making yourself conspicuous." O'si muttered in his ear. The demon was perched on his shoulder, small and imp-like. He was right and Tomas calmed, forcing himself to relax.

"Now you look constipated."

"Will you shut it! You're not helping you know," Tomas growled. It was bad enough walking the streets in clothes that weren't his and didn't quite fit. Having a demon perched on his shoulder helped not at all. "You sure no one can see you."

"My answer is the same as the other three times you asked me. Only you and the gifted can see me and I assure you I will see the gifted well before they see me."

By gifted, Tomas understood O'si to mean magi. He walked on, passing under a gate flanked by a pair of guards in the Kingsholme livery of red and gold. They spared him only a cursory glance before he was through.

He breathed easier. The clean streets and cleaner people of the Nobles made him edgy. Stealing in the Nobles would be rich pickings but no street thief ever bothered. For one thing, it wasn't crowded like the rest of the city. The people were all well to do and commoners always moved on, so a street thief stood no chance of blending in. Besides, getting caught in the Nobles was a death sentence.

Needing information, Tomas headed for the All-Ways, a large square in the Trades that served as a focal point for all the major roads in and out of the city. It was said all roads in the Nine Kingdoms lead to the All-Ways. Tomas didn't know about that, he'd never been past the city walls before but the All-Ways was certainly busy enough that he had no reason to doubt it.

Tomas had thought long about what Renix had told him. It had the ring of truth and he believed the man, even though he knew so little about him. It went without saying he didn't trust him. Hells, Tomas didn't trust anyone except himself.

So, he needed information. He was hunted according to Renix, but how badly? Was there really a bounty on his head and if so how much? That at least would tell him how much trouble he was in. If it was bad and he had to run, where could he go and what would he do? Thieving was all he knew. Tomas didn't want to think much about that.

As if that wasn't enough though, he now had a demon to contend with as well. It was hard to believe one rode his shoulder. Everyone had heard tell of demons but no one had ever seen one. Well, apart from old Ned Baker but Ned had claimed to have travelled the world and seen monsters in the Endless Sea, wherever that was. But Ned didn't count; he wasn't right in the head most days.

* * *

It was a long walk to the All-Ways and the wide street he was on was crowded with people. At each intersection guards stood, in their red and gold livery, looking out on the masses. Tomas knew that should he step off the road and down any of the hundreds of smaller streets and alleyways, there would be no guards. It was those streets where he plied his trade most days, although that held its own dangers. Most were claimed by one crew or another and care was needed where you thieved.

Tomas felt uneasy. The streets in the Trades might be more crowded but he stood out in his rich clothing. He could feel eyes on him, marking him. Now he thought about it, it was a mistake to have come dressed as he was. Still, it was too late for that now and it wasn't like he had his old clothes to slip into.

The All-Ways, when he reached it, was busy and familiar. At its heart stood a tall pillar on a raised plinth that towered into the sky. At its base, four stone lions guarded each point of the compass. Atop the pillar was a statue of King Royce on a rearing stallion, sword held aloft. It dominated the large square.

Tomas moved past it, slipping around the edges of the market stalls and towards the entrance of a small street just off Westway.

Willie-the-Hand had a shop there. Tomas could just make it out from where he stood leaning against a wall and through the throng of people.

Willie was a fence for the syndicate. He was a friendly, affable man who could sell wood to a blacksmith. He'd lost his right hand on a campaign with the Kingsguard when he was younger, or so he said. Tomas heard it was for thieving on the wrong patch at the wrong time, and thought it a far more plausible story. Suggest that to Willie though and he wasn't so affable anymore.

It went without saying that Tomas didn't trust Willie. But he wasn't here for the Hand; it was Sparrow he looked for. Sparrow was the closest thing he had to a friend and if he knew Sparrow like he did, she should be handing her takings over to Willie about now.

Tomas waited but there was no sign of her. A few people noted his presence, hard to hide it dressed as he was, and he knew it was foolish to linger overlong. He was about to move off, back to the relative safety of the square, when he caught sight of a familiar ruff of brown hair leaving an alleyway.

Sparrow paused just as a gap opened in the press of people and her eyes latched on to Tomas. He looked a rich mark at first glance before her eyes flared in recognition.

Tomas nodded, inclined his head to the right, and stepped away from the street, walking slowly towards the statue of King Royce. Slow enough that Sparrow would catch him.

Despite waiting for it, the brush when it came was so expertly delivered, Tomas almost missed it. Then Sparrow was gone. He didn't see her. There were no words, no banter.

His heart sank, it was serious then. His hand moved to his jacket pocket and feeling inside found what he dreaded. Pulling it out, he stared at the small red thread of cloth.

Tomas glanced back, couldn't help himself but Sparrow had already vanished in the crowd. He sat leaning against one of the lions feeling deflated and upset. She hadn't risked talking to him. He felt suddenly alone. What could he do now, where to go?

"What's wrong? You look like you're gonna cry." O'si tugged Tomas's ear.

"I'm not crying. It's just things look bad is all." Tomas flicked a hand trying to dislodge the demon's grip.

"But you've spoken to no one, how do you know anything?" O'si whispered. There was a rumble and the demon looked up warily to see a troop of red-cloaked riders appear at the edge of the square. They were escorting several ornate carriages.

Tomas held his hand out twirling the red thread between thumb and forefinger. "No, but someone has spoken to me, and trust me it ain't good."

The riders clattering past drew to a halt as the way ahead became blocked.

"I think we should move on," O'si whispered urgently.

"Where? I've nowhere to go," Tomas said, looking at the carriages not ten paces from where he sat. They were decadent.

An errant thought flashed through his mind. Stealing one of those would mean never having to work the streets again. He dismissed the notion; he'd never sat on a horse let alone driven a carriage. Besides, he had neither the means nor the method to pull it off, and if he did it wasn't like Willie-the-Hand was going to take it and fence it for him.

"Let's go, now!" O'si hissed.

The curtain to the lead carriage suddenly parted and Tomas watched with interest as a man's head poked through to look about. Tomas grinned, that must be one fat man he thought. The face was round and bloated with folds of flesh hanging loose on cheek and jowl. Small beady eyes cast about the area until finally coming to rest on Tomas. His grin faltered. The eyes were black, completely black, no colour to them at all. That they regarded him so intently made his heart skip and his blood surge in warning.

"I think we should go," Tomas muttered. He realised suddenly he could no longer see the imp on his shoulder despite the fact he felt the demon's weight perched there. O'si didn't reply.

Rising quickly, Tomas slipped into the crowd. He glanced back one last time to see the fat man pointing him out to one of the red-cloaked riders. Fear rose inside him as the red cloak turned to look, his eyes fixing on Tomas. Shouting orders, he turned his horse into the crowd, and people scattered as he rode towards him.

Fuck, Tomas ducked behind a group of merchants. Crouching low he ran for the nearest street. It was the one he'd just left. He baulked suddenly, Sparrow stood at its entrance. She was tiny, just a kid, younger even than him, but the man that held her didn't seem to care much about that. Her cheek was red, one eye puffed and swollen closed where she'd been struck and blood dribbled from her nose and the corner of her mouth.

Tomas turned aside but not before the man caught sight of him. He dropped Sparrow in an instant, gave a short sharp whistle behind, and then lurched menacingly towards him.

There was no finesse then, Tomas just ran. He knew the streets better than anyone and he was small and agile. The crowds helped as he ducked and weaved through them. He felt O'si leave him, the weight on his shoulder vanishing. Treacherous little shit, but Tomas couldn't really blame him.

Tomas steered for the Southway back towards the Nobles, instinctive rather than planned. It was the least likely place to run and besides everywhere else held danger.

"Three men tracking you from the street to your right," The ghost whispered in his ear. O'si was back. "The Red Cloaks are held up a bit but they will see you as soon as you cross the street ahead."

Tomas changed direction, veering away from the strong arms to the right. He'd take his chances with the Red Cloaks if he had to choose. Bortillo, he knew instinctively, meant his death.

"Can you describe the men?" Tomas ducked behind a wagon staying alongside it as it moved around the square.

"One big and two little ones," O'si offered.

"You're no help," Tomas gasped, breaking for a narrow street as he drew level with it. He heard a cry go up behind but didn't waste time looking back. Tomas weaved and bobbed in and around people, trying to put them between him and his pursuers. He ducked down an alley running as hard as he could.

"You've lost the Red Cloak's but those men are still behind. One has split off and I've lost track of him," O'si said.

Small mercy then, Tomas thought ducking down another alley knowing it would bring him back out on the Southway. As he burst out onto the wide thoroughfare he spotted a flash of Red and Gold ahead. An idea burgeoned and he dodged around a delivery wain and headed for the guards.

There were two of them, both stood leaning back against the wall looking bored. One spotted Tomas running towards them through the crowd and nudged his partner. By the time he reached them, they were both alert and wary. The young boy was well dressed, clearly from the Nobles, and looked scared.

"Ho there, you alright, lad?"

Gasping and out of breath, Tomas turned and pointed back the way he'd come. He saw the bobbing heads of his pursuers pause as they caught sight of him.

"Those men and others like them have attacked my father." Tomas pointed out the two men, obvious because they stood in a tide of moving people. The guards swivelled, following his outstretched hand.

"Where's your father, lad?" One asked, the other taking a step towards the men.

"Alleyway on the right just down there," Tomas panted, hands-on knees as he struggled for breath.

"Wait here." Drawing swords the guards moved towards the men who glared balefully at Tomas before turning and slipping back into the crowd, the guards in pursuit.

As soon as the guards left, Tomas stood breathing easy, all pretence gone. Walking onto the road he moved off, not running this time. Running drew the eye, attracted unwanted attention. He moved briskly nevertheless and soon disappeared in the sea of people.

It was a while later that Tomas arrived back at the gatehouse that led to the Nobles. The guards paid him no mind as he walked warily past.

He huffed, resigned. His options so few they were selecting themselves. The demon for his part was good enough to say nothing. A lot of use he was anyway, Tomas groused.

A hooded figure watched Tomas from the shadows of an alley but made no attempt to follow the boy. The Nobles was not his demesne to wander. As Tomas disappeared from sight, the shadow turned away.

## Chapter 20: The Good Father

**Greentower, The Holme**

Nine riders followed the west road out of Greentower as it curled up and around the hills and valleys. It led both to Higholme in the west and Merik further south. The ilfanum led through the night having no trouble seeing the way despite the darkness and the deteriorating weather.

As the sun rose, the road remained quiet and they made steady progress. The people of Greentower, content it seemed to escape the invading urak using the south road to Kroy.

The storm front moved away by mid-day leaving grey clouds in its wake and a crisp freshness in the air. Darion breathed deeply taking in the autumnal scents of the countryside. It felt good to be out of Greentower and better yet to be back on horseback.

The white-robed Father Melbroth rode just ahead of him and sat his horse well enough. That Father Melbroth had stood up for James Encoma with Duke Brant was a good deed well done but he wasn't entirely convinced by him. There was a duality about the priest. On the one hand, Melbroth appeared both thoughtful and considerate; admirable qualities in a priest. On the other, he'd finagled his way into their company under the pretext of wanting to help them.

That he'd acquired their horses from Witter ahead of time before they'd even made their escape, took planning and scheming. Melbroth said he'd produced a signed order from Duke Brant to acquire their horses. The writ made out earlier that day before they'd even arrived, 'To aid the evacuation of the White Church.' The order wasn't specifically for their horses, as Darion understood it, but Father Melbroth was persuasive and with a sweetener, Witter hadn't argued the point since he'd have to find the horses from somewhere.

Well, he wasn't buying it. It didn't sit right. There was more to the White Father than met the eye and Darion resolved to keep a careful watch on him.

He looked at the two other white-robed figures ahead. Another of Father Melbroth's ideas and a pretty good one, Darion grudgingly admitted. The ilfanum had donned priest robes and with the hoods up it hid them well enough from casual inspection. M'rika had understood the necessity but R'ell less so, declaring that it was an affront to hide who and what he was. Only M'rika's intervention and insistence made him relent.

Late afternoon saw them descend from the hills and valleys onto grassland. They passed the village of Little Wick on the banks of a small lake, eerily empty of people. The larger settlement of Cross Wick lay only a league ahead and it was there they would rest and there that they had a decision to make.

*  *  *

They rode into Cross Wick as night was falling. It was a large market town that sat at a crossing of ways. West led to Higholme and south to Merik. Passing the outskirts they found it was not the deserted ghost town of its sibling to the east. Many people had gathered using it as a staging post to meet and rest before deciding their course.

The darkness proved a blessing. The ilfanum bore no close scrutiny and the night proved as good a shroud as the robes they wore. Luckily, the few people they did pass close to, were too absorbed in their circumstance to look much at another group of travellers riding by.

Father Melbroth knew the town and so took the lead. Taking them through several winding lanes he brought them to a small square with a church on its northern edge. The building was of solid construction with high walls and a flat crenellated roof giving it the appearance of a fortification rather than a house of worship.

"This is our church and chapter house," Melbroth announced. He dismounted stiffly and bid them follow before walking his horse around the side.

At the back, they found a stable block and chapterhouse with light peaking around the edges of a shuttered window. A dog barked from inside and Bindu growled in response, Darion calming her with a word. Moments later the chapterhouse door opened, spilling light into the yard.

"Who's there?" A woman in white robes was backlit in the doorway, squinting into the darkness. "Father Melbroth?"

"Mother Sophia, very glad I am to see you," Melbroth called out, genuine warmth in his voice.

"Father, what are you doing here? You should be away south with the rest of our brothers and sisters?"

"As should you, Mother," Melbroth replied. "But come, let us unsaddle our horses and take our ease. Then I will explain all."

"Of course, Father, I'll put a pan on to boil." Mother Sophia did a quick headcount, noting that two others were priests of Nihmrodel although she could not see them clearly beneath their hooded cowls. She turned, the church's ratter almost tangling her up as it glared out at the company. The little dog's hackles were up and glancing back over her shoulder, Sophia saw the glint of yellow eyes in the depths of shadow at the edge of the courtyard, another dog. "Come away, Midge."

"James, please see to my horse. I'd best talk to Mother Sophia and prepare her for all our guests." Melbroth nodded at the ilfanum by way of explanation.

"Yes, Father." James took his reins and went to follow Kronke to the stables, but hesitated. Darion and the ilf lingered still in the yard. The woodsman was statuesque as he stared at the Father's retreating form, his eyes dark and unreadable. Not a woodsman an Orderman, James corrected. He felt Father Melbroth was being judged and found he didn't much care for it.

"Told ya already, the Father's no Red Priest," James said. Then at Darion's continued silence, "I spent the day with him. Saw him with the people of Greentower, helping them, giving them food, preparing them for the road ahead. He gave them hope where Duke Brant gave them nothing. He's a good man Darion. I swear it."

"Maybe so. Let's get these horses unsaddled, eh," Darion said. A shimmer of light from the open doorway reflected off his eyes as he turned towards the stables, pulling Marigold along behind.

It sent a shiver up James' spine. For a moment the eyes had taken on an otherworldly aspect but Darion's words were enough to ease his worry and he followed after.

The ilfanum watched the exchange silently. As the two humans disappeared into the stalls, R'ell signed. *"I do not trust humans. They are weak of mind and body."*

*"They live such a short time it is to be expected."* M'rika signed back. *"There is strength in some and greatness in a few. It is in those Da'Mari says we must trust in."*

R'ell grunted in response, then, whispering to his mount, led her to the stables.

*  *  *

They ate a good meal and drank hot tea. Darion was watchful and quiet throughout, content to listen and observe.

Morpete laughed at something James said. The two men were young and of an age and it pleased Darion. James had suffered much and it was good to see him getting along.

By contrast, Pieterzon and Jess were subdued and spoke little but for differing reasons. Pieterzon's one good eye did the work of two; never still, it roved the room like he was casing the place. Jess on the other hand was unsettled. She fidgeted constantly to the point it was distracting and Darion was not the only one to notice.

"What the deuce is wrong with you, Crawley. It's like you got lice in your smalls," Kronke growled. A sullen apology and Jess sitting immobile for five minutes was her only response before the fidgeting started again.

Darion's attention switched to Mother Sophia as she stood. She was old, her hair grey and fine. Her face was wrinkled, the skin mottling and starting to loosen around cheek and jowl. Bright eyes and a ready smile gave her a warm homely countenance.

"Can I get you anything else?" Her question was directed at the ilfanum, she was captivated by them.

"No."

The blunt response made Darion grin. The ilf didn't like being the focus of Mother Sophia's attention. That she was a considerate and accommodating host required them to respond when clearly they wanted to be left alone.

Kronke shovelled in a mouthful of food. Darion had watched the big sergeant preside over his depleted command, making sure they ate and drank their fill like a mother would her children.

There was a reassuring familiarity about Kronke that recalled Darion to his own time serving with the Black Crows. It was the same doctrine for all warriors in the field and he knew it well. Drink, eat, and sleep. If you can, whenever you can.

Needing no encouragement, Kronke happily followed this aged wisdom himself, heaping whatever he could fit on to his plate and wolfing it down.

Darion's gaze slid to Father Melbroth. The priest had chatted amiably to Mother Sophia and the others over the meal. A quiet word here and there but for the most part he observed as Darion did. Feeling Darion's scrutiny, Melbroth acknowledged him.

"Our meal is done. Perhaps we should talk about the path ahead?"

Kronke paused, his spoon halfway between mouth and bowl. He shrugged, the spoon continuing its journey.

"The south road to Merik is best," Darion said. "It leads more directly away from trouble. In a day or so you could even turn for Kroy should you wish it."

"It sounds like you'll not be taking the road with us," Father Melbroth said.

Kronke's spoon rattled against his bowl, forgotten. He stared at Darion accusingly. He'd assumed they would all take the southern route but the priest was right. "What's this?"

"Our paths crossed for a while but now you're safe it's time we each go our own way," Darion said.

Kronke grunted. He'd gotten used to the big woodsman. There was a calmness and surety in what he said and did. He realised he would miss his company.

"Where do you go?" Melbroth asked.

"No offence but I'll be keeping my own counsel." Darion looked at each of his companions. Brought together in adversity their comradery forged by their trials in the north. He'd not felt that for twenty years and found he would miss it.

Father Melbroth laughed. "Please Darion. I didn't aid your escape to be cast adrift at the first opportunity."

"What's your game here, Father? What does a white priest want with the ilfanum?"

Melbroth looked at the ilf who sat quietly, watching the interplay. "The ilf are endlessly fascinating." He inclined his head at them. "But it is not them that interest me. It is you, Orderman."

Darion cast an accusing glance at James.

"I didn't say anything," James said defensively.

Mother Sophia interjected, worry on her face. "You tread a fine line, Father Melbroth. The Order is banished in this land. It could impact the church."

"Yes, yes, Mother." Melbroth waved away her concerns turning back to Darion. "The church of Nihmrodel, the Lady, knows no borders or boundaries. Until Jenah our High Priestess, Nihmrodel bless and honour her, commands differently it will remain so."

Darion listened, still waiting for an answer.

"It's no game, Darion. It's an opportunity I seek. I would meet with the Keeper of the Order."

"Father Melbroth, you're a priest of the White serving Greentower," Mother Sophia snapped, her gentle demeanour vanishing. "Under whose authority do you speak?"

"Greentower is no more. It's gone, the people fled. I'm a priest without a congregation," Melbroth retorted.

Darion was angry.

"The Order isn't on good terms with any of the Trinity. Red Priests persecute us. Hunting and murdering whilst the churches of Nihmrodel and Ankor say nothing, do nothing. You are guilty for your silence." Darion's face contorted. "People dragged from their homes. Tortured, then burnt alive, just on the suspicion they were of the Order. Where was your church then priest? Tell me, why should I trust you or take you anywhere?"

"Because of the times we live in. The White church has its own histories and Nihmrodel in her teachings prophesied the end of days," Melbroth said, erstwhile and passionate. "I believe this prophecy has come true. What if this is the end of days or at least the start of the end."

There was an audible gasp from Mother Sophia.

"You blaspheme, Father. The word will come from Nihmrodel herself, through the office of her representative, Jenah, High Priestess. It is not for you to subvert her teachings."

"Ah phish to that, we cannot wait. Don't you see? The horde is at the gate. To wait is to die. If we are to survive we must bring the people together. The last end of times was prevented by the people standing together and working in unity. We need representation with the Order."

"To appoint your self is a vanity too far, Father Melbroth. I thought better of you than this," Sophia retorted, waspishly.

"I am here and there is a way. If Jenah, Nihmrodel bless and honour her, sees fit to appoint another in my place I will accept it gracefully. But for now, we need a path. I feel it as if the Lady herself pushes me along it."

Darion was taken aback. The Order held no faith in churches or the Trinity. One life, live it well was one of the principal tenets of the Order. The Order would not perpetuate a lie. His old masters had taught him that the Trinity was a human construct used to subvert and control the people, no matter the moral teachings they hid behind.

In large part, Darion knew this was catalyst and fuel for the enmity between the Churches of the Trinity and the Order. It had not always been so, but in these trying times, to bring a priest to the Order's Halls would be unthinkable. He couldn't do it even if he wanted to.

Father Melbroth saw the rejection on Darion's face and the denial that was coming.

"Please, Darion. It's a big decision, an important chance for the Order and Church of Our Lady alike. I'm not asking that you decide now. I'm asking that you give me a chance. You must have a means of communicating with your brethren. I would make my case to them. Get word to Keeper. Let him decide."

"Sounds reasonable to me given what we've seen and witnessed," Kronke interjected. "Besides, you and two ilf running over the countryside are gonna stand out. Better to hide in plain sight especially if'n you need to head east. East means crossing the Rivers then Cumbrenan. What better disguise than with a priest of the White, eh!"

"I'll be faster without you," Darion insisted.

"You'll be safer with us," Kronke shot back. "I'm guessing if you take the west road to Higholme you plan on following the Fossa to Rivercross. Ain't no other way of getting east," Kronke rumbled. "Give yourself time and keep your options open I reckon. Think on what the good Father says and decide later if you want to part ways. The Fossa runs close enough to Merik if you decide to take that path. In the meantime, there's safety in numbers. Let's all take the south road, eh."

Kronke picked his spoon up and scrapped another helping of stew, he'd said his piece.

## Chapter 21: Burnt Man

**North of Fallston, The Rivers**

Amos could see nothing. The night was as black as any he'd experienced. He should have been miserable, the intensity of the rain soaking him in moments, but he wasn't. The storm was a blessing and he prayed it would continue through the following day.

Jerkze and Jobe held the paddles and steered them into the middle of the river letting the current pull them along. A loose rope had been thrown between the boats to keep them in touch in the darkness and the two men spent much of their time trying to keep the line taut without slowing the other vessel down.

As the night faded to the grey of dawn the river banks slowly appeared as indistinct smudges through the rain. It was perfect. Able to see each other but hidden from casual observation they increased their tempo, paddling hard. They didn't stop to eat or rest wanting to put as many leagues behind them as they could.

Amos glanced down into the boat. Junip was as wet and bedraggled as he felt, Annabelle too, though neither complained. The young girl had dogged him since her rescue. It seemed whenever he turned around she was there, quietly watching with big sad eyes. Amos felt responsible and he knew it wasn't just him she got to, Jerkze and Jobe felt it too. Amos grinned, thinking of his sister. Children weren't his thing and Mercy would wet herself laughing if she could see him with skinny little Annabelle in tow.

Late morning saw them pass the village of Mappels-on-Oust. A solitary wooden jetty jutting out into the water the only evidence it was there, the village itself was hidden by the rain.

Amos noticed that Junip spent much of her time in a trance, judging from the stillness of her body. War changes a person, he'd experienced it himself, but Junip had changed more than most. Since the battle for the walls, she was harder than before. She'd lost whatever vestige of naivety she'd had. No young mage apprentice now, she'd graduated through the forge of battle.

They ate hard cakes in the rain, a bit damp where water had gotten to them. Junip huffed at her offering.

"It still tastes good. The wet just makes it easier to eat." Annabelle offered, biting into hers.

Encouraged Junip took a nibble but was unable to stop her face from scrunching up. It was a soggy, tasteless paste in her mouth. "Umm, delicious,"

"You're funny," Annabelle laughed, pointing. "You got some stuck in your teeth."

"Hush, Belle," Amos admonished. Despite the wind and rain, her high pitched laugh sounded loud to his ears.

They paddled on silently, Junip forcing her hard cake down before resuming her meditations.

\* \* \*

To Amos's consternation the storm moved off in the afternoon and the rain changed to a fine drizzle. The banks of the river and surrounding countryside were visible now and reluctantly they pulled for the south bank, dragging the boats into a small copse of beech trees.

Ned Wynter and Jerkze were sent to scout whilst the rest huddled in the densest part of the thicket, taking what little respite they could. The grove offered shelter from the wind but the passing storm had left a wintery chill in the air. Constance and Annabelle both shivered in the cold and Amos had them huddle together with Junip for warmth.

Ned and Jerkze returned a short while later. They'd found no sign of urak but had been loath to stray too far. Beyond the wooded copse and bulrush abutting the river, the land hereabouts was mostly flat grasslands with the occasional patch of hardy knorcha bush. They ate and rested as best they could until darkness fell.

\* \* \*

They paddled softly, the night sky was clearer than they wanted with only sporadic cloud. Two of the moons were out Ankor and Kildare, reflecting a pale light on the landscape. As midnight approached they saw their first signs of urak. Firelight speckled the northern bank ahead sparkling like glow worms, growing steadily larger as they approached.

Jacob steered them towards the south bank to a natural break in the foliage. He was worried. "It's too risky to try and get by them. If they have watchers on the river they will surely see us, there is too much moonlight."

"How far to Fallston do you think?" Amos asked. It couldn't be far, by his reckoning, no more than five or six leagues.

"Seven leagues," Ned Wynter muttered. "Take us till morning on foot, maybe longer in the dark and carrying our gear and supplies.

"And if we find urak this side of the Oust, then what?" Jacob whispered.

"Then we find a way around them," Amos said, uncomfortable at the thought but accepting they had little choice in the matter. They couldn't stay here.

"Don't make sense to blunder about in the dark through bush and long grass." Jobe scratched his chin. "We're as like to stumble into something we ort not ta."

Amos knew he had more to say, he'd known Jobe long enough that his tell was a familiar one. "Spit it out then." He gave a half-smile. His friend always did like a bit of melodrama.

"Simple. Give 'em nought to see," Jobe said. "Cut us some of these here bushes and branches and lash em to the boats. Its night, moons are out but it's still dark enough that we'll look like a tree or bush washed away in the storm. Just hunker down low and let the river sweep us on by."

Wynter nodded. "A sound plan; we've passed enough on the river ourselves this last day. It could work."

"Anyone else got anything to add?" Jacob asked, looking around the group.

Amos was impressed. Most young Lord's he knew would not have accepted the idea so readily or acted on it with the same surety and conviction.

"Then let's do it," Jacob said when no one responded.

They worked quickly and efficiently once the decision was made. Jerkze, quiet up till then, saw the two girls standing together. He couldn't see their faces clearly but they fidgeted nervously and spoke to each other in a muted whisper.

"You two lend a hand," he growled and moments later he had them gathering bulrush and was showing them how to cut them off low to the ground and use one of the long stems to bind the cuttings together.

"That was well done." Junip brushed a hand against Jerkze's arm. "Master Lutico always said an idle mind makes its own problems. Now, what can I do?"

\* \* \*

Bartuk didn't want to be there. After his escape from the massacre at the ford, he'd been careful to avoid any urak patrols. Nothing good would come of telling his story, far as he knew he was the lone survivor and lone survivors could be seen as coward as easily as hero.

He'd found the Toreen four days after running, camped on the plains around the human settlement of Thorsten. The whole clan it seemed were moving south from the Blue Sky Lakes and in the mass of urak a lone warrior could pass without too much attention, most thinking him a scout or messenger.

At first, he'd been surprised. Word was they were wintering at the Blue Sky Lakes and waging war in the spring but he knew now that the Blood Skull had provoked it, adding yet another reason to avoid the clan's warchief Mar-Dur. The murderous bastard would not like having his hand forced.

The battle for the human settlement of Thorsten was over by the time the Toreen were on the field. Its high walls had been breached in less than two days and now served as a pen for its inhabitants; providing a blooding ground for the young and a ready food supply. Only the stone tower at its centre remained unbroken and Mar-Dur would not waste warriors assailing it. Time would take it for them.

Word had reached him shortly after re-joining the Toreen that Grimpok looked for him. Grimpok was Mar-Dur's right hand and there was only one reason that vicious cunt wanted him. So he headed south with a Toreen war party his chief put together. After all, a moving target was much harder to hit. So for his troubles here he stood on the banks of the river pulling watch.

"Watching for what?" he muttered in annoyance. The humans were crushed at Thorsten. Their high walls had been no match for urak strength. The warbands ahead of them had sent word back that the human settlement of Fallston had been sacked and raised by the Blood Skull, leaving nothing for the White Hand. So watching was a complete waste of his time, there was nothing out here to challenge them. He should be back in his bedroll. Ah well, at least his relief was due.

Needing to relieve himself, Bartuk walked to the river's edge and hooked his kilt up. A strong steady stream arced out into the river. You weren't meant to piss in the river but Bartuk was beyond caring. Somehow he was near the frontline of this whole mess. Fighting humans was one thing but it seemed to him the Blood Skull were intent on stirring things up, despite whatever the clan warchiefs had agreed. He didn't much relish the thought of fighting Blood Skull.

As his bladder emptied, he gazed out across the river. The night sky was mostly clear and a pale light cast across the water from Jud'pur'tak the largest of the tri moons. He watched the vague outline of a bush or tree as it floated by on the far side of the river. Then another, a twin almost, ten paces behind it. Something struck Bartuk as odd about that. He trusted his instincts and screwed his eyes up trying to discern what bothered him. So absorbed was he that he didn't hear the tread of feet.

"Bar, what the fuck is you doin?" The voice was loud and gruff and sounded right behind him. Bartuk lost grip of his leather kilt, as he jumped, then scrambled madly to keep from falling in the river.

"Damn it, Murhtuk you gone and made me piss meself."

Murhtuk laughed. "Not meant to piss in the river, eh. You're meant to be watchin' for shit."

"You said it. Watchin' for shit! There's nought to watch. Shoulda fuckin put the dogs out here if Grot-tuk's worried. Tortak's belly, me leathers are soaked wet through," Bartuk grumbled, brushing his kilt down as he walked past his relief and towards the campfires.

"That all ya got to say then?" Murhtuk laughed.

Bartuk glanced back. "Nah, don't piss into the wind."

Giving no further thought to the river or the floating bushes that had caught his eye, Bartuk turned away. Food, sleep, and dry leathers were all he was interested in now.

* * *

Amos had his bow strung and an arrow loose in his hand as they floated past the urak encampment. A lone sentry was all he saw, joined moments later by another but no alarm was called, no challenge rang out. Then they were passed.

Once clear, they paddled softly but efficiently, determined to reach Fallston before the first light of morning. It was a surprise then when Junip stirred herself, sitting straight and arching her back as if to stretch a kink out. Her head pivoted toward the right bank as something caught her attention.

"There is something odd here." Junip twisted awkwardly to face Amos, causing the boat to rock gently. "On the bank up ahead, I sense something."

"Dangerous?" Amos asked turning and casting his own eyes over the passing bushes and reeds.

"I don't think so, it is most curious. It's like a void in the aether," Junip replied. "I would like to take a look."

Amos wasn't convinced. To him, it was a solid reason to avoid said area and he was about to say so when the look on Junip's face stopped him. It was not fear or idle curiosity he saw. Her eyes were hard, she wasn't asking. War changes a person he reminded himself.

"Okay a quick look," he agreed. "Jerkze, give that rope a snap will you."

Everyone on the little boat heard the exchange and all were curious. Leaning forwards, Jerkze pulled the rope and gave a sharp flick, not much but Ned, on the stern of the boat ahead, felt it and looked back. Jerkze made a circular motion in the air with one hand before pointing to the right.

Ned couldn't quite make it out in the darkness and using his paddle, slowed the boat until his stern brushed the bow behind. "Problem?" he asked.

"Might be, Junip needs to take a look at something just ahead," Amos replied.

Listening, Jacob scowled. He liked Junip but this wasn't the time for idle curiosity. What was she playing at? He opened his mouth to say as much when Amos shook his head.

"We should go see. I could do with a stretch and a bite to eat too." Amos said.

The night was passing and it was only an hour or two until dawn. Reluctant to stop, Jacob grudgingly conceded. "Okay, ten minutes. No more."

They pulled into the bank and disembarked, dragging the boats up into the bushes.

"This way," Junip said, walking off and following the river bank. Despite the muted light from the two moons it was dark enough that she stumbled a few times on root and branch. Thankfully she didn't have far to go. The void she sensed was right about here.

She heard it before she realised she was in it. There was a crunch and crackle as she set her foot down. It startled her and she froze.

"What is it?" Jerkze murmured directly behind.

"I think we're here," Junip whispered, not quite sure where here was. There was a sound, a low keening, so soft it was barely audible. "What was that?"

"Let me take a look," Jerkze offered, stepping carefully around her. He too stopped as his feet crunched. Crouching down, Jerkze ran his hand over the ground. The grass and leaf under his fingers crumbled at his touch.

"That staff of yours; think you can raise a little soft light? It should be safe enough in the bushes here if'n it's not too bright," Jerkze said.

Junip lowered the head of her staff, "Lumousim echiguus."

A soft light sprang to life. It was pale and weak but in the darkness, it seemed harsh and Jerkze had to blink to adjust his eyes. When they had he frowned trying to comprehend what it was he saw.

Before him the grass, shrubs, and bushes were black, like burnt husks, only they had no smell of charcoal and nothing was withered or perished like it would be by flame. It was as if everything had been sculpted in black marble.

Reaching out, Jerkze pinched a leaf between his fingers. It was stiff and brittle before suddenly crumbling to dust. Curious, the wind and rain had no effect on it but his touch had.

Junip must have thought so too. She brushed past him leaving powder black footprints on the ground. "This, this… I've read about it but… I didn't think it possible." She spoke to herself but all heard her.

"What is it?" Jacob asked.

Junip turned to look at him. She made out other faces at the edge of her light. Jobe, Amos, and Ned had followed as well it seemed.

"I think a Taken has been here. I can't believe I'm saying it," Junip said.

"A Taken?" Jacob was unable to keep the scepticism from his voice.

"I see no other explanation." Junip was fearful now. Her pulse was racing as her own revelation hit her. She knew she was right.

"Slow down lass. Tell us what it is we're seeing at least," Amos said softly.

Junip took a deep breath, composing herself, and ordering her thoughts. "Every living thing has an essence that connects them to the world, a life force that is not tangible to most. You can't see it or feel it but it exists. As a mage, I can sense it. It is what drew me here." Junip said. "Only, it was the lack of it. This place is void of life. Like it's been consumed, leaving nothing but a shell of what was. No mage can draw power like that. Master Lutico taught me that and in the books he gave me to study, it only ever mentioned this happening once before."

Junip left the rest unspoken but Jacob filled it in.

"The Taken. You're saying something from a thousand years ago has come to pass again? That this was done by a Morhudrim?"

A low moan interrupted them and Junip spun about, nervous. Speaking her conclusions out loud made it real. A bird lay crumpled on the ground, perfectly formed but as black as the bed it lay upon.

Jerkze walked by the bird. A humped mass lay on the ground nearby. It was a body.

"Over here." He slipped the tie off his sword. He didn't know anything about the Taken or Morhudrim but Junip looked truly frightened and that was good enough for him.

Jerkze felt Junip move alongside, Jacob and Amos at his back. Extending his boot he nudged the man for that was surely what it was. His foot met hard flesh and a soft moan whispered out of the body. The black head turned and pale blue eyes stared out, stark in the white surrounds of his eyes. "Fuck me, he's alive!"

Unmindful of her grey robes, Junip knelt beside the man, nose wrinkling at the smell. Unlike the surrounding undergrowth, he did smell burnt. Holding her staff so its light fell upon him, Junip examined him with her eyes.

It looked like he'd been set on fire. The man had no hair and his clothes were charred and falling off him. In a few places, the cloth looked to have stuck to his flesh. His blackened face was cracked, skin stiff and suppurating. It was safe to say he was in a bad way.

Junip felt hopeless. There was nothing she could do for him. How he still lived was beyond her ken. He must be in agony and she had not the means or ability to help him. She stood, feeling despondent, making room for the others.

Amos reached a similar conclusion. Moving off away, he waited for the others to join him. Only Jobe stayed with the man whilst they talked.

"The best we can do is to slip a knife in his heart and ease his passing," Amos said.

"Junip, is there nothing you can do?" Jacob insisted.

"I'm no physiker. I don't have the art to help him. I'd likely cause more suffering."

"If'n you could save him, my Lord, what would you do with him?" Ned offered. "There's nowhere to take him. He's more like to slow us down, give us away, and get us killed."

"Er hey, he's talkin'," Jobe said from the darkness.

Turning, Jacob hurried to his side, determined at least to hear the man's last words. Jobe stood, making way as he sunk down beside the burnt man.

Pale blue eyes regarded Jacob. There was something about them that was both familiar and unsettling. Air hissed between the man's lips and up close, Jacob could see they were cracked and dry. Slinging the pack from his back, Jacob untied his water skin and removed the bung. He could at least wet his mouth and slake his thirst, how long had he gone without water?

Slipping an arm under the man's shoulders, Jacob raised him a little before tilting the bladder up, trickling water onto swollen lips and into the man's mouth.

A pink tongue licked out. Jacob watched as black flakes peeled away from his mouth, revealing smooth clear skin beneath. It was the strangest thing. The mouth moved and a croak came out.

"Who are you?" Jacob asked, leaning close.

"Suunn."

Jacob didn't understand. He gave more water and waited, noticing as he did that more black skin flaked away where water dribbled down his cheek. Jacob splashed water over the man's brow and cheeks and watched in fascination as bits of black flesh washed away.

"How is that possible?" Junip gasped from behind.

Jacob ignored her. The flesh was smooth and pink but it was the eyes that held him. They were like mirrors.

"Suund," groaned the man, his arm raised from his side and his hand gripped Jacob's shoulder. "Jaak."

Jacob started to shake, shoulders trembling his head rocked forward.

"My Lord?" Ned asked, concerned.

"Jacob?" Amos called reaching a hand to his other shoulder. Jacob peered back at him. Tears flowed freely from his eyes.

"What is it, who is he?" Amos asked.

Jacob gave a pained look, his voice catching. "He's my cousin, Sand."

Amos swallowed his mouth suddenly dry. Bending, he lifted the water skin and took a slug, studying the burnt man as he did so. He'd changed much in the minutes since he'd last looked. The face was no longer black but scabbed with burnt lumps of skin amid smooth and pale flesh.

"Ned," Jacob called out.

"My Lord?"

"Get Mahan and Thornhill and have them bring a canvas. We need to get my cousin back to the boats," Jacob ordered.

"Ai, my Lord." Ned disappeared into the night.

## Chapter 22: Wraith

**Grimhold, The Rivers**

It was a common misconception that the Grim Marsh was flat and featureless and that people got lost in its waterways and constantly shifting channels because of this. But that was wrong, or at least not entirely right.

The vast lake of fens and mire held many small hillocks and mounds, rising like warts out of the marsh. These knolls burst with a diversity of plant life so varied that each was distinct and provided the perfect habitats for the denizens of the Grim.

The Grimmers, understanding the uniqueness of each hummock, used them as fixed points in the ever-changing landscape to navigate by. It was something few outsiders that braved the Grim knew of and fewer still learned.

For those venturing into its depths ill-prepared, collecting the flora and herbs that were so in demand by physikers across the Nine Kingdoms and beyond, it was not uncommon to find them stranded or lost. And for any that holed a boat or brushed with the wild of the marsh, it was often fatal.

For the most part, the creatures of the Grim posed little threat if avoided but most outsiders knew no better. Then there were those few predators that had no qualms hunting anything that moved, including humans. From Razorback eels, seven feet of sinewy muscle whose rancid bite could incapacitate a man in minutes, to latchers that burrowed into the marsh bed in the deeper waterways and ambushed anything large enough to cross its path, exploding out of its trap to fasten hundreds of needle-sharp teeth in its victim.

Of all the dangers though, it was the Grimmers that proved the greatest.

\* \* \*

Energy coalesced over Tom's hand, eliciting a warm tingling sensation in his palm. He grinned, a few short days ago he could barely summon any aether long enough to manifest and control it. Now he could draw it forth at will if he concentrated. He still had to figure out what to do with it mind, other than feeding it to Wraith.

Wraith, the name he'd given to the woman lying in Hett's workroom, who was now something else. He wasn't sure what else exactly but he couldn't keep calling her 'the woman' or 'dead woman' as Hett did and Wraith just seemed to fit.

Hett had given him a strange look when he named her but nodded after a bit as if it would do. He didn't know what Wraith was but Tom got the distinct feeling Hett did even though she denied it.

"You feed its essence and I'll feed its body. Then we shall see what is what," Hett said. And so he had, for four days, and damned if Wraith didn't look better for it. She might even live despite Hett's assertion she was already dead.

The energy ball twisted silently in the air. Tom cast it towards a cattail sitting proudly out of the marsh a dozen paces away, only for it to roll clear of his hand, barely clearing the gunwale of his boat before plopping into the murky water. It dissipated with a hiss.

"Damn it," Tom cursed. He wanted to try again but was late already. Reluctantly, he picked up his paddle and guided the skiff with practised ease through the reeds surrounding the mirepool. Back in the main channel, he turned for the Grimhold and home.

Tom skirted Willow Brae, a pimple of land hosting a small glade of its namesakes, their leafy branches trailing out like locks to kiss the muddy brown water.

The marsh chorus went unheard as Tom paddled past a boamers stack, giving it a wide berth. Named for their barking call, boamers were aggressive, fiercely territorial, and large enough to tip his skiff over if he wasn't mindful.

He watched as a dozen bluefishers flew in darting bursts across the water feeding on sprats and dragonflies. Sometimes, in his idler moments out on the Grim, he would sit and cast his mind, imagining he was the only person in the world, and finding the thought oddly pleasing. Now though wasn't one of those times. As late as it was his mind instead turned to food, hoping he'd not missed the evening meal, and Hett.

The old hag's temperament hadn't softened any these past couple of days. Her venom at his lateness was a bitter expectation to come that sat like a pebble in his gut ruining his good mood.

The Hold's dilapidated tower rose out the reeds and Tom saw the guard atop it lean against its wall. It was Nadine Varla, picking out her distinctive bush of curly black hair held back with the washed-out red band she always wore. Tom smiled; Varla had some sass and was a troublemaker. No doubt she'd gotten on Black Jack's wrong side since this was her third stint in the tower in four days.

As Tom's skiff emerged from the bulrush and into the waters surrounding the Grimhold, Varla's hand rose in greeting and Tom returned it.

Guiding his craft into the docks and past the holds wooden jetty, Tom saw his was the last boat to return, and worse, a large crowd had gathered near the landing. His heart sank and along with it any chance for food.

Beaching the boat, Tom tied its painter to one of the wooden posts before grabbing the plant-filled hemp bags he'd gathered earlier. Hoping his return had gone unnoticed; Tom quietly approached the gathering, anxious but intrigued.

"Don't slink in here, lad. You're late." Black Jack's gruff voice boomed, silencing the muttered conversations. "Skiving again, eh? Guilt's plain to see, boy."

Tom froze. The belligerence in Black Jack's tone told him he was in trouble. It would be tower duty if he was lucky, a beating if he wasn't.

Black Jack's tall frame parted the crowd, giving Tom a brief glimpse of a large body lying on the ground and the pale faces of several commons gathered beside it. His attention turned to the Grimhold's leader as he sauntered close and the hunger knot in his belly turned to fear.

"I was gathering," Tom murmured looking down, holding up one of the hemp bags.

Snatching it, Black Jack looked inside. Face darkening he cracked Tom openhanded across the cheek.

Pain lit the side of Tom's face, rocking him stumbling onto a knee.

"Fucking weeds and flowers, can't even smoke 'em. I won't tolerate daydreamin' boy. You're useless as tits on a boar hog." Black Jack thrust the bag at Tom, knocking him sprawling into the mud.

© 2020 A D Green

Cheek stinging, Tom tentatively worked his aching jaw. He cast his eyes to the ground, not wanting people to see the fear in them. It pulsed through him like a poison, so bad he barely had the strength to stand.

There was a howl and a shadow fell over him. A small meaty hand latched onto his ear yanking it so hard, Tom thought it would come off.

"Get out of the mud you fool. If you've damaged my plants I'll strip the skin from your arse." Hett's shouted command drew a laugh from the crowd as she dragged Tom up, twisting his ear as she did.

Tom couldn't help crying out. He'd taken Black Jack's blow without a sound which made this all the worse. Any sympathy he might have garnered from the others vanished in that instant and the troll didn't relinquish her grip until he'd gained his feet. Humiliated, he chanced a glance up.

Many stood silent; uncomfortable no doubt at what they witnessed, but some looked amused a few openly laughing. Tom's eyes flickered to Black Jack. Cruel eyes in a hard face stared back, looking angry and, if Tom didn't know any better, disappointed. With a jerk of his head, Black Jack indicated he could go.

"Get on with you," Hett said, picking up a hemp bag where it had fallen to the ground. She thrust it at Tom, ushering him in the direction of her hut on the far side of the island.

Tom stumbled by, moving around the gathering. He passed the commons, huddled together, their fear so tangible it hung from each, like a translucent cloak. They were seven all told; two women, three men, a boy, and a girl, who looked to be brother and sister from their blond locks and blue eyes. All looked dirty and tired.

The body on the ground drew Tom's attention. It was dead whatever it was. He'd assumed it to be a man but it wasn't quite. It was too big and heavyset for one thing but it was the grey skin, bony ridged head, and large eyes set wide that confirmed it, urak. The name muttered around hearth fires these past five days. Seems they are a thing, Tom thought as he was shoved from behind.

"On, On," Hett barked.

"That an urak?" Tom hissed over his shoulder, unable to help himself.

"Time enough for questions later," Hett retorted.

The commons watched with nervous eyes but Tom ignored them. He had more pressing matters, a fact punctuated by another push from Hett. Then he was past the crowd and the excited babble, with Black Jack's bellicose voice rising above it all, slowly receding.

They followed the track to Hett's house, a short ten-minute walk. Taking a large iron key from her satchel, Hett unlocked the door to her workroom and apothecary. Lifting the latch the door squealed as she pulled it wide.

Tom paused on its threshold then followed the old woman. Inside it was dim but still light enough to see by and his eyes stole, as they always did, to the table in the middle of the room.

Wraith lay upon it still, her skin deathly pale except for her face where black tendrils sprang from mouth and eyes, tattooing her flesh. She was covered in an old tunic of Hett's that was both too large and too short but at least did the job of hiding her modesty.

Wraith's breathing had gradually improved over the past few days, growing steadier and stronger. Her body too had healed uncommonly well from the knife wound. Hett, having stitched the flesh together, packed it with a herb poultice to draw out infection, changing it morning and night. But even so, it didn't account for the speed of the recovery.

Tom sniffed. The faint tang of putridity that arrived with Wraith had lifted, changing to a dull earthy smell. He didn't like it much better, it was unnatural.

"Put the bags on the bench," Hett ordered, indicating the far wall. Moving to the table she placed the back of her hand against Wraith's brow whilst Tom shuffled, doing as he was bid. With a grunt she lifted her patient's hand, holding it by the wrist.

Tom waited, looking about, Hett's routine mundane. He was waiting for it and felt the subtle shift in the aether as the physiker's sense settled over Wraith like a blanket. He didn't understand all of what Hett did but knew enough that she examined her patient, maybe even performed some healing through her art, who knew.

Tom's mind turned to the dead urak and the commons, wondering where they came from and what news they might bring. Were there more of these urak? If so, how many and where? Questions he would like to ask and have answered; only it wasn't his place. Still, he'd hear soon enough. The Grimhold was small; no more than three hundred souls all told. Word would spread. It always did.

Detecting a hint of movement in the half-light, Tom ducked. Something small and hard struck above his ear with a crack drawing a cry of surprise more than pain. With a scowl, Tom rubbed his head half expecting to see blood on his fingers but there was none. He picked up the missile as it rolled ungainly on the floor. A harknut, no wonder it stung. The bitter nut was a favourite of Hett's and Tom looked accusingly at her.

"What was that for?"

"Pay attention." Hett scowled, "Now pass that bottle behind you and the pin hammer."

Truculent, Tom did as instructed, watching as Hett took the small hammer and tapped it lightly at various points on Wraith's body. Despite his sulk, this part of Hett's inspection intrigued him. Wraith's body never responded to whatever Hett did; it just lay like a slab of meat, the only movement being the gentle rise and fall of her chest. Only this time was there a slight flex of the knee?

Hett grunted and taking the bottle uncorked it. The pungent aroma of smelling salts filled the air. The bottle was wafted under Wraith's nose and Hett watched, as nostrils flared, before removing and recorking the container.

"Hmmm," Hett muttered, "interesting."

"What? Does she awaken?" Tom blurted.

"Tomorrow or the next day I would guess," Hett replied, "Or maybe not at all. Only the old gods know for sure."

Tom was excited at the prospect and nodded, not trusting himself to speak. He felt strangely invested ever since naming Wraith. Drawing aether and feeding it to her was important. She needed him. Everyone used him but no one had ever needed him before. Not even his mother. Out in the Grim these past few days, his idle mind would oft drift to Wraith. The memory of her lying naked on the table was as fresh as the day he'd seen her.

A sudden banging on the door made Tom jump, breaking his guilty reverie. He saw Hett gazing at him, a strange look on her face.

"Go let him in, Tom."

Moving to the door, Tom opened it only for Black Jack to barge through knocking him aside. Towed behind was one of the women from the landing and trailing after her the blonde girl. The woman looked defiant but the girl, no more than eight, Tom guessed, was terrified.

"Jackson Tullock, don't dare sully my doorstep with commons. The answer's no, take them elsewhere. I've no time or patience to teach them our ways." Hett shouted.

"I ain't asking and you'll do as I say," Black Jack snapped.

"No, I'm too busy. Fixing your bit here is not the least of my work," Hett said.

"How is she?" Black Jack asked, his eyes roving to the table and lingering hungrily on Wraith. "She looks better."

"Ai, her body heals. Her mind though is changed. She's not what you think she is Jackson or more to the point not what you want her to be." Hett stated, bluntly. "If she wakes I can't say how she'll be or what she'll be like."

"I'm made up, Hett, she's mine. I can't say why but there's something about her that draws me. Just, fix her."

Tom blinked in surprise. Hard, violent, and vicious, Black Jack was uncompromising. He ruled through strength and fear but the way he spoke made him seem almost normal like he cared. Finding the thought outrageous, Tom grinned, unable to stop himself.

Sensing it, Black Jack spun and like a snake striking, grabbed Tom by the throat.

"Find something amusing you little cunt." Pushing Tom back against the door frame, Black Jack squeezed.

The little girl cried in fear and the woman drew her close, pressing her head into her midriff to shield her from the violence.

Hett saw the terror in Tom's eyes as they bulged. His face turned beet red as he choked for breath with no sign from Black Jack he had any intention of letting up. The woman looked at her imploringly.

"Don't kill him, Jackson," Hett said, "I've need of the boy yet."

"I bought you the woman and girl. They can do his work," Black Jack growled, his stare not leaving Tom's face, fascinated to watch the life struggle as the boy died.

"No, they can't," Hett stated. "They know nothing of the Grim. Not how to survive it nor what plants to gather or where to find them. I need the boy!"

Black Jack's face screwed up in annoyance.

"You want the woman. Give me the boy," Hett insisted.

Tom collapsed gasping to the floor, hands clutching his bruised throat. He was unprepared for the boot that caught him in the stomach. It lifted him, the breath he'd sucked in exploding out so he had none left to cry. Landing on his back half out the entrance he rolled into a ball, eyes screwed shut, sucking in air that hurt with every ragged gasp. On each exhale, bile spewed from his empty stomach which cramped in pain.

"Fine, he's yours," Black Jack said, glaring. "But fail me with the woman and I'll stake the lad in the Stench. Let the lizards eat him piece by piece." He stepped over Tom, avoiding the pool of vomit.

"What of the woman and girl?" Hett called after.

He paused in the doorway, "Told ya. Teach 'em our ways, my rules, and what they need to survive." Then almost as an afterthought, "Woman can read, write too. Might be she's of some use." Not waiting for an answer he disappeared into the evening dusk.

The two women stood a while, one giving comfort the other with a scowl on her face. The muffled sobs of the little girl and Tom's moans were the only sounds.

The woman was the first to move. Disengaging the little girl from about her waist she offered words of comfort before moving to kneel beside Tom.

"Are you alright?" she asked. Her hands moved lightly as she assessed the boy. The livid marks on his neck would bruise but his breathing was unimpaired. Pulling his hands away she probed his abdomen.

Tom groaned in response.

"Why did he do that? Why beat him so?" she asked, turning to Hett.

"Cause he can. Does what he wants to who he wants that one." Hett stated with a shrug. "Life's cheap in the Grim. That's your first lesson and one you'd do well to remember."

"He's a monster."

"Yeah, but a monster that's kept us free folk safe enough this last ten year. Some advice dearie, don't cross him and don't attract his attention. I guarantee it'll be unwanted." Hett looked the woman up and down. "Might want to lose the dress and un-pretty yourself a bit, there's worse than beatings on offer for the likes of you. Now follow me."

Hett stomped to the door brushing past the woman and stepping over Tom. She looked back at him, her face inscrutable. "Clean the sick off my floor, Tom, afore I get back. Then feed Wraith." She disappeared from view.

The woman stood, chest tight with worry, and held a hand out. "Come, Millie."

The little girl grasped it, holding it tight, tears streaking her dirt-smudged face. Together they followed Hett into the gloom.

* * *

Tom wasn't sure how long he'd lain on the floor. Not too long he thought, the sky outside was darkening still. The pain in his gut was intense and he worried something had torn inside. His throat was raw and breathing hurt, but he couldn't just lay there. The wounded and the infirm never lived long in the Grim.

Gathering himself, Tom rolled onto his front and levered himself up, gritting his teeth against the sharp pain in his abdomen. Hett's instructions sounded in his head and he staggered across the room to the water bucket. Thankfully it was full.

After sluicing and washing his vomit off the floor he refilled the bucket from the water butt outside. Clasping his ribs with one hand and the bucket in his other he sloshed it back down in its spot by the far wall. The job had taken him far too long and he feared Hett would return at any minute.

Facing the table, Tom walked tentatively to Wraith's side. She looked peaceful lying there, oblivious to all his hurt and pain. Good, he didn't want her to see him like this. He wiped a tear from his cheek angry with himself for it, why did he have to be so weak.

Clenching his jaw, Tom held his hands above Wraith's chest; so close he imagined he could feel the heat radiating from her body. He cleared his mind, pain receding, and spread his sense. Aether was all about, strong as it always was. Drawing on it, Tom conjured a ball of energy in his hands, watching it slowly manifest and grow. With practise, it had become easy for him.

Tom held it spinning and pulsing for what seemed a minute, then with a sudden blink, it was gone. A moan, this time not his own. Lifting his gaze, Tom saw Wraith staring back, her eyes like obsidian. Her tongue slipped between blackened lips, moistening them before slipping away again. The corners of her mouth rose and her head tilted as she regarded him.

Tom felt his breath catch. His heart thumped so loud. Pain forgotten, he stared in wonderment unmoving until finally, Wraith's eyes slowly closed. They didn't open again.

## Chapter 23: Hunted

**Near Greenholme, The Rivers**

<Thank the One. Where have you been?> Keeper asked.

<Keeping low. The Morhudrim hunts that which you seek or me. I am unsure which,> Hiro replied.

<And?> Keeper conveyed much in that single word. That the Morhudrim had risen, acknowledgement they were in the Rivers and a question.

<Marron is dead, killed by a Taken. I've no word of Darion though Nihm lives. I have her here with me now,> Hiro countered.

<A Taken!> Keeper exclaimed. <Show me.>

Hiro concentrated, recalling the river bank and his investigation, sending the memory of it down the link in a moment to Keeper.

<Did the Taken seek that which we sought?> Keeper asked, concern leaking through to Hiro. <Has it found this new power?>

<No, I do not believe so. The Taken is gone and I believe the new power moves south. It is shielded and difficult to track but I am sure of it,> Hiro replied, disgruntled. <Have you any news of Darion?>

<No, I've heard nothing from our assets in Greentower or Higholme. He could be anywhere,> Keeper paused, <I am sorry. You thought well of the Castells, as did I. If Darion makes contact I will tell him of Marron's passing and of Nihm.>

<If he lives, he will know of Marron already,> Hiro replied thinking of the rings he'd bonded them with all those years ago.

<You must find this power. It is a new piece on the board and I would know if it is for or against the Order,> Keeper persisted. <Find it my friend. Bring it to me.>

<I will do what I must.>

<Ironside sails the Emerald Lake. He will be in Rivercross the day after next. I will send him to aid you,> Keeper advised.

The link terminated, leaving Hiro a moment of unsettled contemplation.

\* \* \*

"Ha, you sleep anywhere." Lucky clapped Hiro on the back as he stirred, "One of these days you'll turn over and find yourself drowned in the river," he said cheerily.

Hiro flexed his back working a crick out of it but made no reply. Lucson talked too much and he'd not encourage him. He closed his eyes again taking up his vigil.

They were three days out from Longstretch and still on the river. Passage though was slow, as Hiro had them stop on the west bank and hide whenever urak warbands roved the east side pillaging south. The first time there had been much grumbling for there had been no sign of any urak. But ten minutes after they lay hidden, a large contingent had passed by. There were no protests after that.

Hiro's eyes snapped open, "Urak!"

Immediately the canoes veered for the west bank, the routine familiar.

"We are discovered," Hiro said, pointing out distant figures on the road. They were clearly urak and were stopped. Their guttural calls reached them moments later.

"Damn it," Mercy swore from the boat behind. The western bank was steep and high lined with bushes offering no break to land the boats and though the river was a hundred paces or more wide, they would soon be in easy bow range.

The current drew them inexorably downriver. The urak left the southern road and loped across the meadow grass to stand upon the eastern bank. Unlimbering bows they stuck arrows in the dirt and waited. Their targets would be in range soon enough.

"There," Stama said. A fallen willow sloped into the water, the mud bank surrounding it collapsed and crumbling. It wasn't much, the branches an encumbrance and the soil full of tree root and foliage, but it was enough.

Steering for the break, Stama drove the point of his canoe between branch and bank until it snagged tight. The other boats followed, Morten and Nihm struggling to find a gap instead caught on the branches further out.

"We'll have to abandon the boats." Mercy said. "Lucky, Mao, get to the side. The rest pass the supplies ashore."

The next few minutes proved perilous. The mud bank was wet and sucked their feet in up to their shins. Each step proved arduous and energy-sapping as they pulled themselves free. Thankfully they hadn't far to go and the fallen tree offered some support.

Mao, despite age and injury managed surprisingly well and, with no complaint, was the first up the side. Likewise, the dogs had no trouble. Bounding from boat to boat, sending them rocking with each jump, before leaping almost clear of the bank, claws scrambling the last few feet through dirt and roots.

Of all of them, Morten suffered most. He and Nihm had to clamber over the fallen tree through branches mere inches from the flowing river. Nihm was surefooted, showing no signs of her recent ailment. But Morten's fear of the water made him nervous and tentative, each step slow and unsteady.

Seeing Morten's fear up close, Nihm struggled to understand it. It was only water, there were plenty of branches to hold onto, what was to fear. But he did, she could see his hands shaking and sweat bead his forehead that had nothing to do with his exertions. Watching, chest tight, Nihm found herself encouraging him, offering advice.

Eventually, he made the river's side, pale-faced he gave a rueful grin. Nihm smiled back, pleased for him.

"Come," Hiro hefted Morten's pack. "You've wasted time enough already."

Catching it, Morten swung it about his shoulders then clutched his staff as Hiro thrust it at him.

They pushed inland, directly away from the river, and found it tough going. The undergrowth was dense and they had to avoid thickets of needle bush and brambles. Lucky took the lead putting his bulk and strong arms to use forging a passage.

"A blind babe could follow the trail you're leaving," Stama quipped.

"Ai, come and take point if you can do better," Lucky grumbled back.

A hundred paces inland the going eased. The landscape changing from thick bush to plains of long grass tall as a man and interspersed with the occasional grove of hark trees. Both were durable and well acclimated to the soft ground. The grasslands extended over two leagues where the ground rose, meeting the rolling hills of the Grimwolds.

They moved more quickly then, their urgency unspoken, stopping only once to rest and take sustenance as the sun dipped towards the western horizon.

"Do you think they will follow?" Mercy asked Hiro.

"Maybe," he said, "but if they cross they'll be downriver a good way and will have to trackback. It's likely they will send a hunting party at least."

"How do you know?" Stama asked.

"I studied the urakakule once and remember still my learning. The Order never forgets."

"Urak have been gone fer hundreds of years. Reading about someat in some book ain't the same as knowing a thing I've found," Lucky offered, unconvinced.

"You can read, Master Lucson?" Hiro's eyebrows rose expansively, "Clearly not the right books then."

He looked up at the sun, judging its position.

"We should keep moving. We have hours at most to reach the foothills." Hiro lifted his pack onto his shoulder. "I'll know better there if we are hunted or no."

He held a hand out to Mao who sat cross-legged on a bed of grass and who eyed it a moment before clasping it. Rising wordlessly, Mao followed Hiro as he parted the tall grass.

Nihm had listened avidly to the conversation, finding it a distraction from the deep melancholy that seeped into her bones whenever she was idle. In those moments, her mind would constantly return to her mother, Marron, falling into the waters of the Oust whilst she lay helpless on the ground. Or to her father, Darion, lost in the wilds of the north, unable to shake the fear that he too was gone. Sai proved no help or at least no comfort, though he offered advice enough. Being on the move again then would be a relief.

Barely hesitating, Nihm stood searching for Snow and Ash. They were away in the grass doing whatever it was wolfdogs did. She whistled the recall and heard the rustle of grass as they tracked towards her even as she trekked after the two old men.

* * *

They reached the low foothills of the Grimwolds as the sun was setting. Atop a small bush filled rise overlooking the grasslands, they stopped again. Nihm watched, as Hiro sat cross-legged facing the northeast, back the way they'd come then closed his eyes. There was a calm economy to everything he did that fascinated her.

<I am unsure what to make of Master Hiro. He seems a good man but there is an edge to him, an aloofness,> Nihm observed.

<He is very functional for a human,> Sai replied. <Given his apparent age he performs at a level exceeding those of your other companions.>

<Our companions,> Nihm corrected. <He is of the Order. Like my parents. He is more though. I think he is or was an Order Knight. Maybe he is retired given how old he is.>

<Your knowledge of the Order is insufficient for me to confirm your hypothesis. However, given his performance at the Loud Water establishment and subsequently, there is a 93.6 percentile probability he is enhanced. He is not normal,> Sai concluded.

<Like me you mean?>

<His speed and movement exceed our own, at least for now. There is insufficient data however to draw a definitive conclusion. My conjecture sub-routines though suggest it is a strong possibility. Your thought raises an interesting question.>

<Which is?> Nihm pressed.

<If he is like 'you' why is he so aged?>

<Okay, that is not interesting. Just so you know. When humans get old they look… old… worn like.> Nihm laughed, drawing a few strange looks from Stama and Morten who were nearest. She ignored them.

<Nano micro-cells pervade your body. We are one. Your organic cells will grow until maturity provided they receive the correct bio-chemical mix. After that they will renew,> Sai said.

<What does that mean exactly?> Nihm asked.

<Cell maturity occurs at different stages for the various organs within your vessel. However, to approximate, once you reach twenty-five you will no longer age.>

Nihm was too stunned to say anything for a moment. It was impossible, wasn't it? What did it mean? Am I even human? She must have thought it out loud for Sai responded to her questions in order.

<It is possible. It means you are more than you were and mostly…>

"You alright, Nihm, ya've gone all pale?" Morten asked. Dropping to his haunches he placed a hand on Nihm's arm.

"I'm fine," Nihm muttered moving her arm away from his touch.

Morten stood. Much had changed since Marron's death and none for the better. Before, he might have pressed her. Not now. Their friendship was different, brittle. He moved away.

Nihm felt him go but gave it no heed. Her mind was ablaze, unable to hold one thought or emotion before latching onto another.

<I have caused distress. There is much to discuss. Calm your mind. Order your thoughts. In time, when you are ready, ask and I will explain what I can,> Sai offered.

The monk rose suddenly from his meditations brushing and smoothing his robes down.

"They are ten and follow an hour behind," Hiro announced. He peered at the western horizon. The sun had already set behind the Grimwolds but the fading glory of arching reds and purples still provided light to see by. The sky above was clear and the moons of Kildare and Ankor were visible and he knew their sister, Nihmrodel, would join them later.

"The night will provide no shroud for us I fear. They will track us through the witching light and catch us before dawn."

"Damn it, you're sure?" Stama said.

Hiro gave the Duncan man a stony look. It was Mercy that answered.

"He reads aether like a master. Something sadly I lack. If he says it is so, it is so."

"Then we need ta move. We'll lose them in the hills." Stama started repacking his bag.

"I think not," Hiro said, "at least, not all of us."

"Think ya can do better on your own, old man?" Lucky said voice raised, "With Mao slowin' ya down."

Hiro frowned. "You misunderstand me; though Mao is not an issue, believe me."

"He means to hunt them." Nihm surprised herself with her interjection. Everyone but Mao turned to look at her.

"Do I?" Hiro said. "Explain."

It was so like her Da, Nihm was flustered. Conscious as well that everyone looked at her.

<Go on. Your thinking is sound if Master Hiro's assessment is correct,> Sai offered in support.

"Hunting man is dangerous," Nihm blurted, face reddening.

<Good. Continue,> Sai said.

Nihm bowed her head, closing her eyes. Was it on purpose or coincidence that Sai echoed her father's words? Did it matter?

Resolved, she opened her eyes and looked at each of her companions in turn. Da would agree with her, it was enough. With a hint of a smile she began.

"Hunting a man is difficult, unpredictable. A man lays a trail like any beast. But, if the man knows he is hunted then he knows the path the hunter follows and suddenly the man is the hunter if he chooses," Nihm said. "If we cannot escape the urak we must change the rules of the hunt."

"You're suggesting we attack? There are seven of us and ten of them." Lucky laughed, shaking his head. "You and Mort aren't even blooded and Mao over there had the living snot kicked out of him less than a ten-day ago. Four against ten are bad odds if they were men. Against urak, we'd be slaughtered."

"Maybe," Hiro said, "But I don't think Nihm here is proposing we take them on in open battle."

"No," Nihm agreed. "We've three bows. One goes with the main group and sets up on that bluff." Nihm indicated a steep rising hill behind them. "The other two bows hunt."

"Crazy, so now two take on ten?" Lucky said. "No offence girl but you're sixteen. You know nothing of war or urak."

Nihm's blood boiled.

<Calm yourself. He goads you. Make your point clearly and with conviction. You have their attention. Apart from Mao who is picking petals off a flower head. You can ignore him for now,> Sai prompted.

Nihm took a breath.

"You're right," Nihm conceded, "I know nothing of war and little of urak, maybe even as little as you."

It brought a chuckle from Stama. "Okay lass. I'm listening." He slapped Lucky on the shoulder, forestalling his friend before he could reply.

"I know how to hunt. We slow them down, make them fear us. Their trackers will be out front. Shoot them first then run," Nihm stated.

"Kill their trackers. Need ta get close in the long grass to even see them; one or three they'd chase down any fool enough to try... " Lucky snapped, angry now. "S'pose ya want me ta be the fool too."

"Not kill, wound. The wounded need care, the dead not so much," Nihm said, "And no, I would be the fool. I'm best with a bow and I'm fast."

"Bold statement lass considering we've not seen you shoot and brave considering a while back you could barely stand," Stama said, "I'll do it."

"What!" Lucky exclaimed turning on his friend.

"Enough!" Mercy said, joining the discussion. "Nihm's right. We need to change the game. Stama will take point, I will go with him."

"No, it must be Nihm and I," Hiro said, "Stama will cover our retreat from the grasslands with the third bow. The rest make for the bluff, it is defensible. Now, we've no time to waste on further discussion."

"That ain't right! Nihm's just a girl. She almost died before," Morten shouted, stopping them all. The hard look on Nihm's face told him he'd erred but Morten continued, committed, "I promised Marron I'd look after you."

"You're the one as needs looking after," Nihm snapped. "I'm not a child. Not now."

Turning her back, Nihm bent to retrieve her bow. It would be the first time she had used it since the hunt in the forest, what felt like a lifetime ago. She found the thought oddly calming.

Snow and Ash, aware of her shifting mood sat quietly on their haunches watching and ready.

\* \* \*

Rutgarpok considered the path ahead. The sun had set an hour past leaving the silvery gloom of moonlight. It made tracking difficult but, skilled as he was, it was impossible for his prey to hide their passage through the long grass. They were closing, no more than an hour behind he judged.

Highly alert, Rutgarpok raised his head at the barely perceptible flutter of shifting grass. The arrow struck high on his chest, embedding itself with a thunk, just below his collarbone. Howling he stumbled to a knee.

The rest of the hunters didn't see the arrow strike but his cry and fall were enough. Bellowing, they bounded past charging ahead.

He saw Makjatukh, his brother, stumble then fall, crashing heavily onto his face. He didn't get up. A groan told him that his brother lived still. It was a trap plain as the red moon, Naris-Krol, in the sky above.

Rutgarpok shouted a warning but the blood rage burned in his brethren and they took no heed. With a grunt, he staggered upright and grimacing checked on Makjatukh. The broken shaft of an arrow protruded from his leg leaking blood into the dirt, his crash to the ground knocking him senseless.

War cries echoed across the plain and Rutgarpok limped after them, biting back his pain.

\* \* \*

"Try not to stick me with an arrow, eh," Master Hiro told her. That had been fifteen minutes ago, though in truth it felt like an hour to Nihm.

Watch and listen. Patience is the hunter's friend her Da always told her. In the end, it was her nose that gave the first warning. The wind blew from the northeast carrying a hint of musk that her refined senses picked out. It was familiar, matching the urak she and Da had found in the forest though Nihm could not recall taking note of the scent at the time.

Ash and Snow had followed her into the grasslands and sat like sentinels on each side of her, ears erect, heads fixed on an unseen point ahead. They smelled it too.

A bestial roaring carried over the tall grass and Nihm felt her heart beat faster. Her arms felt suddenly heavy as she placed an arrow on the bowstring ready. Her mouth was dry and she needed to pee.

<Calm your breathing and focus. Lockdown your emotions and remember your father's lessons,> Sai intoned.

Nihm closed her eyes and breathed deeply. A rustling sounded, close enough to hear over the shouting urak. They were near. The dogs stood alert, hackles raised and shivering with tension. At a sign they crouched low and disappeared into the grass, vanishing in moments.

Nihm blinked her eyes and the dark-light suddenly took on a different aspect. Everything appeared leeched of colour but was crisper and sharper. There was a blur of motion, moving to her right. A flash of brown leaked through the stalks taking shape as it neared. It was Hiro, moving quickly and making far too much noise, drawing the urak on behind him. They were close, the sound of their passage loud as they spread out trying to corral their prey.

Nihm's pulse quickened and a slither of fear worked its way into her brain. It told her to run. Run like the wind, now.

But she didn't. Lifting her bow, Nihm took the tension, drawing the arrow back to her ear. Everything slowed and a calmness overcame her. The shadow of an urak lumbered into view. Her mind filled instantly with calculations. Wind speed and direction, distance to target, movement, and lead angles. It was as her father taught only so much more.

A line appeared in her mind's eye, the flight her arrow would take from bow to target. Releasing her breath, the arrow sped away slipping through the grass like parting smoke.

It was a difficult shot in bad light through long stalks but the arrow never wavered and a moment later thunked into the urak's chest dropping it to the ground without a sound.

<I thought we were disabling rather than killing?> Sai said.

<My mistake.> Nihm had already drawn another arrow.

Eyes scanning, they latched onto a shadowy figure charging after Hiro. Turning to align her body she drew and launched. She didn't watch the arrow knowing it struck true, eyes already searching for her next target. Cold dispassion filled her.

<Three approaching from the east, it is time to go,> Sai urged, picking out sounds of movement over the noise of wounded and enraged urak.

Nihm turned, hands reaching for another arrow when the grass exploded twenty paces ahead. Nocking, drawing smoothly she released. Luck or fortune favoured the urak. The arrowhead deflected off the blade of its war axe and into the meat of its arm. Painful, but not enough to stop its charge as it roared in rage.

As if called, the grass on either side of the urak erupted and two more appeared.

Nihm phased, time dilating. Grasping an arrow in one hand she fell, rolling fluidly to the side then back onto her knees. Notching and drawing Nihm released point-blank. The arrow punched into the left eye socket, driving into the urak's brain. Collapsing, it skidded to a heap before her, blood and gore splattering its face.

There was a snarling tearing sound, Nihm registered. Then she was in motion again. Jumping up onto the balls of her feet she met an onrushing urak. He was huge, face pulled back in a rictus of a snarl, eyes wild. Its hair was tied in long queues down its back and knotted in many places. A warrior, not sure how she knew or whether it was Sai's observation or her own.

It was fast for its size, its large blade weaving a pattern in the air. Nihm did not doubt that, should it connect, it would cleave her from shoulder to hip. She felt fear but it was a distant thing, held back and contained as if in a jar, something to be looked and wondered at. In its place was a cold analytical indifference.

Nihm watched the rhythm of the blade, the subtle shifting of the urak as it closed. The scene slowed again so that it seemed as if the urak moved through water. It was so near, its arm flexed, muscles tightening imperceptibly and Nihm was spinning. Dropping her bow, she drew a knife and arrow both.

Somehow the urak managed to divert her blade and follow her spin. Nihm's fear looked out from its glass jar. She moved, coolly assessing the arc and quickness of the scything sword, and knew it would clip her side. She had misjudged the urak's power and speed.

Arching her back, Nihm brought her knife to bear, making contact with the slicing blade. Pain exploded through her wrist and the knife was wrenched, spinning from her hand. But it was enough. The sword passed, so close the air of its passage felt like a kiss on her skin.

Continuing her arching turn, Nihm tucked and rolled coming up behind the urak as it staggered by. The resistance anticipated, of sword hitting flesh was gone, overbalancing him.

Bringing her arm around, Nihm stabbed the arrow she held deep into the urak's calf. Rising to her feet, Nihm skipped back and away, easily avoiding the returning backswing, watching with a morbid fascination as the blade cut the air.

Her senses searched for the third urak and she was instantly aware it was down, Ash and Snow ripping and tearing at its inert body.

The urak limped round to face Nihm taking a step towards her.

Mirroring him, Nihm took a step back eyes never leaving his face. She had underestimated the urak once already.

<Go. There are five urak unaccounted for. It is illogical to take more risk,> Sai ordered. As if to punctuate his point the sound of movement came from deeper in the grass.

The urak took another hobbling step towards her, glaring defiantly. The earlier rage it exuded though was gone, in its place something else.

Nihm stepped away and to the side. Bending she picked up her fallen bow before slowly receding into the grass, the urak watching in silence. Turning she ran, whistling the recall for the dogs as she did. Her wrist throbbed abominably with every step until it suddenly abated. The pain was still there but muted, no doubt Sai's handiwork.

She became aware of Hiro. He was stood not ten paces away and held an arrow ready on his bow. Everything had happened so quickly he couldn't have been there long but he must have seen her fight with the urak. With a curt nod, he turned for the hills leaving Nihm to follow in his path.

## Chapter 24: The Defile

**The Defile, The Rivers**

The massive fortress atop the Defile was ancient and formidable. It dominated the surrounding land. On its far side, a granite cliff face fell to the river below leaving only one approach, a hard road that was steep and winding. The final turn undercut a bluff as it rose to an imposing gatehouse. No enemy had ever breached its walls.

It was built after the war of the Taken. The wilderness then was newly populated by men who came, carving out the land to claim for their own. Many named themselves king and it was a bitter and unruly time as each vied with his neighbour to take what the other had.

Named for the hill it sat atop, the Defile was originally built by Jorgen the Faithful after his ascension as the first One King; so named for his devotion to the old gods of wood and stone, water and earth.

Jorgen Varthenon was twice a king before becoming the One. He lost his first kingdom to Handel the Just, a friend, and ally who betrayed him. Forced into hiding, he lived in the unclaimed wilds to the north. Life was hard and the country harder. To survive, Jorgen preyed on the new settlements where he earned his second kinghood. Jorgen, King of Reavers. It was a title well named for he was ruthless taking only those he needed and killing the rest.

Fearing him, the many kings banded together to bring Jorgen to heel but they could never follow him through the wilds. It wasn't until the Defile that there was to be an accounting, but not of the sort they anticipated.

Jorgen claimed it was the gods who bid him take up the mantle as the One King. They sent visions of the Defile where he would settle his throne and lay his walls. So it was he led his people there and started to build.

That first fortress was little more than a wood stockade. But its position was well chosen and the hill highly defensible. By the time the many kings gathered to challenge him, Jorgen was well prepared. His fort was provisioned for the winter and his Reavers ready for war.

Heavily outnumbered it looked grim for Jorgen and his people. All the many kings had to do was hold fast, they had him trapped, or so they thought. However, bulled by their superior numbers they did not wait. Up the hard road, at that time little more than a rocky footpath, they ascended and suffered grievously as rocks and boulders were rained down upon them. Thousands of men perished on the climb up and thousands more in the retreat down.

That night, as the kings bickered in their pavilions and the remnants of their shattered soldiers rested, Jorgen and his Reavers lowered themselves down the far cliff. It was a strategy they'd planned for; the rope ties pounded into the rock face in the weeks leading up to their encirclement.

A great battle was fought then and the many kings were defeated. Jorgen himself striking the heads from each, except for Handel, for Jorgen had loved him as a brother. Handel, it is said, he neutered; his sack and balls hung on a rope about his neck as a reminder of his treachery.

With none to challenge him, Jorgen Varthenon, King of the Reavers became Jorgen the Faithful, the One King.

Scorned by the southern kingdoms, his realm was not so easily rid of its violent birthing. They named it the land of the Reavers and it was derided by all but those who lived there. To them, the name was borne with pride.

\* \* \*

Zoller stomped down the musty corridors of the Defile and rounded a corner bumping into a servant. The man was so startled he stumbled, spilling the linen he carried on to the floor. Distracted, Zoller hardly registered it as he barged past.

Tuco, trailing in his wake grinned, knocking the few remaining blankets the servant held out of his arms as he sauntered past.

Zoller didn't see; his mind elsewhere. Three long slow days it had taken to reach the Defile from Appleby. A journey that should have taken half that. But checkpoints had sprung up on route and whilst he and his Red Cloak's were summarily waved by, each became a choke point as a glut of people queued to be passed through.

Zoller had wondered at the point of it until he cleared the first checkpoint. There, goods were inspected and tagged; appropriated by the High Lord. Dockets then had to be written and exchanged accounting in large part for the holdup. Worse though was to come. There was another checkpoint, five leagues further down the road where the process was repeated, only this time for livestock and harvest. Then, a final checkpoint as they approached the Defile itself. Here, any with useful trade skills were hired, with not much choice given to those that had, whilst those without but deemed fit and able were conscripted. It all took time, a delay that rankled.

To add salt to his tea, on arrival at the Defile, the High Lord had bid him wait, assigning him and his men the fortress chapel and chapter house. That was over a day ago. A day! He should be in Rivercross by now. That Twyford had just turned him away again only darkened his already dour mood.

Approaching a large iron-bound door, Zoller waited, moving to the side to allow Tuco by. The swarthy cutthroat didn't hesitate; unlatching the door and pushing it open with a groan of hinges. A brisk cold air assailed them both as they stepped through.

They found themselves in the upper courtyard, a large almost square arena, filled with tents and soldiers. All wore the High Lord's steel grey colours with the Rivercross emblem, a wolf's head enclosed between merging twinned rivers.

Tuco waited for Father Zoller to lead off and neatly took station again at his back. Crossing the square between avenues of tents, they made their way to the chapel. There was nothing much to distinguish the chapel from the other buildings around the courtyard. Like them, it was built so as to form part of the wall, a buttress adjoining the cliff face that overlooked the river.

A pair of Red Cloaks stood guard outside a similar iron-bound door to the one they had just passed through. Spying Father Zoller both stood a little straighter and, at his approach, uncrossed their spears with one opening the door for him.

"Blessings to you, Brothers," Zoller intoned as he disappeared inside.

The chapel interior was large and high and together with a few ancillary rooms provided ample accommodation for his dozen Red Cloaks and their two guests. An internal balcony ran around the facing walls, providing access to numerous shuttered and barred windows that when opened, looked out over the courtyard on one side and the plunging cliff face on the other.

There was no furniture or ornamentation. No symbols of the Trinity other than the hastily erected red banner on the far wall. This depicted Kildare. A golden-haired warrior dressed in red armour with a flaming sword in one hand and the book of death in the other.

If not for the four pillars that stood, one in each corner, the room could pass for a barracks as much as a church. Zoller had studied the columns with interest whilst waiting for the High Lord's summons. Stone, like granite yet not. Harder, more durable, they were ancient and etched with script and pictograms that were fine and clear despite time's passage.

Each pillar was different, appointed to represent one of the old gods; gods he had no knowledge of. Still, it was clear that was what they were. He was learned and had interpreted the symbols for wood and stone, water and earth. Heathen gods for a heathen people from a time before the Trinity made themselves known.

Zoller moved through the chapel, nodding in response to his men as they bowed at his passing. Normally he found the whole thing tedious but today their deference soothed him.

The largest annexe onto the chapel, Zoller claimed for his own and furnished it with the few possessions he had. After his first night, stiff and sore from sleeping on the floor, Holt had appropriated a bed from somewhere. He asked no questions and gave no thanks and Holt, faithful as ever, expected none.

The reason for the Defile's lack of accoutrements was obvious to Zoller now that he'd spent a day here. The fortress, whilst imposing from the outside, had seen no real use in many years and was in sorry disrepair.

Its commander was Sir Simon Hempthorn, a young Lord from out near Merik. He had garrisoned with a contingent of twenty men at arms and another fifty or so servants and support staff. It was barely enough to fill the gatehouse.

No doubt, like the many commanders before him, Sir Simon had seen no reason in trying to maintain the whole place. It was too big an undertaking with too few to carry it out, despite the stipend paid by the High Lord requiring just that. Bringing fewer men at arms and ancillaries meant more money.

Hempthorn's command of the fortress was for two years. Then another would be appointed, hoping to increase their stock with the High Lord. Zoller recalled the body staked outside the gatehouse, head spiked alongside it, a grisly warning from Twyford. He supposed with Sir Simon's tenure ending prematurely, a new commander would need to be found.

Zoller closed the door to his room, shutting out the noise with it, before walking to his bed. It stood alone, head up against the far wall looking too small for the space it was in. He sat on its end with a heavy sigh. Nothing was ever simple.

\* \* \*

Zoller woke with a start. He hadn't meant to drift off. It was not like him. His mouth was dry and he reached for the watered wine he kept at the side of the bed. He took a swig, swilling it around his mouth before swallowing it.

Where was Holt? He'd not seen him when he'd come in earlier, no doubt tormenting the boy again. The giant Red Cloak wasn't much for standing about and there was little else to keep him occupied. A failing of my own not to keep him so, Zoller conceded. Thoughts of Renco resolved him. Rising, he brushed his cassock straight, smoothed his hair back, and then headed for the door.

The annexe next to his room had steps down to a basement. A storeroom, perhaps, in days gone by, certainly there was evidence of it from the detritus in the room. It was a large space and interestingly the pillars in the chapel above appeared to flow through the ceiling to the basement's floor, the etchings and carvings seemingly unbroken.

Crates and barrels of supplies had been stacked at the far end, arranged in such a way as to partition the room into sections. More supplies were being brought down every day and the space was slowly filling up.

Zoller heard Holt before he saw him. Muttering profanities, his voice rough and bellicose, directed presumably at the boy. The boy who would not speak.

"Where ya goin'?" Zoller heard Holt exclaim.

"There's no need to subject Lettie to this," replied a voice, Thomas Perrick. "What you do to the lad is wrong, Brother. I can't stop you but be sure I will speak to the good Father about it. This can't continue. We're not animals."

Zoller had hardly ventured down to see Renco. He had no use for him other than as bait for the monk. The trap though was set for Rivercross; the lure was in the wrong place.

Quickening his stride, Zoller stepped around a high stack of crates. A bloody body was strapped to a pillar. He knew it was the boy but only because it could be no one else.

Renco was stripped naked, hands and feet bound so that he faced the pillar, his back a mess of welts and cuts. In several places, flaps of skin hung loose and blood oozed leaving dark trails on his already red-painted body. Holt has been busy, with the knife as well as the lash, Zoller mused.

Holt saw Brother Thomas stiffen. It was enough to alert him and he turned to find Father Zoller staring back, eyes both discerning and disapproving.

"Father," Holt dropped to his knee and bowed his head.

Perrick followed awkwardly a moment later, relinquishing his hold on Lett's hand.

"Father," Thomas said, then blurted, "Brother Holt has been torturing this mute. For no reason I can discern other than his own pleasure." His eyes darted to Holt as he spoke. Not liking the violence he saw, he looked back to the priest.

Zoller made no immediate reply. He stared at the girl and the guilty blush on Perrick's cheeks. Then at Holt who was unmoved.

Walking about the pillar, Zoller inspected Renco. His wounds appeared bad at first glance but up close the cuts were shallow, the skin expertly peeled. The raised welts and torn flesh looked painful but would heal given time, provided no infection set in. Two of the fingers on the boy's left hand were broken and all of the nails torn out. Strangely, his right hand was untouched. No doubt Holt was saving it for later.

"Has the boy spoken?"

"No, Father," Holt replied, smirking in vindication at Perrick.

"Well then. That will be enough for now. If he's not spoken since you've had him, he's not going to."

He glanced at the girl. Her eyes were dead.

"Brother Thomas, be so kind as to fetch Brother Patrice. Have him bring his physikers bag," Zoller said. "No, leave the girl. She will attend the boy."

Perrick spared a glance at Lett before brusquely walking past the crates heading for the stairs.

They waited. The girl was unmoved, head downcast. Holt, gaining his feet, observed his victim and handiwork whilst avoiding Father Zoller's eyes.

Zoller himself finished his circuit of the pillar, studying the hieroglyphics. The ancient symbol for stone was clearly defined; its edges, dark with the boy's blood, stood out against the other script. So much so that Zoller brushed his fingertips over it, expecting to find it raised but instead it was smooth to his touch. Only the blood seemed to find its edge. It intrigued him.

At the heavy tread of boots, Zoller turned, just as Brothers Thomas and Patrice rounded the crates to the makeshift room.

Patrice was the oldest of the Brothers in Zoller's command and was well respected, not least because he was the company's only Physiker. His slate grey eyes took in the scene, lingered on Renco's wounded body before returning to the good Father who was watching him.

"Brother Holt, take Brothers Thomas and Diadago. We need provisioning for the road ahead," Zoller ordered.

"We leaving, Father?" Holt asked.

Zoller turned in surprise. Holt rarely questioned him, "Preparing for different eventualities, Brother."

Holt grunted, gave a curt nod, and left to do as bid.

Perrick spared a glance at Lett but her head remained downcast and she did not acknowledge him. Heaving a sigh, he turned and followed Holt.

"Stitch and dress his wounds, Brother Patrice. See he is made comfortable."

"Of course, Father." Stepping past Zoller, Patrice set his bag down and set about untying Renco.

Turning to leave, Zoller found Tuco waiting, a leering grin on his face.

"Sorry to interrupt, Father. A messenger from Twyford arrived," Tuco said. "I left him in your room."

Back upstairs, Zoller found a young man dressed in Rivercross livery waiting for him. He looked nervous and jumped when the door was opened.

"Father Zoller?"

"Of course, you have a message for me?"

"Yes, Father. Lord Trenton Twyford of Rivercross, High Lord, Knight-General and Defender of the Rivers, asks that you attend him immediately in the great hall."

"Let me refresh myself. Then you may lead the way."

"He said immediately, Father," the messenger blurted, nervously.

Zoller held his hand up, fingertips red. "I can hardly see the High Lord, Knight-General, and Defender of the Rivers with blood on my hands now can I."

Not waiting for an answer, Zoller moved to a bowl set down in a wall alcove. Thankfully it had been changed, the water fresh. Zoller bent to wash his face and hands.

\* \* \*

The bright red cassock with gold trim stood out immediately Zoller entered the great hall. It gave him a heavy feeling in his gut. A Red Bishop, one of five in the Rivers.

High Lord Trenton Twyford sat languidly on a raised dais in a throne chiselled out of a massive, jagged-edged rock that looked as if it might swallow him.

Zoller had met Twyford on several occasions. A dangerous man, his mind was as sharp as his arrogance. It was the eyes though that told. Bright blue, they were every bit as penetrating and shrewd as the Black Crow's. The comparison with Bouchemeax was apt too. For both men shared a similarity of construction; dark-haired, lean, and of medium height. The Crow though was older and hardier, like worn leather. Whereas Twyford held a softer, more refined countenance. The beard was immaculately trimmed. The hair neat and oiled, face powdered, clothes rich. In truth he looked kingly, Zoller conceded.

His boots rang out on the stone floor and the waiting Bishop turned to observe him as the hall doors boomed shut behind. In the seconds since entering, Zoller had already filtered possibilities. The blond hair ruled out four of the bishops leaving Kentworth, Bishop of Charncross. But it was not Kentworth that looked back at him. In fact, he had never met this man. His step faltered.

The Bishop held his hand out and Zoller dutifully knelt kissing the back of it. "You're Excellency."

"Rise, Father." The Bishop withdrew his hand. "We've not met. I am Jon Whent, Archbishop of Killenhess and Lord Commander of the Faith Militant."

Zoller was stunned, though hid it well enough. Killenhess was in Cumbrenan to the southeast. Home of the Red Cloaks, Killenhess observed no provincial borders and answered only to the High Cardinal in Kingsholme. Whent was spoken of with reverence by all Red Cloaks.

"Make your introductions later. I'm a busy man," Twyford drawled, interrupting from his throne. "Let's to business."

Whent turned to Twyford. "Indeed High Lord. We were discussing the garrison at the Defile and the urak horde infesting your lands."

Twyford paused. Whent's tone had been neutral enough but his words rankled all the same. Twyford's fingers drummed against the stone rest of his throne. "I'm not sure why we needed to await Father Zoller but he's here now. As for my proposal, how many Red Cloaks can you spare me?"

"None, High Lord."

"None?" Twyford repeated, "Cardinal Tortuga and I reached an accord. Does the Red Church renege on this agreement?"

"I'm afraid I do not answer to Cardinal Tortuga only High Cardinal Worsten Lannik. I have received no missive from his High Holiness of any accord. Though, I would be interested to hear it."

Twyford's eyes narrowed. "Five thousand Red Cloaks landed at Rivercross. They ride north as I speak. Do not play with me. This is my kingdom and my people we are talking about."

Whent smiled; Twyford indeed looked like a king and sat as if he was one. "You mean your province, High Lord? There is only one King."

"Do not waste my time with semantics. What are you doing here if not to aid me?" Twyford growled.

"His High Holiness bid me come and assess the situation. If the urak are as many as reports suggest, I will help evacuate your people to Rivercross. I also have a sealed missive from High Lady Arisa Montreau. I am given to understand she offers sanctuary in Cumbrenan for your people."

"I need her armies, not her land. Does she not understand? If the Rivers fall Cumbrenan will be next?"

Whent stood silent, waiting. Zoller watched the interchange and wondered at it. The High Lord was right, what was the archbishop doing here?

"Bah, you play a game. One that will cost me and my people dearly," Twyford snapped. "If you will not help then I bid you leave."

"I apologize, High Lord. Distress was not my intent."

"Then what is?"

"What do you know of the urak? What is your latest intelligence?" queried Whent.

Twyford waited, considering. Then grudgingly, "They have reached the Fossa in the west. Greentower and Higholme have fallen. I have received no bird from Merik or Kroy today and fear the worst. To the north, Marston, Fallston, and Longstretch are lost and in the east, Chortonwood and Greenholme. At last report, the urak have moved no further south than that." He paused but was not yet done.

"All but a third of the Rivers is gone. The most populated third to be sure but that brings its own complications. Two thousand men fought a pitched battle north of Greenholme, only a few mounted survived." Twyford shook his head. "The only success we've had, if you can call it that, is with cavalry. We've bloodied their noses but little else."

"I see. You are in dire straits indeed, High Lord." The Archbishop's voice was flat and his demeanour had changed little, Zoller observed. The man had ice in his veins.

"It seems the enemy is difficult to meet, moving as they are upon many fronts. Who is your field commander and what are your plans?" Whent asked.

"Lord Nesto of Charncross commands. As to my plans," Twyford grimaced, "we'll fall back to Rivercross."

"So swift to abandon your lands?" Whent frowned.

"Yes, my lands. My people bleed and die as we speak," Twyford snapped, rising from his throne. "I like it not but face a stark truth. Lord Nesto cannot defeat them in the field. I know not their number but it is many times our own. In the end, our survival, stand or fall, will depend on Rivercross."

"This place has not been well maintained but it is still your strongest fortification. You choose to abandon it?" Whent raised an eyebrow.

"The Defile is formidable but the urak have shown no willingness to siege any of our castles. They do not fight like men. They do not covet our towns or riches. It is the land they seek. The Defile is guardian of a hill and the river. Strategically it is not enough." Twyford stroked his well-trimmed beard as he spoke, a sign of his nerves, Zoller thought. The High Lord continued.

"Rivercross is the seat of power in the Rivers. It has high walls and is flanked by three rivers. There we can hold out indefinitely, with relief and supplies possible from the Emerald Lake. If I lose here or elsewhere I may not have the numbers to defend her."

It was a sorry revelation and after speaking it aloud Twyford slumped wearily back onto the throne. He kneaded his temples with his fingers and shook his head, lost momentarily to those in the room. It was only a moment though. When he looked up again his eyes were hard.

"In answer, Archbishop, I'll not abandon the Defile. It can be held by a hundred hands and that is my intent. Tomorrow, I withdraw all my armies to Rivercross."

Whent barely hesitated in response. "Thank you for your candour, High Lord. The Faith Militant is ready to aid your withdrawal. For what it's worth your strategy is sound."

The archbishop glanced at Zoller, his look thoughtful before returning to Twyford. "I have an offer to make."

Twyford sat forward. "Will I like this offer?"

Whent shrugged. "Maybe. I received instruction, approved by his High Holiness, from Cardinal Tortuga. His Eminence offers five hundred of his Faith Militant in defence of the Rivers. My suggestion would be to deploy them here at the Defile. They are disciplined and have trained under duress, which will serve them well."

"How generous of the Cardinal," Twyford quipped. "As usual the Red Church offers too little too late. Tell me, who will lead this heroic band of Brothers." His eyes swivelled to Zoller, the reason for his attendance suddenly clear.

"Indeed. Cardinal Tortuga has high regard for Father Zoller's tactical acumen. He is well studied."

"Tell me, Father," Twyford asked, "How many men have you led in battle and how often?"

"I have seen no war and fought no battles, High Lord," Zoller offered. His heavy gut was threatening to expel its contents. All the while his mind raged.

With an acerbic smile, Twyford shook his head. "Well then, I can rest easy knowing the Defile is safe in your hands Father. It's a rather apt place to spend your last days."

Twyford stood, suddenly energised. "I accept. I will leave five hundred men of my own and my cousin, Duke Brant in command of the fortress when he arrives. That, I do not cede to the church. You are dismissed, both of you."

"Your will, High Lord," Whent inclined his head, before leaving. Zoller did the same falling into step behind the Archbishop.

Outside the great hall, Whent signalled Zoller forward.

"I am staying in the main keep but would like to see this pagan chapel you're staying in. I will see you tomorrow after morning prayers. I would have words before I depart."

"Your Grace," Zoller dipped his head in acquiescence, shuffling to keep pace.

"I'm given to understand one of your Red Cloaks is a Brother Tuco," Whent continued. "Strange, I have an impeccable memory but recall no Brother passing my halls by that name. I would be interested to reacquaint myself. Please have him attend in the morning."

"Many Brothers take a new name do they not, when they pass and take their final vow?" Zoller said.

Whent was unmoved by his words. "Indeed. Nevertheless, I will see him."

"Of course," Zoller agreed. It was hard to read the Archbishop, given he couldn't see his face. "He will be there; you will see that he is a troubled soul. Maybe you can reach him where I have not. I fear for him."

Abruptly stopping, Whent forced Zoller to a halt and stared at him. "You pique my intrigue, Father; until morning."

"Your Grace," Zoller ducked his head but Whent had already moved off, his stride long and purposeful.

Zoller watched him out of sight and waited. Moments passed, then Tuco materialised beside him.

"He looks pleased with hisself. Who is he?" Tuco asked.

"Archbishop Whent, Lord Commander of the Faith Militant," Zoller answered. "It is said he passes all Red Cloaks, takes their final oath himself. It's also said he never forgets a face."

Tuco cursed. "Best I keep out of sight then."

"Unfortunately, Whent insists on meeting you after morning prayer tomorrow. So don't stray far, Tuco. We'll need to resolve matters before then. You'll have need of me, and I of you," Zoller said. "Someone has betrayed me."

## Chapter 25: Burning Woman

**Grimwolds, The Rivers**

The woman screamed. High pitched, full of terror. The sound tore at her mind and shredded her heart.

It was her mother, though she knew her not. She watched transfixed, unable to do anything but observe and feel.

The screams reverberated and her view shifted. She was aware she was in a cage looking out at a crowd of people in a town square, lit by torches and sconces.

She felt tears, though did not cry them. Hands extended and gripped the bars of the cage. The hands were that of a child's, only rough and lacerated. They left bloody streaks against the iron.

Moaning. Like that of a wounded animal, scared and full of pain. The hands squeezed and the arms strained as she watched her mother, who was not, burn.

She was bound naked to a stake, arms tied high. Her blonde hair matted red. Blood dribbled from mouth to heaving breast as she fought her bindings. Flames licked her feet. She thrashed, but there was no escape and in moments her lower legs were engulfed. Her cries pitched higher, changing from fear to agony.

The child's view shifted again, sweeping past the crowd to another cage. This one held a man. It was her father, but again she did not know him. He wore horror on his face as he knelt, slumped, watching in silence. She saw no rage in him, his eyes were dead, the light behind them gone. He was broken and she couldn't bear it.

Looking back to the pyre, the woman who was not, was still alive, still screaming her suffering. Her breathing became ragged as if she couldn't catch enough air and her body started shaking uncontrollably.

The fire fed.

Then quiet. Just the crackle and spit of flames occupying the silence the woman's cries had left.

The child was weeping and she was aware that the tears were not hers. That she bore witness to another's pain and terror. It was the child's mother that was dead, her burning husk merely fuel now for the fire.

Beyond the flames, she became aware of the hushed ranks of the townsfolk, illuminated by the firelight. She saw fear and shock on many. It felt as if she knew them and they, in turn, knew her. Why had none stepped forward to help? Why had they merely stood by? Watching... Pity, anger, shame; they wore it all and she felt hatred for them, boiling through her blood. The hatred, too, was not hers; though she felt its scouring effect.

Her view stole back to the mother, unrecognisable now. Leaning forward her face mashed against the child's hands, eyes screwed tight shut to block out the image. Heart wrenched, she sobbed raggedly but couldn't escape it. The flaming body was imprinted in her mind and the wood smoke carried the sulphurous stench of burnt hair and sickly sweet aroma of charred flesh.

She collapsed to the cage floor, shaking. The grief and fear, though not her own, was overwhelming.

A figure approached, silhouetted by the firelight. It stepped in front of the cage and spoke. The voice was gentle and she found herself straining to hear it.

"Your mother was a heretic who refused to recant." The priest crouched in the dirt before her, red-robed and solemn.

Emotion flipped, turning to a towering rage. Head raised, hatred glared through tear-filled eyes at the holy man.

"It's not too late for you boy. Save yourself. Repent…" The priest intoned, flinching as a crash and scream tore out from the adjoining cage.

"Get away. Don't you touch him!" An arm flailed, grasping but not quite reaching.

Staring at her Da who was not, she saw his anger and grief and felt a tiny hope kindle inside. There was life in him still.

The priest was smiling, the glint of his teeth bright in the reflected firelight. Extending a hand through the bars he placed it on her head. It seemed a benediction. Then he patted her like a man would a favoured dog.

Madness filled her, a madness observed and which she had no control over. The child's hand lashed out through the bars.

The priest moved, but not quickly enough. A nail gouged his cheek narrowly missing his right eye, tearing off a bloody strip of skin and flesh.

Falling backwards the priest roared. Standing slowly, breathing heavily, he brushed his red cassock down where dirt had soiled it. Blood tracked like a teardrop down his face and she watched him touch a hand to his cheek. He examined the blood on his fingertips then glared at her.

"You'll burn in hellfire boy, but not before I have the skin stripped from your back." The words were spoken softly, but his eyes gave lie to the calmness in his voice.

She felt afraid and found herself scrambling to the back of the cage, her small act of defiance spent. Piss soaked her breeches though she could not recall wetting herself.

The priest stared stony-eyed through the bars.

"After the lash, I will give you a night to contemplate your sins. Then it'll be your turn at the stake."

The man, who was not her father, was swearing and spitting still. Flailing, he tried and failed to reach the priest, who turned, watched for a moment, then spoke, his calm manner disturbing.

"You can save him. It's too late for you but you can save your boy." He cocked his head to the side. "No? Got nothing to say?" The priest's lips pouted in mock sadness. "At least have the courage to admit you're of the Order?"

The child's father lapsed into silence. She saw his nostrils flare and his jaw tense.

The priest shrugged as if he cared not one way or the other for his confession. "I'll ask once more in the morning. Your answer will determine if your boy accompanies you to the fourth hell, or not. Until then, make peace with your gods, heretic."

She watched the priest daub at the blood on his cheek before turning and walking away, back straight. His red cassock seemingly alive as the light of the burning pyre played across it.

Nihm sat bolt upright. She was breathing hard and felt hot sweat on her brow.

<Your heart rate is elevated. Your brain patterns show heightened activity and I am sensing increased oxygen and hormone levels. There are no external threats and your body's recharge is functioning as expected. What is wrong?> Sai asked.

<A dream. A… a nightmare.> Nihm took a deep breath, steadying herself. <It was real. I was there Sai, like it happened.>

She was upset, the memory of it so vivid; the child's hurt and suffering, all that she'd borne witness to….

To her consternation, Sai seemed uninterested.

<Didn't you see it?>

<Dreams are a succession of images, ideas, emotions, and sensations that occur involuntarily in the mind during certain stages of sleep, most typically REM sleep. I am not fully aware of their purpose, though my information databases indicate they have been a topic of scientific, philosophical, and religious interest. Numerous theories abound.>

<Yes, yes, forget all that. If you didn't see or feel it just say so,> Nihm snapped. <But I'm telling you Sai, it was so real. I think it actually happened. It was like watching through somebody else's eyes. A child's eyes. I saw what they saw and felt what they felt. It was… horrific.>

<Mercy approaches,> Nihm thought she detected a hint of relief in Sai's tone.

The moons of Ankor and Kildare were out, casting a pale light, more than enough to spy Mercy as she picked her way through the camp. Nihm was aware of Ash's shaggy head settling back down beside her. Snow hadn't bothered to raise hers but her ears were erect and locked towards the far side of camp.

Mercy was on the last watch, dawn would not be far away. The tall woman stepped carefully around a snoring Maohong and the still form of Master Hiro and crouched beside her.

"You cried out. Are you alright?" Mercy touched a hand to Nihm's shoulder.

"A bad dream is all," Nihm whispered.

"Want to talk about it?" Mercy asked, squeezing her hand gently.

Nihm shook her head, no.

"Fine, I'll get back to my watch then. If you change your mind, come find me." Standing, she moved off, threading her way back through the camp.

\* \* \*

It was no use, sleep eluded her. Lately, it was dreams of Marron that kept her awake; at least this time it was something else.

Reluctantly Nihm rose, leaving her bedroll and its warmth for the icy chill of the early morning air. A hard-frost had settled overnight. Autumn was deepening, tightening its hold; the countryside a tawny riot of golden browns, yellows and reds. Winter was not far away.

Their makeshift camp lay in a small hollow, a dimple on one of the wolds, two days south of their encounter with the urak. Picking her way easily through the camp, Nihm started up the crest towards the treeline where Mercy kept watch.

Her footing slipped on the frosted slope but Nihm caught her balance without thought, refraining from using a steadying hand. Her wrist, injured during the fight with the urak, had hurt abominably at first but the last day the pain had receded to a dull ache.

<Your wrist is at eighty-one percent of operational capacity. Repairs will take another day to complete. Your material reserves, however, are low,> Sai reported.

Nihm took it in but said nothing in return. Acknowledging every interjection Sai made would drive her mad. For his part, Sai took no offence.

"Couldn't sleep?" Mercy asked as Nihm approached. Her eyes flickered to Snow and Ash who, as ever, trailed after their mistress.

"No," Nihm replied, curt.

Mercy nodded agreeably then turned back to her duty. Her post was well chosen, just inside the treeline at the crown of the hill. It afforded a clear view north and east as well as providing cover and shelter.

Nihm wasn't entirely sure why she'd come and now that she was here, quite what to say. The silence grew and she found herself listening to the night. There was plenty to hear if you paid attention; screech owls calling out among a host of other bird calls. In the distance, the belching coughs of red stags and the clash of their antlers could be heard; it was the season for rutting.

"You've had a hard time. Lost a lot, more than you should." Mercy husked. "Bad dreams are normal. My mother always said, the body heals at night and so too the mind." She grimaced at the mention of her mother, thumping a fist against her thigh. She looked across at the young woman. Nihm was as still as the tree she leant against. Mercy tried again.

"Taking a life can be hard. Tough as losing a loved one some say. It changes a person. I guess that could be true even if it's an urak. Never actually killed anyone myself. Not till the river." Mercy bit her tongue, her voice trailing off. Once a fool, twice a fool always a fool she berated herself.

The silence stretched.

"It was easy," Nihm finally said, unmindful of Mercy's clumsy attempt at consoling her.

"What was?"

"The killing," Nihm turned and stared at the mage. The livid scar on her face was hidden by the shadow of night and the worry lines of the past weeks were all but invisible. She was pretty. "I didn't feel anything when I killed those urak. Not then and not now. How did you feel?"

"What?"

"About taking that thing's life? You hit it with a ball of fire. If I close my eyes I can recall the sight and the smell and the sounds of it. You must too. Do you want to talk about it?" Nihm said.

Mercy blinked, taken aback. "No... I don't think I do."

"Same," Nihm replied.

Mercy nodded, understanding. "I'm here if you need me," she offered. "Amos says I'm a better listener than a talker."

"Same." Nihm grinned, taking the edge off her reply, and was surprised to find she meant it. Mercy's brother was lost in the North, the same as her father. They shared that at least. It was reason enough she supposed.

They sat in companionable silence for a while, comfortable with each other until the question bubbling away in Nihm's mind finally broke to the surface.

"I was told dreams are random pictures and thoughts that occur when you sleep; that there's no rhyme or reason to them. Do you think that's true?"

Mercy considered the question.

"Sometimes. But not always. Some dreams seem real until you wake. Then the memory of it is lost. Other dreams I think are memories that play out differently for whatever reason. Those I think are tangible, familiar at least and easier to retain," Mercy said. "Some show the future or what might be, or so some say. The bad ones, the night terrors…" Mercy stopped herself.

"Go on," Nihm prompted.

"It's written that some dreams cross boundaries. Different times, different places, even different people. I don't give much credence to it myself but my mother does and my father always says there's a little truth in every tale. So, who knows?"

"I think I stole a dream," Nihm said, uncertainty edging her voice.

"You mean the dream was not yours?" Mercy asked.

"It was a child's dream. A nightmare really," Nihm qualified. Now she'd started she found she needed to talk. Sai didn't understand her need and Mercy… well; she was a mage and a woman. It didn't feel quite so foolish talking to her about it.

"It was a boy's dream. I think it was real. I think he relives a terror from his past. I felt his hurt and despair. His horror," Nihm wiped a tear from her eye before it fell. "I think I know him, kind of."

She heard movement and turned. Master Hiro was climbing the slope to join them.

"Don't say anything," Nihm hissed. "I'm still working it out. Maybe I'm just being foolish."

"As you wish." Mercy laid a hand on Nihm's arm. "Let me know how it goes though okay and… you're not being foolish."

They waited for Hiro to join them saying nothing more. Nihm thought he must be cold in his cloth leggings and shirt with just his brown monk's robe over the top but if so he gave no outward sign of discomfort.

"I'm not disturbing you both I hope?" Hiro asked. Snow brushed up against him and he laid a hand on her in greeting.

"Nihm couldn't sleep, thought we'd watch the dawn come in," Mercy replied.

Hiro grunted. He crouched easily onto his haunches and considered them both before looking eastward. Yellows and reds blossomed on the horizon, sunrise indeed approached.

"We will clear the Grimwolds later today. A further two days should see us to the road from Karsten Abbey. We need to make some decisions between now and then," Hiro said.

"You've made all the decisions since Fallston and we're still alive," Mercy said grudgingly. "If the urak haven't beaten us south what are you proposing?"

"I am taking Mao to Kingsholme. The fastest way is through Rivercross and then a boat south," Hiro said.

"You're an Order Knight, Hiro. We all know it even though you don't talk of it," Mercy said. "You know fastest is not always quickest. There is danger for you in Rivercross. Nihm as well."

"Just so. Nevertheless, I have an errand in Rivercross. It is my path. Mao's as well."

"You mean to save Renco don't you," Nihm said.

Hiro inclined his head.

"You mean to part ways with us then?" Mercy said, reading his intent. "You know this priest Zoller lays a trap for you."

© 2020 A D Green

"Still I must go," Hiro replied.

"What? No. I can help. We all can," Nihm said. Mercy laid a hand on her arm, stilling her protest.

"What do you propose?" Mercy repeated.

"Keeper searches for you, child." Hiro looked at Nihm. "But he doesn't know who you are, yet." A quick glance at Mercy then back to Nihm. "I have reservations. I'm not sure you're ready to meet Keeper. Not yet anyway. Besides, it should be your choice when and if you do and it should be an informed one."

Hiro turned to Mercy, "When we reach the road to Karsten Abbey, head to Fastain and cross the Fossa. Then make your way to Wooliston, a village two days south of Rivercross on the Emerald Lakes western shore. If you would wait, I will meet you there."

"And then?" Mercy asked.

Hiro shrugged. "South certainly, I must get Mao to Kingsholme as I said before but I would stop and see your father on the way. I have need of his counsel.

"What of my father," Nihm blurted. She'd thought little about him the past day. He was always present in her mind, he never left her but it was like she had closed that part off. Unwilling to consider the possibility he was dead and gone. She felt guilty for it.

"Darion is capable. He will come for you if he is able. First though, he'll make contact with the Order. When he does, I will know and from there we can plan. I would tell you, Nihm, that if you do go to the Order Halls it may be many years before you're allowed to leave. You should know that at the very least."

As Nihm considered Hiro's words, hope for her father kindled anew. Somehow she knew he lived, he must and he would come for her. Nihm saw that Mercy was deep in her own thoughts. Whatever they were though, she didn't share them.

"I will rouse the others." Hiro rose to his feet. "We've many leagues to cover today. Since half of us are up already we may as well make an early start."

Nihm watched as he headed back to camp leaving them to mull over his words.

## Chapter 26: He Came, He Whent

**The Defile, The Rivers**

Renco groaned. He was in pain; deep, intense, physical.

The pain, though unwanted, was familiar. It had been a part of his life since he was a child. Master Hiro had taught him long ago how to cope with it. He knew how to wall the mind and mask the pain so that it did not become all-consuming. Why then today did he struggle so? It gnawed at him making it hard to think or focus.

He was laid on his front on padded sackcloth on the cold stone floor. It was how the Red Cloak physiker, Patrice had left him after stitching his wounds and splinting his broken fingers.

He stank as well. Patrice having painted a solution over his injuries to ward against infection or so he claimed. The evil-smelling concoction smarted as it went on and his skin still stung with it now.

"You spoke." An accusation.

Renco twisted, facing Lett where she sat on her own sackcloth bed. She looked immeasurably sad. He shook his head.

"Yes, you did." Lett insisted. "You thrashed about so in your sleep I was worried you would tear your stitches. You were dreaming, or else delirious. But you spoke a name. I heard it, clear as anything. Marron."

Renco recoiled at the name. He knew no Marron but nevertheless, it rocked him.

As if looking through a frosted pane, he had a vague sense. A reminiscence; of looking up at a woman as if he lay upon the ground. She had a dagger in her chest and a man reaching, grasping for her as she fell disappearing into a fog. Moments later a roar of flame and the young, bedraggled man exploded in a ball of fire.

In his recollection, Renco screamed a name but no voice came out, he had no voice. But the name, it was Marron.

Shaking his head to clear his mind, Renco pulled himself gingerly into a sitting position and looked at Lett. He shrugged his shoulders and shook his head again.

"I heard it plain and simple. You can talk, Renco," Lett said. She sighed, tired of his denial. At least you have a mother to remember, she bit her lip at her turn of thought. A tear glistened at the corner of her eye. Angry, she gritted her teeth and glared.

"Keep your secrets. It's of no matter to me." Lett got up and crossed the floor to the shuttered window. Throwing them wide a sharp icy wind entered, ruffling her hair.

"We have to get away."

Gazing out, Lett was afforded a magnificent panorama. In the fresh light of a new dawn, the whole of the land seemed to stretch away before her. To the north on the horizon a shadowed verge that must be the Grimwolds. West, hillocks framed the river and past them, verdant flat grasslands and wilderness. Through it, a road traced like a vein slowly disappearing into nothing.

A sudden urge took hold and feeling emboldened, Lett lay across the deep ledge and looked down. A faint sense of vertigo tickled her gut and fear trickled down her spine. They were so high up and the cliff face sheer to the river below.

She startled. Renco was behind her, silent as a ghost. Shuffling upright again, Lett wrinkled her nose; this particular ghost stank of liniment. His breath was warm on her cheek as he leaned past her, looking at the vista beyond.

Easing Lett to the side with his good hand, Renco felt her flinch. She was scared, of him?

He lay where Lett had been moments before. The fortress wall was thick and the ledge easily wide enough that he could jump up on its sill and throw himself out if he chose. Foolish, the fall would kill him. Even if he could leap far enough to clear the rock face and make the river, still it was too high.

His eyes scanned the Defile's wall and then the cliff face searching for something, anything.

"What are you doing?" Lett's hand pressed into the small of his back as if she thought he might fall. Pain flared at her touch and he grimaced pulling himself upright again.

"There might not be bars on the window but this is a cell, Renco. The only way out is up the stairs we came down." Lett said. Then, suddenly, "Why won't you talk to me?"

Exasperated, Renco shook his head. He couldn't, why didn't she understand?

He took a slow breath to calm himself. He might have no memory of it but her assertion that he'd spoken was real. She believed it, he could tell that much from her eyes. Renco opened his mouth but the only sound was as he gagged. Frustrated, embarrassed, he turned away sitting back on his sackcloth.

Footsteps echoed on the stairs and moments later Tuco appeared around the side of the crates. A large coil of rope was looped over his shoulder. Looking between the two of them he leered.

"Lovers tiff, eh."

Tuco walked to the embrasure sending Lett scurrying backwards. Her fear of him was obvious and he enjoyed it a moment before shrugging the rope coil onto the ground.

Whistling a tune as he worked, Tuco bent, picking up one of the rope ends, and measured off five paces. Looping the end around the ancient pillar, scarred still with the boy's blood, he cinched a knot and tugged upon the line. Satisfied it was secure he walked back toward the window. Picking up the other rope end, Tuco turned.

"Who's first then?"

Lett looked at Renco then back at Tuco.

"What are you doing?" Lett asked.

"You need to get out. I need to get out. So we're getting out," Tuco explained. "Any more questions?"

Lett glanced at Renco who shook his head, no.

"That rope ain't long enough. Not by a long chalk," Lett challenged, unable to keep the quiver from her voice.

Tuco laughed, "This 'ere is over a hundred feet of rope. Ten ropes like this wouldn't reach the bottom, girlie. But it's more 'an long enough fer what's needed."

Renco shook his head again and Tuco rounded on him.

"You got someat to say. Oh wait, you don't do you, never got nothing to say." Tuco grinned and Lett shivered. His expression the same as when he ran his knife blade across her father's throat.

When it was clear neither would move, Tuco scowled.

"I've never known folk so reluctant ta get rescued. Look, between the footing and cliff proper is a small ledge. Only a foot at most but it's the best we got. Get to that and untie yourself. Inch your way to the right, sixty, seventy paces and you'll make the side. The rock climbs another twenty feet or so after that but there's plenty of handholds. Once over, we pick our way round to the front and join the carters and traders going down. Slip away, easy as pie."

Lett looked uncertain. The view and the vertigo were still fresh in her mind. It was a long way down. She jumped as Tuco lurched towards her.

"Fuck sake, you wanna die here? With that cockhead Perrick bangin' ya whenever he wants? Ya think he gives two shits about you?" Tuco snarled. "You're just a cunt to him whatever he whispers in ya ear. Now come on."

Lett recoiled at his touch but he was persistent and before she knew it the rope was around her waist, tied and knotted.

"Me and the boy will lower you down. Do not freeze. Keep the weight over your feet, small steps and you'll be fine. The sooner you untie the rope and move away the sooner loverboy here can join ya. Then me. Quick now." Tuco's tone brooked no argument and he backed Lett up until her legs brushed against the embrasure.

She had no time to think. Body shaking, her mind numb with fear, Lett sat on the ledge. "I can't do it, I just can't."

"Fuck me. I don't know why I bother."

With no warning, Tuco thrust forward, pushing Lett hard in the chest. Flying back, her hands flailed but got no purchase on the stone, and with a screech, she pitched backwards out of the window. Tuco gripped the rope as it spooled out before her exit could gain momentum and sinews straining, arrested her fall. He could hear her mewling cry below.

"I can't do it. Please, please, pull me up."

Ignoring her pleas, Tuco played out an arm's length of rope. "Boy, come help. Bitch is heavier than she looks."

Moving behind, Renco reached out. He didn't take the rope though. Instead, he slipped the knife from Tuco's belt.

"Woo, what are ya doin' lad?"

Renco thought he detected a hint of panic. Good. He leaned forward to slip the knife in but the assassin was already in motion.

Relinquishing his hold on the rope, Tuco dropped, rolling away.

Renco phased. Time dilated and his mind spun weighing options.

Tuco seemed to hover before him, falling slowly to the side. Time enough for a killing blow. But the rope hissed on the stone as it played out, Lett was falling. Tied as she was, a hundred-foot rope fall with a sudden stop could prove fatal or badly injure her. With the fingers of his left hand broken and splinted his choice was already made.

Releasing the knife, Renco grabbed at the rope. It burnt as he gripped it, tearing at his skin and threatening to pull him through the opening. Planting his feet against the stone wall beneath the embrasure, muscles screaming, he held on.

Renco phased back and Lett's faint cries reached him from below. How far had she fallen? Not too far he judged. There was a scrape of metal on stone and he knew Tuco picked up the dagger from the floor.

"Kildare's cock, ya surprised me there, boy." Tuco blasphemed with a wry chuckle. "Ya've restored my 'lack' of faith in humanity."

In his periphery, Renco sensed the Red Cloak move behind him and was helpless to do anything except hold onto the rope. Master would berate him. Better one should die than two he would say but Renco couldn't bring himself to let go. He waited for the blade to come. Felt blood trickle down his back where his stitches had torn. It was of no consequence now.

But the blow never landed. Instead, Renco felt the rope shiver and tremble through his hand. Twisting his head, Tuco hacked at the rope and it parted with a snap. Were he to let go now, Lett's fall would be to the bottom, smashed upon the rocks at the foot of the Defile.

The mere thought of it seemed to increase the pull on his grip. He grabbed the rope with his other hand trying to ease the burden but his broken fingers couldn't bend or grasp it.

Throwing his head back, Renco strained, the veins in his neck bulging at the effort. He couldn't afford to let the rope slip an inch. Tuco had cut it leaving no length behind. How long could he hold her? Long enough he hoped for Lett to find and reach the ledge the assassin spoke of if it was there at all. Distantly, he became aware of a sound. Footsteps, two sets he counted. He groaned.

"What goes on here?" Father Zoller.

"Where's Lett?" Thomas Perrick.

"Girl's out the window and probably halfway down by now," Tuco said, "Caught 'em trying to escape."

"Brother Thomas, assist young Renco please in holding the rope. We don't want any accidents," Father Zoller said.

Perrick moved to help but Renco was already wedged with his feet lodged beneath the window.

"Hurry up man, before he lets go," Zoller snapped.

Straddling and reaching past, Perrick leant across the sill and braced himself before getting a firm grip on the rope. Taking the weight, he shouted out the window.

"Lettie. Lettie. It's me, Thomas. Hold on and I will pull you up."

"Well now, let's not be too hasty," Zoller said.

Something in his tone made Thomas twist and look back over his shoulder. "Whatever do you mean, Father? We have to pull her up."

"Yes, but first, what did you tell Archbishop Whent?" Zoller asked.

"What do you mean? Father Zoller please, I've not spoken to his Excellency. I swear it."

"When you swear an oath to Kildare you pledge your soul. Give up all worldly ties. The church is your first family." Zoller said. "Still, Brother Patrice tells me your brother from before is also a Red Cloak. That he's in the Archbishop's personal guard no less. More than that, you met with him on arrival. Before I even knew his Excellency was here. I ask myself. How can this be?"

"Happenstance, I was at the gatehouse when they arrived. I knew not they were arriving, I swear it, Father. I spoke briefly with my brother whilst they were billeted, nothing more."

"You are subordinate to me and yet felt this was somehow not worthy of my time or attention?" Zoller pressed.

"My brother asked me to keep my peace. His Excellency wished to make enquiry first before calling upon you. That is all."

"So your brother, from before, ordered your silence," Zoller said, his tone neutral.

"I'm sorry, Father. I saw no harm in it."

"What of Brother Tuco? It seems his Excellency has taken a rather keen interest in him and I wonder why that might be."

"I don't know, Father. Please, let me pull her up."

Zoller nodded and Perrick turned in relief. "Thank you."

As Perrick strained, pulling up an arm of rope, Renco grimaced. The numb ache of tired muscles screamed at him as the weight was relieved; his back was afire with sudden pain.

He was aware of Tuco stood next to him. The swarthy Red Cloak's hand was empty, his knife returned to its sheath on his belt. Tuco glanced at him, his eyes bright with cruelty his lip curling. Renco saw death in that smile. Casually, reaching a hand out, Tuco pushed and sent him stumbling to the side.

Perrick cried out as the rope bit, pulling him hard against the embrasure. Leaning forward, Tuco bent grabbed Perrick around the legs and hoisted with surprising strength.

A scream of shock and raw terror ripped from Thomas's throat. Relinquishing the rope, he flailed wildly at the stone sill as he was launched up and out of the window. The rope too would have followed had Renco not still grasped it.

The diminishing scream seemed long then cut off abruptly.

"Stop admiring your handy work Tuco and pull the girl up. I presume she's still on the end." Zoller said.

A grinning Tuco seized the rope and started heaving. It was hard work and Lett, a dead weight to begin with. She found her feet though and steadied herself and Tuco was soon pulling the rope in arm over arm until finally, a blonde dishevelled head appeared at the aperture.

Pale-faced, eyes full of terror, Lett was half dragged and half slid across the wide stone sill until she collapsed on the floor. Her whole body trembled with shock.

"Very good, Tuco, now, make yourself scarce. The Archbishop will be here after morning prayers. Speaking of which, I best get myself back upstairs."

\* \* \*

"Explain it to me again." Archbishop Whent asked, looking about at what was clearly a storeroom.

"Excellency," Zoller inclined his head.

"Brother Thomas fell to his death from this window after trying to escape with the young woman he was meant to be guarding. I did not question his faith. An error in judgement I now realise. Talking to my Red Cloaks they say he was besotted with the girl. I believe he thought he was in love. What else could turn him from Kildare?"

A Red Cloak, one of four attending Archbishop Whent, looked agitated. Now he knew to look, Zoller could see the family resemblance.

"I see." The archbishop gave a leery stare at the hulking form of Brother Holt and next to him the older brother, Patrice. Both were arranged behind, Father Zoller. Holt impassive, Patrice pensive. He dearly wanted to question them but couldn't, not directly. Unless he had clear evidence to the contrary it would call into question the integrity of the church. A Red Cloak's word could not be held above that of a priest.

"And you say Brother Tuco is missing," Whent said, "If you were not a Holy Father of the Red Faith, one might say rather conveniently so."

"I do not believe it convenient for Brother Tuco, Excellency," Zoller replied. "He was on duty here at the time of Brother Thomas's demise and given the fact he is not here now, I fear the worst. The stairwell and these windows are the only exits. Brother Holt has assured me that he has questioned his Brothers and none saw Brother Tuco take the stairs."

Walking to the window, Whent leaned out. It was a long drop to the river below. A splash of red could be seen on the rocks edging the river. A red cloak shrouding a body or blood, he wondered. He saw no sign of a second such marking.

"Have some men recover the body below. If it is not Brother Thomas maybe it is this Brother Tuco. Either way, we will send it onward. Kildare will be their judge now." Whent touched a clenched fist to his stomach and bowed his head in brief obeisance. A gesture repeated by all in the room.

"Now, I would like to see these prisoners," Whent announced.

Zoller gestured to a pair of Red Cloaks watching from the edge of the crated room and turning they disappeared from view.

Whilst waiting for their return, Whent inspected the room. It didn't take long. It was packed with barrels and crates of supplies. The window and the ancient pillar were the only features of note. The pillar was like the ones in the chapel above, finely etched with pictograms and symbols. This one though had dried blood smeared across it.

The clatter of many feet sounded on the stairwell and Whent turned expectantly. Moments later the two Red Cloak guards reappeared pushing a young man and woman before them.

"This is Renco. A mute," Zoller said. "The woman is Letizia, a bard's daughter. They are both detained for their association with the Order."

"You have questioned them?" Whent asked.

"Yes, and I still do."

Whent gave careful regard, the Father's tone was neutral and he appeared composed. He glanced at the pillar then the prisoners.

"Take your shirts off," Whent ordered.

The young man barely paused before reaching and unfastening buttons using just his right hand. Whent noted the fingers on his left were bandaged and splinted. The woman didn't move.

"Both of you," Whent drawled, his eyes boring into the woman's. Cowed, she reached tentative hands to her shirt and slowly unfastened buttons until finally, the shirt slipped from her shoulders. He saw she wore a strapping across her chest, but even so, she covered herself with hands and arms.

Whent found both man and woman breath-taking but for entirely different reasons. The woman was stunning despite the mussed hair and pale, haunted face. Her blue eyes were downcast and stared at the floor but even so, they were captivating. He could see the trouble such a woman might cause.

The man on the other hand looked wretched; his body a rich bruising of browns and yellows. His eyes were clear though and his face composed as if his battered body troubled him not at all.

"Turn," Whent ordered.

Slowly the man turned. His back was worse, so much worse. Fresh blood did little to hide the stitched cuts that crisscrossed his flesh or the massive welts of new and old scar tissue. He didn't look twenty summers old, to have borne so much.

"Did the mute say anything?" Whent asked his voice dry.

It was not difficult to sense the archbishop's unease and Zoller knew he already trod a fine line. "We did not know him to be mute. Still might not be."

"Has he spoken a single word?" Whent asked.

"No, Your Grace."

"Very well. I'll take them both. Gather what belongings they have. I leave within the hour."

"Your Grace, if I may, they are part of a larger plan. The boy at least," Zoller said.

"No longer, Father. Your sole purpose now is the defence of this fortress," Whent said. "Turn your mind to that."

"He is bait for an Order Knight. Excellency, I beseech you," Zoller pleaded.

"Enough. If this Order Knight you speak of believes you have his man, he will come whether or not you have him," Whent reasoned. "You have larger concerns now. Do not test my patience any further, Father."

Zoller bowed. "Forgive me, Your Grace."

Watching, Renco was intrigued at the sudden turn of events. He saw the subtle tightening of skin at the corners of Zoller's eyes and the clenching of his jaw. The priest was not happy. His demeanour didn't improve any when Brother Patrice rolled up his and Lett's bedrolls.

At a sign from Whent, Renco shrugged back into his bloodied shirt and grasped his things from Patrice. He put his leather jerkin and cloak on, Patrice helping him with the clasp, before tucking his sackcloth bedroll under his arm.

Satisfied they were ready, Whent spun and glided from the room his red cloaks forming up behind and around Lett and Renco.

As he left, Renco spared a final glance back and locked eyes with Zoller. *Nothing is forgotten, nothing forgiven. I will kill you*, Renco's eyes said. A look mirrored by the priest.

## Chapter 27: Dead Metal

**Confluence, The Rivers**

The ring was uncomfortably cold on his finger. Darion twisted it out of habit. Nothing. Not a glimmer of warmth. There hadn't been since that day. Now, it was just dead metal.

He should take it off. String it on a neck chain or keep it in a purse now that part of his life was over and gone. But he couldn't bring himself to do it. The ring had been a part of him for sixteen years. Its icy touch was a small price to pay for the remembrance.

Inevitably, his thoughts turned to his daughter. Did Nihm live or had she perished with Marron? Not knowing hurt. It was like a thorn in his mind and every day that he couldn't pull it free it lodged a little deeper. At night, when he lay in his bedroll, the guilt ate away at him. They had failed her, him and Marron. Hadn't ever told her who they were or why they lived as they did. Nor about the Order and their place in it.

If she lived, Nihm would be lost. She knew of no one to help her. Other than their occasional excursions to Thorsten, she had experienced nothing of the world. They had coddled her, Darion realised; kept her isolated, and told themselves it was to keep her safe. Instead, they'd endangered her. He'd taught her hunting and survival and a thousand other skills but still left her ill-prepared.

If, she still lives. The barb was set deep.

The town of Confluence lay ahead. It was a distraction from his moroseness. It was one of the few settlements on the Fossa where the river bordered the Old Forest.

Rivers folk were rightly superstitious of the Old Forest. Many who entered its dark interior were never seen again. It instilled a mysticism and mythical fear of the ilfanum lands. Despite this, the Fossa still drew humanity like a lodestone. The river was too valuable not to utilise. It provided water and food for holdsteaders and townships alike as well as passage for trade and commerce.

Confluence itself lay at the juncture of the river where it split, diverging around a rocky formation called the Blade, so named because it appeared to slice the river in two. The southern branch of the river became the Rosen and flowed into Westlands. The eastern branch remained the Fossa reaching to Rivercross and emptying into the Emerald Lake.

The original town of Confluence was established on rising ground and was contained behind an earthwork foundation upon which a solid, drystone wall was built. Renowned for its artful construction and strength, it attracted much interest from Master Stone Mason's from across the Nine Kingdoms.

The citizens of Confluence though held it in different regard. Over the years the walls embrace had not managed to contain the burgeoning population. As the town expanded the wall delineated the well to do, who lived within its bounds, and the rest, who lived without. Wood mills, tanning yards, stonemasons, and other manufactories were typically arranged outside the walls, extending from the river docks and surrounds, right up to the wall.

Earlier in the day, Darion and his fellowship passed several mining villages as they crossed the Pemloc Knolls. The smelters and forges were cold though and the mines lay abandoned. The roads too were empty of travellers. The few people they did pass were holdsteaders further removed from Confluence that had received word late of what was coming.

Clearing a small wood, they crossed a bridge over a winding, swollen brook. Fields and orchard groves stretched before them with neatly thatched buildings scattered between. No smoke rose from their chimneys and they could see no one toiling. Smoke did rise though from the distant town. Thin black laces, spiralling skyward before eddying and dispersing, picked apart by the wind.

Bezal, circling above, flew down. With a beating of wings, the raven alighted upon R'ell's shoulder.

"Many riders come," R'ell stated.

"Soldiers?" James Encoma asked.

"Riders." R'ell shrugged.

"They'll be soldiers right enough, lad," Kronke said.

It wasn't long before they came into view and Kronke's assertion proved right. The many riders being a regiment of lancers two thousand strong, riding three abreast.

As they drew close, Darion led his party off the road and into a field of barley stubble to wait for the procession to pass. Father Melbroth, with his newly acquired acolytes, moved to the back with their white cowls pulled up to cover their faces.

The soldiers all stared as they rode past, many of them hard-eyed and grim-faced. They wore the brown and gold of Confluence and bore banners depicting three rivers all meeting in the centre with a sword overlaid. A rider peeled away from the column and approached. Drawing his horse to a stop he looked them over before settling his eyes on Kronke.

"Black Crows unless I miss my mark. You're a long way from home?" His look was flinty and the question barbed.

"Ai," Kronke replied.

An uneasy silence, the thud of hooves loud, as the moment stretched. The man's horse fidgeted, feeling the tension from its rider.

"Four black crows, two holdsteaders, three white priests, and all I get is 'Ai'. Think you'll have ta come with me, the knight-commander will want more than that."

Darion shook his head exasperated. Kronke was a thick-headed mule sometimes. He opened his mouth to speak but the priest beat him to it.

"Forgive his lack of conversation." Father Melbroth lowered his hood. "It's been a hard road. The good sergeant escorts me and my brethren to Rivercross."

"Heard Thorsten had fallen and Greentower," the rider said. "Strange you travel to Rivercross yet end up at Confluence. A suspicious man might think it a short journey down the Rosen to Westlands."

"A reasonable man would know its five days downriver to Rivercross. You have the right to question my son but the simple truth is, urak have directed our travel as much as our intent," Father Melbroth replied. "We left Merik the day before last and it was all but deserted. And yesterday morning there was smoke in the north. Merik burns and the horde come yet you ride into the storm. Might I ask why?"

The rider grimaced in apology. "I'm sorry, Father. These are strange times." He glanced over his shoulder at the columns of horse clattering by. "My Lord, Idris

Inigo has been ordered to Rivercross but needs time to evacuate everyone so we are sent to harry the enemy. If we can, we'll hold them at Sarton Ridge."

The tail of the column was fast approaching and the rider looked again at it before reaching a decision. "There's a bridge at Miller's Cross a league east of Confluence. Lord Idris moves our people across it to the south bank of the Fossa. You should take it. You'll find no boats in Confluence to ferry you to Rivercross. I bid you good fortune."

"Thank you for the advice. May Nihmrodel aid your travel, Ankor bolster your heart, and Kildare strengthen your arm," The priest replied.

The rider ducked his head at the blessing, touching a hand to his head and heart and a clenched fist to his stomach. Pulling sharply on the reins he spun his horse about and cantered back up the column.

They watched while the last of the lancers trotted past. Father Melbroth, newly inspired, offered blessings to them as they rode by. Then they were alone.

"So, Miller's Cross?" Kronke asked.

"Confluence," Darion said. "There's a woman I need to see. You though should await me at Miller's Cross."

There ensued a brief but heated argument. M'rika insistent she would go with Darion. Father Melbroth was equally adamant as if suspecting the Orderman of duplicity. In the end, a disgruntled Darion led them all across the fallow fields and green pastures to Confluence.

\* \* \*

The town was large, about half again as big as Thorsten, Darion guessed as they entered the north side. It was definitely dirtier and the buildings looked tired and worn. Piles of refuse lay on many of the street corners and in the glooming autumnal light of late afternoon the glint of rat's eyes could be seen as they foraged.

The street they were on was wide but not as busy as it might have been. The people looked anxious with most headed in the opposite direction. Families in the main, carrying what they could or pushing carts laden with their worldly possessions. Seeing the White Priests many called out, begging for a blessing. Only one obliged though. The other two sat tall, shrouded in silence.

Darion had been to Confluence a few times in the past but it had been many years ago and the place did not match his recollection. He did however recognise the column bearing the statue of Richard Varthenon. The landmark could be seen rising above the rooftops and gave him a bearing in the maze of streets. The statue itself was situated in Traders Square and Darion was hopeful he could find her house from there.

Traders Square, when they entered it, was impressive for its size and the tall column at its centre but little else. The stalls that once occupied large portions of the square were mostly gone leaving it open and bare; the discarded evidence of them littering the ground.

The shopfronts and taverns around the perimeter of the square were boarded and closed and if not for the steady trickle of people from the myriad cut-outs, alleys, and streets around its periphery the place would have looked abandoned.

A score of soldiers in their brown and gold livery stood guard at one of the streets. Behind them, a hundred paces back loomed the old town walls.

The fellowship made their way to the water troughs, arranged like bollards around the column, and let the horses rest and drink their fill, Bindu too. The wolfdog placing her front paws on the rim of one trough and lapping thirstily.

"I go alone from here. I'll return within the hour." Darion stated.

"You are my guide. I will come with you," M'rika insisted.

Melbroth's wrinkled face told Darion the earlier arguments of before were about to be repeated. He held his hand up to forestall them all.

"You have my word."

"R'ell will wait with you," M'rika said as if settling the matter.

Darion wasn't entirely happy but the priest at least considered her statement. R'ell for his part said nothing, his demeanour as stoic and unchanged as ever. He did sign with his hands and M'rika signed back. It was so quick, if Darion hadn't been looking for it, he would have missed it. He wasn't the only one to have witnessed it though.

"What's he sayin?" Jess Crawley said.

M'rika stared at the woman regarding her. "The ilfanum are not like humans. We do not speak untruth. We do not covet material things. We are Da'Mari's guardians first and last. Your lack of knowledge and understanding is a familiar one. That you distrust that which you do not understand saddens me."

"So ya not sayin then?" Jess sneered.

There was a ghost of a smile and a hint of teeth from M'rika. "R'ell does not wish to leave my side. But he will because I ask it."

The ilf turned to Darion. "Shall we go?"

"Ai. Bindu stay."

Sitting obediently on her haunches, Bindu watched her master, as still as the statue above.

Darion strode off before any more could be said. He glanced at the distant brown and golds. They had taken note of their small company but had not moved from their post. He hoped that would remain the case.

Giving them a wide berth, Darion headed for one of the southern roads. The tavern on its corner was familiar though its name now read the Golden Tap. M'rika followed, silent but for the swish of her robes.

* * *

It took entirely too long to find the place. It was one dead-end and two wrong turns before he located the lane he was after.

The door he stood before was faded black and bore a sign above it depicting a roll of cloth and needle with the name 'M. Chancer Clothier' etched beneath it. That at least had not changed.

Darion knocked loudly and waited. The street was empty though a dog barked at his banging and he could hear the cries of a child from further down the lane. He was starting to think the clothier's place was abandoned. Its resident having joined the exodus to Miller's Cross.

He knocked again then stood back and looked up at the windows of the second floor. They were shuttered. His heart sank but he had to be sure.

"Someone is inside," M'rika said. Her head canted slightly to one side.

Darion pursed his lips, shrugging his shoulders he leant into the door.

"Meredith. Please, open up. It's Darion, Darion Castell. I need to speak with you."

He waited, listening.

"There is movement," M'rika said.

Darion glanced back. The ilf's hearing was extraordinarily good. He'd heard nothing and his head was to the door. At that moment he detected a sound. A faint shuffle followed by the creak of a loose floorboard.

"Meredith isn't here."

The voice was just the other side of the door. It was a young man's voice.

"Am I too late? Has she left then?" Darion asked the door.

"Who's asking?" The door replied.

"I told my name already. I need to speak with Meredith. It's a matter of great import."

"Got no customers called Castell and business is closed in case you haven't noticed. Leave. Take your friend with you."

Damn it, Darion fumed. He stilled his growing frustration and tried again. "We all need to leave. It's not safe here for any of us. I've come from the north and the urak have never been more than a day or two behind. Meredith needs to go and now."

There was a soft tump on the door, repeated a few times. Darion was about to speak, to try again when he heard the door bar sliding in its cradle. Moments later the latch lifted and the door creaked open.

The man was not quite what Darion was expecting. He was dressed as if for travel with a cloak, tunic, leggings, and sturdy leather boots. The clothes were plain but well-made and neatly stitched. It wasn't this though that surprised him. The man was dark-skinned and his eyes white and clouded over.

"You're blind?"

The man laughed. "Refreshing, most folks tell me I'm black, not blind as if I am unaware. I am of course both of these things."

"I meant no offence friend," Darion said.

Still amused the man stood back. "Guess you better come in."

The young man led them through the shop front to the back rooms. They settled around a large wooden table that was worn smooth to the touch. Fabrics, of various hues and colour, hung on racks and were folded on shelves. In the hearth, a fire crackled chasing the chill from the air and providing the only light.

The man rummaged in a cupboard before he joined them at the table. It seemed to Darion he had no problem finding what he was looking for or navigating the room. As he sat, the man laid a parchment in front of Darion and placed chalk atop it.

"I am Meredith's son. You may call me David."

"No." Darion stood, "Meredith had a son called David when first I met her but he was neither black nor blind."

The man's smile was wide. He gestured. "Please sit, Master Castell." He waited until he heard Darion settle back down. "The story is my mother's to tell not mine and certainly not to strangers."

"You expect me to trust you?" Darion asked. "Where is Meredith?"

"First Master Castell I need you to answer something for me. You are from the north and knew my mother from before. I ask for a sign of your association. Please." David indicated the parchment and chalk.

Despite his blindness, Darion knew what David wanted. With a little trepidation, he picked up the chalk and drew a large circle on the parchment. Inside this circle, he sketched three smaller ones so that each kissed the other. He slid the parchment across the table and waited.

M'rika lent forward to peer at Darion's handiwork before leaning back again, silent and watchful as ever.

David took the parchment and traced his fingers over it smudging the chalk. After a while, he grunted. "Sown from the seeds of chaos they brought order." He sat back and looked at them with his clouded eyes.

"Meredith is with Lord Inigo. She went to see him three days ago. I have not seen her since though I receive an occasional message to say she is well. The last was yesterday, bidding me leave for Rivercross."

"How do you know it was she who sent these messages?" Darion asked.

"We have our methods mother and I. Trust me, it is she," David said.

Darion swore. "It's a dangerous game she's at. It's not safe to play it here and now."

"Mother would say that now is the exact time to play it. When else would it matter if not now?"

"I knew another that would answer the same. Call me Darion." He put his head in his hands thinking and massaged his forehead. He needed desperately to talk to Keeper.

Rolling up the parchment, David got up and threw it on the fire. Parchment was expensive, but Darion couldn't fault his caution even though a prudent man might simply have brushed the chalk from it. It decided him but first, he had another question.

"Does Lord Inigo, know who she is?"

"I imagine so. Else why would a clothier be of interest to him for three days?"

Darion detected a hint of concern in David's voice and couldn't blame him, "Red Priests?"

"They left two days ago. Sealed their church and took a boat to Rivercross along with a hundred Red Cloaks. Whites and Browns still here though."

"And Lord Inigo, what is he like?"

"He's liked well enough I suppose. More so if you live the other side of the walls but they say he's honourable."

"I cannot wait, nor can I risk Lord Inigo. I need to ask a favour of you," Darion said.

"Ask it."

"Tell Meredith I live. Tell her I bring the founders descendant."

David turned his blind eyes to M'rika, "Your companion?"

"Ai,"

"I thought your scent unfamiliar." Rising, David formed a triangle with his hands using thumbs and forefingers. He bowed over them. "I bid you welcome. If your mission allows time may I offer refreshment?"

M'rika rose and inclined her head. "Thank you. I am sufficient."

"We'd best go." Darion scraped his chair back.

"I will convey your message. I will go today," David said.

"Thank you. And urge Meredith to get away." Darion thought of the regiment of lancers that had passed them earlier that day. "The urak will be here in two days, no more."

\* \* \*

It was a much quicker return. Once they found a main thoroughfare it was easy enough to follow it to Trader's square.

The company stood by the statue where they'd left them but as Darion and M'rika crossed the square a detachment of brown and golds broke off from their post, an officer leading them.

Darion had a sinking feeling in his gut. It was clear from their direction the guards were making for the statue. Darion played through all the options he could think of and decided he didn't much care for any of them.

"David said Lord Idris Inigo is honourable," M'rika said, interrupting his thoughts. "If that is so, maybe we should meet with him."

"That didn't go too well for us in Greentower and Duke Brant now did it?" Darion replied.

"Duke Brant was not honourable. His aura was weak."

"Ai, well let's see what they want first. Make sure your hood covers you." He widened his step, increasing his pace so they would arrive ahead of the guards.

Bindu rushed to greet him, brushing up against his legs as if he'd been gone a day rather than an hour.

"Okay girl." Darion scratched between her ears, "Come." Bindu obediently dropped to his side and followed.

"How do you want to play this?" Kronke asked when they arrived.

"See what they want. Hopefully, they just want to know why there's a bunch of Black Crows in town," Darion said.

"I can talk to them. Like before," Father Melbroth offered.

There was no time for further chat. The officer and his guard arrived, halting ten paces away. The man cast a critical eye over each before settling on Kronke.

"Captain Harton," he said by way of introduction. "Don't recognise those uniforms but your black crow emblem tells me you're from Thorsten. That so?"

"Mal Kronke, Sergeant. Yeah, we're Black Crows," Kronke replied.

There was a pause. Darion pursed his lips but managed to stay his tongue. Thankfully Kronke was not finished.

"Been a hard road, followed all the way by urak it seems." Kronke gestured at Father Melbroth, "We're escorting the good Father here to Rivercross. We was hoping to find passage."

"Is Abbot Farley still here?" Melbroth interjected.

The captain inclined his head at Melbroth. "He is, Father. Though they leave for Rivercross on the morrow I understand. Maybe you could join them?"

"It would be good to see the Abbot again," Melbroth mused.

Harton turned back to Kronke. "It seems your charge is over sergeant. I'd like to invite you to meet my commander. You may be able to help if you come from the north." He saw Kronke glance at the woodsman that had just returned with one of the white priests.

"Maybe your companions would like to join us," Harton offered.

"I hear Lord Idris Inigo is an honourable man," Darion challenged. "Are you Captain? Wherein lies your loyalty?"

The brown and golds all tensed at his words. Captain Harton placed a hand on his sword hilt and drew his blade several inches from its scabbard.

"My loyalty is always to Lord Idris. Who are you impugn my honour, sir?" Harton said the neutral politeness gone from his voice.

"Well-spoken Captain and I apologise for my friend," Father Melbroth interrupted. "He is wary that is all and meant no slight. Might I ask, do you favour our lady Nihmrodel the White?"

The captain reluctantly tore his gaze from the woodsman and looked at the priest. He let his sword slide home then almost sheepish.

"I follow the Trinity father but forgive me, I favour Ankor." The returning smile he got from the White Father was unexpected.

"There is nothing to forgive. We are all children of the Trinity after all," Melbroth said. "Perhaps we could ask friend Darion here the reason for his question?"

Everyone stared at Darion. He could tell the guards were on edge still despite Melbroth's words, but his companions and the captain looked more expectant.

"Your reaction told me what I needed," Darion said by way of explanation. There was no apology in his tone. "I need to see Lord Inigo. I have a matter of great importance to discuss with him."

"And I'm just gonna take you like that. If not for the Crows here and the White Priests I'd have you run out of town. Dressed as you are and looking like you've not bathed in a week, I think I still might." Despite his words, Captain Harton sounded more curious than affronted.

Darion was hopeful for a second or two. Getting runoff would be a good result for him but M'rika and R'ell would no doubt be expected to follow Melbroth to meet this Abbot. Resigning himself to the situation, he waved the Captain forward.

"I would talk in private. Then you can decide if I should leave or no."

Captain Harton took only a moment to consider, his interest was well and truly piqued. Telling his men to wait, he followed the woodsman and his wolfdog as they walked just out of earshot.

The guards watched their commander avidly. At one point the captain glanced wide-eyed at the white priests. The woodsman waved one forward and the priest obliged, seeming to lean into the captain as if to speak in confidence.

When Captain Harton stood back, eyes flaring, they tensed. Then of all things, the captain went to bow, until the woodsman whispered something. He straightened up again almost immediately but they'd all seen it and wondered at it.

After a brief discussion, the captain, woodsman, and priest were walking back.

"Cousens and Stickler, on me, rest of you get back to your post," Harton ordered.

\* \* \*

The next hour saw Darion and his company escorted through town. They were passed through a large gatehouse in the walls to the old town beyond. Darion and Kronke both exclaimed at the wall's drystone construction. The large blocks fit so precisely no mortar filled the joins. It was a marvel.

In the old town, the streets were narrower but clean and the houses well-kept. The shop fronts were all closed and, like the townsfolk outside the walls, the residents looked to be packing up and leaving.

They passed a large park bordered by large gated estates that looked both impressive and excessive compared to the humbler homes around Traders Square. It was like two different worlds.

Captain Harton led them past the estates and up a road that climbed towards a large keep contained behind a drystone wall of the same type and construction as the one they had just passed through.

Harton spoke briefly to the captain on duty before they were waved through, passing under an iron portcullis. Crossing a large courtyard they entered into the keep, where Harton led them to a reception room just off the main hall.

To Darion, it was reminiscent of Greentower, and looking at the nervous faces of Morpete, Crawley, and the sweat on Pieterzon's brow he wasn't the only one to make the comparison.

"I will take you and the… er… White Fathers to see Lord Inigo," Harton addressed Darion. "For the rest. If you will wait here I'll order refreshments for you all. Please take your ease."

Darion had Bindu wait, then followed after Harton who led them down the hallway and up a wide stone staircase. They followed a balcony corridor that overlooked the hall below and Darion could see from his vantage point that the hall was filled with both people and supplies of every description. It was unclear though whether they prepared for a siege or an exodus.

Darion had no time to dwell on it any further as they were ushered through a large door into a spacious antechamber. It was empty apart from a pair of guards standing to attention by the door they had just entered through and another pair guarding the far door to the room beyond. A lone desk and chair were the only furnishings and both were empty.

The brown and golds on the far side acknowledged Captain Harton and swung the door open without any preamble. They were expected, it seemed.

Passing through, Darion found himself in a large chamber. An oaken table dominated the centre space and gathered around it were two men and a young boy of about fourteen.

The eldest of the two men had long grey hair gathered tightly and tied back in a tail. Tall and thin he wore an embroidered robe to denote his office and leant upon a hardwood staff. That, together with the prickle of hair on his arm, told Darion he was a magus and no doubt counsellor to his Lordship.

The second man was a few years younger than Darion. He was dressed casually in brown trousers and a black shirt that was of fine quality. He seemed ordinary at first glance. Plain of face and medium of build with brown hair and brown eyes. However, there was an edge to him, a tension in his sparse frame that spoke of time spent in the practise yards. He looked old enough to be a father to the boy alongside but they didn't share the look of father and son, nor the clothing; a swordsman then, a first sword.

As for the boy, he was lean and hawkish with hair the colour of old straw. His brown eyes seemed too old and knowing for the face they were in. He was attired in a similar fashion to the warrior but in the brown and gold of Confluence rather than the brown and black the warrior favoured. There was an air about him, a confidence.

The door thumped closed and moments later Captain Harton walked to the fore. "My Lord Idris, this is Darion Castell of the Order and Father Melbroth of the Lady." He made no introduction for the ilfanum.

Darion watched to see how the captain's introductions were received. The magus's eyes tightened, not exactly a surprise there, Darion thought. The sword, in contrast, looked both amused and interested. But it was the boy's reaction that was most telling. He nodded his head, beaming as if Darion was an old friend long expected.

"You Order people are not very good at staying banished," the magus observed.

"Don't be so surly, Osiris," The boy said. "Welcome Darion of the Order. I would be intrigued to hear why you would risk yourself to see me."

Not waiting for an answer, the young Lord turned to Melbroth. "Welcome to my halls, Father. I don't recognise you as one of Abbot Farley's. It's strange, finding a White Priest as a travelling companion to an Orderman given their current status in this realm."

Melbroth nodded sagely. "We are at a crux in time, Lord Idris, we face a perilous path. Finely balanced, if we move too far one way we doom ourselves. Too far the other we face annihilation," Father Melbroth said. "It's my belief we need to hold together if we are to have any chance. To scorn the Order is a luxury we do not have."

"Urak," Osiris spat. "We may not have seen them in an age but they have come before. Always we have defeated them. Once the Council of Mages and the High King get organised we will kick them back over the Torns where they belong."

"Order histories say that was one clan. Some scribes argue only a few tribes," Darion answered. "At least two clans have invaded this time, the White Hand and the Blood Skull. The ilfanum say at least one other is on the move. We've not seen this in a millennium. Not since the War of the Taken."

"Bah, talk of the Taken is merely a ploy. They are long dead and gone from this world. The Order scare-monger to ingratiate themselves back where they are no longer needed," Osiris argued.

"You have spoken with the ilfanum?" Lord Idris's eyes were bright with interest.

"I have," Darion said.

The swordmaster placed a hand on his sword in warning.

"More lies," The magus said. "What game do you play? You think Lord Idris a fool because he's young?"

"Osiris, he merely confirms what Meredith has already told us," Idris said, his voice oddly pitching low then high in excitement. "Tell me of the Ilfanum."

Darion heard the door open behind them.

"Speaking of the Order, Meredith do you recognise this fellow?" Lord Idris asked a hint of challenge in his question.

Darion spun, his eyes fastening on the woman. They did not speak for a while. It had been a long time since he'd seen her but it was Meredith. She had aged well considering it had been almost fifteen years. Her auburn hair had turned white but her face, though a little looser in flesh was hers, and the brown, thoughtful eyes were unchanged.

"You've dyed your hair?" Darion said, feeling an unexpected happiness come over him.

"Still the same Darion, I see? I'm never sure if you're flattering or critiquing me." Meredith's hand subconsciously brushed her hair. She smiled.

"It is good to see you. We need to talk." Her eyes studied him. His was a face from the past. A few more lines around his eyes and a little grey through his hair but otherwise the same solid, dependable man she remembered.

"Later, if we get the chance," Darion said, aware everyone was watching them. He returned to Lord Idris.

"My Lord, forgive two old friends their distraction. You asked about the ilfanum?"

"Yes, have you seen them? Spoken with them?" Lord Idris asked.

Darion heard the eagerness in his voice. Living the other side of the river from ilf lands the young lord held an obvious fascination for them. Many that lived in close proximity did. Darion didn't reply immediately. Instead, he turned to the white priest and gave a curt nod of his head.

The mage, the sword, and the lord watched as the two white priests hidden beneath their cowls reached up and lowered them.

"By the Trinity," Osiris gasped, shock plain on his face.

The swordmaster bent and whispered something to the young lord who listened briefly before waving him away.

"I am Idris Inigo, Lord of Confluence. I bid you welcome and offer food and shelter," Lord Idris said, his voice breaking high. His face flushed red.

M'rika inclined her head at his offer.

"I am M'rika Dul Da'Mari, Visok, and Kraal. This is R'ell, Visok, and Umphathi. We thank you and accept your hospitality," M'rika replied.

"I have read everything I can find about the ilfanum," Lord Idris gushed. "It was not much and did not do you justice, my lady."

M'rika looked at Darion then back to the child lord. "I am not your lady, I am his."

Startled, Lord Idris stared at Darion.

"She does not mean in that way, my Lord," Darion interjected quickly. "By their custom, we owe a duty to each other. She means, I believe, for you to address her by her name or Kraal. Likewise, you should address R'ell by name or Umphathi," Darion turned to the ilf.

"M'rika, my lady was meant as an honorific," Darion explained.

Lord Idris smiled, his fascination growing. "I see. I would love to learn more. Maybe we can talk later? But my first sword, Si Manko here, reminds me we are in desperate straits. Have the ilfanum come to aid us?"

M'rika shrugged. "Darion will speak for us in this matter."

Darion saw Osiris, Si Manko, and Lord Idris looking at him anew. Osiris troubled but Si Manko and the young lord intrigued. He sighed heavily.

"M'rika is an ambassador of sorts. I am charged with taking her south to Kingsholme." The lie came easily to his lips.

"Your journey to Confluence makes sense then. You hope for passage to Westlands then on to Kingsholme," Lord Idris said.

For one so young, Darion was impressed at his reasoning, even if he was wrong.

"Actually no, I have business in Rivercross. My daughter," Darion paused, closing his eyes. He'd not spoken aloud his hope that she lived. "I seek her in Rivercross. Then we go south."

"Well, it's probably safest you travel with me. Though, putting yourself or your charges within reach of the High Lord is not a good idea." The way Lord Idris said High Lord left Darion in no doubt he held no goodwill for Twyford.

"Captain Harton, bring chairs for our guests and some refreshments," Idris commanded.

"My Lord." The captain hustled from the room.

"I hear you have a wolf?" Idris asked of Darion.

"A wolfdog," Darion corrected.

"I would like to see it," Idris said. Turning to the ilf he bowed from the waist, first to M'rika and then again to R'ell. "We'll speak later Kraal. For now, please take your ease. I will return shortly."

He followed the mage out of the room, Si Manco at his back.

Darion faced the others. "That went better than I expected."

"Do all human towns smell this bad?" R'ell asked. "When can we leave it? And why does a child rule?"

"We will leave when we can," Darion promised, ignoring R'ell's first question. Meredith interjected.

"Lord Idris has several boats to take his household east," Meredith said. "I have been offered a place on them. He will offer you one as well I am sure."

© 2020 A D Green

The ilf looked at Meredith, their cool dark eyes assessing. She bowed and both R'ell and M'rika acknowledged it with a short sharp nod.

"I am Meredith Chancer. Like Darion, I am of the Order. In answer R'ell, his Lordship came to rule after his father, mother and sister died tragically in Rivercross. An accident purportedly, though Si Manco and Osiris believe otherwise. Idris is the last of the Inigo's until he marries and fathers an heir."

"I understand," R'ell replied.

Now they were alone, Darion couldn't contain himself. His fears and worries came bubbling out. "Meredith, I need to get word to Keeper. The urak… Marron…" He didn't finish, couldn't bring himself to say the words.

"Darion, I need to tell you something, about Marron." Meredith took Darion by the hands and looked into his eyes, her face softened in sympathy. His hands were rough and callused and as her fingers brushed against the ring on his left hand she gasped. It felt cold against the warmth of his flesh. She frowned.

"Marron's gone and I've no idea where Nihm is," Darion's voice caught.

"Marron died on the banks of the Oust, just outside of Fallston," Meredith said her eyes gentle. "But Nihm lives. She is with Master Hiro. Keeper didn't know where you were and lost touch with Marron at Thorsten." She squeezed his hands. "I'm so sorry Darion."

"Nihm lives," Darion exclaimed. It was like a great weight was suddenly lifted from his heart. He turned to M'rika.

"She lives." The ilf returned his smile. Even R'ell looked less stern.

"How did you know?" Meredith asked. "About Marron I mean."

Darion raised his left hand and tapped his ring.

"Master Hiro performed our joining ceremony, his gift to us, heart bands. It went cold south of Thorsten. That's how I know. Now it's just dead metal."

## Chapter 28: Honour Be Damned

**The Grim Marsh, The Rivers**

Sand dreamed in a fevered sleep, of death. Of a darkness inside of him, that was insatiable, hungry. It needed to feed and so it fed. As it did, Sand felt the darkness slipping through his blood, seeping into his flesh, penetrating his bones.

His mind fogged, his dream faded to nothingness.

\* \* \*

Awareness and with it a sharp throbbing pain. It radiated from all over his body. It was unrelenting and Sand cried at the hurt.

The darkness from his dreams eddied inside him caressing the pain, embracing it. It was changed though. The crushing force of its malignant will was gone. In its stead a single primal, primitive need.

Sand prayed to the Trinity. Firstly, for death to take him, for the memory of what he'd done, what he'd endured was too much to bear. It played in his mind over and over as he lay helpless. He prayed as well for forgiveness and that the Morhudrim would not return to reclaim him. Finally, to his eternal shame, he prayed for life. He clung to it, weeping inside at his weakness.

Sand sensed light. The darkness uncoiled, oscillating, agitated. He felt moisture on his mouth and face. His lips were cracked and he tasted blood when he moved them. A face from his past peered down at him and he croaked a name before the fog descended upon him again and he lost all thought.

\* \* \*

"Think he's dead. Look." Belle prodded the man to underline her point. She should have been scared to touch him, burnt as he was, but Conn wasn't afraid, so she determined she wouldn't be either.

The man groaned and Belle jumped setting the little boat rocking. Conn giggled at her and after a moment Belle joined in.

"Hush girls," Jacob said, from the back of the boat. "Let Sand rest now. He needs his strength."

© 2020 A D Green

It was night and a heavy overcast covered the sky. It was hard to make much out as Jacob's eyes constantly tracked side to side trying to discern something, anything from the dark shapes sliding by.

He listened for a sound out of place but the marsh was full of noise. Insects mostly, but the flutter of wings as well and the occasional plop as the water was disturbed by some creature or other. The piping of dark larch and trilling of redwings rang out; at least that was what Wynter named them. The lanky ranger had spent time in the Grim, that much was plain, but the man offered no explanation and Jacob didn't press him on it.

Their flight from Thorsten had been difficult. They were dirty, wet, and tired and the constant threat of discovery left them wrung out and on edge. The urak presence on the northern banks of the Oust had grown much more prevalent and it was only luck that they'd not been discovered. Chancing upon Sand had forced a rethink of their escape route and forced them onto a different path.

Directing them down a tributary of the river, Ned Wynter led them south into the grasslands and flood plains that soon turned to marshland. Initially, they intended to make for Hilden. It was a town of dubious repute that bordered the Grimwolds, the Grim Marsh, and the northern plains. But black smoke on the horizon told its own story and instead Wynter took them into the Grim.

Jacobs's attention returned to the now as the boats brushed through reeds and grounded softly.

"We'll camp here the night," Wynter called out. Climbing over the gunwale he dragged the boat further onto the mud bank to anchor it.

Jacob heard the other boat nudge into the bank alongside. Then a soft splash as people disembarked. No one spoke as the boats were pulled through the reeds and into the sawgrass to hide them from view.

They left Sand in the boat with Jerkze and Jobe on guard whilst the rest explored the small mound they had beached on. It was raised and dense with bush. So much so that Junip was forced to incant a light spell on her staff to enable them to see their surroundings.

The little island was about sixty feet across and fringed with spiky sawgrass and bulrush. The interior was full of shrubs and bushes except at the high point where they found a large gnarled tree. Here the bush thinned as if it feared growing too close to the giant and they found space enough to set a camp of sorts.

Sitting heavily with her back against the tree, Junip laid her staff across her lap. She was so tired she could barely lift her head or keep her eyes open but she needed to maintain her casting.

Wynter, Mahan and Thornhill set about clearing the ground whilst Jacob set the two girls the task of preparing food, which meant searching the supply packs for biscuits, hard cheese and dry meat.

Jacob and Amos headed back to the boats to get Sand. Using the canvas he was laid upon and, with Jobe and Jerkze each taking a corner, they lifted him. Then, forging through the bush, carried him to their makeshift camp.

The dull light fluttered and Amos gave Junip a nudge. "Sleep in a bit, lass. Let's check Lord Sandford first, eh."

The mention of Sand stirred Junip sufficiently that she rose wearily to her feet. That he still lived was a miracle of the gods. Leaning close to his prone body she held her staff over him.

He looked awful; the skin on his torso was crusted black. Like his face, a scab had peeled off. Maybe knocked free by his passage through the bushes she mused. Either way, the flesh revealed looked smooth and white.

Junip was no physiker but observing him through the aether she found his essence was stronger than before. He was mending she realised. There was more though. Something else that was harder to define. It was like a mottled stain, only the stain was not fixed. It flowed over his form like a cloud shadow across a lake. She'd never seen anything like it before.

"How is he?" Constance interrupted. She slipped her hand into her brothers.

"Will he live?" Jacob asked. He squeezed Conn's hand in comfort.

"He is stronger. It is quite remarkable. He is badly burnt and has not eaten or drank anything in days. He should be dead. Yet he is not." Junip articulated her thoughts as they occurred.

"His burns are very strange. Where the burnt skin has flaked away fresh epidermis lies beneath and it looks as smooth as a newborn."

"I fear to remove any of the dead skin. An open sore will fester and likely prove fatal, especially here in this place. Still, I suspect were I to do so, his skin would be the same beneath all his burns. It is quite remarkable," Junip repeated.

"Anything you can do for him?" Jacob asked. "I would be in your debt."

"You're my Lord. No debt is owed," Junip snapped. She was tired and irritable. If she wasn't careful she would turn into a grouch like Master Lutico. Thoughts of the old mage made her reflective and melancholy. She looked at Jacob and the wide-eyed Constance.

"Sorry. I'm worn out. But, as I've said before, I'm no physiker. All I can suggest is keeping his wounds clean and dressed, then rest. If he gets black vein or his wounds turn sour I can offer little help I'm afraid."

"Thank you." Jacob laid a hand on Junip's shoulder then peered at his sister.

"He'll pull through. He's a Bouchemeax. They breed us tough, right Conn?" The conviction in his voice sounded false even to his own ears. "Let's get something to eat."

\* \* \*

The company shared a sparse meal that was over all too soon before discussing their options.

"Head due south, we could be in the Grimwolds tomorrow," Wynter said. "It's rough country but I know it well enough."

"We'd have to leave the boats and go on foot. If we cross any urak they will run us down easily, especially carrying your cousin," Amos said to Jacob.

"Don't let 'em see us then," Wynter suggested.

"Big gamble, if they do we're dead. Me and the boys were on horseback and they still almost caught us," Amos replied. "No, I say take the boats east. When we hit the Reach follow it to Longstretch then south. Ain't seen any urak on the river, big as they are I suspect they don't much care for water."

"It'll take too long," Wynter countered. "We need to get ahead of them. They've got the Great North road to speed their passage. Going east will take us three days before we get to the elbow and turn south. It'll be thick with the bastards all the way and risky."

"Let's get some sleep. Better to decide with a clear head." Jacob said.

* * *

The morning dawned. Overnight the rain had cleared leaving a damp mist blanketing the marsh obscuring all but the gnarled tree, which rose above it.

They ate a cold breakfast before taking up the discussion from the night before.

"My Lord," Wynter said, "east is a mistake. We have the marsh to navigate, the Grimmers to avoid and the Reach to cross. We'd be in plain sight on the lake and river. If we go south, the Grimwolds is as wild as the north. Plenty of cover, and I have tracked it before."

"Travel the lake by night. We need the boats," Amos replied. "Lord Sandford is a burden we can't hope to bear, especially if the wolds are as wild as you say."

Wynter grimaced and shook his head.

"Speak freely, Ned. No time for niceties," Jacob prodded.

"Your cousin's a burden as Lord Amos rightly says," Wynter started.

"I'm not leaving him behind," Jacob retorted.

"Pardon milord, the way I see it we got no choice. Your father tasked me to get you safe and the Lady Constance. Cain't with him, he's dead weight and that's the truth."

"On my honour I won't leave him. He's my kin," Jacob declared.

Wynter stared hard at Jacob. His Lord was decided. Lord Amos was in his periphery, face solemn as he digested what was said. It surprised him. Nobles had a strange way of looking at things but they usually stuck together on matters like this.

"Fuck honour."

Everyone turned. It was Jerkze.

"What?" Jacob hissed, his hand subconsciously resting on his knife hilt.

"Well, your father's honour sent us," Jerkze swept his hand in a circle, "to keep you safe. He brokered sanctuary with Lord Duncan here on his honour, for you and your sister. Now your honour is telling ya to save your cousin here. But if you and your sister die, what use honour then? Or Lord Duncan's and indeed your father's. We would all have failed. So yeah, fuck it. Let's be smart instead."

Jacob started shaking his head. He glanced at Amos. "Are your men always this forthright?"

"Annoyingly so, but worse than that, they're usually right," Amos said.

"I can't change who I am, Amos. I can't abandon him whatever the odds," Jacob said.

"I know. You won't like it but I have an alternative," Amos said.

"I'm listening."

"'A Bouchemeax must survive this thing. To reclaim what is ours, to rebuild for our people.' Your father's words, not mine," Amos clarified. "We got two Bouchemeax's, three if you include your cousin. If you'll not leave Lord Sandford then let me take Constance south, two paths, both perilous." He didn't mention the obvious, didn't want to say it in front of the two girls.

"Double the chance," Jacob murmured, bowing his head. After a while, he nodded to himself and his shoulders slumped in weary reluctance.

"Okay."

"No. I won't go," Constance blurted. "I can stay with you. I can help with Sand you'll see."

Jacob clasped his sister to him and she clung back, trembling. Placing a hand on the back of her head he breathed deeply, calming his emotions. After a while, he stood her back so she could see his face.

"What does Da say is our first duty?" he asked quietly.

"To our people." She sniffed.

"Yes, to protect them and to serve them. Above our own wants and needs. That means making hard choices." The irony was not lost on him. That he preached one thing yet did the opposite. He recalled their father's words back at the keep that strangely echoed Jerkze's of a moment before.

'Honour be damned, Jacob. You will take your sister and you will endure. You must. There will be no help for our people. No help for any of us here. The urak are too many.'

The lie came easily to Jacob's lips. "He sent us away in the hope that one day we could come back for our people with help and rebuild what has been lost. We must do what needs to be done."

"No one will listen to me. I'm eleven," Conn whined. "I won't know what to do without you."

"Amos will listen and help, Junip too. First though, we need to survive and for you, that means going with Lord Amos. I need you to be Lady Bouchemeax, brave, and fearsome as a forest cat. Not Conn the girl," Jacob said, burying the guilt he felt for playing on his sister's fascination with the beasts. It felt cheap and false.

"I'm scared. I don't want to lose you too," Conn sobbed.

"I will save our cousin. Then I will find you and we will be together again."

"Promise? Promise you'll find me."

"I swear it, Conn. You have my oath," Jacob said.

Conn gripped her little hip knife and drew it. "Jobe says the strongest oaths are sworn in blood." Before anyone could react she nicked her finger with it.

"I'll go check the boats," Jobe muttered as Jacob's stern gaze settled on him.

Turning back to his sister, Jacob took his knife and without hesitation sliced his finger. Then clasped Conn's hand in his and said the words. "I swear on my life I will find you."

"And I swear I will save our people," Conn replied. It was a child's promise and its simplicity broke Jacob. It was likely their people would be dead come spring and her oath meaningless. No more than his own.

He pulled her to him and they hugged again, fiercely.

\* \* \*

It took only moments to break camp. The supplies were split and the boats packed. Despite his earlier argument for the Grimwolds, Wynter insisted that he follow Jacob, and together with Mahan and Thornhill, they took Sand and one of the boats. No one said much. A heavy disquiet settling over them all as the two boats paddled away from each other, slowly fading into the mist.

## Chapter 29: Tae'al

**Plains of Ramira, The Rivers**

Tae'al. Nihm rolled the name around in her head. She wasn't sure where the word derived from but it sounded otherworldly. Hiro had other names for essence as well, Aether and Allthing but Tae'al was far more evocative. As was ki'tae, the hidden sense, which had newly been awakened in her.

Nihm phased and instantly the world was changed. It was disorienting. The ground she walked on and the grass and bushes stretching into the distance became a hazy riot of colours; a swirling maelstrom, that was hard to distinguish and even harder to understand. She knew however that Morten and Stama walked just ahead and the tightly coalescing splashes of white, with green and brown ghosting, must be them.

At first, they looked alike but as Nihm focused they appeared to expand in her mind. Examining them closely she detected subtle differences between them, with traces of black and gold threading the bolder colours. The longer she looked the more different they became. She wondered why she'd ever thought them the same.

Her head ached and Nihm phased back. Blinking in the sudden brightness of day, she rubbed her eyes at the stabbing pain.

<You were gone for thirty-seven seconds,> Sai stated. <I intervened else you would have fallen.>

<I thought you needed consent to control my body,> Nihm said.

<You were gone,> Sai repeated. <My default protocol allows protection of the vessel.>

<I see.> Nihm lifted her eyes as the pain behind them started to ebb. Ahead, rolling grasslands stretched to the distance with an occasional wood grove or bush thicket breaking the monotony.

They were a day south of the Grimwolds and Stama said the plains ran another thirty leagues until they bumped up against the River Fossa. The town of Fastain, their destination, lay on its banks; a two maybe three-day journey at most.

Late morning, Nihm spotted a lodge nestled up against a copse of trees far to their left and pointed it out. When they investigated it, they found it to be little more than a wooden hut and completely deserted. They rested, eating a cold meal before following the faintest of trails south.

They saw signs of wildlife, trampled grass and cropped bushes, and once caught sight of a dark stain on the horizon. Musk carried by the wind accompanied by the faintest of bellows told Nihm it was a bison herd. The wind switched shortly after from a cool southerly to a cold north-eastern and the herd moved out of sight and sound.

Occasionally, Morten would drop back and talk with her. There was still tension between them but the burning resentment Nihm held was gone. It had taken the events at Fallston to make her see he'd done no wrong and for her to concede, grudgingly, that she'd treated him badly. Not enough to make her want to clear the air with him but enough at least to let go of her anger and for their friendship to renew.

Her thoughts turned to Mao who, much like Hiro, was an enigma. He was old, ancient in fact, and in Fallston, he'd looked on the verge of death. Somehow though, he'd recovered and quickly. It didn't stack up. Old people just didn't heal that fast. He should be abed recuperating but instead was up and not only moving about but having no trouble keeping pace. Nihm stole a glance at him.

Mao's oaken face was no longer swollen and the bruising had mellowed to deep browns and mottled yellows. Catching her look, he winked giving her a toothy leer.

That too was different. In the caves, he had become introverted and quiet, even on the Reach. He had only come out of himself after Longstretch. But, even though Nihm hardly knew him, he was not the same somehow.

Without thought, Nihm phased again. Her head throbbed in protest; hardly recovered, it seemed, from her last shift.

Tae'al swirled into being in her mind. It took a few moments to adjust before she picked out the swirling mass that must be Mao. The now-familiar white with green and brown swirls spun softly but there was another as well. As Nihm focused the black and gold threads became clear but the other also clarified. A thick, blood-red lace seemed to twist around and through Mao's essence. Instinctively, she knew it was not part of him. It seemed oily to her way of thinking, unable to mix as it would if they were part of the same being.

*<Do not do that.>* Hiro's displeasure was evident.

Concentration broken, Nihm shifted back. She blinked and bowed her head at the sharp pain. When she was sufficiently recovered she asked.

*<What's wrong with him?>*

*<He is safe and in no danger,>* Hiro said. *<That is all you need to know for now.>*

*<That's no answer,>* Nihm accused.

Hiro broke the link.

Nihm resisted reconnecting. Frustrated and annoyed with Hiro as she was, Nihm still found him alluring and mysterious. He knew so much and had taught her things, things she had no comprehension of before they met. That didn't mean he couldn't still be an ass though. The thought cheered her for some reason and, widening her stride, Nihm moved up to join Stama and Morten.

\* \* \*

Farms and holdsteads started to dot the landscape the further south they went and with them orchards and vine groves, crop fields and pastures. There was a stillness to them that told of their abandonment. Though they did on occasion see livestock in neatly bordered fields; sheep and cattle that the holders either had no time or no means to herd south with them.

Mercy sent Stama to investigate the first holdstead they drew close to. On his return, he reported it abandoned as was expected but also, much to their relief, that there was no sign of forced entry or indication the urak had raided the place.

In fact, they'd seen no sign of urak since their encounter three days past, and Nihm was starting to think they'd gotten ahead of them. As if betrayed by her very thoughts a call rang out from Hiro.

"Urak, lay flat and still."

Slinging his pack from his shoulders, Hiro settled into the grass lying on his back.

"Be quick," Hiro urged.

Nihm eased off her pack and bow and dropped low. Then, following Hiro's example went down onto her back. Despite it being late autumn the plains grass was long enough still to cover them. Cold and damp as it was, it was the best they could expect.

"How many and where?" Mercy hissed.

"A score, a league out and," Hiro paused, "heading this general direction it seems."

"Hells, a score you say?" Mercy sounded calm to Nihm's ears and wished she felt the same.

"And you plan to lie here and wait for them?" the mage said.

"Yes and no," Hiro replied. "I suspect they make for that holding to the east. They should miss us comfortably. I suggest resting and silence. We may have to wait for dark before we can move on."

Nihm glanced at the sun. It was an hour from setting. Ash and Snow, curious as to what she was doing, sniffed at her and walked around before settling next to her. At least they were warm.

Despite her recent practise at it, Nihm found lying and doing nothing quite hard. It was tedious for one thing. For another, her back itched incessantly, as if something crawled across her skin even though Sai assured her that wasn't the case. She heard the rustling of grass not far from her. Morten was finding it no easier.

"Mort, stop fidgeting lad. Urak get close enough to see the grass twitching they're like to think there's game here," Stama hissed. "Shut your eyes and try ta sleep. Might be the only rest you get tonight."

The rustling stopped and Nihm tried to settle her own nerves. Taking Stama's advice she closed her eyes only to find that sleep wouldn't come. It was the urak. Blood soared through her veins at the thought of them.

With nothing else to do, Nihm found her mind drifting inevitably to her Ma and Da, then to Tae'al and Hiro and the lessons he taught. Finally, she thought of Renco and her dream of the burning woman. It was his dream. She knew it somehow. A hint of him had washed across their link as they dream shared.

An idea occurred. It was ludicrous, ridiculous but the thought of it excited her. Examining it she saw no reason not to try.

Nihm phased, her eyes were closed but she didn't need them to sense tae'al. It sprang into being all around her. Face to the sky, it appeared as a uniform honey gold vista, like the most brilliant of sunrises. Focusing her mind on the gold, Nihm's consciousness elevated and spun above her body. Hiro hadn't mentioned this, she thought, not quite sure how she had managed it.

Casting about, Nihm sensed a riot of colour below. A sea predominantly of purple and violets but also interspersed with a multitude of other colours. There amongst it, the white, green, brown essence of her companions including her own, though her colours were muted from her shielding. Resisting the temptation to remove it and look upon her tae'al in its fullness, Nihm focused instead on the two white brown swirls next to her own.

Ash and Snow. Concentrating on them they expanded in her mind. Tell-tale traces of green and gold washed through the brown. They were near-identical to each other. Nihm felt deeply happy, their tae'al somehow was clean and pure, and… she grasped for meaning… honest. That was it; their signatures were good and true.

Her Da told her once everything had an aura and that, if you could read it, you could tell a lot about a person; healthy or sick, good or bad, even their mood. She understood now what it was he meant.

Nihm's mind drifted back to Renco. She remembered a faint taste of tae'al. At least that was how she thought of it. She cleared her mind of everything but that taste.

Nothing happened. The sky was golden, the sea of grass still purple and violet. It seemed an age she waited but still, nothing. Nihm wasn't sure what to expect or what she was looking for. She let her mind drift, lazy and without purpose, suspended between the gold and the purple. She felt something. Exactly what she didn't know, it was like a hair tickling the back of her hand only it was her mind that felt it.

It came again, a barely perceptible thrum. Now aware of it she could discern it more easily. Like a spider feeling the vibrations in its silken web, it told her she had caught something.

Nihm's mind followed the thread. Faster, the golden sky blurring, the purple sea rising and falling with occasional islands of yellow and green pockmarking it. It was too much. Everything went dark.

What's happened? Nihm asked. Sai would normally have chimed in at this point but he didn't and it panicked her. She was alone in the void. She was about to shift back when something caught her attention. It was a star, a lone star, nothing more. It was distant and pulsed faintly but against the black it was obvious.

Curiosity overriding fear, Nihm approached it. The star grew brighter and larger until familiar greens and browns twisted through the white and she knew then what it was. Her approach sped up and suddenly it was as if she were falling. Unable to stop herself, the light grew impossibly fast until it hit her.

Nihm opened her eyes and blinked. Her head did not ache as it had before. That was a wonder. There was no time to dwell on it though. The darkening blue sky she expected to see was gone. In its place was a column of horses with red-cloaked riders atop them. Her gaze shifted without volition to the horse alongside hers. Did she dream?

The rider was a young woman with golden hair and deep blue eyes. She was wearing, a dirt-stained yellow smock under a scuffed yet neatly embroidered jacket and a black cloak with dark deerskin pants and brown leather riding boots. She was pretty but there was a weary despondency about her too. Her shoulders were slumped and her blue eyes sad. She seemed familiar.

I've found him, Nihm realised. Surely I'm looking through his eyes and seeing what he sees. Just like the burning woman.

The question of how sprang to mind. How could she see through his eyes? How had she found him? She didn't have an answer.

Twisting, her point of view changed, looking back. The column of horses and red-cloaked riders stretched out behind them and into the distance. Above them, rising like a jagged tooth, was a steep hilltop and atop that was a fortress, its walls easily distinguishable.

Her gaze swung forward again then down to the saddle. A groan and hands suddenly clasped her head, his head.

"What's wrong, Renco?" The golden-haired woman's voice was full of concern. It was a nice voice that annoyed her for some reason, though Nihm couldn't say why.

Then, in a blink, she was gone, ripped out, back into the void. Renco's essence swam before her receding rapidly to a single point of light that grew fainter.

An explosion of golden light and Nihm was back, hovering over her body. With a thought, she sank into it. It was like sinking into a warm bath and she sighed in pleasure. That simple action felt so good.

As she phased back Nihm was immediately aware of a coldness seeping into her side. Snow and Ash were gone. Opening her eyes, Nihm screwed them tight shut against the spike of pain that immediately exploded in her head. It was all she could do to not cry out.

<You were gone for five minutes and thirty-seven point four seconds,> Sai announced. <You are in pain. Compensating.>

<Really? It seemed so much longer. Are you sure?> Nihm gasped.

<Yes.>

The pain abated. Nihm opened her eyes again and mercifully it stayed away. Above her was a blue sky, darkening with the setting sun.

<Where are Snow and Ash?> Nihm wondered.

<On my mark, they left forty two seconds ago………mark. Their destination is unknown to me.>

<What? Okay don't worry.> Nihm was worried though. Had they heard the urak? Had they gone to investigate? What to do? They were young dogs, still learning. Damn it.

Nihm thought of Hiro and felt her will link with his.

<The dogs have gone. How far are the urak? Can I call them back?> Nihm asked. She immediately felt foolish for asking. If she had taken the time in the aether she could have found out herself, maybe. She wasn't quite sure how to judge distance. Maybe it wasn't a stupid question.

<The urak are close but there are riders from the south; they will fight, I think.>

*<How many riders?>* Nihm asked.

*<Twelve,>* Hiro said.

*<Twelve against twenty. That makes no sense, even if they are on horseback why would they attack?>* Nihm asked.

*<They are here for me, two Order knights and their hands. If they ask, you're my apprentice.>* Hiro broke the link.

That's getting to be annoying, Nihm thought. As she pondered what to do there was a rustle of grass and she raised her head to look.

Hiro had gained his feet but was hunched over to keep his profile low. Staff in one hand, bow and quiver in the other, he started running.

Lucky swore. "What in the seven hell's is he playing at?" He rolled to his feet and was followed moments later by Stama and Mercy.

Nihm rose and spotted the crouched figure of Hiro moving swiftly away. Taking a string out of a belt pouch she quickly strung her bow.

"Shit in hells," Mercy swore; her knuckles white where she gripped her staff. "Nihm, Morten wait here with Mao and guard the packs." Not waiting for an acknowledgement she set off after Hiro.

"Stay low and out of sight," Stama offered. His bow was already strung as he headed out, Lucky running easily at his side.

Nihm watched them go with a sense of frustration, desperate to join them. She'd fought in the fields on the edge of the wolds and proven herself, hadn't she?

"Where are you going?" Morten hissed. "Mercy said to stay here."

Nihm had taken several steps. Looking back at Morten there was concern in his eyes. He was afraid, his hands trembling faintly.

*<He is no fool at least,>* Sai said. *<The optimum course of action would be to remain hidden and avoid conflict. The odds are not favourable. There are too many unknowns in battle.>*

*<Sometimes you have no choice,>* Nihm retorted, knowing she meant to follow.

*<Your fight or flight instinct is clearly broken,>* Sai said.

<My what? You say the strangest things, you know that right?>

"Nihm!" Morten hissed.

"I have a bow. It might make a difference. Wait here with Mao. I'll be right back." Nihm turned away abruptly ending their discussion. Breaking into a loping jog she followed the trail in the grass left by her companions.

Nihm heard Morten swear profusely, then the swish of grass as he chased after her.

## Chapter 30: Ironside and Castigan

**Plains of Ramira, The Rivers**

They seemed to be running for an age. Nihm avoided getting too close to her companions, afraid she'd be ordered away and was thankful they never looked back.

A fearsome battle cry that could only be urak carried to her, followed by the distant crump of armour meeting flesh and the clashing of blades.

Ahead, the ground rose and Hiro stood at its crest launching arrows into the half-light. Mercy, Stama and Lucky ran up beside him. Without a word, Stama set his feet and pulled an arrow from his quiver. In one smooth action, he nocked, drew then released.

Nihm felt the prickle of magic on her skin and the raw power emanating from the mage.

Planting her staff, Mercy bowed her head with her free hand open and held up. Symbols flared to life on her staff and a ball of red-green fire swirled into being over her hand. Mercy raised her head. Eyes tracking, she launched the fireball.

Nihm lost sight of it almost immediately as it disappeared behind the downgrade but a muffled whump and an inhuman scream announced its impact.

The time for subtlety was gone and Nihm ran up the rise. Mercy's annoyance was obvious but the mage said nothing and Nihm had no time to worry about it.

The sound of fighting was visceral and Nihm's gaze was drawn down the slope to the battle raging less than a hundred paces away.

A dozen armoured knights had charged the urak, three of them having fallen before ever reaching them. The rest though must have crunched into and through the line, since half-a-dozen urak were down with long spears buried in them.

Hiro's arrows had struck with deadly precision and the evidence of Mercy's fireball was a wreck on the ground. An arm, ripped loose by its impact, smouldered beside the burning body.

In all, nine urak remained standing, the rest were dead or dying.

Her analysis took a split second. To Nihm, the horsemen evoked images from her books. Two of the knights wore burnished gold armour with square helms, the rest tarnished grey. Each warhorse wore barding to match their riders.

The momentum of the knights' charge was spent and the unexpected assault on the uraks' flank had thrown them into disarray. It brought time for the knights to draw their longswords and spur their armoured chargers back into the fray.

The ensuing battle was intense and frenetic. A rider's sword swing was blocked. Then, his horse was cut out from under him, sending him crashing to the ground. Dazed and weighted down by his armour he was slow to rise. The urak stepped in and crunched an axe into his helm. It crumpled and rang at the blow, sending blood flying and the man fell, lifeless.

The fighting became too close for arrow work and Stama, Lucky and Mercy drew their swords and followed Hiro as he ran to join the battle.

Except for her dagger and bow, Nihm had no weapon for fighting like this. Her mother's sword lay strapped to her pack, forgotten in the excitement. Even if she had it, the sword lessons Da gave her seemed inadequate for the brutality she witnessed.

Blood surged in her veins, a cocktail of fear and adrenaline. Holding an arrow loose on her string, Nihm stalked the downgrade looking for a target. Morten, covered her back, armed with the battle staff Hiro gave him in the caves. She prayed he knew how to use it.

A grey knight swung a longsword at an urak that stood head and shoulders above his warhorse. The urak deflected the blow with its blade then grabbed the rider's sword arm. With a wrench, he was pulled from his saddle and slung to the ground. As the urak raised its sword, Nihm lifted her bow drawing it back without a thought.

As before, in the grasslands by the Grimwolds, a line superimposed Nihm's vision. As the arrow's fletch grazed her cheek the lines arc stretched and tightened. Instinctively she adjusted her aim, tracking until the arc centred on the urak's torso. With a breath, she loosed.

The bow thrummed and the arrow, silently transcribing the arc, buried itself with a wet thunk into the urak's back.

© 2020 A D Green

Another horseman was down. Nihm nocked an arrow but the horse, now riderless, stepped in front spoiling her aim. The sword rose and fell, then rose again, this time red with viscera. Swearing, Nihm relaxed her aim, eyes searching the battlefield whilst she waited for the horse to move.

Only three knights were left mounted, two of them gold. Nihm watched, as the golden knights slid from their saddles. Despite the fact they wore mail, there was a fluid grace to their movements. They discarded their helms, revealing them to be a man and a woman. Both exuded an air of stoic certainty as they hunted the battlefield.

The man had strong sharp features; his long black hair, curled into tight ringlets, was held back with a cloth tie. The woman, in contrast, looked stern, her red-gold hair cropped short on top and shaved at the sides. She spun her longsword once in an easy circle as if it were made of balsam.

Grinning, the man swept into the path of an urak as it struck at the remaining horseman. Catching the urak's blow on his sword, Blackhair deflected its blade into the ground.

The urak reacted instantly to backhand the man, who seemingly blurred and ducked beneath the swinging arm. Turning, straightening, Blackhair drew his sword from low guard to high, its edge biting and slicing through skin then bone and severing the arm. Continuing his turn, Blackhair avoided the gush of arterial spray and, using the momentum of his spin, punched his sword with force between the urak's shoulder blades.

Not far from him, the stern woman fought an urak that dwarfed her and seemed intent on bludgeoning her with a cleaver sword. For all its ferocity and brute strength though it failed to break her guard.

Like the man, her liquid movements blurred as she switched from one guard to the next, flowing around each blow. Most were deflected, the angle of her blade enough to direct its swing wide, whilst avoiding the jarring impact. Often though, she avoided contact altogether by stepping to the side or back.

Blocking an overhead cut using a long point guard the woman abruptly, rolled her wrists and lunged. In a haze of motion, her rear foot slide forward and her sword swept up. It sliced into the urak's neck, cutting deep. Twisting away, she wrenched the blade free. The wound gaped like an obscene smile vomiting thick dark blood. The urak grunted then collapsed. Stepping away, her eyes were already searching for her next opponent.

Nihm was transfixed. Belatedly, she scanned the battlefield looking for an opportunity to launch an arrow but it was over. Hiro had reached the fighting in time to take the last of them. His staff clattering an urak on the back of the head as it swung at a downed rider. It keeled over and didn't move.

Only five knights had survived the battle. All were wounded except for the golden knights who wandered the battlefield, clinically dispatching any urak still breathing whilst checking the fallen.

Hiro and Mercy had those still standing, gather the fallen, whilst they unbuckled straps and removed armour to attend injuries.

For Nihm the air was oppressive. It was foul with the smell of blood and laced with a pungent undertone. Sai made an adjustment to dampen the worst of the effects but Morten had no such luxury. Dropping to his hands and knees he started retching.

Smiling broadly his task complete, Blackhair approached Hiro. "Well met, old friend. What has it been, ten years?"

His eyes were tight, his smile a little too wide, Nihm thought, and he did not seem overly disturbed by the carnage of the battle.

Hiro looked up from the wound he ministered to.

"Ironside," he acknowledged, his tone stiff, "fourteen, I believe."

Ironside whistled his grin widening. "Ten, fourteen, either is too long."

Finished with his binding, Hiro stood and regarded him. "Ai, if only it were under happier circumstances."

Ironside pulled on his right gauntlet tearing it free and they gripped each other's forearms in greeting.

"Hiro, you old rogue." The woman flung her arms around the monk as he turned to face her. She clasped him hard.

"Castigan," Hiro grimaced, gasping. "Much as I've missed your warm welcomes, I'd rather it not be whilst one of us is wearing plate."

"Sorry," Castigan laughed, breaking from their embrace. "Iron is right though, it has been too long. Now, where's Mao? Don't tell me you've planted the old bugger."

"No, he's very much alive. Guarding the baggage I hope." Hiro spared Nihm a glance, one eyebrow cocked high in question.

Shit, Nihm had forgotten about Mao. As she turned to leave, Ash and Snow rose like wraiths in the long grass. There came a rasping sound as two swords cleared their scabbards then the reassuring voice of Hiro.

"It's alright, they're with us."

\* \* \*

Anxious to leave the stink of death behind, Morten went with Nihm and together they traced the path back to where they'd lain hidden. The two wolfdogs, seemingly knowing their destination, bounded ahead.

They found Mao where they'd left him. He was laid in the long grass with his head on his pack, eyes closed and snoring gently.

"Cannae believe he slept through this whole thing," Morten grumbled.

Nihm thought he sounded more than a little jealous. They let Mao be whilst they gathered the packs. They were just wondering how they would move them all when Mao finally stirred and sat up.

"You wake, Mao," he moaned, clambering to his feet. He stretched, arching his back.

Morten shook his head, "Whilst you took your leisure we battled urak ya silly fool."

Mao looked down his long slightly crooked nose at Morten then at the battle staff in his hand and finally, at the stacked packs. He sniffed loudly.

"Fighting not for Mao and you smell of sweat, not fighting." Hoisting his pack he walked away, following the crushed grass south.

"You could help us," Nihm shouted after him.

Mao waved as if bidden farewell but didn't look back, calling over his shoulder. "Boy, no use staff fight. Use staff carry pack."

It was sound advice, or so they thought. Using the staff as a pole they threaded the packs along its length and each hoisted an end to their shoulders. Nihm found the load surprisingly bearable but had to wait whilst Morten grunted and adjusted his grip.

Burdened as they were the return trip was a lot longer, Morten having to stop several times to switch his hold and change shoulders. Normally quite chatty, Nihm couldn't help but notice he seemed perturbed and reflective.

"You okay, Mort? You seem quiet," Nihm asked.

"Just thinking is all," Mort replied.

He seemed unwilling to elaborate and Nihm respected that. Sometimes all she wanted was to be left alone.

Sai disagreed. <Morten is lost. No home, no family, everything he has cherished in life is gone. Keep a careful watch on him. He may not wish to talk but he may need too and he is your friend. The burden should be yours. You are all he knows from his past life.>

<We've all suffered loss and are all dealing with this shit,> Nihm snapped, feeling judged.

In response, the memory of her isolation in the roaring cave and her near-death played through her mind.

<If Hiro had not been there things would have ended very differently for you. He was a rock in the storm, an anchor when you needed it. Morten's needs may differ but he may still need an anchor.>

Somehow, Sai was right. Infuriatingly, he was always right. Morten was suffering and she'd been no friend to him in recent times.

"You know, Mort. If you ever need to talk I'm here for you. You're the only friend I have. The only one I ever had really," Nihm muttered.

"I know." Morten panted. "I had friends once but you're all that's left, far as I know. The only one I got. What more is there to say?"

"Okay, but just so you know. You're not alone," Nihm said. It elicited a grunt in response but no more and they made the rest of the journey in silence.

On their return, Hiro took a dim view of Morten's misuse of his battle staff and castigated him roundly. Mao's smirking face in the background didn't help any and Morten glared at him.

A lot had happened in the time they were gone. The survivors had set a makeshift camp a hundred paces downwind of the dead. The wounded knights had been moved and the horses staked out, still in full harness. Night had fallen but all three moons were out, casting a baleful light over the plains and this was augmented by several conjured light globs that hovered low to the ground.

Mercy and Hiro were busy attending to the injured still. Stripped of their armour the wounded knights looked pale and wan. Nihm watched as Hiro lent over one, bowed his head, and murmured what sounded like a prayer, her acute hearing picking out the words.

"Earth blessed.
Sun-kissed.
From dust, you came.
To dust, you return."

Reaching out a hand, Hiro closed dead eyes.

Nihm was curious. Hiro dressed as a monk but was of the Order and the Order worshipped no gods. She wondered at the duality of it.

There was no time to ponder further. The dogs were up and staring to the south, ears erect. Nihm heard the indistinct rattle of wagons rumbling in the distance. They appeared a short while later over a far crest, two of them, each with a train of horses in tow. Castigan, one of the golden knights, was riding beside them, her red-gold hair clear to see in the moonlight.

Nihm watched as the carts drew near. The drivers looked ordinary. They were dressed in dark brown leather breeches and pale linen shirts. One wore a dark greatcoat the other a padded leather jerkin with a winter cloak to guard against the cold wind.

Castigan spurred her mount into a canter, riding directly for Nihm. Pulling up sharply, her horse skidded to a halt and she slid from its back. Clattering past in her armour, she gathered Mao in her arms.

"Vagabond, still leading Hiro astray I see." She laughed.

"Always," Mao smiled. "You feast for old man eye, Lyra Castigan."

"Silver tongue, we'll talk later. The day's been a grievous one. I've lost many brothers and a sister. I must attend them." Giving another quick embrace, Castigan walked away.

\* \* \*

That night was sombre and long.

Eight knights had died and the two surviving golds and two greys spent much of it preparing their fallen comrades. They removed the armour from the dead, then their bloodied and soiled clothing. Naked, their bodies were cleansed then bound in muslin.

The two drivers, introduced as Regus and Gatzinger, unloaded one of the wagons, neatly stacking its supplies on the grass. Nihm thought at first it was to carry the dead but instead, they climbed aboard and headed out with Ansel, one of the grey knights.

"They go to gather wood," Lucky said.

It was after midnight when they returned. By the light of the moon and stars the wagon was emptied, the wood laid and a pyre built with the dead resting upon it.

Everyone gathered to pay final respects with Ironside and Castigan standing together. They had long since removed their armour and were dressed now in black leather leggings and tunics with studded plates sewn into them.

Ironside spoke words over four of the fallen, naming them and recalling their character and spirit. Two had wives and children to remember them. For these, Ironside knelt and cut a lock of hair, folding each in a white cloth and tucking them into a pocket inside his tunic. Finally, Ironside commended the dead for their service to the Order and their valour. As he stood away, Rutigard his grey knight stepped forward and spoke his own words and memories of the four, his voice sombre but steady.

Castigan then spoke for the remaining dead. She followed the same formal process as Ironside. None of Castigan's knights was married but one of the dead was a woman. Kneeling beside her, Castigan stroked her hair gently, smoothing it back in place where the wind had disturbed it. As Ironside had done before her, she cut a lock and rolled it in a white cloth. A single tear fell but no more. When the time came for Ansel, her grey knight to speak, he placed a consoling hand on Castigan's shoulder, before standing forward.

Afterwards, Ironside, Castigan, and their greys bowed formally to the fallen and gave a final blessing.

"Earth blessed.
Sun-kissed.
From dust, you came.
To dust, you return."

It must be an Order thing, Nihm surmised, it was the same blessing Hiro had uttered earlier that evening. The hairs on her arms tingled with charged energy as the two knights held their hands out to the pyre.

"Ignatituum forus arctum." The pyre ignited with a roar, sizzling and spitting as the moisture in the wood superheated, the steam blending with the smoke. In moments it was ablaze and tall flames licked the night sky, heat radiating out and over the gathering.

Ironside turned away, his eyes resting on the two wagoners. "Regus, Gatz, get everything loaded. We move out in twenty minutes."

The ceremony concluded, the assembled dispersed to prepare for travel.

Nihm found herself at a loose end. Morten had wandered over and was speaking quietly with Regus. Nihm gravitated towards them watching as Regus slapped Morten good-naturedly on the shoulder before the two men turned and started loading the wagon.

<*Nihm,*> Hiro interrupted. <*Come see me. Keep yourself shielded at all times, just as I taught you.*>

Nihm changed direction, sensing his worry and wondering at his concern about her shield. Once in place, it took no effort to maintain it.

<*Ironside wishes to speak with you. Do not share that we mind speak or any of your other abilities. Not with anyone unless I say otherwise.*>

<*Why? They're Order knights same as you.*> Nihm approached Hiro, his diminutive frame sandwiched between Ironside and Castigan. The woman spoke

animatedly to him and Hiro it seemed had no trouble holding two conversations at once.

<I was a knight once but no longer, not in an age at least. I ask that you trust me.>

"Nihmrodel, we've not been formally introduced." Ironside flicked accusing eyes at Hiro then back.

"I'm Ironside, Knight of the Order. My friends call me Iron." He held his hand out in greeting and Nihm took it automatically.

"You're friends with Master Hiro then?" Nihm smiled.

"Hiro and I go way back. We've known each other longer than either probably cares to remember." His teeth flashed and his smile seemed genuine but his eyes lacked any warmth.

Nihm felt conflicted. She wanted to like him, he looked heroic and brave like the knights of old she'd read about in her books. But there was something about the Order knight that told her, beware. Always trust your instincts, Da always told her and she did. She released his hand.

"My mother worked for the Order. She's dead now," Nihm said.

Ironside nodded, "I know. I was sorry to hear of it. I knew her when she was younger than you are now. I always liked her. Though, I must say your mother didn't work for the Order. She was of the Order."

"Same thing," Nihm said, irritated at being corrected and thinking his expression smug.

<His demeanour is self-assured and confident,> Sai countered.

<Same thing,> Nihm said, repeating her assertion of a second before.

"No. It isn't," Ironside said. "Work is a job. Being of the Order is a choice, a way of life. Like family." His eyes slid to Hiro. "I feel your pain."

Nihm felt her jaw clench.

"Is that what you wanted to speak to me about, my pain?" She sounded bitter and petulant to her own ears but she was beyond caring. Thoughts of her mother and his empty words filled her with both longing and anger.

"No, we didn't ride all this way to talk about your pain," Castigan said roughly, interceding. "We rode for you and Marron. I'm sorry she didn't make it but we've all lost people we love. Now, do you want to sulk or listen?"

Biting back a retort, Nihm took a calming breath.

Barely perceptible, Castigan dipped her head then stepped back as if to give Nihm her space. The knight didn't smile at her but Nihm saw the tension go from her shoulders and was wise enough to say no more.

Nihm glanced at Hiro, who remained impassive and difficult to read, then to Ironside who wiggled a thumb in Castigan's direction.

"You'll find Lyra blunt and to the point." He winked. "She grows on you though."

"I'm listening," Nihm said.

"Keeper has made a place for you in the Training Halls at the Orders Academy. You're to begin your initiate's training. I'm to bring you to Tankrit."

"I don't even know what that means. Two months ago I didn't even know my mother or father were of the Order." Nihm stressed this last. "I don't know you and I don't know this Keeper but I do know I'm apprentice to Master Hiro. What do you say, Hiro? Should I go?"

"I say you are unruly and impertinent, child." His staff tip tapped her lightly on the shoulder. She hadn't sensed him move and she jumped.

"Address me as Master or Master Hiro at all times. As to your question, Ironside has not finished with his news." Hiro directed Nihm's attention back to the knight.

"I didn't know you took apprentices, Hiro. Keeper will not be pleased I think," Ironside said. He looked at Nihm, his green eyes penetrating.

"The other news I bring is about your father. Darion is alive and well. He will be in Fastain in the next day or two and I will take you to him."

Nihm felt her heartbeat skip. Hope flared; she knew it, had felt it in her bones. Always doubt had plagued her that her Da might be dead but always she had refused to believe it. Even so, hearing it was as if the fist clenched about her heart had finally released its grip.

She found herself on her knees sobbing gently, her cheeks wet with tears. As if listening from afar she heard Hiro speak.

"Iron, next time lead with that."

## Chapter 31: Tankrit Red

**Kingsholme, The Holme**

The guard knocked loudly on the door. Princess Matrice waited impatiently behind him and Gart Vannen, her first sword, a step further back. She heard movement from within followed moments later by the sound of the door bolt sliding back.

As the door cracked open the guard shifted, bumping into the princess. "Sorry, Highness."

"Wait downstairs," Matrice hissed.

"I was ordered…"

"I know what the High King, my father, ordered. Now wait downstairs and guard the way up, unless you mean to impugn the honour of Lord Renix." Matrice stared the young guard down.

"Yes, Highness." The guard shuffled awkwardly past the princess, then Sir Vannen. Noting as he did that the swordmaster held a casual hand on the hilt of his long knife. Mail clanking, he retreated down the stairs.

Matrice watched the guardsman go. She liked the young ones. They were easy to flatter and easier to intimidate. The veterans were always harder to bend.

The door swung wide and the hallway beyond was dark but for a single candelabra. It shrouded the man who waited upon its threshold. Matrice felt a chill crawl up her spine. He looked every bit an assassin. Gart moved alongside her protectively.

"How unexpected." The voice was soft and refined. The man turned, throwing his face into relief, a well-groomed, aristocratic face. "Please come in, Highness. Sir Vannen too is welcome, though I ask that he take his hand from his weapon. I am no threat."

Renix led them down the hallway through a large door and into a drawing-room. A small open hearth fire filled the room with rosy warmth, augmenting the light from two open windows.

"Please, take a seat. Can I get you any refreshment?"

"Wine please." Matrice smiled artfully. Then, smoothing her skirts, she sat in one of the two armchairs. Vannen took station behind her.

Renix pursed his mouth, both impressed and amused. Young the princess might be but she was well versed in the travails of court politics and the art of manipulation. Barely fifteen, the high king would not approve her casual consumption of wine.

It impressed him because her test was cunningly simple but no less effective for it. Would he treat her as a child or a woman?

It amused him because he really didn't care.

"I have a nice Tankrit Red, grown from the Order's own grape. It's your father's favourite and very rare," Renix replied.

"That sounds acceptable."

Renix gave a slight bow, the corner of his mouth rising before he disappeared back through the door they had entered from.

Standing, the princess paced. Curious eyes examined every part of the room and Matrice found herself oddly disappointed by it. The Order ambassador was the subject of many whispers and rumours and whilst the Order's influence may have waned in recent years it still held a certain mystique.

The room then was underwhelming. It was tidy and well-appointed but boringly normal. Bookcases lined two of the walls. On another, a map of the Nine Kingdoms and, more interestingly, Tankrit Isle home to the Order. None went to the Isle unless invited and no one was unless to join the Order and swear fealty to the enigmatic Keeper of the Order. Or so Master Wendell told her.

The books, the maps, the furnishings, were all of the best quality but still, it could just as easily belong to a rich merchant or a minor noble.

Gart coughed and Matrice turned to find the ambassador standing silent by the armchairs. He held two goblets and a dark glass bottle in his hands. His face was pleasant and friendly enough but Matrice saw it for a mask, like those worn by the nobles in court. She saw through most but found the ambassador harder to fathom and wondered briefly if coming here had been a mistake. But as quick as the thought came, so it went.

"I wonder, Lord Renix. Would you serve me as well as you do my father if I were the High Queen?"

"Sit Highness; let me pour you a glass of wine before I answer," Renix said.

Setting the goblets and bottle on a small table, he waited while the princess was seated. Her eyes watched his face as he poured the wine. As was the tradition with royalty, Renix raised his goblet first and supped. Sitting, he casually crossed his legs and regarded her.

"I do not serve your father. I serve the Order and the Order serves all. Your question was ill-phrased," Renix said. He was intrigued when the flash of annoyance he expected did not materialise. Instead, Matrice pursed her lips in a mock pout.

"Come, my father speaks highly of you. You offer him sound advice and friendship do you not? If I were High Queen would you not offer me the same?"

"I offer nothing. Offers are for dealing and I'm no merchant, I do not deal in bargains. Your father gets the same as any that care to ask. Honest advice. Some on occasion even listen to it." A small smile played across his face as he spoke. "Your father and I are friends, I grant. A friendship evolved from mutual trust and respect, garnered over many years from shared experiences and ideals. If you were High Queen, I would hope, given time, similar regard would grow between us."

Matrice took a sip from her wine, the red staining her lips. She rolled her tongue over them, "I can see why my father likes the wine. It's delicious."

Renix inclined his head at the compliment. He was aware as the princess supped that Sir Gart Vannen's hand was back on his dirk. His demeanour was tense and the swordmaster looked ready for violence. There is darkness in him, Renix thought sadly. On a whim, he allowed a little mischief into his next question.

"Surely you need not worry about the throne, princess? Your father is in good health and Crown Prince Herald will ascend should anything befall your father."

"My brother is a pampered oaf and not fit to rule," Matrice scowled, green eyes glinting in anger. "But after my father passes, rule he must. Even if I were the elder this would be so. Both law and custom dictate this."

"Life is inconstant and humanity yearns for certainty," Renix said. "Laws and traditions bring a semblance of this, along with a large dose of idiocy at times it has to be said. Still, if you're concerned about your brother's competence, perhaps you could help him to aspire."

Matrice covered her mouth to hide her amusement but couldn't stop a giggle escaping. "I see why my father likes you. Honest advice you say? Humour I counter."

"As I said before, some heed my advice; others ignore it or are amused by it. You may take it however you wish, Highness," Renix said.

"I meant no offence, Lord Renix but you do not know my brother," Matrice replied. "Maybe you think me an idle and feckless girl, daydreaming of being the first High Queen. But war has come. I must prepare for every eventuality. I have no doubt that my brother, the crown prince, will try to prove himself in battle. If so, his incompetence is likely to get him killed and the many that will no doubt follow him."

"Why did you come here Highness? It was not for my counsel since you clearly keep your own." The princess was bold but Renix had not thought her quite so brazen.

"I came to see 'it'."

"It? You'll need to elaborate I'm afraid," Renix said.

"I was hoping you would do that," Matrice countered. "I mean of course the 'it' causing a death marker to be placed against your name. The rumour is spoken of openly in court. You have taken something from someone and they are not best pleased."

"Ah, now that is strange," Renix said. "You're the first to ask me and a neat bind you've placed me in. If I deny you, the rumours will continue unabated. If I show you, I'm not sure you would understand."

Matrice frowned. "Your answer is telling despite its vagueness. Come, I would like to know. Maybe I can help."

"You can't and I would not seek to embroil you in this affair. It's a personal matter, highness."

There was a slide of steel as Gart Vannen drew his knife and stepped out from behind the princess. Renix stood smoothly to meet him.

"Gart, what are you doing?" The princess scolded. Straining her neck, she looked up at her first sword. His eyes were fixed not on the ambassador but the doorway.

"Sheath your knife, Sir Vannen, and step away," Renix commanded. "There is nothing here to threaten the princess."

Vannen's eyes never wavered. "Tell whoever's out there to step forward Ord. Then I'll decide for myself."

"Don't be so vulgar, Gart. Whilst you're with me you will show proper respect for the ambassador," Matrice admonished. Not liking the two men towering above her she stood.

"Forgive his bad manners, Lord Renix. He's unwavering in his protection of me, often to courtesy's detriment."

"A duty he performs well I am sure," Renix twisted his head slightly. "Tomas, come here."

Silence stretched.

A muscle twitched on Vannen's neck, impatience was starting to show on his face and in the tension of his shoulders, when a boy suddenly appeared in the doorway.

"Sorry, Lord Renix. I only wanted to see the princess," Tomas mumbled.

"Come in, lad. Take a look. Apparently, her highness is as intrigued by you as you are her." Renix waved the boy forward.

Tomas walked slowly into the room, wary of the red-clad man bearing a knife. His face was hard, eyes intense as if he was considering even now where to bury his blade. Tomas shifted nervously, his mouth dry.

"Gart, put your knife away you're scaring the boy," Matrice ordered.

The man grinned but Tomas saw nothing friendly in it. Even after sheathing his knife and returning to his post behind the princess, his eyes still glowered at him.

"Step forward boy. Let me look at you," Matrice said.

Tomas glanced at Renix who gave a slight nod. Nervous, he moved before the princess, his cheeks colouring as she inspected him. He bowed awkwardly from the waist. He must have done it right because the princess gave a beautiful smile. She smelled of flowers.

"Your clothes are well-made boy but slightly too big and are obviously not your own." The princess wrinkled her nose in thought. "Who are you I wonder?"

"I'm Tomas," Tomas blurted. He felt blood rushing to his face. What was wrong with him? He'd seen plenty of women before and it never bothered him. From the ugly and dirty living rough in the alleys to the beautiful painted ladies on Harlots Row, who men paid good coin to spend time with. She wasn't like them ones though. She was like a sunrise in comparison, even if she did call him boy all the time.

Aware he'd compared the princess to a whore he bowed again to hide his further embarrassment and heard her titter.

"Well Tomas, you're no Lordling. But that's no bad thing, most are pompous prigs. Perhaps you're a protégée of some description." She glanced at Renix questioningly. "Strong rumour is the council of mages has placed the death marker."

Tomas glanced accusingly at Renix, unsure what to say. He'd not overheard their entire conversation only the latter part. What had Renix told the princess and what was a protégée? Thankfully Renix answered for him.

"He is no mage apprentice I assure you. Tomas was just a boy living on the streets."

"Was?" Matrice questioned.

"Was," Renix said agreeably. He turned to Tomas. "You may go now. No more loitering outside of doors. The princess and Sir Vannen are my guests and deserve better."

"Yes. Sorry, milord." Tomas was pleased to get away from scrutiny. It was only when he got to the door that he remembered the princess. He turned, bowed stiffly a third time. "Pardon me, princess."

Matrice watched in amusement as Tomas disappeared. "He's adorable. I want one."

© 2020 A D Green

"He's no horse to be owned Highness," Renix admonished.

Matrice laughed. "Are you always so serious? It was a jest." As if in contradiction, her humour suddenly died. Her face turned thoughtful and serious.

"Still, you've not told me why the boy is important. Just that he lived on the streets. A child, surviving alone for so long, it must have been hard. I'm guessing he stole something. Probably from someone he shouldn't have. It must be valuable indeed if your protection of him only brings a death mark on your head."

"You may be right," Renix conceded. "The Syndicate has placed a bounty on his head after all but that is not the same thing as the death mark placed upon my own."

Renix bid the princess sit and sipped from his wine before taking his seat. "Maybe Tomas stole something or witnessed something he shouldn't have. But most likely his bounty and my death mark are not related."

"The Order is under attack. Many call for our banishment or go further. Foremost are the Churches of the Trinity, in particular, the Red Church but also it has to be said the Council. The mages have long set themselves against the Order. It's short-sighted, foolish, and completely unnecessary. Especially now and in these times, but humanity has oft been flawed with these traits."

Matrice frowned. "If that is the case, why take the boy? If what you say is true, you both suffer the other's ill fortune as well as your own."

"Tomas is no prisoner. He's free to leave as he wishes. As for me, I am of the Order. If a ten-year-old boy is not worthy of protection I betray my honour and our creed. I said earlier I wasn't sure you would understand but I hope you do. Your father does."

At the mention of her father, Matrice sighed. "He's angry at me still."

Eyes sullen, nose wrinkling in a grimace, she clarified. "My father blames me over Herald's horse, King's Champion. I went to see him but he's always so busy, especially now with these urak invading and organising this war council. Did you know, High Lady Hardcastle arrived yesterday and High Lords Ostenbow and Trevenon are already here? The last time the Nine Kingdoms gathered like this was for my father's coronation."

"I recall. Still, I do not think he blames you. He has a lot to contend with," Renix consoled, pleased at the digression.

Matrice took a large swig of wine, wiping at her chin where some had spilt leaving a red trail against her pale skin. A rueful look came on her face.

"You must think me a child moaning at nothing. I fear I'm a burden my father does not need. But how can I say sorry if he'll not hear me?"

Renix considered the princess. Right now she seemed like the fifteen-year-old girl she was rather than the woman she pretended to be. He watched her sip again at her goblet. Edward would have harsh words with him if she turned up drunk at the Palace. Her eyes lifted to his, coquettish and playful.

"I would like to begin our journey of friendship, Lord Renix. To start, I would ask for your advice regarding my father."

Renix hid the surprise he felt. She was a complex creature he was starting to realise. Bold and certain one minute, young and unsure the next, she was hard to know. One thing he was sure of though, she was highly intelligent. Her request was made naturally enough but there was artful device in it as well.

"Very well. Firstly, no more wine. It's delicate to taste but strong. It will go straight to your head if you drink it too fast, Highness. Secondly, write your father a note of apology if you cannot see him. I will give you a bottle of Tankrit Red from my stores. If you leave it with your note it will hopefully sweeten the apology."

Matrice beamed. "Thank you Lord Renix. I will do as you suggest. Already I feel happier."

"You are most welcome, princess."

"I should go. I fear I've already taken up far too much of your time," Matrice said, excited and animated. "In my girlish fancy, I came looking to find something parlous and adventurous. Instead, I found a boy and gained an insight."

Renix smiled at her sudden zest. "Oft, the treasure you find is not the one you seek."

"Indeed, Lord Renix. You are so right," Matrice said, rising to leave.

"Now, if you could fetch that bottle for me I'll be on my way."

## Chapter 32: The First Rule

**North of the Defile, The Rivers**

Renco's fingers ached abominably. The only good thing was it masked the pain in his back unless he moved suddenly. It made his early morning forms interesting, to say the least. The practice was so ingrained that it was natural to perform them now he was no longer constrained.

Renco's exercise provoked many comments and much amusement from the nearby Red Cloaks who watched him slowly glide through his moves, holding each position for a while before changing to the next. By the time he was done, fresh blood dribbled down his back. It elicited a scolding from Henreece, the Red Cloak physiker when he came to check his patient.

"Damn fool. If infection sets in your wounds could turn fatal and that will not do. The Lord Commander would hold me to account," Henreece lectured, as if getting the young physiker in trouble was an unforeseen consequence Renco hadn't considered. Which, in fairness, he hadn't.

One benefit of their minor altercation was that Henreece marched Renco to the river insisting that he bathe. It had been a while and Renco found the water sharp as ice and invigorating. It leeched the pain from his wounds until they were numb and turned his skin blue. The cold though did not bother him and it was Henreece that lost patience first and called him in.

Afterwards, Henreece inspected his injuries afresh and cleaned them with a solution before applying the stinging, stinking salve the Red Cloak medics seemed to favour. There was one troubling incident following his ablutions.

"You appear to have a stain on the left side of your face and chest," Henreece told him.

"It's visible only at a certain angle and I would think it a bruise but," the physiker seemed intrigued, "the pattern is too regular. Design, symbols of some description I would say. But to what I wonder?"

Renco shrugged, staring at his chest. He saw nothing but the faintest shimmer, markings he couldn't quite discern. Renco did not think himself cursed with vanity but nevertheless, hands rose unbidden to probe his face and it caused him to wonder at whether it was marred. His hands dropped to his sides; he had plenty of scars, what mattered one more.

There was an added bonus to bathing when Henreece handed over one of his own clean shirts. They were of a similar build and it fit him better than his soiled one. And, whilst most Red Cloaks wore red shirts under their gambesons, their physikers it seemed wore black, which suited him just fine. He abhorred red.

Henreece left him back at camp with a promise to check on him later in the day.

"You look better for a wash," Lett told him. "Here, I got bread rolls off one of the cook wagons."

Lett threw it to him and he deftly caught it with his uninjured hand. The crust was hard but his stomach didn't care and growled impatiently.

Biting into it, Renco was pleasantly surprised to find the bread inside was soft. He chewed, idly watching the Red Cloaks as they broke camp. Tents and gear were packed and campfires extinguished with an efficiency that spoke of practise and routine. Archbishop Whent had a pavilion and it collapsed suddenly as a hand of men worked at taking it down.

Last night, he'd dreamt again of the woman, Marron. As sad and troubling as it was, it gave blessed relief from the nightmare of his burning mother and he felt guilty for it. That another's pain should ease his suffering was wrong but it was more than that. Marron was real, the dream a memory that was not his. It was unnerving. Almost as much as the presence he'd felt inside his body the day before. He'd hardly been aware of it to start with but, when he was, his sense of it was not malevolent. It simply saw what he saw. Felt what he felt.

He knew it was her, the girl with the wolf dogs. Felt it in his core. Somehow they shared a bond. One he didn't understand. Her name was Nihm, though again he couldn't explain how he knew it. Maybe Marron and the dream was hers. Renco wiped a hand over his mouth and the soft stubble of his chin. It was crazy; maybe his torture at the hands of the giant Red Cloak had affected his mind.

"We'd best hurry, that sergeant will be back soon with the horses," Lett said. "If we're not ready, he promised we'd ride in the caged wagon."

Renco knew Lett didn't much care for the sergeant. For a Red Cloak, he seemed friendly enough but Lett said his eyes always lingered. Hungry eyes she called them. That they both didn't already occupy the cage was a mystery, but he was not about to complain or give reason to change that.

Kneeling, Renco grabbed his bedding awkwardly in his good hand and rolled the sackcloth into a tight bundle. He was done. The clothes he wore and the bedroll were all he had. His few possessions, including his precious weapons, were lost in Fallston and he knew he'd not see them again.

Comter, the burly sergeant Lett spoke of, turned up with their horses a short while later and it was not long after that that the lead elements of the Red Cloak army headed out, Renco and Lett among them.

It was an unusual feeling not to be bound with only the red-faced Comter appearing to pay them any mind. But Renco was under no illusion they were prisoners still.

"Why head north when everyone else travels south?" Lett asked.

"It's where the urak are girl," Comter replied.

"Five days running south with Father Zoller to escape them. Now Whent races us north to meet them. I didn't know you were all so keen to die." Lett's voice sounded brittle.

"It's Lord Commander, Archbishop Whent; his Excellency or his Grace to you. Anything else y'all feel the back of ma hand. You've been warned," Comter growled.

Unperturbed, Lett turned to Renco and spoke loudly enough that the riders ahead and behind would hear. "I don't think the good sergeant knows, Renco. He's only good for escorting a bard and her companion."

Comter leered, unfazed. "A bard ya say? Guess y'all have a new tale ta tell and song ta sing. Make sure you get me name right, eh."

"The only tale to tell will be of you basting on an urak roasting spit with an apple up the arse for flavour," Lett retorted.

The Red Cloaks all laughed and Comter with them, enjoying the banter.

"Waste of a good apple," A Red Cloak quipped, and the laughter grew louder.

Renco grinned, as much at Lett's sour face as the joke. It earned him a glare and she hissed so only he could hear.

"Glad you're amused, Renco. I'm trying to find where we go. We need to escape and you're not helping any."

Renco had been trying to teach Lett some of the sign language he used. Sorry, his hands spoke. He mangled it badly, his broken fingers making the simple gesture hard to form. Lett though seemed to understand and, mollified, sat back in her saddle.

Riding left plenty of time for thinking and talk of escape turned Renco's mind to Master and Mao. They were all he had in the world. He wondered if they were alive and, if so, where they might be. He could no longer assume his rescue. Master Hiro would be searching for him in Rivercross. If they were to reunite he'd have to affect his own escape and make his way to the city.

He glanced across at Lett. Despite all they'd been through, somehow she managed to look good. Her clothes might be dirt-stained but she'd washed her face and slicked her hair back, binding it in a ponytail and her cheeks were flushed red by the cold lick of wind.

Lett was an added complication. He should abandon her. It was him the Red Church needed to trap Master Hiro. Lett would only slow him down, making any escape doubly difficult. With him gone they'd have no reason to detain her, surely.

\* \* \*

Mid-afternoon a messenger rode back from the front and spoke quietly with Sergeant Comter. Immediately, the sergeant signalled Lett and Renco to follow and in short order, they were cantering past the columns of horses up to the van where they joined the detachment around the Archbishop.

Listening and observing as he did, Renco had learnt much in the last day. He knew Archbishop Whent was Lord Commander of the Red Cloaks, their highest general and head of their training academy in Killenhess. The Academy of Divine Right, they named it. Pretentious, he could hear Master Hiro say. The thought of Master brought a smile to his face just as Whent turned.

"I'm sorry I've not spoken with you both sooner. I've been preoccupied as I'm sure you both appreciate." Whent's voice was disarmingly normal. The steel, from his confrontation with Zoller, was gone.

Renco's smile faded until his face became inscrutable. 'When in an unknowing situation, give nothing to your adversary,' Master taught. Still, there was a charisma about Whent that drew him. Or maybe it was that he'd locked horns with Zoller and slapped the priest down. The pain of his broken fingers had almost been worth it to see that.

"Why bring us here?" Lett asked. "Your five thousand is not enough. We're all going to die."

Whent raised his hand, stilling the men in his guard who were agitated by the question. One, in particular, glared hatefully at Lett.

"It's a fair question," Whent conceded, looking directly at Renco. "We're here because of the first rule of war."

"If getting massacred by urak is the first rule I'm guessing there is no second?" Lett quipped.

Whent gave a terse grin. "Amusing I'm sure. I'm a patient man ordinarily but I've no time for childish posturing. If you listen more you may learn something for your betterment."

"The first rule is, know your adversary. We fight urak but we do not know how to fight them except from books and books alone will not do. Books make statements but that is not the same as understanding and books don't always hold truth. War is a fluid, visceral beast that is in constant flux. We must learn, adapt to it, or die. So here we are; the first rule."

And so it went. With autumn well advanced and winter knocking the day was short, and for the rest of it, the Lord Commander spoke with Lett. He was civil in his questioning and it was subtly done but Renco saw it for what it was; an interrogation.

Whent's manner placed Lett at ease and his insightful, sympathetic tone soon had her recounting everything. From when she first met Renco to how they ended up with Father Zoller at the Defile.

At one point, as Lett told of her experience at Greenholme, it provoked an angry outburst from one of the Red Cloaks and Lett's voice quivered and trailed off.

Renco saw a flash of annoyance cross Whent's face and it brought the steel back to his voice.

"Your lack of control disappoints, Brother Perrick. Tonight, after prayer you will meditate until morning. Think about your actions. Open your soul to Our Lord Kildare and seek his forgiveness. Until then, I do not wish to see or hear you, now go."

As soon as Whent named him, Renco saw the similarities to Thomas Perrick; same eyes, same chin. It explained much. He watched as the Red Cloak nudged his mount out of the line letting the column ride by. His face was contrite but there was no disguising the venom in his eyes as Lett passed him.

As the sun-kissed the horizon in the west an advance scout arrived and spoke with Whent. They talked quietly and away from the column but Renco's hearing was exceptional and he discerned enough to know that urak had been sighted.

It seemed to be the news the Lord Commander waited for. Turning his army away from the road he led it up a path that slowly wound its way into the surrounding foothills.

That night they lit no campfires. In the morning they would practise the first rule.

## Chapter 33: Carvathe Shit

**Abanna Ranges, The Rivers**

"Muruin, god of fates, is a fickle muck-fucker," Bartuk declared.

The Toreen had moved to the southern front in the White Hand invasion of the human lands. His tribe was filled with pride at the honour Mar-Dur accorded them. It meant not only glory in battle but the first claim to any spoils.

Bartuk's feelings on the matter though were decidedly different. Being one of the Toreen's foremost trackers he'd been on many raids and they always made him nervous. He could fight, had passed his trials. But experience and his relatively mediocre size taught that being at the front of anything was a risk.

'Big kills little.' The old words echoed in his mind. Words spoken by his vicious-tongued, gnarl-faced mother. He believed her. Had seen it too many times on countless occasions not to; in battle, the smallest and weakest were always singled out.

Still, maybe Muruin favoured him. The humans fled, leaving no resistance and offering no fight. They'd run down a few stragglers but little else. Not only that; Grimpok no longer hunted him. His focus had shifted elsewhere.

It was said by the Toreen elders that Grimpok led the White Hand's eastern war host against the Blood Skull and pursued them all the way to the Dragons Spine.

Rumour was that Krol led the Blood Skull east to the lands beyond the Dragons Spine. Lands filled with a different breed of humans called Norders; warriors all that fought, tooth and claw, and died hard.

Bartuk grimaced as Murhtuk nudged him sharply in the ribs.

"Grot-tuk comes."

Biting back a retort, Bartuk turned and looked.

Fuck.

The solid bulk of Grot-tuk was hard to miss. Big seemed a prerequisite for leading a Warband and Grot-tuk was no exception. He wended his way through camp unerringly towards them.

"Bar, Murh." His voice was deep and rumbled, "Got a job for you."

Bartuk scowled. They'd just gotten back from scouting their eastern flank. He could smell food cooking.

Murhtuk was more forthcoming, "Yeah?"

"Maliktuk and his boys scouted the stone path by the great river. Found someat needs looking into."

Grot-tuk smiled and Bartuk knew then he wasn't going to like it. Gritting his teeth he waited, determined not to give Grot-tuk the satisfaction of asking. He didn't have to wait long.

"Shit," Grot-tuk said. "Carvathe shit, Malik says."

Bartuk couldn't help himself. "You want us to go out and look at carvathe shit?"

Grot-tuk's face turned hard, eyes furrowed. "Malik found several piles of it just off the stone path two leagues south. Says it was still warm and he found markings in the ground shaped like crescent moons. The shaman, Orqis-tarn, says it is from the metal shoes the humans fit to the carvathe."

"Humans, running south?" Murhtuk suggested.

But Bartuk knew different, the unease twisting his gut told him so. And, he conceded, Maliktuk knew his business.

Grot-tuk shook his head. "Malik says no. And the only carvathe we've seen, till now, have been dead ones."

"How many?" Bartuk asked.

"Four."

Bartuk nodded his head, knowing what that meant. Resigned, he picked up his pack and strapped his axe across his back. Murhtuk hesitated, before gathering his gear.

"We'll need dogs if we're to track at night," Murhtuk grumbled.

"No dogs," Grot-tuk said.

"Four humans, riding tamed carvathe, moving the moons knows where. They'll outrun us," Murhtuk argued.

Grot-tuk's chest puffed out and he seemed to rise several inches. "No. Fucking. Dogs."

Bartuk sighed under his breath. Murhtuk wasn't going to let it go. His friend was big but stupid. Further argument would be seen as a challenge. Already, the musky scent of violence filled the air. He laid a hand on Murhtuk's sword arm.

"We do not look for the scouts, Murh. We look for their masters," Bartuk explained.

Murhtuk stepped back, shrugging Bartuk's hand off. His friend played a dangerous game touching him like that.

"Come. Let's go." Bartuk turned, glanced briefly at the overcast sky, before setting off in an easy, ground eating jog.

Murhtuk followed.

\* \* \*

Night descended quickly and a sharp wind blew from the northeast, right off the Dragons Spine. The cold though did not faze them. They had borne much worse in the tundra of the Norde-Targkish.

The darkness proved more challenging. It slowed them, but there was enough ambient light they could track still, despite the clouds obscuring the tri-moons.

They ran south and west a league before picking up the stone track built by the humans. Bartuk debated walking its path for speed or staying in the undergrowth for stealth and opted in the end for the path. It was a risk, but Bartuk reasoned, if the humans posted lookouts, they would hear them in the dense undergrowth before ever seeing them on the path. Sound travelled further than shadows in this witching no light.

They stopped often to examine the stone track and the verge. Every time, Bartuk found signs of passage but always it turned south. It wasn't until they'd travelled a further league before he found what they looked for.

It was impossible to miss really. What had once been a simple dirt trail leading up into the hills had been churned and trampled as if a herd of longhair had passed through. But longhair didn't roam neatly, two or three abreast. They foraged as they migrated cutting a swathe hundreds of paces across or more.

Bartuk ran his fingers over the dirt, tracing the smooth, uniform rut marks. Nor do they pull wagons, he observed drily. He tried to gauge how many might have passed but it was impossible. Many certainly, but that could mean a hundred hands or a thousand. Intuition told him the latter. To be here in such numbers meant the humans had come to fight.

Instinct burned at him to go, that he'd seen enough, but he resisted its urging. Grot-tuk would not be happy with a guess. He'd want to know how many and where.

Rising, Bartuk moved to Murhtuk, who waited in the long grass. There were no words. Holding his hand up in front of Murhtuk he clenched it into a fist, the sign for a hundred hands. Opening his hand he tapped the edge of it, lightly, five times against the palm of his other hand.

Murhtuk nodded understanding. They clenched, as brothers would, hand to forearm, then Murhtuk turned and disappeared, back the way they'd come.

*** 

"Alone in the dark, tracking humans; what the fuck am I doing?" Bartuk bemoaned. Every step closer threatened danger and fear coursed through his body.

Fear was good. It heightened the senses and kept him alert. It was the lack of it, back in the forest with Gromma and No-nose, which had almost cost him his life. Thinking they were safe, in terrain already scouted, he had been lax. Well, there would be none of that here. Every sense was attuned to his task.

Time was hard to judge with no stars or moons for guidance. But he thought an hour, maybe two had passed when he got his next tell. It was not the trail that gave it but the air.

Approaching the brow of a hill, keeping to the tall bush and trees, it was borne on the wind; the musky, grassy scent of many carvathe and beneath that a subtler smell that could only be humans.

He slowed. Any sentries guarding the path would hear or see him if he was not careful. He moved deeper into the undergrowth, each step carefully placed.

A cough in the darkness, so close it almost made him jump. He waited, listening and eyes straining. There was a faint rustle as the watcher shifted restlessly.

Bartuk took several long breaths to still his hammering heart. Then, carefully, he stepped away, holding the branches of the bushes as he passed to still any noise.

Bartuk was proud of his craft; he was the best tracker the Toreen had, though Maliktuk would no doubt argue it. But these were new lands; everything here was different than in the north. The terrain was alien with undergrowth that was thick, lush, and more varied than the tundra of the Norde-Targkish, from hardy thorn bush to rowans and hornbeams and a hundred more that he had no name for. Each step was unknown and with it his fear grew, warring with his pride.

Parting the bushes in front of him, the ground fell away steeply and Bartuk reasoned he had crested the hill. The smell of carvathe and human was so strong he could almost sense them in the valley below. No fires were lit but sound carried and he could hear carvathe nickering and, despite the late hour, the muted murmur of humans.

It was a mistake to have come. With no light, there was no way to gauge numbers. He glanced at the sky but it was a black canvas still. A hazy sheen showed where Jud'pur'tak, the largest of the tri-moons, tried breaking through the cover.

Then, as if Ampor-tak, the god of luck, witnessed his plight the clouds parted and the baleful face of Jud'pur'tak cast its light on the valley below. Undulating herds of carvathe were revealed and alongside and around them, a patchwork quilt of blocky shades and darker shadows. It vanished as the cloud once again obscured Jud'pur'tak's face but he'd seen enough.

Bartuk retraced his steps, careful of how he placed his feet. Leaf litter was everywhere. Unlike the tundra and forests in the north, half the trees and bushes seemed to shed their plumage. It made moving quietly, in the dark, a tricky prospect.

Scrapping aside leaves with his foot, Bartuk placed it on the soft loam beneath. As his weight shifted over it, the ground suddenly crumbled and fell away. Stumbling, his ankle twisted and flared in pain. Biting back a cry, he fell forward, hands grasping blindly. One grazed a branch and he latched on to it without thought. Razor-sharp spikes of agony stabbed into his fingers and palm. A grunt escaped as he fought back a scream that threatened to burst out.

© 2020 A D Green

It wasn't enough. The rustle of bush and snap of branch sounded so loud. Light flared, glaring and sudden, as a lantern was unshielded. A whistle sounded over the rasping ring of steel.

"Who passes?"

There was no time for subtlety. Lurching to his feet, Bartuk crashed through the scrub and bush towards the light. His ankle protested furiously at every jarring impact. It threatened not to hold his weight but it did, just. Stiff and sharp with pain, Bartuk's spiked and bloody hand pulled the knife from his belt.

The challenger was masked behind the lantern's light, which threw the ground between them into stark relief. Drawing his arm back, Bartuk flicked his wrist and sent the knife spinning into the night. It smashed into the lantern and the human cried out in surprise and the light extinguished.

Following hard behind his throw, Bartuk tore through the low scrub and, dropping his shoulder, threw himself forward at where the light had been. Something grazed his left arm and shoulder before the sickening, dizzying crunch of impact.

Not big for an urak, he still out massed a human and they tumbled to the ground. There was a snap and a scream of pain.

Rising from on top, Bartuk pummelled his fist once, twice then a final time into the human's face. The screaming stopped at the first blow and the body flopped, limp and lifeless beneath him.

Blood coursed down his arm. He'd taken a cut but strangely felt no pain from it. His thorn scarred hand ached more and his ankle throbbed abominably.

Rolling off the body, Bartuk felt around the leaf litter for his knife but couldn't find it. Fear and instinct overrode his pain. The alarm had sounded and who knew how close the next guard was or how many. Heart pumping furiously, he had to get away.

Rising to his feet, Bartuk tested his ankle and winced. It was bad. Already he could feel it swelling, tight against his hide boot.

Darkness was his only chance now and turning, he stumbled downhill making far too much noise.

© 2020 A D Green

Bartuk felt the air shift and flinched, turning just as something smashed into the back of his head.

## Chapter 34: Barden Vale

**Barden Vale, The Rivers**

The old dream was back, reasserting itself in his unconscious psyche. It was a dream he could never sleep through and so it was that Renco was awake, with images of fire and the acrid scent of burning in his mind when the whistle sounded. He hurried to the tent's opening and cautiously peered out. The alarm was shrill but distant in the quiet of the night. It came from one of the pickets in the low hills to the west.

Lett stirred. She'd been huddled close to Renco for warmth and the cold air chilled her where his heat had been moments before. Groaning, she opened her eyes.

"It's dark still. What're you doing?"

Renco sighed in frustration. He turned back in time to see her stretch and yawn. It was not a totally unpleasant sight as it pulled her shift in interesting directions, but it was clear from the way she stared over his shoulder that she couldn't see him as easily.

Guilty at his turn of thought and trapped by his silence he turned and looked west again. People were moving in the dark. Lanterns suddenly sprang up as shutter guards were opened.

"What's going on?" Lett sat up in concern.

A whistle sounded again in the distance just as a squad of Red Cloaks shuffled past, several still fighting with buckles on their mail as they dressed.

The camp was alive with sudden activity. A slash of light beamed fifty feet to Renco's left and he watched with interest as a large, barrel-chested guard held back the canvas flap to the pavilion. Moments later, Archbishop Whent strode through it. He was dressed not in a church cassock but in red plated armour with elaborate gold filigree etched on the pauldrons and at the joints that glinted in the lantern light.

Whent spoke briefly with the large Red Cloak, who bowed then turned and spoke with several others that stood guard near the pavilion. The Red Cloaks swiftly departed, heading to the west of camp and towards the alarm.

Awkward with his broken fingers, Renco grimaced and slipped his boots on. Lacing them roughly, he dressed quickly.

"What are you doing?" Lett hissed.

Renco gestured with his hands, 'prepare' 'watch'. In the new half-light of the lanterns, she could see him but Renco wasn't sure she understood his signing. Whether she did or not Lett rose and started pulling her clothes on.

"Do you mind?" she hissed when she realised he watched her still.

Renco held his hands up in apology. It's not like you're naked or anything he thought. Lett was an enigma that confounded him. He felt so confused, embarrassed, guilty, and annoyed all at the same time and he wasn't quite sure what for. A sudden pang struck him, a longing for the simple life of the open road with only Master and Mao for company.

Raised voices and the sounds of booted feet and rattling armour dragged Renco from his introspection. A column of Red Cloaks approached, though it was more a crowd funnelled through avenues of tents than an orderly file.

"Order and discipline, Captain Warwick, I will have it," Whent told the burly Red Cloak. They had moved unnoticed and stood waiting in a clear space near Renco and Lett.

Captain Warwick promptly shouted commands and his sergeants moved through the camp screaming orders. Like mist parting in sunlight, the mass of Red Cloaks melted away, suddenly finding some other duty to attend to.

It left a dozen Red Cloaks on the approach, four of them carrying something between them in a canvas sheet. At Whent's urging, they dumped it on the ground at his feet. Spears and swords were levelled, whilst one pulled back the covering to reveal an unconscious and inert urak. Rope ties bound it hand and foot. The rise and fall of its chest was the only sign it lived.

Renco stared in interest. It was the first chance he'd had to study one close up. It looked large, bigger than the Red Cloak Captain who stood over it, though not by much. Its skin was grey-hued and its hair teased into small spikes. It had large eyes set in a broad face with a wide mouth and flat nose. Its ridged forehead had an ugly scar running across it that looked puckered and sore and was clearly recent. Blood from a wound, oozed at its temple, so dark it appeared almost black.

"Very good," Whent stepped close and nudged the urak roughly with his boot as if to reassure himself it was indeed alive. "Fetch Brother Henreece. It won't do for this thing to die. Not yet anyway."

"Your will, Lord Commander," Captain Warwick nodded at a guardsman who promptly turned and disappeared between the tents.

"It won't be alone," the captain said.

"Indeed, we must assume the urak know we're here," Whent said, glancing at the black skies above, "But maybe not our number, unless they can see in the dark. Have the men readied. We move at first light. Let's bait the trap."

The physiker, Henreece, arrived and moved to the prone urak. He muttered a belated "Lord Commander", as he knelt beside it.

Setting his bag down the physiker opened it, took out a small bottle, and rinsed his hands with the solution it contained. He started his examination, fingers and hands moving over his patient as he pried and prodded. The rest observed in silence.

"Hmmm, interesting," Henreece said, lifting the urak's eyelids and peering intently. Finally, sitting back on his heels, he looked up at the Archbishop.

"Well?"

"If you're asking if it will live, your grace, then yes. The urak was hit hard here." Henreece touched the side of his head. "But there is no haemorrhaging in the eyes and no bleeding from ear or nose. From my observations, I would say that they are remarkably similar in design to us. Though more solid it would appear in both bone density and muscle mass. I'll know more after carrying out a detailed examination and some tests. I don't suppose you have a dead one I could look at? It would be a shame to waste a live one if we don't have to."

Renco blinked, a chill tickling the nape of his neck at the matter of fact way the physiker spoke; it was as if he talked of carving a joint of meat.

"I'm sure we'll have something for you by day's end," Whent assured him. "Now, secure the urak in one of the wagons, tend its wounds then make sure it has food and water."

"Your will, Lord Commander," Henreece snapped his bag closed and stood. The urak was hefted once again in its hammock by the guardsmen, who followed Henreece as he led them away.

Whent watched them go, his expression thoughtful before turning to Warwick. "Captain, have the wagons and support auxiliaries withdraw south as planned. Have Captain Maeson's cohort guard them and secure a line of withdrawal."

Warwick clenched a fist to his stomach and inclined his head, "Your will, Lord Commander."

Renco watched the captain move off, whilst keeping Whent in his periphery. The Archbishop looked over as if only now seeing him but Renco wasn't fooled. He had that same smug air of calculation the priest did. That he detested Zoller above all things was personal. In all likelihood, he conceded, Whent was likely no better.

There was a creasing of leather on steel as Whent crossed the small space between them.

"You're a fine puzzle, Renco. If Father Zoller is to be believed, and that is my tendency; then you're a mute apprentice to an Order Knight. That means your Master is either a fool or a genius. I am undecided on the matter."

Renco listened warily, keeping his face impassive.

"I was going to send you with the support auxiliaries but I think I've changed my mind. Sergeant Comter."

"Lord Commander." Comter materialised from behind Renco and Lett.

"Make sure they're both ready to move by first light. They'll be accompanying me." Whent waited for Comter's acknowledgement then swivelled and strode back to his pavilion, two Red Cloaks shadowing him.

* * *

The hamlet of Barden Vale lay in the valley it took its name from. Its handful of wood and thatch cottages was situated on high ground, west of the stream that neatly bisected the vale. The lands around the hamlet had been cultivated and were a combination of pasture and crop fields.

The surrounding hills stretched into the distance and were a patchwork riot of colour. Tall evergreens clashed with the muted greys and the dull browns of naked trees and against a carpet of autumn leaves and hardy bush.

It was in these hills just to the west, that Renco and Lett observed the hamlet. They stood atop a small hillock, with Archbishop Whent and his elite guard, hidden by the trees and bushes that crowned it. From their vantage point, it was apparent the cluster of buildings laid abandoned, with no sign of life, human or otherwise.

Renco wasn't entirely sure why they were there. But assumed from Whent's earlier comment about 'baiting the trap' and the fact they'd been sat observing the hamlet for the past hour, that it had some part to play in matters.

Behind them and just below the hill's crown, a cohort of a thousand Red Cloaks threaded the trees. To Renco, it begged the question: where was the rest of Whent's army? And why had he split it? Master had often lectured on the art of warfare and it seemed to Renco that, not knowing where the enemy was or in what numbers, Whent's strategy was a poor one.

But the Archbishop seemed unbothered, appearing relaxed and exuding a quiet confidence. It led Renco to conclude that Whent knew more than he divulged.

Something on the opposite side of the valley drew Renco's eye, ending his speculation. He seemed the first to notice it for it was a full ten seconds before one of the guards raised a hand and pointed.

Red Cloaks passing through the low forest to the east. Riding clear of the trees and into the open grasslands of the vale, they headed towards the cluster of buildings. At first, Renco thought it might be the main body of the Red Cloak army but only fifty riders cleared the treeline.

"What are we waiting for?" Lett moaned, her frosted breath pluming the air. It drew a scowl from Comter and she lapsed into silence. Moving next to Renco, she slipped an arm through his and pressed her body close.

Renco felt her shivering. The overcast skies of the night before had remained and the same chill wind blew from the northeast. It was bitter and he knew it would only get worse for Lett. Other than her cloak and hood, the rest of Lett's attire was not suited to the cold weather and the day was set to get worse. He could smell rain in the air.

Willing some of his warmth into her, Renco felt concerned and protective all of a sudden. He patted her hand and Lett seemed to appreciate the gesture. She snuggled closer and her trembling abated. Her head brushed his and her warm breath tickled his ear. He smelled carrok seed, used to clean and refresh the mouth. He about jumped out of his skin when she spoke.

"Today, if chance permits, we should make a break for it."

Renco squeezed her hand. The idea had already occurred to him, only he'd not been able to convey it. Whilst it was reassuring they shared the same thought, he felt discomfited, for Lett had not featured in his plans.

Enjoying her closeness, his attention switched back to the valley. The riders had forded the stream and were entering the hamlet. Whatever they were about they appeared in no great hurry. They gathered in the centre and moments later dismounted in unison. Several broke off, entering a large barn, pulling the doors wide. Renco wondered at first if they foraged, searching for feed for the horses but they were gone too long for that.

A tendril of smoke trickled its way through the thatch of the barn, barely noticeable at first, as the stiff breeze tore it away. Soon however, it thickened and tall spirals of dark smoke plumed the sky.

"That's somebody's barn. Why are you burning it?" Lett asked.

"Quiet girl, I'll not tell ya agin." Comter loomed up behind her and Renco felt Lett flinch.

"Now, Sergeant. That is no way to speak to our guests," Whent admonished; his voice was calm and reasonable but it stopped Comter in his tracks.

"Sorry, Lord Commander," Comter ducked his head and took a step back.

"We are sending a message, my dear," Whent said.

Lett frowned. "Torching a place is a message? Who too? Everyone's either left already or dead."

Whent's brow furrowed. "I understand your father was a bard. I imagine you get your fiery disregard and curiosity from him. Fine qualities for a bard, I'm sure, but that shouldn't stop you from engaging your intellect or common sense. If you cannot reason it, perhaps friend Renco here might elaborate. I'm sure he understands the message."

At the mention of her father, Lett's face dropped. Renco gave her hand another squeeze, glaring at Whent, who shrugged indifferently before returning to his surveillance.

Turning his own eyes to the valley, Renco saw the barn was burning steadily and could smell the smoke on the gusting breeze. From this distance, the riders looked small. Mounted again, the Red Cloaks turned their horses north and left the hamlet. They moved slowly, following the winding path of the stream.

The sky darkened as rain swept in. It rolled down the valley from the north and over the riders, until they were just a vague blur before disappearing altogether behind its veil.

The leaves sang a symphony, as rain suddenly pattered down around them. As one, hoods were raised and cloaks pulled tight. Renco could feel the unease pervading the Red Cloaks as they stared restlessly into the downpour.

The sky rumbled and the rain intensified. Straining his senses, Renco picked out something. It was indistinct, a clash or noise that tantalised the edge of reason. It could have been the wind and rain or distant thunder maybe, but its pitch was off.

Renco detected movement among the blocky, indistinct shapes of the hamlet. A shadow moved between the buildings, its hazy outline slowly resolving.

"Lord Commander," shouted a guard, pointing redundantly to where everyone already looked, "a horse, with no rider."

"So I see." Whent spared an accusing look at the sky but made no further comment.

Another shape turned into another horse. Then more, until suddenly there were many. Some still bore riders and these gathered in the centre, near to the still smoking barn.

"Lord Commander?"

"If you speak again, Brother Morgan, you will join your brethren in the ranks behind." Whent raised his voice above the crescendo of rain.

The downpour suddenly tapered off to a soft drizzle as the squall passed. Below, the remnants of the Red Cloak company had regrouped. Renco counted twenty-two of them but a hand of those did not sit right in the saddle.

"Where's the rest?" Lett asked. Then, to no one in particular, "I bloody well hate the cold."

Renco touched a hand to her shoulder to quiet her and draw her attention. A sour-faced Comter was in view behind, jaw grinding, eyes boring into the back of Lett's head. Renco repeated the sign for 'watch' adding another for 'stillness', hoping she would understand, if not his exact meaning, then the intent.

Below, the riders faced north, forming a skirmish line with shields out and long spears extending before them. The horses danced nervously. Something was coming.

As the drizzle faded, shapes emerged from the wild grass at the edge of the far fields. At this distance, they appeared as men would and could have been mistaken for them, but Renco knew they were not. Judging by the stone drywall they climbed over they were bigger than a man and their movement different. Their strides were longer, more loping, with bodies stooped slightly forward as they moved.

They outnumbered the surviving Red Cloaks by a score or more. Renco felt the urge to use his hidden sense but knew they were too distant. Master could navigate aether that far but it was beyond his ability.

The urak slowed, half of them stopping altogether and pulling heavy bows from the covers on their backs. The remainder walked on, calling out in challenge. Their barking cries carrying down the valley and echoing up into the hills.

The riders waited, calmly it seemed to Renco. Why? *It's madness.* To his left, Whent suddenly raised a hand and the guard by his side lifted a silver horn to his lips. A long, low wail stretched out. It reverberated and set Renco's ears buzzing in protest so that he raised his hands to cover them.

Below, the urak advance stopped. At the same instant, the horsemen spurred their mounts into a canter, spears lowering as they rapidly closed the distance.

The urak roared in response, breaking into a run. A ragged, uneven volley of arrows rose from their archers. The impact as they struck staggered several of the riders, whose shield or armour blocked and deflected most of the strikes. The rest either missed or past harmlessly overhead, their closing speed causing many urak to misjudge the lead required.

Not all Red Cloaks passed unscathed. A horse was struck sending it tumbling to the ground, its rider crushed under its flailing body. Another was hit flush in the chest, the arrow piercing his plated mail. The saddles high back prevented him from cartwheeling off. Instead, he flopped back then forwards before sliding slowly to the side and tumbling to the ground.

The two sides met in a thunderous crash. Spears sought flesh as the chargers clattered into and through the urak. Lightly armoured, the urak were easily impaled if a thrust landed; most missed though. The urak were spread out in a staggered formation whilst the Red Cloaks' charge was uneven as those carrying injury lagged behind, breaking the solid line of spears and the armoured wall of horseflesh.

A handful of urak fell to the spears and a handful more to the iron-shod hooves of the battle-trained chargers, their bones snapping as they were trampled.

In return, several horses went down, killed or hamstrung, and the riders that fell with them died too. Weighted down by their armour, they were slow to rise and the urak simply clubbed them or ran the men through as they struggled to regain their feet.

Momentum carried the surviving Red Cloaks through the first line of urak and into a hail of arrows. The withering volley slammed into horse and rider alike, the close range and heavy arrows devastating in their effect. A few arrows were deflected or became lodged in shields but the rest punched through, over matching the mail, to pierce flesh and bone.

The charge faltered then broke as the Red Cloaks were assailed by urak front and back. In a battle-fuelled frenzy, they were pulled from their mounts and bludgeoned to death.

And then it was over.

The battle had lasted no more than a minute and the urak stood victorious, whooping and screaming.

"You sent them to be slaughtered," Lett accused.

Renco gripped her arm as she confronted Whent but she shook him off, angry.

Whent ignored her, his attention fixated still on the battlefield, a look of eager anticipation on his face.

Puzzled, Renco's gaze was drawn back to the valley. Flickers of red tantalised the eastern fringes of the vale as if some huge serpent slithered and undulated through the scrub and trees.

It wasn't over.

The sounding of the horn had been more than just a signal for the dead men below, Renco realised, just as riders burst from the forest. Hordes of them; their red cloaks billowing out behind.

The urak reacted immediately. To Renco, they appeared fierce and brutal and he half expected them to charge the Red Cloaks but they didn't. They turned tail and ran, heading north up the valley, back the way they'd come. He wondered at that. The deep undergrowth and forest on the western slopes of the valley would offer the best chance to escape. Running up the valley they would be ridden down in minutes.

In his periphery, the guard with the silver horn lifted it to his lips. Whent said something and raised his hand to forestall him. The guard immediately lowered it and Whent returned his attention to the battlefield.

His mood has changed, Renco realised. Whent was faced away from him but his body language told him much. He was tense whereas before he was eager.

A sudden cognizance struck him. The Lord Commander had predicted the attack, planned for it in fact. The urak had sprung 'the trap' only Whent had expected them to break for the western slopes. With abrupt clarity, Renco knew then where the rest of Whent's forces were. It was followed almost immediately by a deep foreboding.

Numbness infused his body, uncertainty settling like a fist in his chest. Renco took a faltering step. Unsure exactly what he was doing, only that there was danger in the fields below, even if it could not be seen.

"Step away." The barrel-chested, Captain Warwick interposed himself between Renco and the Lord Commander. "Sergeant Comter, why am I doing your job for you?"

"Sorry Captain," Comter knew better than to offer an excuse. Gripping a handful of cloak, he pulled Renco back.

Without thought, Renco spun; twisting beneath Comter's outstretched arm and broke his hold. Flaring his cloak up and over whilst unhooking its clasp it settled over the Red Cloak's head. With a stumbling step backwards, Comter slipped on the wet ground and ended up on his backside, grunting in pain as his mail tugged harshly against their straps.

There was a rasp of drawn steel and Renco turned slowly to find a blade poised inches from his chest. Captain Warwick held it. His hand was steady, arm slightly bent, ready for a killing thrust.

Strangely, the numb uncertainty Renco had felt moments before was gone. He had taken an action and the altercation had been enough to clear his mind. His eyes shifted from the hard-faced Captain, seeking out Whent.

The commotion had drawn the Archbishop's attention away from the unfolding drama in the valley and Whent glared at him, a vexed expression on his face.

Renco signed, badly, his broken fingers screaming in protest. No one would understand but what else could he do. At the puzzled looks, he pointed at the Red Cloaks down in the vale and shook his head, no. He banged the edges of his hands together hard, to emphasize his point.

Whent's face cleared; his eyes thoughtful as understanding dawned. At the same time, Brother Morgan spoke despite his order to remain silent.

"My sister's child is deaf, Lord Commander. The boy's signing differs from what I know but I think he signals danger or warning."

Whent sighed, breath misting in the chill air. Decided, he barked out commands.

"Sound the withdrawal, Brother Hamish." He instructed the bugler, before addressing Warwick. "Captain, have your cohort fall back. Our adventure it seems is prematurely ended."

Warwick had not moved his sword point an inch from the mute's chest. The corner of his mouth curled derisively and he withdrew his blade, returning it with practised ease to its scabbard. Turning on his heel, Warwick started shouting orders. At the same time, a long low wail peeled out, rising and falling in pitch.

"What's going on? I don't understand," Lett said, as the horses were brought forward.

"Master Renco believes the urak have laid their own trap. I agree so we ride south," Whent replied, "My purpose is untested but we have gained some insight and a prisoner."

Lett laughed derisively. "Just words to make you feel better. You sacrificed your men and at the first sign of trouble you run with your tail between your legs."

The Red Cloaks in earshot bristled and Whent's eyes narrowed. "Why Miss Letizia, I do believe you try to goad me. If you're unhappy with your rescue from Father Zoller I can always return you to his company, Renco too."

Lett scowled at the mention of Zoller.

"Well then, might I suggest you show a modicum of humility and gratitude?" Whent said, gathering his reins. Brother Morgan, standing behind, grabbed the Lord Commander's raised sabaton and boosted him up into the saddle.

Sensing movement, Renco turned, catching his balled up cloak as Comter threw it at him. The Sergeant glared at the both of them, waited till Whent trotted out of sight, then spat. "I don't need no excuse to brain the pair of ya. Now get on ya fucking horses and ride."

## Chapter 35: The Holes

**The Grim Marsh, The Rivers**

"We're being watched." Wynter's certainty was unquestionable.

"Grimmers?" Jacob queried.

"Ai," Wynter sounded resigned. "Bin watching us an hour or more I suspect. Only now there's more of 'em."

Jacob, Mahan and Thornhill looked anxiously at the surrounding reeds and mud banks but couldn't see anything.

They were already on edge, as the deeper into the marsh they travelled the more alien it seemed. Mist hovered over the dark, fetid waters and they were reliant completely on Wynter to guide them. At times, islands of dense foliage sprang into relief around them or they'd find themselves paddling through forests of tall reeds or fields of bright lilies. Occasionally they would grind over a hidden mud bar.

Sometimes, large bubbles globbed and puttered to the surface, hinting at something lurking beneath. Always, Wynter steered wide when he saw these, though he offered no explanation. Talk was infrequent.

"What do you suggest?" Jacob felt his chest tightening. He'd trained with arms since he was six and barely able to lift the child's blade his father had made for him. His training though hadn't prepared him for the helplessness he felt now. In Thorsten, surrounded by urak, he'd felt despair but there at least he could see the enemy. Fight if he chose. Here, he was lost.

"We've drawn 'em, like blowflies to a body. There ain't no escaping 'em. We'll wait on that island ahead," Wynter declared.

The island turned out to be a massive rock. Incongruously out of place in this land of mud and stinking water.

"It's like a Rock Giant placed it here for some purpose," Mahan muttered, as he clambered up on to it. Bush roots and vine hugged the rock's surface making it easy to scale.

"Ain't no such thing as a Rock Giant," Thornhill argued.

"Quieten down the pair of you," Jacob said. He looked back into their boat, at Sand lying helpless between the gunwales. Wynter insisted they leave him there, since pulling him up and onto the rock would be tricky with no means to anchor the boat and it would serve no real purpose. Jacob agreed but that didn't mean he had to like it.

Standing atop the rock, they were above the cloying fog and Jacob could see another rock island no more than fifty paces away. It looked a twin to the one they stood upon, if not for the gnarled willow that clung to its crown like a malignant growth, its roots extending like fingers across its surface and into the marsh.

"There's four of 'em." Wynter said, nodding at the pimple of stone, "Lined up perfect like one after t'other. Grimmers calls 'em the giant's knuckles."

"Told ya, Rock Giants," Mahan nudged Thornhill.

Thornhill grunted, too busy scanning the sea of mist for the watchers to offer any argument. "Don't like this a piece. Not a piece of it."

Jacob agreed wholeheartedly. He turned to Wynter. "What now?"

"We wait," Wynter said.

The wait wasn't long. A figure slowly emerged from the mist, at the prow of a narrowboat. A small mast, with its sail wrapped tightly around it, split the middle of the craft, and as it neared the rocks, two more figures resolved at its tail.

The skiff drew to a stop as the man at the stern back paddled expertly, hardly drawing a ripple from the still water.

"Hail gentles," the prow man called. He was short and solid with a tangled beard that fell to his mid-riff. The face behind the beard was lopsided, with one rheumy eye sitting higher than the other.

"Seems you is lost in this gods' forsaken swamp. Bad place to be doin' that if'n I do say so meself."

"Hail friend," Jacob said. "We're not lost, just passing through."

This drew a derisive laugh from the other two in the boat.

"Seems you've a problem then, 'friend'," the bearded man drawled. "See, if'n you ain't lost that be tellin' me you's here a purpose. 'Scuse me cussing but ya weren't fuckin' invited. Which means you is trespassing."

Wynter laid a hand on Jacob's arm, his expression hard to fathom as he stepped forward.

"Thought ya'd be dead by now, Odd-John?"

The bearded man made a show, cupping his hand above his eyes and straining his neck forward. "Ned? That you ya treacherous cunt? I confess the same thought as just run through me own 'ead."

Odd-John beamed, flashing dirty yellow teeth, and gave a shake of his head. "Ya should'na come back, Ned."

"Ai, I know it."

"He'll want ta see ya," Odd-John stated. "Ya know the drill. Hissings here'll come up, collect your weapons. Tell ya, friends, to make no trouble else they'll find it right enough."

Wynter gave a barely perceptible nod and started unbuckling his sword belt. The rest followed his example. All looked askance at him but Wynter offered nothing.

\* \* \*

The journey through the marsh was long and vague in Jacob's recollection. Wynter was held in another boat, bound hand and foot with a weighted rock around his ankles. The rest of them, including the still comatose Sand, rode unfettered in their own boat. A lanyard was tied from its prow to the stern of Odd-John's skiff though they were encouraged to paddle rather than be towed. They were surrounded by a hand of boats, each bearing three Grimmers, two paddling, one armed with a light bow. The possibility of escape was none and had there been any they had no idea where they were in this cloying mist.

Night had set in when the twinkling sparkle of lights appeared like fireflies in the dark. As they drew near, a thick mass against the black sky hinted at a large building or structure of some type.

Their captors followed the shoreline around until finally drawing into an area bright with torches. It revealed a wooden jetty protruding out into the marsh and a stone ramp slowly rising from its murky depths.

A disordered crowd awaited them. Their numbers were hard to gauge in the gloom of torchlight but hundreds strong, Jacob guessed. A heavy trepidation settled over him.

As the boats beached on the ramp, the Grimmers leapt from the skiffs and dragged them high. Their canoe, with its slightly deeper hull, forced them into the inky cold waters. Slipping and stumbling on the slime coated stone they waded ashore pulling the prow half up the ramp to anchor it.

A man detached from the crowd and sauntered towards them. He was tall though not overly so. Wide shouldered and narrow hipped he walked with an ease and swagger that told his story. This is my domain and these are my people, it said.

The man carried a torch that flickered in the breeze, casting his face into sharp relief. It was a hard face with harsh lines and strong angles with eyes that glinted like quartz, silver in the torchlight. Casting a cursory glance at Jacob, Mahan and Thornhill he dismissed them, his gaze instead settling on Wynter. Approaching the bow master he gave a grim smile.

"It's good to see you, brother."

Wynter stared back. He took a deep breath, a resigned look crossing his face.

"Jackson…."

If he would say more, Wynter never had the chance. Suddenly he was doubled up, the breath he'd taken whooshing out of him as a fist drove hard into his gut. Coughing and gasping for air he dropped a knee to the mud.

"You should'na come back, Ned. Death waits for you here. The crone foresaw it and I warned you." The man turned to face the crowd, holding his arms high and wide. The crowd looked like it had grown, the mass of people swelling and shifting as they watched the drama unfolding. Not one made a sound.

"NED TULLOCK!" Jackson shouted, his voice lifting and carrying. "SEE, MY PRODIGAL BROTHER RETURNS. NOW PISS OFF! SHOW'S OVER CUNT FUCKERS."

Jacob watched as the assembly dispersed, needing no further encouragement it seemed to go about their business. The trepidation he'd felt earlier deepened. This man, Wynter's brother if it could be believed, seemed unhinged. He wasn't sure what to expect but Jacob knew whatever it was, it would be nothing good.

The man turned to Wynter again and regarded him in silence a while. The bow master for his part stared right back, unflinching. It drew a crooked smile.

"Names Jackson Tullock, Lord of the Grimhold," He announced, his eyes flicking to Jacob before sweeping to include Mahan and Thornhill. "Black Jack is what folks call me. That or Lord Tullock'll do when you speak to me."

The guards about them shifted impatiently and Black Jack nodded at them.

"Put my brother in the hole. His friends too, I'll deal with them in the morning."

"There's another in the boat. Burnt bad, like that fella we found on the river, only not so much," One of the guards lisped.

Black Jack strode down to the waterline. Holding his torch over the canoe it illuminated the man lying within. He whistled, as if both impressed and surprised.

"You're right, Hissings. He don't look so good; more dead than alive."

"What should we do with 'im? He won't survive the hole," Hissings said.

Black Jack drew his knife and stepped closer, his boot sinking into the water.

Jacob stepped towards the canoe about to call out but Wynter beat him to it.

"Leave 'im be, Jack. He's worth more than his weight in gold alive, nothing at all dead."

Black Jack stopped and paused before taking a slow step back, shaking his wet boot off as he did.

"Okay, I'll bite. Who is he, Ned?"

"Lord Jacob Bouchemeax, son of the Black Crow," Wynter said.

Black Jack whistled again, this time long and low, "That so. These here his men I s'ppose, they're wearing Black Crow livery."

"You s'ppose right."

© 2020 A D Green

"Do I? We'll see. Kill the young buck," Black Jack said. Hissings and Odd-John glanced at each other, shrugged then drew their knives. Mahan and Thornhill immediately stepped in front of Jacob.

"Wait," Jacob implored. This was senseless, they stood no chance.

Hissings sidled close brandishing his knife, weaving it back and forth through the air in an intricate pattern. Odd-John, however, glanced back at Black Jack.

"Hold," the command reluctantly given, "Talk. If you lie, the tall one dies." Black Jack indicated Thornhill.

Jacob spared Wynter a look, wondering who the bow master was. The former Grimmer returned it, his stony-eyed gaze conveying nothing, giving no indication if he thought Jacob about to make a mistake or not.

"Well come on boy, spit it out. Who the fuck are you? And who the fuck is he?" Black Jack hitched a thumb at the canoe.

"I'm Lord Jacob. That's my cousin Sandford, Lord of Redford," Jacob said.

Gratingly, Black Jack whistled again.

"Lord William's boy, eh. Bad Bill, mad Bill……" Black Jack trailed off in silence, lost in thought. After a time he looked up, casually spun his knife before sliding it smoothly into the sheath at his hip.

"Put 'em in the hole like I said. All of 'em. If his Lordship here survives till morning, the gods will have spoken."

\* \* \*

The hole turned out to be several large circular pits within the dilapidated ruins of an old keep. Ancient stone formed the walls of each cell, rough to the touch but surprisingly whole despite their age. No mortar held the joins, though lichen and moss did grace the sides where damp moistened the stone.

Separated, they were cast, one each to a hole. A foot of water filled the bottom of each with a perfectly round stone block rising in the centre. It provided the only dry space and was just large enough to sit upon. Unable to lie down or sit comfortably, each man perched with their knees tucked in tight to their bodies.

Unconscious still, Sand was the only one unable to support himself on the stone block. Hissings and Odd-John left him propped, half-naked, against the cell wall. His stomach and legs submerged in the surprisingly warm water.

"He'll be gone afore an hours past," Odd-John predicted cheerily. Hissings smirked in agreement but his mind was on other things.

"I could eat a rat I'm so hungry," he declared, dropping the last of the metal grills in place.

"I can do you better than that," Odd-John said.

"Got a catfish curing in the smoke hut…." Their voices grew fainter until a door boomed closed and they were gone. It was pitch black.

"What do we do now?" Mahan's voice wavered.

"We wait," Wynter said.

"Are you really brothers?" Jacob asked more accusation than a question.

"Half and a bit," Wynter replied, "Mothers were sisters. Same father."

"Blood binds but he don't like you none," Thornhill stated. "Why is that?"

"We was close once when we was young," Wynter explained, "Necessity and need. Surviving this place is easier with someone watchin ya back."

There was a long pause as Wynter collected his thoughts. After a while Jacob prompted him.

"So what happened?"

"The short of it, Da was a sadistic fuck, and I the elder. I was mean enough, guess I had to be, but I'd no intention of staying in this shithole let alone rule it afterwards. Jack though was like him, twisted. He wanted it bad. When he was big enough and had the balls for it, he murdered our Da and tried to kill me. Blood don't bind Grimmers so much as mark'em. Me, I was an obstacle."

There was more to it than that, Jacob was sure of it. Odd-John had called Wynter treacherous. It left him wondering more about what Wynter hadn't said as did.

"Argh, I can't stand this," Mahan wailed suddenly. "The walls are gonna cave in. There's someat in this water too, I know it and by Kildare's hairy ball sack why is it so warm?"

"Stay out of the water. There are lice and leeches in it and other things you don't wanna know about. They won't kill but stronger men than you have come out of this place with the wasting sickness," Wynter said.

"Fucking great," Mahan cussed.

"Place like this asks questions of a man. Gives him perspective."

"Now you're a philosopher? How about you give us back the ranger and get us the fuck out of here instead?" Mahan shouted, his voice rising hysterically.

Wynter's reply seemed distant and vague. As if he spoke to himself. "Rage all you like it'll do no good. Save your strength. Harness your anger. Suppress your fear. Plan your vengeance."

"What the fu…"

"Mahan. Give it a rest," Jacob snapped. "Like it or not we're here. Rest up if you can. We need to be ready."

"For what?" Mahan sulked, "My Lord."

"For whatever comes next," Jacob said.

"What in the Trinity is wrong with you Mahan?" Thornhill interjected. "Lord Jacob has enough to contend with. Don't need you whining on."

"Whining on? You lanky bastard…."

A loud chuckling silenced the rest of his insult. It rose from Wynter's cell and echoed in the vaulted room above.

"Only just got 'ere and already you're losing your shit. This place will mess you up if you let it." Wynter's gruff pronouncement followed his laughter.

"Stop it," Jacob, ordered. "He doesn't like small spaces; that's all. He's scared, hells we all are. And here, I'm Lord of nothing. I'm just Jacob. We're all the same in this place."

© 2020 A D Green

They lapsed into silence; alone, with only their thoughts for company. Thoughts, that offered no comfort. Hard to sit easy, impossible to sleep, it was the longest night of their lives.

* * *

The darkness was not complete. Now his eyes had adjusted, Jacob was sure the black above him was deeper than the rest. Imagined as well he could see the faintest filaments of light on the cell wall. Not the whole wall, just one spot. It was not enough to provide ambient light to see by but he found it comforting nevertheless. 'I am blind,' the thought was unwelcome.

Sound, scent, and touch were his only senses. Touch was the rock he sat upon and nothing else. To abate aching muscles he would stand and stretch, reaching up. The grate was above him. Too high to reach unless he jumped but he couldn't jump because he couldn't see. He was more likely to break a finger on the grating or land badly on the rock-seat or in the water.

Scent was the turbid mud and damp of his cell and the stink of his own body. To relieve himself he pissed in the water and was grateful at that, though it added another layer to the cloying miasma surrounding him.

Sound was enhanced in the stillness. Every subtle noise was revealed; the rustle of cloth against stone, of bones cracking, water stirring, and insects prowling, skittering and buzzing. Sound in many ways was the worst of them.

It was impossible to track time in this no space no place. But time was constant and marched on regardless. Eventually, the black circle lightened until it was a grey disk and the high ceiling above his hole faded into being, the beams and brickwork looking dirt-stained and worn.

He heard the footsteps long before they reached the door. It groaned open on angry hinges, the feet padding into the room. A scraping of wood on stone and Jacob recalled the table and chairs from the night before.

Whoever it was approached his hole. A face appeared above. A young face, fair-haired and fair-skinned, surprisingly clean with the fuzz of a beard threatening to break out. The youth sniffed.

"I've got food and water for you. The food ain't great but you'd best eat it." His blue eyes looked solemn for someone so young.

"Thank you. I'm Jacob, what are you named?" Jacob asked.

"Tom, Tom Trickle, and I know who you are. The whole town is talkin' about it. You should'na come here, my Lord."

"Just Jacob."

Tom nodded. "I'll lower a bag down. Take the food and keep the water skin. Don't drink it all at once."

A sackcloth bag was squeezed through the bars and lowered. Jacob caught and opened it. A stale hunk of bread the size of his fist was inside and a bone with a rind of skin on it and little else. The water skin was only half-filled.

The sack was pulled back up. "Thank you, Tom, could you check my cousin. They laid him in one of these cells."

"I was told to check him last," Tom said. "Hissings said he'd be dead and I'm like to lose my stomach if I check first."

He moved off and repeated the same task, offering the same advice to Thornhill and then Mahan. When he got to Wynter though there was silence and Jacob wondered if he'd forgotten him.

"Hey Ned, I was only given water for you." The voice was tentative, uncertain.

"It's good to see your face, Tom. Sorry, I left you like I did lad." Jacob had to strain to hear Wynter's reply.

"I was only a boy. Besides, if you hadn't I'd be in the hole next to you."

"Ai, most likely," Wynter chuckled, "What's this?"

"It's nought, Ned, especially if you eat it afore Black Jack gets here, eh."

There was the sound of rope over metal as Tom pulled up the bag. Then, the shuffling of boots as he walked to the next hole. There was a pause then a curse and then he ran for the door.

"What is it?" Jacob yelled. But Tom was gone, the slap of boots on stone quickly receding. 'Fuck' what had the lad seen? Was Sand dead? Eyes grainy, head pounding from the lack of sleep, Jacob gathered himself. Awkwardly rising, he stood, bones aching, his muscles cramping in protest at every movement. The iron grating was mere inches above his outstretched hands. There was no lock on it.

Booted feet sounded in the corridor outside. Barked orders by the doorway, then the room seemed to fill with noise.

"Quiet, all of you. Busk, Egg, guard the door."

Jacob recognised the gravelly voice of Black Jack. The noise died almost immediately. He heard the clunk and whine of metal, followed by a loud clang.

"Fuck me. Varla, go an' fetch the witch."

"On my way, " a woman's voice replied.

"Tom, come here," Black Jack called. "You did right getting me. He like this when you saw him?"

"Yes." A single word but it conveyed more than a simple answer. Jacob could hear the fear in it.

"It's alright lad, I said ya did good didn't I?"

"Yes,"

"Tell me, was his eyes open like that when you saw him?" Black Jack asked.

"Yes, only they were different," Tom said. "He stared straight at me and they was black as coal, I swear it. Cold and dead they were."

"Hey, look at me," Black Jack shouted. "That's it. Can you speak?"

Jacob didn't hear a reply but Black Jack must have heard something.

"Tom, fetch some water."

It was torturous listening and not seeing. Jacob again heard the scuffle of feet.

"What's that black shit floating in the water? You see that?" Black Jack said.

"No, just saw his eyes and ran," Tom confessed.

"Tell me true, boy. Why was you 'ere? Come to see Ned, eh?" It was calmly spoken but even Jacob could sense the hidden menace in the question.

"Hissings asked. Says he was feeling rough. Someat he ate," Tom said.

"More like Odd-John's whiskey mash. I'll string that lax cunt up by his ball sack." Tom's answer, however, seemed to mollify Black Jack. "Now, get your arse down there. See if his Lordship will drink someat. An' see what that black stuff is whilst you're at it."

There was the scrapping of wood as a ladder was lowered down the hole and the sound of someone scrambling down it.

"His eyes are watching me but he won't take the skin hisself." The voice was muffled and distant.

"Fucking get in the water and help him then." Black Jack shouted.

"This stuff… its bugs and suckers. They're dead and black as tar. I don't like it," the voice echoed.

"Dead, you say?"

"Yeah, if I touch one, they just fall apart to nothing."

"I'll lower a rope. Tie it under his arms and we'll pull him up. Let Hett take a look at him," Black Jack said. "Egg, Busk lend a hand here."

Black Jack's face suddenly loomed above Jacob's hole. "What the fuck's wrong with him?"

"Don't know. He was worse than that when we found him. Let us up and we can help."

That brought a laugh of derision from Black Jack. "Nah, my Lord, you'll do just fine where ya are."

The witch Black Jack called for was named Hett. At least Jacob assumed it was her, for no one called her witch when she arrived.

Jacob knew she was old from the way she moved about the room but if he needed confirmation her voice provided it.

"What 'ave ya brought me now Jack," she croaked.

"A Lord apparently," Black Jack said, "Need ya ta tell me what's wrong with 'im."

"Hmmm, let's see…" Hett said, humming to herself. "Hold the torch steady, fool." Her voice was acid. After a moment she resumed her tune. "Interesting. Not entirely sure. Take him to my hut. I'll need to examine him more thoroughly to be sure."

"Just tell me if he'll live, Hett. If not, I'd as soon slit his throat and be done with it."

"With care, I think he'll live. But there's a taint on him I need to understand. Might help with Wraith, it seems similar to her affliction."

"Okay," Black Jack said.

"You should let these others up too if you plan on keeping them. The hole breaks the mind before ever it breaks the body. It always does," Hett said.

"What I do with 'em is my business. Attend yours and leave me to mine."

"Ai, I will. But don't go asking me to fix your toys once you broke 'em, Jack."

Jacob shouted up, out of the hole. "You have my word, Lord Tullock. We will do no harm to you or your people. I give my oath on it."

The heavy tread of boots then Black Jack's grim face appeared above.

"One a day can come up if you behave yourselves. Fuck me off you'll be back down here or worse. That's my bargain and I always piss on my bargains." Unhitching his belt and unlacing his breeches he dropped them to his thighs. Pulling his small clothes aside he eased his penis out.

A strong-smelling stream of yellow piss rained down. Jacob could do nothing to avoid it.

## Chapter 36: Sparrow, An Observation

**Kingsholme, The Holme**

"I ain't never left the city. It's my home."

"You've little choice. The city cares not for you Tomas and I cannot protect you here indefinitely," Renix replied.

"Ain't going, don't fit in nowhere else. Don't know nothin' else," Tomas moaned.

"That's exactly my point, my boy. You've lived your whole life hand to mouth, taking what you can, thieving to get by. That is not living Tomas, that is subsisting. It's no life. You can be so much more," Renix said.

Tomas dipped and twisted his head to the side. "Shut up!"

"Pardon me?" Renix was taken aback.

"Sorry, talkin……to meself?" Tomas murmured, face colouring up.

"Are you asking or telling me?" Renix's piercing grey eyes regarded Tomas shrewdly.

"Look, Tomas, I can't make you go to Tankrit but you would be safe there. You could become whatever you wanted. You've already taught yourself to read. That is an incredible thing. You know, we have a library the size of Saints Light Cathedral. It's said to hold a copy of every book ever written."

Tomas was tempted, sorely tempted. What Renix offered sounded like a dream and… well Benny the Weasel said anything too good to be true was a con. But he believed Renix or wanted to. The Orderman was different than anyone he'd ever met. Renix had never once treated him lesser than any other man or woman. Not even the princess that day she called.

This past month, Tomas had left the apartment every day. He never went so far as that first time though and his excursions were almost exclusively at night. The lure of the thieves' highway and the freedom of the night called to him and Tomas found it impossible to resist. So he mapped the rooftops in his head, learning the routes and dead-ends, finding the hidden nooks and the safe pathways to the ground. I should go, he would tell himself, but always he would return to the safety of the apartment.

The thing was, Renix knew and never once tried to stop him. Every time he returned, a glass of fruit juice awaited him on the table by his bed. He had never tasted anything so sweet. Freshly squeezed, it was enough to make him want to go, just to come back. It got to be a game between them. One that neither admitted to.

Tomas was scared. But it was a different kind of scared to any he'd experienced before. Wasn't even sure what of, or so he told himself. But deep within, where he feared to look, he knew. It was hope. Renix had given him hope. Belief, that things could be different and it frightened him.

This though wasn't his only fear. It warred with another, older, more familiar one; a fear that was easy to know but proving just as hard to admit or accept.

Tomas had been forced to face many realisations these last few weeks and this was the greatest of them and the cause of his biggest terror. His life was over, finished. Or at least the life he knew, the only life he knew. Bortillo Targus placed a bounty on him, a mark that would always follow him and he would never be safe. Renix was right.

"Okay, I'll go to this Tankrit Isle place you talk of. But I've no money and no idea how to get there."

Renix smiled. "You will not go alone and if you will accept it, I offer you my token." They were in his study and Renix walked to a framed picture on the far wall.

"Trakoris optim." Like a blessing, Renix touched the frame three times in three different places with his fingers and it swung wide to reveal an opening.

Tomas couldn't see what lay inside. I'll look later he promised himself. He'd already memorised the pressure points Renix had touched and the words spoken.

Renix turned and in his hand was a simple necklace with a metal disk threaded upon it. Crossing to Tomas, he extended his hands. "May I?"

"I'll probably fence it," Tomas said. Renix stared silently into his eyes, his lips tugging gently at the corners of his mouth.

Tomas nodded, not trusting himself to speak. This was significant, though he couldn't say why. After the clasp and chain were fastened, Renix lifted the token and slipped it beneath his tunic.

"Look at it later. It bears my house crest," Renix said.

"What does it mean?" Tomas asked.

"It means many things but principally that I am your sponsor. Do you know what that is?"

Tomas shook his head, no.

"It means I vouch for you. I will provide for you and, by my name, you'll be admitted to the college at Tankrit Isle and receive training. You're a little old and late to your studies but my name carries some weight. Do not squander this chance I give you Tomas. All I ask is the best of you."

"You're not coming are you?" Tomas accused.

"No, I remain here. But I will come and see you in the summer. I promise."

"I want Sparrow to go too," Tomas demanded. "She saved me in the All-Ways."

"Sparrow is your friend?"

Tomas shrugged. "Don't know. We look out for each other is all."

"Well then, we shall go and find her," Renix said. "I cannot guarantee she can go with you but at the very least I can keep her safe, take her out from harm's way."

"Why are you doing this? Why are you helping me?" Tomas asked. "Why not Sparrow or a thousand others in this city just like me?"

"It's a fair question," Renix conceded. "I'll try to give a fair answer, though in truth I am not entirely certain myself."

Renix propped himself on the edge of his desk and Tomas resigned himself to a long answer, the Order man liked to talk.

"It is my belief that each of us follows our own path. I can't help everyone as I have helped you, that much is true as much as I might wish it otherwise," Renix began. "The simple answer is that our paths crossed. Your book almost poleaxed me when you fell from the sky. It didn't and you got up with nothing more than a few bruises."

"I am old, Tomas. I have lived many lifetimes and trust me when I say this - a boy falling from the sky and walking away from it does not happen very often. You are in fact my first." Renix smiled at his jest.

"Then to discover that boy is a thief, wanted by the Syndicate with a bounty placed upon him by Bortillo Targus no less. Well, to say you intrigued me would be an understatement. These, however, are not all, or indeed even the most enticing or relevant of reasons."

"Tomas, you can read. An impoverished boy, doing what he must just to survive, can somehow, miraculously, read? I'm afraid it was all too much for me to ignore." Renix drummed fingers against the wood of his desktop. He looked down in a moment of reflection. Then, as if deciding something he nodded, raised his head then stared at Tomas.

"I would be lying to say they were the sole reasons. Truthfully, I think mostly it's because you remind me of the son I lost, in looks as well as spirit. I see you, Tomas."

Tomas shifted uncomfortably. No one ever spoke to him like this. He wasn't entirely sure what it all meant. There was a deep melancholy in this man he'd not sensed before and he wanted desperately to ask Renix about the son he never named.

His courage failed him. "I still don't understand what you see in me."

"Tomas, you have witnessed and experienced many bad things in your short life and it has not broken you. That is what I see. I also see that you are decent despite these travails. I believe you can be a force for good in this world."

Renix shrugged. "Knowing all this, I would be a fool to ignore it. I'm afraid you chose yourself as much as I ever did, my boy. Now let's go find this Sparrow before you turn me into a sentimental old fool. Though perhaps on that score it is already too late."

Renix stood and Tomas faced him awkwardly. He felt funny and didn't know why. The Orderman reached out and laid a hand on his shoulder.

"Get your cloak, let's go, and ah, maybe you should wear this, hidden preferably." In his hand, Renix held a slim dagger. The hilt was plain and wrapped in leather that made it easy to grip. The sheath too was ordinary to look at.

Tomas took it and slid the blade out, finding the centre balance almost immediately. Its edge was blue-tinged and keen. He knew quality; the knife was probably worth more than he'd stolen in the past year. He snapped it back in, unwound the strapping it came with then fastened it about his waist, twisting it so that when he donned his cloak it would be out of sight.

A polished metal mirror hung in the corridor and Tomas hardly recognised himself when he passed it. He was clean and dressed in the refined clothes of high society. It wouldn't do. He'd be marked as soon as he left the Nobles and set foot in the Trades, not to mention Old Town and the Stacks.

Striding to his room, Tomas closed the door. He still wasn't used to thinking of it as his, or that he'd a wardrobe and a selection of outfits. He changed quickly into simpler, hardier clothes. Brown leggings, a long shirt and a dark leather jerkin. Leather boots and a black cloak completed his ensemble. He took his knife out and admired it in more detail before strapping it again around his waist.

"My, my, you've turned into quite the little Lordling," The voice was sultry and feminine.

Tomas didn't startle. The demon seemed to take great pleasure when he did but frankly, O'si had become all too predictable.

He'd manifested as the scantily clad princess, dark-skinned, dark-haired, and brown-eyed. It was the guise Tomas found most alluring and most disturbing and hence the reason it was used more than most.

"Thank you, but you'd best hide. You know Renix is gifted. If he sees you…well, I'm not sure what he'd do but best not to find out, eh."

O'si ignored Tomas. "I command you not to go to this place Renix speaks of. It is full of the gifted. I will not allow it. You must stay in the city. The Tetriarché will come here for us. Do as you have sworn, open a way, and send us back."

"Yeah, well as I told you already, this Sházáik Douné Táak book says I need all this shit for the casting. I don't even know what most of it is and you've been no help at all in finding it, except to say the mages have what's needed. I ain't breaking in there, especially since we don't even know where they would keep any of this stuff," Tomas reasoned.

"Look, I think this Tankrit place could be the answer for both of us. Renix seems to think it's the font of all knowledge. Surely they will have what we need?"

"You say what I want to hear to get what you want. I am no fool, human." A sharp pain flared through Tomas's hand as the hidden mark from his contract with the demon blazed into life.

"Fuck, stop that," Tomas hissed. The stamp faded as quickly as it came and the pain with it.

"We struck a bargain," the woman purred. The demon leaned forward, arms squeezing, pressing her cleavage together.

"Ew, would you cut that out?" Tomas pulled a face, shifting uncomfortably.

"Never forget, the seal is set. Until the deal is done you are mine." The dark princess pouted and blew him a kiss.

"Yeah so you say, and you're mine too remember. The deal goes both ways," Tomas argued.

The sensuous woman vanished. The door opened and Renix stuck his head in. He glanced around the room then back to Tomas.

"Thought I heard voices?"

"Just me, I talk to myself sometimes and you've given me a lot to think on."

"I could've sworn there was more than one and one a woman's voice. I must be losing the plot. You ready?"

"Yeah, let's go," Tomas said, a little too abruptly for Renix scrunched his face up in suspicion. He said nothing more though as they left the apartment.

They found a problem awaiting them as they descended to the street in the form of the Crown Prince, Herald Blackstar. He was accompanied by his first sword, a tall, languid looking man, later introduced as Horyk Andersun, a Norderman from his pale skin and blonde hair. With them were a score of guardsmen in the red and gold livery of Kingsholme.

"Lord Renix, I appear to have caught you just in time." Herald glanced dismissively at Tomas before his deep, hazel brown eyes fixed firmly on the ambassador.

Tomas took an instant dislike. The prince was dressed brightly in red velvet hose and silk shirt, embroidered with gold thread. Over the shirt he wore a honey and dark weave jacket and finished with a black silk cape, lined and trimmed in ermine. The clothes were expensive, Tomas had no doubt, but they were garish and clashed badly. He wouldn't last five minutes in Old Town and even less in the Stacks, the thought was oddly comforting.

"You are early highness; our lesson is not until later this afternoon," Renix replied.

"I have a social engagement this afternoon. Since it's at father's insistence I see you, I've brought our appointment forward," Herald said testily.

"The High King asked that I teach you as I once taught him. I agreed. I set the agenda and the time for our lessons, Highness. If that is not acceptable then I bid you a good day," Renix stepped past the prince, striding purposefully away.

"You dare speak so, to me?" Herald's voice was rising. "You've my father's protection Orderman but one day I will be High King. You would do well to remember that. Now give me my damn lesson and let's be done with this farce."

Stopping, Renix turned and considered the young man. That the prince was here against his wishes was obvious, the anger he exuded made that clear should his words have left any doubt, which they did not. He noted the guards shifting nervously and Horyk Andersun alert but bored. No doubt Herald's first sword had seen all this before.

"Tomas, where is it we go?" Renix asked.

"The Stacks," Tomas said, aware the fabric merchant from across the way was avidly watching proceedings from her shop front. No doubt it would be rich gossip for her customers. She was not the only one though. A few people he noticed had stopped and idled. It was not every day you saw the Crown Prince.

Approaching Herald, Renix stopped uncomfortably close. Refusing to back away, the prince had to raise his head to meet his eyes. It pleased Renix. A pampered fool he might be but Herald had some fire in him. It would be interesting to see if it was genuine or not once he stripped everything away.

"We go to the Stacks. This can be your first lesson, observation." Renix took a step back.

Herald's face turned beet red and incredulous, "The Stacks! I'm not…"

"I should warn you," Renix interrupted, "it could prove highly dangerous, Highness. The choice to come or not is entirely yours."

Whatever Herald had been about to say he didn't. Instead, he glared. "The people love me. I am their prince."

Lip curling, Tomas couldn't stop the smirk rising on his face but it died, heart hammering, when the crown prince saw him. If it were possible, Herald's colour deepened.

"You think me afraid, boy!" Herald spat. "Or stupid?" He directed this last at Renix. "I know the game you play Ord. You have a death mark against your name. It is you that is in danger and it's my protection you seek. For no one would dare harm me. That, Lord Renix, is my observation."

"As you will, Highness." Spinning on his heel, Renix marched off.

"Tomas," he called out, "lead on, my boy."

Tomas had to skip to catch up. Behind them, a brief argument ensued.

"Stacks is dangerous and your safety paramount your highness," drawled Horyk Andersun, in a deep northern twang.

"This is my city and my people. I go where I will." Herald's voice was raised.

The large Norlander tried a different tack, "The Stacks' is filthy, stinks of piss and shit. You'll not get the stench or muck out of your clothes."

"Horyk, are you arguing with me?"

"Yeah, I'm pretty sure that I am."

"Well don't. Now come along," Herald commanded.

There was a clatter of armour and Tomas looked back to see the Kingsguard rushing to form up behind a swiftly approaching Prince. He groaned.

"Problem?" Renix asked.

"Hard for the two of us getting in and out of the Stacks unnoticed. With that lot along it'll be impossible."

"I confess, I did not think he would come," Renix admitted. "We will have to go for loud and obvious. That shouldn't be too difficult."

The prince caught them and fell into step beside Renix. It forced Tomas to walk ahead, leading the way through the broad, tree-lined avenues of the Nobles.

The only good thing, Tomas decided, was that everyone moved out of their way. At the gates, when they crossed from the Nobles into the Trades, the guards merely stood to the side and saluted the prince as he walked past. It was surreal and unsettling for someone use to going unnoticed.

Tomas followed the wide thoroughfare north towards the All-Ways. The stone architecture, with its elaborate frescoes and carved reliefs, gave way to tall wooden buildings with slated rooves and chimney stacks. Shops with awnings displayed merchandise to lure customers and the road was busy with the bustle of people. Tomas loved it. It was easy to disappear amongst the crowds and easier still to ply his trade.

Not now though. Now, it was the complete opposite, the mass of people offered no anonymity or place to hide. The prince and his entourage drew too much attention for it to be otherwise.

Thankfully, the focus was exclusively on the prince. Many called out Herald's name and waved, some even cheered as he walked by. As much as Tomas hated it, he saw the prince revelled in it. His chest puffed up like a popping jay. How could the princess be so alluring yet the prince so repugnant?

The All-Ways, as ever, was busy when they reached it and Tomas had trouble forging a path through the crowd. The market stalls in the square's centre created their own maze of pathways and Tomas angled them around, skirting its edge.

He was grateful in more ways than one when Horyk Andersun suddenly moved up alongside him. His size and bulk had no trouble clearing the way. It gave Tomas the chance to scan the faces in the crowd. He'd not forgotten Bortillo Targus and knew a knife thrust could easily come and the deliverer gone before anyone realised.

"Tomas the boy is wound tighter than a bowstring," Horyk said. "A man wonders why?"

"Don't like crowds," Tomas muttered, his eyes constantly roving.

Horyk grunted unconvinced.

Turning west, they passed the All-Ways without incident, despite Tomas's fears, and he relaxed as the crowds of people thinned. The wide boulevard started to narrow the further they went. The buildings became shabbier; their white-washed walls dirtier and stained.

Their transition into Old Town was unclear. Unlike the Nobles, there was no wall or gate to delineate the one from the other. It was more a metamorphism of old and shabby to old and run down. The guard stations became less frequent, the streets more cluttered with refuse and detritus, and its people less well to do.

Old Town had its own, base smell too. A mixture of earthy and sour from the gutters, damp wood, and smoke from the houses, Tomas loved it. It was home. Sure he lived in the Stacks but this was his stomping ground more days than most.

Seeing people he knew, Tomas relaxed. There was a rhythm to the streets. A thousand little things that happened every day carried out by the same familiar people. Most he knew only by sight but that didn't mean he didn't know them. It was important for a thief to understand who they were. The baker would give a tanning if he caught you stealing a loaf, but no more than that. The blacksmith on the other hand gave beatings that would lay you low for a week. He'd even been known to break bones. Then there were those you didn't touch at all, like the trader on Carlton Lane. A fence for the Syndicate, she was protected. Stealing from her meant you were disappeared.

Old Town was by far the largest area in the city, curling around the Trades like a cupped hand. Its northern boundary was formed by the original walls of Kingsholme. Tall and formidable, the walls were well maintained and all entry into and out of the city was through one of its three gates, Morngate on the eastside, Highgate in the north, and the Gloamingate to the west. Each gate was guarded by an immense barbican and accompanied by its own military barracks.

Of all the districts inside the city, Old Town's Gloamingate was the poorest. It contained the tanneries and abattoirs, the dockside and warehousing. Labour was cheap, its people hardy but poor and this reflected in the houses and the streets.

Over the years, as Kingsholme grew, a township had grown up outside the walls of the Gloamingate to accommodate the burgeoning population. The Stacks, its residents called it, after the tall, poorly constructed, wooden buildings they lived in.

As was the way with humanity, everyone strove for something better. The people of the Stacks longed to live in the Gloamingate district. Gloamingate folk strived for Highgate or the Morngate. Always people looked south, up the rise, following the white road to Anglemere, wishing to be one step closer to its provenance.

For a motherless and fatherless boy abandoned on the streets of Kingsholme, the Stacks were the only place he could live and that was where Tomas led them.

Sparrow lived at the top of a bell tower across the street from the dilapidated building Tomas called home. No one knew Sparrow's real name, not even Sparrow and it was Tomas that first called her so. 'A street thief needs a name else they're a no one,' he told her once and since nothing lived in the bell top but the birds and given her diminutive size it seemed natural to name her so. Sparrow had liked it well enough at least.

In the Stacks, the streets were not paved but packed mud. Rain from the night before had wet everything and the roads were churned to a viscous mush by countless feet as people carried on regardless.

"I thought Old Town smelt bad. This place reeks of shit." Herald scrunched his nose in disgust. "Look at my boots, they're ruined."

Herald's complaints had started in the All-Ways and grown steadily louder ever since. Tomas had stopped listening a while back.

"How can people live like this?" The moaning continued, unabated.

"A prince asks and a man shall tell." To Tomas's surprise, it was Horyk Andersun who answered.

"They live here because they must. If they are lucky they work for coppers. Coppers put food on the table, pays rent but little else. So the cycle continues. They are trapped with no opportunity to better themselves, my prince."

"I don't think I could stand it. They live like animals."

"They are not so different from anyone else. They laugh and cry. They moan, they sing, they fuck, they dance and they dream. They want more, better things for themselves and their children. But they make do because they must. They are not animals, they are your people."

Tomas decided he liked the Norderman. He talked differently from everyone else. His deep, resonating voice was matter-of-fact.

Herald raised his eyebrows. "Why Horyk, you're positively chatty today. I wonder why? Could it be my companions? I know you have a thing for the Order."

Horyk's forehead creased into a frown, "The Order is honourable and worthy of my respect." He nodded at Renix, the gesture noticed by Herald.

"So, Lord Renix, now that you've dragged me to the asshole of the city, where is this person you've come to find?"

"Tomas and I will go fetch her. I suggest you wait here." Renix replied.

"I did not come all this way to stand in filth waiting like a common servant. We'll all go." Herald commanded.

"Best I go alone," Tomas ventured. "Sparrow'll be gone if'n she ain't already at the sight of all this."

Tomas swept his arms around, indicating the prince and the Kingsguard. It was true as well. Sparrow's Bell Tower gave a grand view of the street they stood in and already their entourage had drawn a small crowd. Intrigued no doubt, for the prince had never been seen in the Stacks before.

"Nonsense, I am your prince and I've spoken. Now lead on," Herald said.

Tomas's nostrils flared and he glared at Renix accusingly who gave a half-smile in apology.

"Sorry, my boy."

A reluctant Tomas crossed the street. He saw Joe Danver with his five children watching from the side and Fat Mole Preston with her babe propped on a hip, eyes wide with incredulity as she recognised him.

The crowd parted, though it was more for the prince trudging through the mud behind than for him. Tomas had never felt so conspicuous and didn't much like the sinking feeling it gave him. It wasn't natural.

Milly Danver, Joe's youngest, wriggled through to the front of the crowd. Glancing wide-eyed all around she hissed at him. "Da says not to go up there, Tomas."

Milly was gone, slipping out of sight before he could ask her why. His chest tightened and his mind started racing. Before Tomas knew it he was running.

The Bell Tower was home to several families. Tomas knew them all. People looked out for one another in the Stacks. The looks they gave added to his sense of dread, adding to his impetus as his feet pounded the steps, round and up to the next level, then the next until finally, he reached the top. A flat walkway surrounded the landing with a ladder propped at the far end giving access to a trap door and the bell room.

"Tomas, wait." Renix's voice echoed up the stairwell.

Leaping onto the ladder, Tomas scampered up as he had done a hundred times before. Hand extending, he pushed on the trap, flinging it back with more strength than he knew he possessed.

The putrid stench of death struck before he had a chance to step out onto the boards. So sickly sweet and cloying he gagged.

Eyes already wet with tears, Tomas forced himself up the last few rungs, to turn and see what he already knew but couldn't quite comprehend.

The Bell room was devoid of its bell, Tomas had never seen one. Sold for scrap most people said. Where it should have hung was a body. So small it could only be a child's. It was Sparrow, he knew it in his soul but on his life, she was beyond recognition.

Stripped naked, her skin had been flayed and hung in tattered strips, flesh raw and livid. Her face was unrecognisable. The nose was gone, sliced clean off. Eyes sunken pits of black that stared accusingly no matter where he moved in the room.

Tomas fell to his knees, covering his face with his hands to block out the nightmare. He bowed, head sinking to the floorboards. He was numb, couldn't feel or hear anything as his world condensed. In his mind, he could still see the black orbs of Sparrow's empty eye sockets boring into him. Heat and anger and pain, she blamed him, it was his fault.

"Ssshh, shhh, shhh." Distantly, Tomas became aware of arms wrapping around him and a voice whispering. "It's not your fault. This is not your fault."

Slowly, life returned. His limbs were heavy. The voice was familiar and Tomas knew it was no whisper as his hearing regained and with it, heard his own heartrending wail.

"It is not your fault. Come, let me take you down." Renix lifted Tomas gently away, cradling the boy's head against his shoulder.

Face damp with tears, Tomas shook his head and sobbed. "I can't leave Sparrow like this. She was my friend."

"We won't my boy, we won't." Renix's eyes creased in sympathy. "Let me take you away and I will come back for her. I promise. I will treat her with the greatest care and dignity. Please, will you wait downstairs for me?"

There was a gagging, retching sound and they both turned to look. Horyk Andersun stood, head bowed so as not to crack his head on the tall beams. At his feet, sagging on hands and knees was Herald, a pile of vomit and bile adding its sour stench to the reeking atmosphere of death.

Renix looked grimly at the prince. "Take him away, Horyk. I think his highness has seen enough for one day."

\* \* \*

Afterwards, Renix returned as he promised. It was worse than seeing Sparrow the first time. Up close everything was more nuanced, more detailed; more personal. He disturbed the flies that moved like a shadow over her flesh. Fat bloated maggots crawled in every crevice and orifice. It was clear she had been dead a while. In her torture, the girl had soiled herself and the stain of excreta ran down her legs, mixing with blood and urine to gather on the floor beneath her feet like the cruellest of tombstones.

The worst of it was her ties. They had cut into the flesh of her arms and legs which had distended in putrefaction making removal painstaking and nauseous.

The agony and fear she must have suffered, Renix thought. It made his heart ache with pity and his blood boil with rage. He felt murderous, which shocked him, for it had been several lifetimes since he had last felt so.

Finally, freed of her constraints, Renix laid the girl named Sparrow onto his cloak. Wrapping her gently, reverently he carried her out.

Renix had lived an age and right then felt every year of it. A deep melancholy struck him.

"Will we never change?"

## Chapter 37: Reunions

**Fastain, The Rivers**

The stick rapped against a hand then an elbow. "Keep your arm up and in towards your body."

A scowling Idris Inigo did as instructed, gritting his teeth against the sharp pain.

"And again," Si Manco commanded.

Darion watched with interest as the boy attacked the inert wooden buttress with his blunted training sword. Listening to the loud sharp cracks as the sword clacked against the block, and the low, even tones of Manco calling out the strikes.

"Three highs cuts, two low." Manco wandered around his charge, eyes constantly analysing.

Darion fidgeted in discomfort. The room they were in was hardly big enough for Lord Idris's exercise and he was hemmed in at the stern bay window. He noted that, despite the tight space, the swordmaster had no trouble avoiding the boy as he practised.

"Enough," Manco grunted. He gave a lopsided grin. "To master the sword you must…"

"…first master your mind and body," Idris finished.

From the smooth familiarity and returning grin, Darion realised the words were a ritual for master and student.

"Now we shall eat." Idris wiped his brow with a cloth, then his hands. "Let's see what cook has managed to scrape together on this barge."

The *River Arrow* was hardly a barge, Darion thought. Lord Inigo's boat was not wide enough for that and its keel was sharp and sleek rather than curved and rounded. It had a mast and bench seats for rowers like a barge but that was the only similarity as far as Darion could see. On the journey from Confluence, the vessel seemed to carve its way through the widening expanse of the River Fossa, arriving in Fastain half a day earlier than expected. Now they waited.

"Think I'll take Bindu out. She's not used to being cooped up."

Idris scrunched his face. "You shouldn't fret Darion. Meredith says your daughter is with Order Knights. They'll see her safe. Now come, she'll be here soon enough. Break your fast with me."

The lad meant well, but sitting, eating and idle chat wasn't something Darion could stomach right then. His body was a bag of anxious, pent up energy. He needed to walk and breathe.

"Come, my Lord," Manco interjected. "Food is not what our friend needs. I on the other hand could eat a hog."

With an exhale of air, Darion nodded thanks to Si Manco. At the same time, he saw a flash of annoyance cross the young Lord's face. So Darion was surprised when, instead of arguing or insisting, Idris turned away. With deliberation, he placed his practise sword in its case and snapped it shut.

When Idris turned back he gave a rueful smile. "Si Manco tells me a Lord should never apologise. Instead, let me say he is right. I do not mean to monopolise your time, especially when you have worries of your own."

He looked chagrined. "It's just the ilfanum are not very forthcoming and I confess a fascination with them. They seem more amenable, more approachable when you're about. Well, M'rika is at least."

It brought a wry chuckle from Darion. "Ai, R'ell's hard to talk too that's the truth."

"I don't think he likes us very much," Idris stated, pursing his lips. "I mean humans in general not me specifically."

"Maybe," Darion was noncommittal. It was hard to know what R'ell felt or thought. "Some folk don't like talkin' overmuch. Maybe some ilf are the same," Darion offered, not wanting the boy to think badly of R'ell and not sure why he cared one way or the other.

Idris nodded, "Of course. It makes sense when you put it like that."

"By your leave, Lord Idris," Darion unfurled himself from the bench seat, ducking his head to avoid a beam that ran the length of the room.

The boy waved his hand. "Maybe when your daughter arrives, we can all share a meal? I would like to meet her."

"When she is ready, I'm sure she would like that," Darion said. He strode across to the door, nodded to Si Manco once again, before pulling it wide.

Outside in the corridor, Darion squeezed past a pair of guards and onto the main deck. Bindu was curled up on an old blanket one of the servants had thrown her, waiting. As his boots rang on the wooden timbers her head came up, ears erect and she bounded to greet him.

"Hello, old girl." Darion knelt and ruffled her neck, giving a cursory look to the wound she'd taken. It had healed well, leaving a jagged scar that was still a little raw to look at. He scratched his beard with one hand whilst rubbing his other hand over Bindu's flanks. "That'll be one to tell Nihm about. Come on, let's go stretch our legs a bit."

Bindu's eyes flitted past his shoulder and her tail wagged. Darion turned in his crouch. R'ell and M'rika stood silently above him. He'd not heard or sensed their approach. Both wore their white priest robes with the hoods lowered to conceal their faces and gloves upon their hands.

"Good morn to you both." Darion squinted up at them. And it was a good morning. A watery sun had risen that day in a powder blue sky with only a scattering of cotton clouds for company, and he'd see his daughter. What could be better?

R'ell, as usual, said nothing. M'rika though was more forthcoming. "Good morn, Darion." Then, as if echoing Darion's thoughts, "You will be pleased to see Nihm today. I look forward very much to meeting her."

"I'm overjoyed and nervous, anxious…" Darion admitted ruefully.

M'rika's face creased. "I don't understand. Why be other than happy?"

Darion shrugged. "Marron is dead. My wife, Nihm's mother, and I weren't there and she was. I should've been. Nihm's had to deal with that alone and it ain't right." That he'd spoken his admission aloud was disturbing. He'd only ever spoken to Marron in this way and even with her; well, he was not renowned for his displays of emotion. Stoic, Marron called him and he liked that. She never will again, the voice in his head whispered. He tapped his hand angrily against his thigh and rose to his feet.

"I'm taking Bindu out. Need ta stretch ma legs and clear my head."

Unexpectedly, R'ell spoke up. "I will join you. Bezal too is anxious. He does not like this place, too many humans."

Now that R'ell mentioned it, Darion couldn't recall when last he'd seen the raven. Hiding his disgruntlement as best he could, Darion sucked his lips. "Sure, be glad of the company."

"I will leave you both to enjoy your walk," M'rika said, her dark eyes glinted, the corner of her mouth curving.

With a grunt of resignation and R'ell in tow, Darion walked off, Bindu pacing quietly by his side. If he thought that was it though he was mistaken. Approaching *River Arrow's* gangplank, Kronke intercepted him.

"Darion."

"Kronke."

The giant Black Crow's face was pinched into a frown. "If you see Pieterzon, Morpete, or that Encoma lad, tell 'em to get their butts back on board."

Darion gave an ironic grin. "You've lost your entire command."

Kronke's brows knitted together. "Not Crawley. She's in the hold with Inigo's fletcher; got this thing about needin' more arrows," he said. "But yeah. Rest of 'em took off last night."

"A man's gotta sleep," Darion consoled, knowing without needing to, exactly what had happened.

"Yeah, it's that shitter Pieterzon, I know it. Waited till I was out, then lit off. He'll be pissing out his arse when I get my hands on him."

"I'm guessing he knows that," Darion said, the rough talk lightening his mood. "If I see 'em, I'll tell 'em."

Kronke slapped him on the shoulder in thanks. "I'll hunt them down meself if they're not back by midday. The gods help them when I do."

Onshore, Darion led R'ell through the streets of Fastain. It was much smaller than Confluence, little more in fact than a market town. At first glance, Fastain looked almost normal. The streets were filled with folk as might be expected. Only, it didn't take much to see that the people looked harried. They moved in small groups and were loaded down with whatever they could carry. Passing carts and wagons were piled high with all manner of things. One, Darion saw, even had an expensive copper bath in it.

Most of the shop fronts were boarded shut and those few that weren't were in the process of it. Refugees, from Karsten Abbey in the north, had been arriving for days and, like a spreading plague, a strange air of panic and fear had suffused the town.

Darion couldn't blame them. Fastain's lord, Mical Hanboek had visited with Lord Inigo the night before. Urak had been reported as close as a day to the north. Roving bands that left burnt out holdsteads and destruction in their wake but very few bodies. Hanboek complained he'd only a hundred guards. Of these, only half were mounted of which only three were knights with full armour. He was one of them.

Like Lord Inigo at Confluence, Hanboek was evacuating his town. Boats had been used to ferry people east to Rivercross, the rest crossed the town's long bridge over the Fossa. The river was wide and grew wider the further it travelled east. It would be their best defence. Hanboek's intention was to hold the bridge until the urak arrived, whereby he would drop it into the river.

It was a sound plan, Darion thought but Lord Hanboek had raved in anger. The High Lord had sent no help. Instead, Twyford issued him the same orders as Lord Inigo. Orders, commanding that he 'move to Rivercross in all haste with his entire garrison'. Hanboek had ranted about it until the fourteen-year-old Lord of Confluence intervened to calm his older peer.

The memory of it brought a grudging smile to Darion's face. Despite Idris's age, or because of it, he found the young lord quite compelling. Something about the lad resonated.

A growl intruded on Darion's thoughts. A man approached. The purposeful way he crossed the street to intersect them made it obvious. Not wanting anyone to get too close to R'ell, Darion turned to greet him.

"Can I help you, friend?"

The man was thin and of middling years, with a weathered face and tired eyes. It looked like he hadn't shaved for three days from the black, peppery stubble of his beard and his clothing was stained from travel. A sword was strapped to his hip but its cracked leather grip told Darion it had not seen use in a while.

The man ignored him, his red-rimmed eyes fastening instead on R'ell. "White Father, my daughter is injured. Can you help us?"

R'ell's hooded head turned to Darion and an uncomfortable silence followed. Bindu sniffed the man, who twitched nervously as the big wolfdog circled him. Deciding the man was not a threat, Bindu returned to Darion's side and sat, tense and alert.

"Please, Father," The man implored. "She can hardly walk and I can carry her no further."

Darion sighed. If Marron were here she'd not have wavered. By comparison, his healing skills were paltry but just thinking about Marron left him no choice. He looked hard at R'ell. "Can you help?"

Whatever R'ell had been waiting for he barely hesitated. "I will see the child."

The man's worried eyes travelled between them, watching the interplay. At R'ell's announcement, a look of relief broke across his face and he gushed, "Thank you, Father. I'm Pieter and my daughter is Ada. It's this way, over here."

"Perhaps I too could be of assistance," a familiar voice called out.

Father Melbroth stood behind them and Darion's eyes flared in suspicion.

"Now friend Darion, do not look so at me," Melbroth said. "I was returning when I saw you depart the jetty and it is true that I followed. But only to intervene should you bump into unforeseen circumstance." He spread his arms wide as he spoke this last.

Pieter was elated, oblivious to the sudden tension between the two men. "I was told the churches of the Trinity left the day before last. My prayers have been answered finding two priests of the White."

He led off before they could change their minds with the large, bearded man striding next to him. Pieter spared a nervous glance at the huge wolfdog trotting alongside. The hound though seemed uninterested in him and Pieter breathed a silent relief.

They were led through town and past its outskirts to where a makeshift camp had been set up in a field. It was mostly devoid of people but Darion saw from the crushed grass and rubbish left behind that thousands must have passed through here. Of the people he did see, most were either breaking camp or already moving towards the road and heading for the long bridge.

A tall lone ronu tree stood in the middle of the camp and it was to this Pieter led them. A small group of people was camped nearby and upon spotting Pieter and the white priests they gathered expectantly.

"Look," Pieter declared as he walked up. "I've got two Holy Fathers for Ada."

Then, as they crowded close, all chattering at once, he shouted at them, "Stand back. Let the Fathers through."

Conscious of the ilf at his back, Darion helped to clear a path, ushering people away. All of them looked as haggard and travel-stained as Pieter.

A young girl, eleven or twelve summers old, Darion guessed, sat with her back against the ronu tree. Her right leg was propped on a rucksack. Her knee was bloody and scuffed and a crude bandage was tied around her calf.

"Ada tripped, sliced her leg on a rock a day back. Had to carry her here and it weren't easy," Pieter explained as he knelt beside the girl.

Ada gave a whimper, her large eyes staring up at them.

"It's alright the Fathers here will help." Pieter hugged his daughter and she clung to him.

"Keep everyone away, Pieter," Father Melbroth instructed. Then, at his troubled face, "With the Lady's blessing, we'll do what we can for her."

"Yes Fathers, thank you." Pieter rose and bowing awkwardly backed off. He didn't go far though and Darion couldn't blame him.

"How would you like to proceed?" Father Melbroth asked R'ell. "My own physikers gift, granted me by The Lady, is somewhat limited."

R'ell huffed, the only sign he'd heard Melbroth speak, and knelt beside the girl. Her eyes widened in surprise as he removed his gloves and she saw beneath his hood. Before she could say anything though, R'ell pressed a green, leaf scaled hand over her eyes.

"Tar nada bein."

R'ell removed his hand. Ada's eyes were closed, her breathing deep and even.

Father Melbroth stood back, captivated, watching everything. Using his body to shield R'ell and Ada from view, he signed for Darion to do the same.

R'ell sat back on his haunches; his white cassock stained with dirt as he considered the human child. Concentrating his mind he opened his second sight. A luminescent glow appeared around the girl as he observed her body in the tae'al, or aether as humans called it. The thought disgruntled and he remonstrated with himself. Now was not the time for idle distractions.

Her leg was damaged. R'ell did not need to remove the covering to see that, nor the feather thread of darkness that indicated infection. It traced all through her tae'al.

R'ell removed the bandage, revealing a nasty gash that sliced deep into the muscle. Blood seeped from the wound and the surrounding flesh was inflamed and red. He could smell the taint of corruption.

It would take power to heal and his ability was not that of Ruith's. He could not tap tae'al as Ruith could. That was not his calling. Searching the tree litter on the ground, R'ell brushed dead leaves aside until he found what he looked for. Two seeds, both hairy and dry on the outside, looking as dead as the leaves they hid beneath. But the green pulse of tae'al from their hearts told him otherwise. They were sufficient.

Laying one seed on the ground by his knee, R'ell enclosed the other in his fist. His free hand hovered above the wound, so close he could feel the heat from it.

Closing his eyes to help focus his second sight, R'ell drew a sliver of tae'al from the seed and like a seamstress wove it around the threads of pollution in the child's body. It was difficult to bind the two, like oil and water the strands of tae'al naturally repelled each other.

Satisfied at last, R'ell used a little of his own tae'al to incise the corrupted strands from the girl's body. With each cut, the dark thread wound more tightly to the green until with a final slice she was free. R'ell released the threads. Curling and writhing they snapped back, into the seed. Opening his eyes the seed looked unchanged in his palm.

"Ignatituum," R'ell breathed.

The seed withered, turning black as onyx. He touched a finger to it and the seed crumbled to powder. Lowering his head he blew the dust into the air.

Like the wind tickling the margins of his leaf scale, R'ell could sense Father Melbroth behind. The priest was bursting to question him and R'ell was grateful the human restrained himself, for he was tired and his work was just begun.

Picking up the second seed, R'ell again clasped it in his hand. Closing his eyes he concentrated, this time focusing on the wound. Whilst his hand worked the flesh his will drew tae'al from the seed, using it to knit the wound together, a long and laborious process. The tae'al was easier though to marry with the girls own which at least made the intricate work possible.

When he was done, R'ell sat back, spent. The seed in his hand was dead, not black like its twin, just dead, the tae'al left inside insufficient to sustain it. He rolled it out of his palm and onto the ground.

Rising, R'ell turned to the others. Melbroth's eyes watched eagerly and behind him, the worried face of the girl's father, Pieter.

"How did it go?" Darion stared at the ilf. "You okay, you were gone a while?"

"I am thirsty and weary." R'ell's voice cracked.

Father Melbroth took the small knapsack from his back and opening the ties pulled a small metal flask out. He offered it to R'ell who stared at it.

"It's blessed water. Perfectly drinkable," the priest assured, unscrewing the intricately designed cap.

Reluctant, R'ell took the proffered flask and sniffed at the opening. Satisfied, he raised it to his mouth and drained it in one before offering the flask back.

Melbroth took it, eyebrows rising, "I meant a sip. That's the last of my holy water."

R'ell shrugged. "It was just water."

Lips tight, face pinched, Melbroth said no more as he returned the empty flask to his knapsack.

"Ada? Will she be alright?" Pieter pushed in, face creased with worry.

"The human child will mend. I have drawn out the corruption and healed her flesh," R'ell stated, pulling the gloves back onto his hands.

Pieter glanced at his daughter. She was asleep and looked at peace.

"Her leg will be painful for many days. The healing has only started. Bind her leg with a clean cloth boiled in water then cooled. Change it morning and night," R'ell instructed.

"Can she walk? We must cross the bridge. People say the urak are near." A loud caw sounded from the tree's branches above and Pieter glanced up. The biggest raven he'd ever seen sat perched in its upper limbs.

"Fashion a crutch. The child should bear no weight on it for three days else she may go lame and lose function," R'ell cocked his head to the side. "Urak are close and watching even now. Too few I judge to attack a settlement this size but their numbers will grow. I would cross the river today if you are able."

"It's late Father. The sun fades early this time of year."

R'ell studied the sky. The sun was sinking fast towards the horizon. Much time had passed it seemed since he began his work.

"The night is no barrier. Do as I say or do not, the choice is yours," R'ell said, tired of talking to the human.

The girl stirred, a moan escaping her lips and Pieter immediately went to her.

Taking the opportunity, R'ell left. An anxious Darion followed with Father Melbroth bringing up the rear. Bezal flapped by overhead, circling and calling out to R'ell before eventually flying away to the north.

Darion realised the ilf was headed back to town. He'd stood patiently for hours watching as the ilf silently did whatever it was he did. He'd healed the girl, there was no doubt about that, but R'ell had not moved for hours. It differed somehow from Ruith's healing but he had no expertise or experience to know in what way. It was just a feeling.

"I still await my daughter," Darion said. He'd kept an eye on the north road whilst the ilf worked but few people it seemed were left to travel it. Certainly, there had been no sign of his daughter, Hiro, or the Order knights that had found her. "I will wait here for her."

R'ell stopped and studied Darion. "Forgive me, ilf friend, if you desire it I will wait with you."

Darion stared into the shadowed cowl, the dark eyes within flickered but he saw nothing else other than a vague outline. Solitude was what he desired. The last time he'd had any was in the old forest a lifetime ago, in a different world. One where Marron was alive and the Rivers did not burn in flames.

"No. You go on."

\* \* \*

<Blood pressure is elevated. Sympathetic nervous system is showing increased activity and your body is producing excess levels of hormones. Are you in distress?> Sai asked. <I detect no imminent threat.>

<I'm just excited. I'm going to see my Da,> Nihm said.

<I sense more. Please clarify.>

Nihm sighed. Sometimes she missed being alone with her thoughts. Sai was ever-present and whilst he was well-meaning it was also bloody annoying at times. There was little point arguing though. That only led to more questions and what all too often felt like a lecture. <I guess I'm mixed up a little. Mostly excited but scared too.>

<Having analysed the memory of your interactions with your father there is no need to be afraid,> Sai replied

<What if he's disappointed in me? I did nothing but lay helpless whilst my mother was murdered. What if he blames me? And where was he? Da was to meet us in Thorsten. If he had, none of this would have happened. I wouldn't have been attacked and ma would still be alive.> Nihm blew out a heavy breath, relieved at finally expressing the thoughts that had plagued her mind since that day. Thoughts she had suppressed, too afraid to face them. <What if we're never the same?>

<Nothing is ever the same. Everything is in constant motion,> Sai replied.

<That's very helpful, Sai, thank you,> Nihm thought back, irritated.

<I detect sarcasm in your response. But you are welcome. With time and thought my words will bring understanding. Understanding will bring comfort.>

Nihm switched off, letting her eyes wander ahead. She was sat on a wagon next to Gatzinger, a burly man with a bald head and lined face that made him look severe. His brown eyes though were warm and friendly and he spoke often and in a manner that immediately put Nihm at ease.

The road they were on was wide and well-kept but eerily devoid of travellers and they saw no one until they neared Fastain. The few people they passed looked tired and fearful.

The sun was touching the horizon, painting the sky in warm oranges and reds, when the cragged outline of Fastain appeared. A lone tree stood in the near distance as if to watch over the approach and something drew her eye to it. Focusing, Nihm picked out the dark outline of a man in the tree's shadow and by his side the blocky shape of a dog. By their stances both peered northward, watching the road. It was instantly familiar.

Nihm knew who it was but didn't trust herself at first. She didn't want to be wrong. Her mouth was dry and she distracted herself by taking a swig on Gatzinger's water skin. When she looked back they were still there, like statues, unmoved.

Glancing about she sought Ash and Snow and found them trotting in the long grass beside the road. They never let her out of their sight these days.

A howl sounded, fighting against the northerly wind. Immediately the dogs' heads came up, ears erect. Another howl and Nihm knew beyond any doubt it was Bindu. Ash and Snow bounded ahead in a sudden rush and Nihm found herself leaping from the wagon. It was too slow.

"'Ere, miss," Gatzinger shouted.

Nihm didn't listen to whatever else he said. Already her legs were propelling her in a mad sprint down the road, arms flailing to keep her balance. It was the hardest and fastest she had ever run; the ground seemed to fly beneath her.

As fast as Nihm was, Ash and Snow streaked ahead, bounding effortless and graceful across the grass. And there, rushing to greet them, was the imposing, familiar, wonderful shape of Bindu. At the last second all three dogs skidded to a halt, cavorting and sniffing each other in greeting. Then Bindu was past them, rushing towards her until suddenly Nihm was collapsing, falling to her knees before the old dog knocked her flat; licking hands and face until Nihm thought her heart would explode with happiness. Whatever fear and uncertainty she felt was blown away in that instant.

Nihm knew he was there, had heard his hurried approach and his rasping breath as he gasped air into starved lungs. She was almost afraid to turn and look at him.

"Nihm," Darion's voice tremored, it was enough.

His voice was a balm to the rift in her heart and Nihm lifted her head from Bindu's ruff. Her Da was thinner than she remembered but he looked good despite it. She met his eyes and the joy and sadness in them mirrored her own. Abruptly, Nihm was pushing Bindu off and rising to her feet. They stared a moment, each drinking in the sight of the other before suddenly they were embracing, hugging each other tightly.

"I missed you fierce, lass, I should'na left ya. Not you nor ya ma." Darion's voice cracked with emotion.

Heart-wracked, unable to speak, Nihm sobbed into his shoulder.

\* \* \*

That so much joy can also hold so much pain is a wonder, thought Hiro, watching as father and daughter embraced. The two held each other a long time as their dogs milled about pressing against their legs. They could feel it too, shared in it, for they were pack.

It warmed his heart and not a lot did these days. He felt a pang, not jealousy exactly but an ache a longing. Mao rode beside him and Hiro glanced at his friend's wrinkled face, mottled still with deep yellows and browns from his beating but they were fading.

Inevitably, his mind turned to Renco, lost out there somewhere with Zoller. It was a betrayal, something he knew all too much about. He should have gone for him sooner. Instead, he'd allowed himself to become entangled. Firstly, with the wondrous magical impossibility of Nihm and secondly, with his old friend who should be dead, would be dead if not for the intervention. A deal had been struck.

Hiro let his eyes track again over father and daughter. Like a balm, it eased his soul, if only he believed in such a thing.

Ironside, riding at his side, also watched. "Last time I saw Darion he was unmarried and childless. I pity the path he chose. He would have made a good hand, maybe even have taken the trial and become one of us." He sounded wistful but Hiro knew him of old.

"Save your pity. At the academy, he was a face and name to you, nothing more." Hiro turned dark eyes to the Order Knight. "You knew him not. Darion chose his path and who of us can say it was wrong."

"Blunt as ever, old friend." Ironside laughed, "Who of us indeed. Still, Keeper knows more than is said. Maybe even foresaw this 'path'. The girl too is interesting, no?"

A chill swept Hiro, one he suppressed. Outwardly he gave no reaction, no emotion, projecting the self-same calm he always did. Nihm shielded herself masterfully well but he couldn't help but wonder if Ironside sensed she was something more. Ironside was ruthless, an enforcer. That Keeper sent him and that he arrived so quickly gave more questions than answers.

A cackle rang out, so loud it drew everyone's attention. "Mao knows, eh. Mao sees. You interest in girl but girl no interest in you. Aggh toooo young! Mao say look for fun elsewhere."

Ironside's cheeks and neck reddened. He glanced angrily at Hiro. "Why do you insist on keeping that old fool around? Thought he'd be dead by now but tell him if he opens his mouth again so to me, I will end him."

A huge beam spread over Mao's face. Opening his mouth wide he lifted a hand to it and made a gesture as if he sucked on something big. Eyes creasing, he roared with laughter doubling over his saddle in mirth.

Ironside was taken aback. That someone should speak so, act so, to him. His rage flared at the affront. Not the controlled burning that possessed him in battle but a cold, calculating, smouldering anger. Impossibly fast he reached for the dagger on his hip but never drew it for a hand covered his own.

As fast as Ironside was, Hiro had been waiting, anticipating. He saw the spark in the Order Knight's eyes and was moving even before Ironside was.

"Forgive me, 'old friend'," Hiro spoke softly but his words carried to Castigan, Mercy, and the others. "Mao is old. Do not let his words unsettle you."

"He doesn't unsettle me. You do." Ironside spoke evenly suppressing the rage within. "We've known each other for a long time, maybe too long. Why piss on that and for what? An old fuck that's not long for this world? In the scheme of things that fool's life is meaningless. Control him or I will."

Kicking his horse into a trot, Ironside rode off, passing Darion and Nihm without so much as glancing at them.

Turning, Hiro studied his friend. "Well played. You seem almost like your old self."

"Welcome, Master." Mao sighed, "Mao's… lodger, content to watch."

"Well, that's good. It's nice to have you returned."

"Yes. Mao old and ready but have time for one last ride, eh." His eyes held a deep sadness and his face screwed into a wistful smile.

"You may be ready but I'm not sure I am," Hiro murmured as Mercy manoeuvred her horse beside his.

"What was that about?" the mage snapped. "I thought the Order played nicely?"

Hiro grimaced, "History mostly. Take the others and go on. I would have words with Darion and Nihm."

"You know, I get the distinct feeling I'm missing something here," Mercy rasped. "Me, Stama, and Lucky have been through a lot with Nihm. Feel… responsible I guess and none of what I just witnessed sits easy with me."

"She is with Darion now. Your charge is complete," Hiro said.

"With all due respect, Hiro, I'll be the one to decide that. We'll talk later," Mercy promised. With a tap of her heels, she moved her horse away.

Hiro watched her join Stama and Lucky just ahead, her back stiff and straight. With a twitch of his reins, Hiro guided his mount off the road, crossing the open grass to where Darion and Nihm still stood, Mao, trailing unspoken behind.

Sitting quietly, Hiro waited as the wagons rattled past and the rest of their party moved down the road and into town. He observed as Morten, with his flaming red hair and face pinched in a frown, twisted in his seat next to Regus. The lad peered so intently at Nihm that for a minute he thought the boy would jump down and join her but the wagon rumbled on and him with it. Hiro pursed his lips; Morten's infatuation could prove problematic.

"Hiro," Darion called. "Meredith said you'd found Nihm. Thanks for bringing her safe ta me."

Turning back, Hiro saw father and daughter had parted, though they both stood so close they touched still.

"That was mostly down to Mercy and the others. Nihm will introduce them later, I'm sure." Thighs aching in protest, Hiro dismounted and the two stared at each other before clasping arms.

With a grin, Darion yanked Hiro into a bear hug, engulfing the smaller man's slight frame in his massive one. "I can't say as I've ever bin happier to see ya."

Hiro grunted in response even as Darion's eyes travelled over and up to meet Mao's.

"Ya look even more wrinkled and ancient than ever, elderly father. You sure ya not dead?"

"Almost. Mao older and wiser but better than fatter and wider, neh!" Mao flashed crooked teeth, pleased with himself.

Releasing Hiro, Darion crossed quickly to Mao's horse and waved a hand in front of the old man's face.

"Eh."

"Just checkin' ya can see," Darion rumbled. "Looks like ya bin kissin tree's instead a lass's." Not waiting for a retort, Darion pulled Mao from his horse.

"Bah, get off Mao, big ox," Mao grumped, but there was no venom in it and he couldn't stop his face from crinkling into a smile as they clasped each other.

"As much as it pleases me to see, we've no time for your foolery, either of you," Hiro stated. "We have a lot to discuss and much to consider. First, before Nihm tells you her story Darion, I would hear yours."

Releasing Mao, Darion studied his old mentor. The tone, dusty in his memory, was still remembered. Hiro was concerned. "Ai,"

The walk back through town was taken slowly, as first Darion then Nihm recounted what had happened to them since they parted. Only a few short months had past but it seemed both a lifetime and world away from their lives of before.

In the town square, they stopped by the fountain as Nihm struggled to tell of Marron's death. That wound was still fresh and raw and looking into her father's eyes she broke down. They had clung to each other then, oblivious to the world around them.

Hiro waited patiently, feeling their grief and pain but apart from it. This thing only a father and daughter could share. Afterwards, they sat in silence as the night deepened. It was then that Hiro broached what had been uppermost in his mind.

"Darion much has changed and most of it for the bad. But not all," Hiro phased briefly as he spoke and surveyed the darkness of the square. Aether ghosted into being in his mind. Satisfied no one was near he continued.

"Nihm was dying when Marron saved her. In the doing, she was changed. As unbelievable as that seems the facts are irrefutable. In surviving, Nihm passed a trial and transcended. Became more than she was before."

Nothing was said for a minute and then it was Nihm that spoke.

"Ma had something, didn't she? I never asked and she never told but I suspected. It was something belonging to the Order wasn't it?" Nihm's eyes glinted in the gloom.

"Yes and no. Your parents possessed part of the creature that bonded with Elora dul Eladrohim a millennium ago but I do not believe it belongs to anyone as such," Hiro said.

"I understand. Is that why I'm like you?"

Hiro's brows furrowed. *She knows already*, the thought revelatory and a little unsettling.

"We are similar but not the same. When I opened my sight to you that first time, your tae'al, your aether was so strong. I have seen it's like only once before."

"What am I then? What am I meant to do?" Nihm's voice expressed her uncertainty as much as her words.

"You are whatever you want to be. Can do whatever feels right," Hiro replied. "It's why you should not go to Tankrit Isle with your father."

"What!"

"No!"

Darion and Nihm both spoke at once and Hiro held his hands up to forestall them, the gesture barely visible with only Ankor hanging in the night sky.

"If you go to Tankrit you will be welcomed, of that, there is no doubt. But somehow, Nihm, you are more than I and the Order Knights. I don't understand how but I know it." Hiro sighed, "If you go, you will become what Keeper wants you to be; what Keeper needs you to be."

Hiro faced Darion. "It was not so long ago a young man and woman begged to leave Tankrit Isle. Keeper let them go because it suited the Order's needs as much as if they stayed. I fear Nihm will not have that choice."

"I am of the Order. It is my blood and my life," Darion exclaimed. "You make the Order sound… sinister. As bad as the churches you so despise. You're a Knight of the Order, Hiro, how can you speak so? Keeper is a good man."

Hiro snorted. "Keeper is not what you think. I made my choice and have long been on the outside, tolerated as an old relic, nothing more."

"You sound bitter, Hiro. How has this come to be?"

Hiro shook his head and laughed. "Bitter, no. Sometimes a man cannot see a thing until he is outside of it observing the whole. I think of myself as enlightened, neh." His eyes sparkled and his face wrinkled in good humour as he continued.

"You know when the Order was founded its primary purpose was to defeat the Morhudrim." Hiro shrugged. "Afterwards, it needed a new purpose and Elora chose well. The Order did much good in the world. Still does. But time claims all things, even reason. The Order has become old and stagnant, wrapped up in rules and lore and self-history. It must change or else it will wither and die or worse."

Darion shuffled his feet, frowning. "Death is final, you taught me that. What could be worse?"

"Tyranny," Hiro replied.

Darion shook his head. "I don't understand you, Hiro. The Morhudrim are back, we both know it. Keeper knows it. The Order is needed now more than ever."

"You are correct. The irony is not lost upon me. But come, we've given each other much to reflect upon. I ask only that you think on my words."

Reaching up, Hiro clapped Darion on the shoulder. "Now, show me this M'rika dul Da'Mari of yours and the umphathi R'ell. It has been many years since I've spoken with the ilfanum."

## Chapter 39: The Kiss

**Anglemere Castle, Kingsholme, The Holme**

The Red Cloak messenger blinked. The only movement he exhibited.

Matrice read the note again. It was from Cardinal Tortuga, one of the nine cardinals of the Red Church of Kildare. She was not familiar with him. In fact, she knew very little about him other than he was from Rivercross and fat. Grossly fat, according to Marta, one of her Ladies-in-waiting.

Lady Marta liked to gossip. Something Matrice relied upon, since she couldn't abide the vagaries of court. It bored her. Other people bored her. Nobles were all so predictable and self-serving. Marta on the other hand thrived on it and her friend could always be relied upon to filter the worthy and interesting from the banal and bring it to her notice.

Now, a fat cardinal was hardly worthy but he was at least interesting. Marta said he was so huge he had to be borne in a palanquin by eight Red Cloaks.

She tapped a finger against the vellum. His note intrigued. It requested an audience on a matter of urgency and hinted at some mutual benefit. People requested an audience with her all the time, usually to wheedle a good word with or intervention from her father. Most she ignored but there was something in the phrasing of the cardinal's message that enticed. Besides, how fat could Tortuga really be?

"I have some time this afternoon. I imagine he must be busy with the Conclave commencing the day after next. Tell the Cardinal I will attend him in his chambers at the Cathedral."

Gart Vannen frowned and gave the slightest shake of his head. The princess's First Sword moved from his lounging post by the door and stood immediately behind the messenger.

Matrice ignored his unspoken warning. It pleased her to do so. Gart was protective and it all got a bit dull. She pressed her lips tight to hide her amusement.

"If I may, your Highness?" The Red Cloak bowed. "Cardinal Tortuga is not quartered at Saints Light Cathedral but near the Convocation of the Trivium. If it pleases you, I will call this afternoon and lead you to him."

"Very well, until this afternoon," Matrice dismissed the man and watched as he swivelled, narrowly avoiding Gart who stood with a dark glower on his face.

After the door closed, he was still unmoved.

"What is it, Gart? You look like you've just bitten a sour fruit."

"I don't like it. Too many damn Red Cloaks in the city. I don't trust 'em."

"You don't trust anyone, Gart. It's one of your most endearing qualities and it's why I like you." Matrice's nose wrinkled as she smiled.

Gart scowled, "The Trinity serve themselves first and the crown second and the red bastards are the worst of the lot of them. Have that fuck Tortuga come to you."

"No, the decision is made. I was too young at the time of the last Red Conclave. This is an opportunity."

"For what?" Gart hissed. "The priests talk endlessly of Kildare's word whilst all the time twist it for their own ends."

Matrice chuckled. "The Red Priests would light you aflame for your blasphemy and yet I know you for a believer. Why do you dislike them so?"

Gart glared. "You'll see. This conclave… it will give the appearance of reason and civil judgement. But look deeper and you will see their true nature. Just like all the rest they vie for and trade in power. This has nothing to do with Kildare's will and everything with greed."

"Hmmm, which is why I go; it's at times like these that opportunities present themselves. Opportunities I can exploit. Tell me, Gart, am I not the same. Does this not make me 'like all the rest'?"

Gart shook his head vehemently. "Never; I've told you, Kildare guides your hand. I've seen it, he has shown me. You will become the Red Queen. You will bow to no man and no paper priests. It's Kildare's will you follow, whether you know it or not."

"Well then. If I follow Kildare's will there is nothing to fear from this Tortuga."

Gart frowned, most arguments with Matrice were losing ones and this was no different. All that was left was to mitigate the risk. "If Tortuga or any priest asks to see you alone you must refuse them. Kildare has tasked me as your protector and I will not be parted from your side. On my life, I swear it, my Queen."

His eyes were flat, his face stern and Matrice read it as easily as any book. She knew it for no idle boast.

"Hush Gart, I've asked you not to call me that, not yet," Matrice admonished gently.

Pursing her lips, she considered his words. "Very well, I agree."

\* \* \*

The Convocation of the Trivium was a vast, domed chamber devoted to the Trinity. It was a meeting place for the gods and their representatives. Its walls and floors were richly appointed and adorned with ornate statues and carved marble reliefs. Hundreds of stained glass murals hung around its perimeter telling the story of the gods. The story of Nihmrodel the White Lady, God of Truth and Justice; of Ankor the Saint, God of Life; and Kildare the Protector called by many the Soldier, God of War and Death. Avatars for The One, it was only through the Trinity that a soul could reach The One.

The dome's curved ceiling held an intricate reconstruction of the heavens with the tri moons, each a home to the gods, hovering around its apex. There to gaze down in observance and to bear witness as their arbiters carried out their will.

The chamber itself was divided into three wedges, one for each of the gods. At its centre, where the wedges met, was a large, raised dais. Perfectly round it was thirty paces across.

Outside, following the tradition of the chamber of Convocation, the Trivium itself was surrounded by three enclaves, each devoted to one of the Trinity. They each contained many buildings all interconnected by corridors and walkways that threaded through a myriad of contemplation gardens.

This was the seat of power for the churches and where the High Cardinals sat. It was where the administrative arm of each conducted business; where the youngest and brightest of acolytes studied and trained for their vocation; where the most senior church figures gave prayer and guided doctrine for the masses. For the followers of the Trinity, it was the centre of all things holy and the most sacred place in the Nine Kingdoms.

Tortuga was sat in an office assigned to him by the High Cardinal's under-secretary for the duration of the conclave. It was large and well-appointed with attendant rooms for his staff. Father Manning, his new secretary, sat at a desk to his right quietly reviewing reports. He was a fastidious man and precise but lacked the insightful intelligence of his predecessor Father Zoller. It was an appointment well-made, Tortuga thought.

A knock sounded at the door and Father Manning placed the paper he was reading neatly on the desk before scraping his chair back and rising. Walking on cushioned feet he moved to answer it.

"Your Royal Highness, the Cardinal is expecting you. Please come in." Manning stepped back pulling the door wide.

Tortuga watched as the diminutive frame of Matrice, the fifteen-year-old Princess, breezed through it. Father Manning stepped in holding his hand out to bar entry to the man following her. Tall and rangy, he had on a blood-red tunic, padded and edged in leather with metal studs. About his shoulders was a sable cloak with the hood down. He wore a sword strapped to his left hip and a long dirk to his right. It was his eyes though that caught Tortuga's attention. They were hard and flat and moved constantly. Tortuga pursed his lips, a violent man if ever he'd seen one.

As if to confirm his observation, the man reached out. It seemed almost casual as if to shake Father Manning's hand, only he didn't. Instead, the man gripped it between his thumb and fingers, stepped in, and twisted. Father Manning howled, collapsing to the floor in pain as his wrist and elbow were wrenched.

Glancing back over his shoulder the man growled. "Don't even think about it."

The Red Cloak messenger stood stock still, hand on his sword but he didn't draw it. Instead, he looked at Tortuga and waited.

Tortuga gave a faint smile, relishing the cries from his secretary. The dark shadow within him, stirred and uncoiled, its appetite whetted. "Wait outside Brother Mercer, take Father Manning with you."

The man released his hold on the priest and Manning clutched his arm to his chest in relief. It throbbed but nothing was broken. Gritting his teeth, Manning stood and glared. "You dare lay a hand on me. I could have you flayed for less."

The man sneered. "Threaten me again, Father and they'll do more than flay me."

"No one is threatening anyone," Tortuga said. "I'm sure it was a misunderstanding. Now, wait outside, Father."

"Eminence this is most irregular," Manning whined.

Tortuga stared at the priest who blanched under his gaze. Cradling his arm, Manning shuffled off without another word. Good, the man was growing tiresome. With a bang, Brother Mercer pulled the door closed, and he was alone with his guests.

"Please Highness, come and sit. Let's put this unpleasantness behind us. It is not how I intended our acquaintance to begin." Tortuga indicated one of the chairs in front of his desk.

"You must pardon Sir Vannen. He is zealous where my security is concerned." Matrice sat, trying not to stare overmuch at the Cardinal. He was immense, the material of his robes alone was surely enough for two or even three men.

"Overzealous is not always a bad thing, Highness," Tortuga said. His flesh hung in pallid folds beneath his chin.

"Highness?"

Damn it, she'd been staring. She couldn't help it. At Tortuga's prompting, Matrice belatedly returned a pinched frown, "I never said Sir Vannen was overzealous, Cardinal."

"Indeed you did not, Princess," Tortuga agreed. "Please, I assure you both that your Royal Highness is quite safe here. And accept my apologies. Father Manning was only following my instruction. You see I had hoped to speak with you alone."

"But we are alone. Sir Vannen is merely my shadow. Anything we discuss you may be assured will stay private between us unless I tell you otherwise," Matrice said, her green eyes glinting.

Tortuga spread his hands wide, "As you wish, Highness."

His thick lips curled; the reports that the Princess was confident and self-assured seemed accurate which lent hope that the rest of his intelligence on her was.

"Your missive intrigued, Cardinal Tortuga, enough at least to bring me here. Tell me, what's so important you wanted to discuss it with a fifteen-year-old girl? I'm sure my father would be intrigued to hear your answer as well." Matrice was matter-of-fact.

Tortuga sat impassive, forming a steeple with his fingers as he pondered her words. The barbed threat of her father was idle and childish. He discarded it.

"Before we talk, may I offer you refreshment?" Tortuga asked.

"Her Highness is fine," Gart Vannen interjected.

"The shadow speaks."

Matrice glanced at her First Sword and raised a telling eyebrow before turning back to the Cardinal.

"Annoyingly so at times," Matrice said. "And, in this instance, accurate; I am indeed fine. You have my attention, your Eminence but only so much of my time."

"I see you favour directness over posturing and the niceties of polite society, Highness. It is in many ways quite refreshing."

Matrice pursed her lips, regretting her impulse to come. Tortuga had that air of self-importance the nobles in court had. Should have gone riding she remonstrated. Now, instead, she'd have to listen to the fat man wax on.

"Might I ask, Princess? What do you know of me?" Tortuga asked.

Matrice pulled herself back to the room, banishing thoughts of riding as she considered his rather unusual question. One that was entirely too easy to answer, she bit her bottom lip and pondered whether to be polite or direct already knowing the answer.

"I know you're the Cardinal at Rivercross here to attend the Red Conclave. Also, if you will pardon my candour, I heard tell of your immensity. Vacuous that may seem and shallow but the Royal Court suffers from both these afflictions I'm afraid." Matrice locked eyes with the Cardinal's, which sat like raisins in his rotund, fleshy face.

Often, she could tell a lot about a man through his eyes but Tortuga was proving hard to read. Matrice pouted, finding it mildly unsettling. "Those are things though. I know nothing at all about who you are. Man or priest."

"Honesty is the first step to enlightenment. Admitting that too which you know not, nor understand," Tortuga intoned.

"I know you mean well, Cardinal but I've heard the same doctrine from the churches of Ankor and Nihmrodel, as well as your own of course. You know what I've learnt?" Matrice barely paused.

"I've learnt that Ankor's path to enlightenment differs from your own god and again from Nihmrodel's. How can that be I ask myself? Surely the Trinity share the same vision? I will not say my conclusions. Some might find my views parlous."

"Highness, you talk about my god when surely he is our god. I serve Kildare and observe the Trinity as all gods fearing people do. But there is more to this than we know. There is more to the Trinity," Tortuga stated.

Leaning forward, his lip curled. "However, I confess some alignment with your statement. It ties in neatly with that which I would discuss with you."

Matrice settled back in her chair, away from Tortuga's bulk which seemed to sag across his desk. "As I have already said, you have my attention."

"These are dangerous times, Highness and I propose that we share some commonality of purpose," Tortuga started. "The Trinity is, by and large, run by men and women who believe themselves holy and pious. Many consider themselves possessed by the divinity of the gods themselves; to speak with their god's voice and to carry out their god's will. It has ever been so. Yet I find myself questioning their faith and doubting their methods."

"I can see why you sent Father Manning from the room? I am curious. Why risk such a revelation on me, an empty-headed fifteen-year-old princess; one with too much time on her hands?"

Tortuga chuckled, setting his jowls wobbling. "Please, we both know you are anything but. I am telling you because of the times we live in. The crown and church are two sides of a coin. Both need to be pure in purpose and strong in belief."

Matrice frowned, "I'm not sure I follow. Do you accuse the Churches or my father of the lack? The former is blasphemous and the latter treasonous? I think perhaps I have heard enough, your Eminence."

Leaning forward, Matrice rose smoothly from her seat and turned to leave.

Tortuga reached out, grasping her hand in his own, and felt her flinch at his touch. "Hear me out, Princess, before you make judgement of me."

There was a smooth, rasp of steel as Gart drew his sword and detached himself from his spot by the wall.

Releasing the princess, Tortuga sat back in his wide seat and waited.

Matrice was still. Her eyes flickered to Gart and her beating heart calmed at his steadying presence. She raised a hand to his shoulder as he brushed, protectively, alongside her. "It's okay. I will hear the Cardinal."

Gart glared, eyes fixated on his target. With exaggerated slowness, he stepped away but only as far as the back of the chair.

That suited Matrice, who abruptly sat once more. Reassured, she crossed her arms and nodded at Tortuga to speak.

"Heathen savages have attacked the Rivers. According to my reports and judging by their line of advance, the urak have taken all but Rivercross. The Norderlands is soon to be invaded and will face a similar outcome. I've lost most of my congregation, Highness, so I apologise if my earlier bluntness startled you. I thought you preferred direct talking?"

"Your loss is ours, Cardinal, I assure you. The Rivers is part of the Kingdoms after all," Matrice demurred. "You mentioned a commonality of purpose earlier but I've yet to hear it. So, make your point, for I grow weary of this conversation."

"If you will allow me some latitude, I will come to that," Tortuga stated. "Firstly, what is your assessment of your brother, Prince Herald?"

Matrice gave a mocking half-smile. "I see. You've met my brother then. No doubt to seek his patronage. An endorsement from the Crown Prince, our future king, would no doubt go some way to strengthening your position. It is High Office you seek. It all comes clear to me now. You wish to become the next High Cardinal." She laughed.

Tortuga's eyes tightened. "I'm glad you find me amusing but you misunderstand, princess. I will become High Cardinal, among other things. I did meet with your brother as I have now met with you, to assess for myself the merits of you both. So please, indulge me. Tell me about your brother."

"My brother is many things. I will not speak ill of him to you. This is not a confessional. But I will say Herald is not for you. You may be the smartest most humble and pious man in the world." Matrice let her amusement show. "But you possess neither the physique nor charisma that might sway him to your cause. He's a romantic and his purpose clear. An instrument of the gods, Herald believes he will save us from the urak. He's even training again with a sword. I'm afraid the only Red Priest that might interest him is Arch Bishop Whent. A fighting man you see."

"I do see, thank you. It must be difficult, Highness. Watching it all and doing nothing. Knowing you could do so much better. Be so much more," Tortuga stated.

Matrice frowned. "Commonality of purpose, I can think of only one. You seek high office and for what? In return for my patronage, you would see me to the throne. I would laugh if only it weren't so… insulting."

"You failed to mention treasonous, Princess," Tortuga offered.

"Yes, that too." Matrice felt Gart shift behind her.

"But you want it. I can smell desire and ambition rolling off you," Tortuga said. "You may not say it but I will. Your brother is a fool and you so much more capable. You were born to rule and yet, even were you the elder, Herald would still take the throne before you."

"Someone told me recently that life is inconstant and humanity yearns for certainty. That laws and tradition bring a semblance of this and they are right," Matrice murmured. She was uncomfortable but nonetheless found herself wanting to hear more.

"Sounds like something the Order might say, Highness." Tortuga watched for and saw the flare of recognition in her eyes.

He leered. "They are right of course. Though that does not mean things cannot be changed. They need to, lest society stagnates and withers. The Kingdom is made up of the nine, after all, each with their different customs and traditions."

Matrice frowned. "It's impossible. Maybe, if I were High Queen I could fashion such change. But I am not and nor will I be unless tragedy strike both my father and brother. Even then, there are blood ties, male blood ties that would seek to claim the throne before me. That tradition we speak of would split the kingdom in a bloody civil war and we are already at war, Cardinal."

"If there were no way to avoid such conflict would you be brave enough to seize your destiny I wonder? Or would you consign yourself to being a bystander in history?"

"You speak of destiny? Of tearing the kingdom apart for the whims of a young girl who wants to be High Queen? I would wish to serve my people better than that Cardinal. I would not do it."

Tortuga's countenance grew stern, his voice firm and assured. "I do speak of destiny. Kildare, god of war and death has sent me visions, Highness; so stark and vivid they are etched in my mind, visions of that which may come to pass. And in all of them, bar one, the nine kingdoms suffer death and destruction, to perish and fade into obscurity. But in that one vision, that one hope, Kildare showed me a Queen sat upon a throne surrounded by blood. That queen I believe is you."

Matrice felt Gart's hand slip onto her shoulder and squeeze it gently, "The Red Queen!"

Tortuga looked up past Matrice and stared at her First Sword. "You have seen it, Shadow. Kildare has spoken to you."

"I have seen it."

Tortuga nodded sagely. "Good, Matrice will need a protector at her side but also at her back. All Kildare requires is an act of faith."

Matrice twisted in her chair and glanced up into Gart's face. She could see the certainty in his eyes. He believed. But did she? Something about Tortuga unsettled her and more than just his gross bulk and fleshy, pallid face. But he spoke to her deepest desire.

"What sort of act of faith?" Matrice heard herself ask.

"A kiss, your Highness," Tortuga smiled, "with me."

Matrice startled, at first taken aback before her ire rose, "Really? A kiss and like a princess from tales of old all my girlhood fancies come true. I'm sorry Cardinal but you're no prince. I'm afraid I must decline."

"There is much I do not understand, Highness. This act of faith is not at my request I assure you," Tortuga argued.

"So Kildare wants me to kiss you as an act of faith?" Matrice shook her head in disbelief.

"I understand your reluctance. As you have pointed out already, I am hardly a heroic or charismatic man. There is a duality of purpose in this request I suspect. Call it a god's whim or humour if you like."

"Duality, there is no fucking duality fat man," Matrice spat.

Tortuga did not flinch at the insult. "I beg to differ. We are both possessed of intellect. You are beautiful yet a woman, trapped to watch other, lesser creatures rule in your stead. I am devout yet ugly, trapped in this body, shunned and marginalised. That I have risen as far as I have is entirely due to Kildare's will."

Tortuga sagged forward, erstwhile. "I assure you, there is nothing wanton or lecherous in this act of faith on my part. It is just that, an act. Can you do something detestable to seek what is rightfully yours, to receive that which is ordained?"

## Chapter 40: Winter Road

**Abanna Ranges, The Rivers**

"The pale skins have gone." Orqis-tarn's voice was terse, his words more a statement of fact than a question.

Grot-tuk bowed his head. He could feel the shaman's displeasure. "They have. We pursue them but they ride carvathe. We will catch them when they make camp."

"Tell me," Orqis-tarn ordered, glaring at the immense bulk of the Warband leader.

At the shaman's command, Grot-tuk shifted uneasily. Convention had changed in recent times and not just because they warred. Shamans, spiritual guardians to the gods, had become much involved in worldly matters. The past ten years alone had seen them insinuate into tribal councils, second in power only to the chieftains. Divine powers, granted by the gods, were no longer confined to ritual but increasingly used in battle. It was against all tradition. How could you die in honour and pass Nos'varqs Gate to Varis'tuks Hall beyond if you could be struck down by magic? It left many urak troubled but none offered a challenge, for to question the shamans was to question the gods.

"The humans sent a small party into the valley and fired a stone house. Then moved north and broke our trap."

"They fired the building to draw your attention and provoke a response," Orqis-tarn said.

Grot-tuk clenched his jaw. That much was obvious; did the shaman seek to teach him his craft now? "Yes, we each baited the other. We killed them and drew their teeth but the rest of the humans withdrew before we could spring our attack."

"A pity I was not there," the shaman said, "Tell me of them."

Scowling at the not so subtle slight, Grot-tuk felt his blood seethe and white heat rise up his spine to lodge at the base of his skull. Violence threatened to burst out. If it did, it would mean dishonour and death. His spirit, unable to pass Nos'varqs Gate, would be left sundered to wither in the Never. The god of death was unforgiving.

Grot-tuk blew a long steady breath through his nostrils and turned his mind away from murder. Thinking instead of what it was the shaman wanted.

"They were warriors, a different tribe to any we have faced. When they attacked they moved as one and held their line despite being few in number. They wore the same red cloth and bore iron plates that turned our blades and arrows."

A hint of a smile ghosted Orqis-tarn's face. "You admire them."

"Admire," Grot-tuk snorted, "Never. They fought well and died a warrior's death. They are worthy of respect, nothing more."

"Very well, chase them south, but only your Warband, no others." Orqis-tarn's eyes bored into the larger urak. He could sense the anger bubbling beneath the surface and waited until Grot-tuk could barely contain himself before speaking again.

"Mar-Dur calls a tribal council at Ous'trak's elbow in two days. Our chieftain, Narpik-Dur is to attend. So for now, harry them. Keep them moving south. You've been given much honour, even though the humans run before us like herds of longhair. Narpik-Dur has spoken."

"As Narpik-Dur commands." Anxious to leave the shaman's presence Grot-tuk held his hands open, arms wide in supplication, and bowed his head.

Orqis-tarn watched in dry humour as the Warband leader turned to leave then offered a final, parting wisdom.

"Winter is soon upon us. Preserve your strength Grot-tuk for the battles ahead will be many."

\* \* \*

It was an arduous ride and Renco's thighs burned as they trekked their horses through the low hills. The terrain was wild and many a diversion was forced by steep ravines and bush filled gullies.

By mid-afternoon, they left the hills behind and the going eased as signs of humanity exerted itself upon the landscape. Empty pastures of short grass were the first evidence; followed next by crop fields, their harvest taken but the ground left fallow and abandoned. The terrain at least was flat and the going proved much easier.

Their pace increased when they found a road and raced the sun to the horizon. It was a losing battle but urgency sat upon them. In a fog of hearsay and half-truths, word had spread of urak. No one knew where exactly or how many. That they retreated though lent momentum to the rumour and fuelled their anxiety.

They passed a sign for Appleby. It recalled Renco to another journey on another day; one with old Mao, grumbling about missing out on a warm bed and the best cider in the Rivers. He grinned at the memory even as his heart clenched.

Then, as it seemed to want to do these days, his mind turned away from Mao and his Master and settled instead on the girl with the dogs. Nihm, her name rolled around in his mind.

Appleby was a large village. Renco and Lett had passed through it with Zoller just eight days past and it was eerily different. Two well-kept double-storied inns were situated at opposite ends of the village square but, like the surrounding shop fronts and houses, they were boarded up. Appleby lay abandoned.

"This place was so vibrant when Da and I came through here," Lett said, her sad eyes wandering. "It seems only yesterday."

Passing out of Appleby they stopped briefly by the village green to rest. The horses were lathered in sweat and steam from their flanks rose into the cold air as their riders dismounted to water and feed them.

By the time the order came to move out again, the sun touched the horizon and dusk was settling. Torches were lit and soon enough they were mounted and moving off, making way for the columns of Red Cloaks following behind in a line that backed up all the way into the village.

Night fell quickly. Two of the three moons were visible in the cloud broken sky; Ankor, large and pale, hung low in the south whilst Kildare, high in the heavens, glared blood red. Both cast a waning light as the vanguard led them west where the path joined the Great Northern Road. There they turned south.

Hours passed and the night deepened. The clouds thickened, tightening their grip and the air turned frigid and ever colder. The Oust flowed to their right, flat and silent with the occasional moonbeam glinting off its surface. The only sounds became the laboured breathing of their horses, the clatter of hooves on the road, and the crease of leather on armour and harness.

A faint glow tinged the southern sky, drawing them on. It was a while later though, as they crested a small rise, that the glow manifested into hundreds of lights. A camp, Renco surmised, made by Captain Maeson's cohort together with the wagons and auxiliaries sent south early that morning.

Calls rang out in challenge, watchwords were exchanged then they were riding through earthworks that were newly dug judging by the musky smell of fresh loam. The camp itself was arranged in a similar fashion to the previous two nights. Quadrangular in design the centre third held the command tents, wagons and auxiliaries, and a corral for the horses. Each corner of the encampment would be occupied by a cohort, though in the hazy darkness, it was impossible for him to tell if all had returned from the forests of the north and been accounted for.

"You two follow me," Comter called, leading Renco and Lett towards the command tents in the centre. There they dismounted and took their bedrolls and packs before Comter had them hand their reins over to Brother Morgan, who led the horses away without a word.

"Sleep while you can. The night's half done and tomorrow will be a long day," Comter said, pointing to a canvas canopy suspended between two poles. It was one in a long row of tents. "An' don't worry. I'll be right here, watching ya both."

Renco's body ached from the ride. His back was tight where the skin healed and his broken fingers throbbed, the tips aching where fresh nail buds seeded. Despite this, he felt good. The pain was transitory and would pass. He was strong and the sharp wind invigorating.

His eyes travelled to Lett. She looked beat, shoulders slumped in fatigue, her face drawn and pinched.

Laying his bedroll out on the damp grass beneath the canvas, Renco took Lett's from her hands and shook it out next to his. He'd gotten used to her sharing his warmth and this night was colder than any before; she'd need it now more than ever. Already she was shivering and hugging her cloak tight.

Taking up his waterskin, Renco could feel from its weight it was mostly empty. He proffered it and watched as Lett gulped from its neck.

Wiping an arm across her mouth, Lett handed it back with a whispered thanks. Removing her heavy cloak she draped it over her bedroll, unlaced and removed her boots then crawled wearily into bed.

Renco looked at Comter; aware the sergeant watched them both. He hefted the water skin in his hands and shook it, signing he needed to refill it. He wasn't sure the burly Red Cloak understood but when Renco moved in the direction of the wagons a gloved hand on his arm stopped him.

"Leave ya skins out and get your arse in." Comter hooked a thumb at the makeshift tent.

With a shrug of his shoulders, Renco handed the water skin over. Unclasping his cloak, Renco laid it over his bedroll before following Lett's example. Lying there, with Comter's boots and legs filling the entrance, he felt Lett wriggle her bedroll closer for warmth as her body pressed up against his. Comter trudged out of sight but Renco knew he would not be far. And he'd be watching, always watching.

He took a deep breath that turned into a yawn.

* * *

A blood-curdling scream shattered the night.

Renco's eyes flared open. His arm ached. Lett's head rested in the crook of his shoulder turning it numb. Her warmth though was worth it and he could feel her softness even through the bedrolls and clothing they wore.

More screams rang out, again and again. Renco could tell they were distant but it was no less chilling for it. Outside, snow gently fell turning the ground white and pristine.

Winter had arrived.

Lett stirred but didn't awaken. Manoeuvring her head from his shoulder, Renco slid out from beneath his covers and pulled his boots on then fastened the laces, awkward with only one good hand.

"Aarrgh, I'm so tired…" Lett husked. "What are you doing?" She yawned and stretched as she peered at the shadow that was Renco, reaching a hand out to touch him.

It was dark outside and darker still under the canopy but Renco could still see Lett. He saw the moment when the screaming pierced the fog of her sleep-raddled mind, when the whites of her eyes matched the pale snow outside.

"My God, what is that?" Lett gasped the constant worry that seemed always with her these days bubbling to the surface.

Renco shrugged, fastening his cloak about his shoulders.

"You're not leaving me here alone, I'm coming."

Lett struggled out of her bedroll. Her eyes fastened on the snow outside and she shivered. The chill air clung to her body, already sucking the warmth from her.

Determined, scared of Renco leaving her, Lett squeezed into cold boots and laced them as quickly as she could. Renco waggled his fingers at her in that annoying way he did, as if she could somehow understand what it was he signed, then abruptly crawled out from beneath their canopy. Any fear he might abandon her though subsided, as his boots crunched once in the snow then stopped as he stood silent guard outside.

Buttoning her cloth undercoat over her shirt, Lett slipped a thin shawl over her head and fastened the blessedly thick cloak around her shoulders.

Lett shivered involuntarily. She'd have to ask Comter again for warmer clothing, hers were lost at Fallston and what she wore was too thin for this weather. Scrambling out from beneath the canvas she stood beside Renco and pulled her hood up and cloak tight.

Satisfied she was ready; Renco grunted and strode off following the growing number of Red Cloaks on their way to the northern earthworks. Scrambling to keep up, Lett had just fallen in alongside when the screaming abruptly ended. The trudge of boots and the crunch of snow seemed suddenly loud.

Calls rang out and shouted orders, then a horn blared, long and lonely. Renco glanced at the night sky but it was dark, no light from the tri-moons could be seen, and no stars. The snow was set to stay.

A new scream crashed the night, a sound of unbridled, tortured pain. It was the same as before but different. This torment belonged to another.

"Seven hells," Lett swore, "What's happening?" She wasn't expecting an answer but got one.

"The sentries miss. Urak 'ave got 'em." A fresh-faced Red Cloak blurted. He looked as scared as she felt and Lett's heart raced fearfully as Renco led them past.

The entrance to the encampment lay just ahead. Red Cloaks were being organised in rows five deep all along the perimeter and several paces back from the earthworks. Sergeants bellowed and for the first time, Renco wondered where Comter was. He was like a shadow they could not shake. Maybe he was here somewhere, shouting out orders. Renco trudged on; no one seemed to pay them any mind.

Atop the earthworks, he spied the familiar figure of Henreece. The young physiker stood with his back to them, gazing northward. Without thought, Renco scrambled up to stand beside him. Hearing a huff and grunt behind he turned, holding his hand out for Lett to grasp before pulling her up.

"Nothing much to see I'm afraid," Henreece said.

No, Renco agreed, following the line of torches spread along the embankment. The light from them destroyed any chance of that. It ruined their night vision and the paltry glow only extended a dozen paces before the night swallowed it.

The screaming was unrelenting and Renco could feel the nervous energy from the massed ranks behind. Lett clung to his arm, trembling. Snow dusted her hood.

"I don't like it. I think we should go back." Lett's teeth chattered. Even Henreece slapped his arms in the cold.

Renco shrugged, she was right. Standing up here was not the most sensible thing to do. Alone of the three of them, he seemed unaffected by the frigid conditions. Orienting on the noise, Renco peered intently into the darkness and thought he could discern the indistinct movement of black against black, else it was his imagination. He could phase into ki'tae. That would tell him what was out there, Renco was sure of it but his oath to Mao still held. There was danger in it. So instead he tried to decipher what it was he saw.

An arrow suddenly flared into the night sky followed quickly by two more. They left a fiery trail as they arced and fell. The first arrow extinguished as soon as it hit the ground, the other two though stuck, casting a dim light over the snowy surrounds.

Renco detected movement at the very edge of the light before it vanished into the inky black. If anyone else saw though, it was not enough to hold their attention as all eyes fastened on what was revealed.

A wooden stake was stuck upright in the ground. It held a man, naked but for his red cloak which stood out against the dull whiteness of the snow. Even from where he stood, Renco could see the man had been impaled. The stake passing through the man's body and out through his mouth. The head, twisting obscenely, gazed at the heavens in accusation. Blood pooled on the ground beneath the body and a trail of it led across the snow into the darkness of beyond. In it, somewhere, hidden from view, came the screaming of another demented soul.

"By the gods," Lett gasped then swore, tightening her grip on Renco's arm.

"Please do not blaspheme. This is not the doing of the gods," Henreece scolded gently.

Turning he glanced at them, his eyes casting up and down. They both looked so young. "Why don't you take Miss Letizia away, this is no sight for a woman."

Tearing his eyes from the grisly scene, Renco nodded in agreement.

"She looks frozen. I'll see if I can find something more suitable for her to wear," The physiker added. Dismissing them, he returned his attention to his staked brother and wondered where the other sentries were. There were more than two out there.

\* \* \*

The screams continued until an hour from dawn, disturbing any rest and creating a fractured atmosphere of fear, angst, and anger in the camp. When the morning sun finally waxed pale it was over a winter landscape. A landscape decorated with eight dead Red Cloaks. Each staked as the first had been. Each planted a stone's throw from the camp's northern perimeter. A threat or warning to the living.

The snow had stopped falling by then but the heavy clouds threatened more to come. A cohort was dispatched north. Fully armoured and bearing shields and long spears they swept the countryside. The dead Brothers were taken down and placed over a pyre of wet wood. It needed a whole flask of naphtha oil for the flames to take. As thick plumes rose into the sky the cohort returned, reporting that the urak had withdrawn to the hills in the east. The steep terrain and heavy vegetation made it impossible to pursue them further.

The order was struck. The horns were sounded. The Red Cloak army turned south. Outliers rode in large bands to screen their flanks, whilst the main body followed the road.

Whent rode at the van, surrounded by his elites, his mood dark and sour. His plans lay broken and all he had for his endeavour was fifty-nine dead Brothers and one live urak. It was a poor return. Still, not all was lost he consoled himself. The battle in the vale had yielded some insight into how they warred. The urak were cunning and well organised, that much was clear. Laying an ambush spoke of strategy and intelligence; that the mute had seen the trap for what it was interested him. He'd intervened and possibly saved them from disaster. How had he and why?

The boy was a fine puzzle, one he looked forward to solving. Maybe that and their urak prisoner would be enough. It had to be, for it was all he had to show for his foray in the north.

As for the urak, it remained surly and uncooperative. He'd spent some time with Henreece trying to coax it to talk but the urak gave no indication it even understood what they said.

Whent had read a few books in his youth on urakakule. Dredging his memory, he recalled the common tongue was spoken but doubt assailed him. They were ancient tomes, who knew if they still held true. It was possible, likely even, that the urakakule spoke their own tongue and that common had lapsed if they'd no cause to speak it. Another puzzle and like Renco, one to crack another day.

Snow started falling again as the clouds gave up their harvest, the flakes larger and heavier than those in the night. The conditions were further compounded by a strengthening wind, drifting the snow.

Whent grimaced, the flanking units would soon find it hard to keep pace, he would have to call them in or face leaving them stranded and isolated. Speed would be their best defence and after a brief discussion with Warwick, the Captain agreed. Shouted orders filtered back down the column and riders were dispatched to the patrols calling them in.

So it was, that when Brother Hamish sounded two short sharp notes, they were ready. In a staggered concertina, the Red Cloak army broke into a steady trot, the lead riders forging a path through the deepening snow.

\* \* \*

The conditions were unrelenting as the clouds darkened and the wind picked up. A storm raged and Renco wondered how much longer they could continue. Beneath the hooves of his horse, the road was buried and indistinguishable from the hard ground. Were it not for the occasional tree, the whitewashed bushes, and the undergrowth lining the way they would have struggled to follow it.

The only good thing to be said was the wind at least was at their backs urging them on. It kept the driving snow out of their faces.

As was usual, Lett rode by his side and Renco knew she struggled badly. During a brief rest stop, he'd appropriated a cloth wrap from a Red Cloak saddlebag. Tearing it into strips he had Lett knot the ends together. Then wound it like a scarf about Lett's neck and face so that only her eyes showed beneath the rim of her hood. Little enough as it was, it was all he could manage. He spared her a worried glance.

Lett's blue eyes were red-rimmed and stared blankly ahead. They were barely visible in the narrow slits of her eyelids as she screwed her face up against the cold. Her body shivered constantly.

A horn wailed forlornly ahead, the sound whipped away by the wind as soon as it finished. At first, nothing much happened. Renco's horse took one weary step after another, following the horse ahead as it had done all day. Then, after passing through a saddle of ground between two small rises, the column ahead veered off the road to the right. The snow was broken and a trail was forced next to the rising ground of a hill. Trees lined its slope and the wind eased noticeably as they came into its lee.

Stretching away from the hillock the ground was flat and open. It ran all the way to the banks of the Oust which meandered by, unperturbed by storm or snow. It was clear to Renco the Red Cloaks had expected to make it to the Defile but if the fortress was out there its forbidding bulk was hidden by the blizzard.

Not ideal but as good as we're likely to find, Renco conceded.

The Red Cloak camp that night was not so orderly. The wagons were circled in the field just outside the treeline with the auxiliaries huddled in their midst. A cohort was sent to a distant copse for shelter and to guard their southern flank. The rest billeted on the side of the hill, under the cover of the trees, which provided a semblance of shelter.

Renco was grudgingly impressed with the discipline and endeavour shown by the Red Cloaks. The sergeants had their men compact the snow and pile it into banks to act as windbreaks before lean-tos were erected to shelter beneath. With the storm raging no fire would start so a sparse meal of hardtack and dried meat was eaten.

"You two, there," Comter pointed Renco and Lett to a newly constructed shelter. The two Red Cloaks who had just finished it looked less than happy.

"Aw sarge, come on," the smaller of the two moaned in complaint.

"Sarge nothin'," Comter snarled, glaring. "Stay with 'em till I gets back. No walkabouts alone. They go for a piss you go for a piss. Got it?"

The mouthy Red Cloak had to look up to meet Comter's eyes. Mollified he'd not lost his shelter entirely, he nodded, "Yes, Sarge."

"Ai, Sarge," echoed the other.

Comter gave both a stern look. Satisfied they'd got the message he nodded. "I'll not be long." He strode off, heading downhill towards the wagons.

"Cock," spat the wiry Red Cloak once he was sure Comter was out of earshot.

"Mind your tongue, Mackey. Evil bastard hears ya you'll be digging latrines till the thaw."

"Shit, Stokes. Sergeant Cunter singles me out for the crap jobs anyways," Mackey sneered.

"Ai, but not me so shut your hole," Stokes warned. "And the last shit for brains he heard call him Cunter got his arm broke."

Stokes pushed Renco and Lett towards the lean-to. "Get in."

His eyes lingered on Lett, groin stirring. Even wrapped up as she was, the lass looked enticing. Better than Mackey to huddle up next to; Stokes leered. She flinched away from his touch and ducked beneath the canvas. The boy didn't budge though, he just stared at him.

"I said get in," Stokes growled; his breath steaming the air. He was irritable, the warmth from shovelling snow and setting up the shelter was gone and the sweat on his back had turned cold and clammy.

Renco signed, he needed a piss. The larger of the two men, the one called Stokes took his meaning. His small, pebble-like eyes narrowed though in suspicion. Renco shuffled from one foot to the next, agitated.

"Mackey, take the mute for a piss. I'll stay with the other one," Stokes ordered.

"It's dark as fuck out there. You take him. I'll stay with the girl," Mackey snarled.

Stokes laughed derisively, shaking his head he ducked beneath the lean-to.

"Fucker," Mackey shoved Renco from behind. "Move it then, shithead."

Renco trudged past the shelter heading deeper into the trees. The night was like pitch as he crunched his way uphill. He didn't go far, only a dozen paces or so, passing several other lean-tos with their owners already huddled deep inside. Above him, the storm raged. The wind whistling as it whipped through the treetops which creaked and groaned under the assault.

"Far enough. Pick a tree an' be quick. Ya don't want your cock ta freeze off," Mackey shouted, raising his voice above the storm.

Moving behind a tree, Renco loosened his trousers and eased himself out of his small clothes. It was cold right enough but it didn't seem too bad to him. He wasn't chilled to the bone like Lett appeared to be. A warm stream splashed against the bark, hissing and melting the snow like acid and he rather enjoyed it. Finished, he shook and tidied himself away before scooping up a handful of snow to cleanse his hands.

He waited.

"Ankor's hairy arse, can you be any slower?" Mackey blasphemed, slapping his arms to beat some warmth into them.

Renco closed his eyes. Listening intently, he filtered out the wind and trees as Master had taught him.

"Come on, dumbfuck!"

There, the scrunch of snow. Renco waited, his senses extending out. The Red Cloak was behind him, arm reaching….

Spinning, Renco snapped his left arm out knocking aside the out-stretching hand. Stepping into the Red Cloak, he planted his feet and drove his right fist into Mackey's midriff.

Caught off guard, air exploded sinking Mackey to his knees. The pain was exquisite. It felt like something had torn inside his gut. He could barely move and had no breath to cry out as a sludge of hardtack, meat, and bile vomited into the snow. He gasped; he couldn't think. His brain was slow but instinct had him reaching for his knife when a weight pressed into his back. An arm clamped around his throat. Constricted, Mackey gagged, lungs already burning. A leg clamped to his waist trapping his dagger and blocking his hand.

The world was already dark, the trees just a vague mass and the snow a grey-black blend, when Mackey felt himself spinning, disoriented. He was on the ground, the arm choking him tighter. With no air and bright spots dancing before his eyes, he panicked. Slamming his head back it met no resistance. His ear brushed the face of his assailant who hugged him tightly. Lungs starving, the light spots left him and darkness descended.

Renco released Mackey and stood looking down at the Red Cloak. His chest moved and, Renco wrinkled his nose, he could smell the ripe breath and dry sweat on him still. Working quickly he stripped Mackey of his cloak and weapons.

A grin escaped Renco's face, he couldn't help it. He felt alive for the first time since Fallston. His blood sang in his veins and he felt energised. The cold was a caress to him, the pain in his hand and back as nothing.

He took a deep, cool breath of air. Time was paramount if he was to make his escape. But his feet wouldn't move. Lett's face appeared in his mind, blue eyes staring accusingly at him.

He had to leave her, didn't he? She was suffering, the cold too much and her clothing inadequate. She would only slow him down and worse, probably freeze to death. With the Red Cloaks, she would be safe. Surely Whent would see no harm come to her. She was nothing, an instrument the Archbishop used to control him. If he was gone then what use was she to him? None, she was just a bard's daughter.

His euphoria died. Empty words; words to justify and excuse his actions but they were not true. Not for him.

'If you lie to yourself you betray who you are.' Master chided, the words sprouting in his mind like a guilty memory seed.

Damn it, Renco cursed. Bending, he removed Mackey's quilted gambeson and the woollen scarf looped around his neck.

Turning Renco took a reluctant step downhill.

## Chapter 41: A River Divides

**The Grim Marsh, The Rivers**

"So far, so good," Amos squinted at the rising sun, his eyes tracing the snaking edges of the marsh.

They'd spent three days in the Grim, navigating the narrow channels at its fringe. At times the Grim became nothing more than a quagmire, forcing them to double back and lug the canoe overland or go deeper into its sour belly. It all added time and slowed them down.

Amos gave a heavy sigh. If Wynter had been with them they would have crossed the wolds two days ago and cut a path due south, but he and Jobe hadn't liked the look of the wild and forbidding terrain. Not without the ranger to guide them. Not when they had the two children and Junip to worry about. Although in truth both Belle and Conn had been golden and it was the mage that struggled. She was not fit and tired easily.

"It all looks the same to me," Junip rasped, "Same stinking marsh, same hills, same bloody bugs." She slapped at an insect on her arm as if to emphasize her point.

"Ai, it's taken longer than we thought," Jerkze said, "Got a choice now though; east till we hit the river or south over the low hills?"

"If it means escaping these infernal bugs I'm for the hills," Junip growled, "I mean seriously, why am I the only one getting eaten alive here?"

"I've got a bite," Belle held her arm out, showing a single red lump. "Jobe told me to spit on it then it doesn't itch too bad."

"Hah, I've got three bites," Conn countered. She looked across at Junip and smiled encouragingly. "The spit helps, only you have to keep doing it. Jobe says not to itch or you'll break the skin and then you might get black vein and die." She was matter-of-fact, her big eyes wide and solemn.

Junip sniffed, feeling both irritated and embarrassed for complaining, but damn-it she had dozens of bites not one or three. She gritted her teeth. "Jobe says a lot of things."

"I know. He's gonna show us how to whittle with a knife later," Belle said, her face scrunching into a smile. "If you like I could spit on you?"

Jerkze burst out laughing at the look of horror on Junip's face. "Sorry," he held his hands up in apology, "your face was a picture. But the girls are right and dare I say Jobe is too." He was sat next to the mage and tapped a finger on her knee. "So, no more scratching, they are looking red and raw."

"If you've quite finished comparing bug bites," Amos said, his tone making it clear that they had.

"Now, from the map, I have a vague notion where we are." He pointed due south towards the hills. "The wolds are lower here and stretch south another day. It's a long trek and it won't be easy. Add another four or five days and we should reach Rivercross."

"If the urak aren't infesting the plains between here and there," Jobe said. "I don't fancy it."

"You don't fancy it? You'd rather paddle around another day in this stinking bog," Junip moaned.

Jobe grinned, amused by the mage's discomfort. "Winds have changed the last day or so. It's blowing almost due south and it's a lot colder. Seem to remember you moaning plenty about that last night."

Junip glared, aware he was baiting her but unable to stop herself. "What's the weather got to do with it?"

"Winter lass." His eyes crinkled at Junip's scowl. "If the snows hit early we don't want to be stuck in the hills. The river is a risk but, if we play it smart, it's our best and quickest way to Rivercross. I reckon half a day till we strike the Oust. Lie up till dark, then float downriver quiet as a log, just like before. Four days, no walking." Jobe dangled that last like a fisherman with a lure. He didn't fancy listening to Junip moan about her blisters if they had to walk all the way to Rivercross.

"Jerkze?" Amos asked.

"It'd be plenty tough on foot and if the urak are on the plains already the river's our best chance. At least, it gives us more options." Jerkze rubbed a hand over his whiskered chin. "Besides, if Lord Jacob made it to the Reach with Lord Sandford, might be we meet them, small odds though that may be."

"Please, Lord Amos," Conn pleaded.

"Ai, Lady Constance, I know." Amos held his hands up. "Masters Jobe and Jerkze confirm my thoughts on the matter. The river it is."

Amos smiled, as her whole face beamed.

* * *

They paddled east and Jobe's words from earlier seemed prophetic, as dark clouds gathered and the cold wind grew icy. The early morning sun that had warmed them became a distant memory.

By afternoon the sky roiled angrily and sleet started falling, at first just a shower but then in sheets. It forced an impromptu stop whilst the covers were unpacked. Junip and the girls huddled beneath them for shelter and warmth whilst Jobe and Jerkze pulled their hoods up, cloaks tight, and paddled on. Amos was left with the miserable task of scooping out any excess water from the bottom of the boat.

The wolds to their south were lowering, the hills and mounds flattening the further east they went until finally, they disappeared almost entirely. Undercover of the canvas, Amos consulted his map with Junip providing a soft light to see by. Satisfied, he folded the map away.

"Make for the edge. I think we'll need to walk a bit from here."

Steering for the side, they broke through a forest of reeds and grounded the boat on a grassy knoll. The ground though was not as firm as it looked and their feet sank up past their ankles.

Conn wrinkled her nose in distaste, not liking the stink that arose or the freezing ooze that muddied her expensive, leather boots. Belle though scrambled past her like a jackrabbit and Conn rushed to keep up.

Reaching firmer ground both girls turned triumphantly. They found Junip peering at them red-cheeked and puffing like a bellows. She was hunched forward trying to pull one foot out of the muck but it was buried to her knee and stuck fast.

"Here girls, grab the rope and give us a hand." Amos had coiled the bow painter into a loop and threw it across to them.

"I think Junip's stuck," Belle said snatching at the rope as it unfurled.

© 2020 A D Green

"I. Will. Be. Okay." Junip gasped, though it was clear she wasn't. Her other foot was buried up to her shin and she had no purchase.

"Pull hard, Lady Constance. Heave, Annabelle. Let's get this boat out. Then we'll rescue Junip," Jobe called, managing to sound both encouraging and amused at the same time.

The boat slipped all too easily across the soft ground. It was with some ignominy that Junip was rescued in a similar fashion, though with considerably less ease. By the time she stood on firm ground again the mage was covered in mud and the fetid, sour stink of the marsh. To make matters worse snow started to mix with the sleet and did little to wash the muck from her robe and cloak.

Junip couldn't ever remember feeling so miserable and bedraggled as she did right then. The cold seeped into her bones sapping her strength and her face hurt where the skin was exposed. Trudging wearily at the back she paid no heed to where they were going. She was too wrapped up in her misery to care. She missed Thorsten.

Thorsten had always been home. She'd rarely left it. Had never had a need, she was always so busy with her studies. Many times though she had stood atop the keep, looking out at the town spread below and cast a wistful eye over the land. The countryside always looked so inviting. She had longed to experience it, to walk the meadows and woods, listen to the birds, and smell the flowers. Junip shook her head ruefully.

"Be careful what you wish for, else it might come true," she muttered. Now, all she wished was to be alone, back in her room at the Keep with only books for company. Pulling her soiled cloak tight around her, Junip walked on, lost in her memories.

Jerkze stopped ahead and Junip bumped into him, yelping as she smacked against his back.

"Sorry," Junip rubbed her head.

"We're here, Mistress Junip. You can rest a minute," Jerkze said. Amos called out and in unison, they lowered the boat to the ground. Looking at the mage, Jerkze didn't like what he saw. The sullen face and sunken eyes beneath her hood; the slope of her shoulders and tired stance all said she was nearing her limits. His face creased.

"I'll be alright. I'm just… I'm…" Junip gave a heavy sigh. "I know I'm not much use. Just slowing you down and complaining all the time. I'm just so tired, and I ache all over and now I'm covered in filth and I stink." A sob escaped and she bit her lip, mad at herself.

"It's been tough. But you're doing better than you know," Jerkze told her. "You need to eat and drink."

He glanced up at the dismal sky. The light was fading already. The Oust gurgled silent, hidden behind a screen of bush and willow. They would be headed downriver soon but there was time enough. He steered Junip past the boat and past the others. A glare at Jobe was enough for his friend to keep his mouth shut. He settled the mage on the trunk of a fallen tree.

"Wait there a while." Jerkze moved back to the boat, picking out one of the cleaner, drier, canvases and one of the food packs.

In sudden concern, the two girls joined Junip on the log, one on each side. Jerkze smiled to see Lady Constance patting Junip's hand and talking softly to her. She had a fierce spirit that one and a caring nature. She'd make a good ruler one day. That was if they ever got out of here.

Throwing the canvas across two low hanging branches Jerkze made a makeshift shelter. It didn't keep the icy wind at bay but it was enough to create a dry space from the sleet and snow.

"Now, eat whilst we get the boat ready." Jerkze handed Belle the pack, casting another glance at the roiling sky. "We'll be heading off soon enough."

Jobe and Amos were stood, scanning the far bank, looking for anything out of place. The weather was deteriorating quickly though and it was difficult to make much out at all.

"See anything?" Jerkze asked.

"Nope, let's get the boat ready. The Sooner we're gone the better." Jobe screwed his face at the sky. "This is only going to get worse, rivers already running high."

The three of them carried the boat through the bush and settled it in the water, securing the bow and stern painters to a tree root. Then, whilst Amos and

Jerkze prepared the boat, Jobe took a hatchet from his pack and trimmed some foliage from the nearby bushes then tied the trimmings to the boat's sides.

"It won't fool anyone much, but at night in this weather, it will break up our outline at least," Jobe muttered to no one in particular.

They boarded Junip first, sitting her amongst the packs to slump wearily like a sack of grain in the gunnels. Conn and Belle followed and Jobe made sure all three were wrapped and covered as much as could be by their thick cloaks and with the hoods pulled up. The canvas sheets were all damp but were packed on top of them for added protection, for the wind was frigid and the sleet had all turned to snow.

Boarding, they cast off and Jerkze directed the small craft into the main channel of the river. They felt the current pluck at them and were content to let it bear them on.

No one spoke. The snow and ice wind was harsher now they were out in the open. Jerkze drew first duty at the rudder, steering with his paddle to keep them in the middle of the river, whilst Amos took watch at the front. Taking the chance to rest, Jobe crawled wearily beneath the canvas and huddled with Junip and the girls for warmth, and fell into a fast sleep.

* * *

They drifted downriver all that night, the wind and current pushing them on relentlessly. Come morning they took shelter in a copse of fir trees, dragging the boat beneath their boughs and out of sight. A shelter was crafted to keep the wind and snow at bay whilst they waited out the day.

Junip got some colour back in her cheeks and, whilst she was still surly, managed at least to rouse herself enough to draw on her magic. Melting snow, she heated it to drink. The warm water was a tonic, thawing frozen fingers and melting the chill in their bones as they sipped it.

As night fell they repacked the boat and set off once again. This time with Jobe steering and Jerkze taking point. During the day the wind and snow had been unrelenting and had intensified into a blizzard. The river had grown rough and fast and they couldn't see the banks on either side.

In the darkest hours of the morning the storm passed. The wind calmed and the snow gentled to fall in large soft flakes. A muted light grew in the east and they floated past the looming shadow of a hill. Dawn was not far off and they looked for somewhere to lie up for the day.

Trees abounded on the east bank but urak were thought to roam there and it was another, anxious league downriver before any trees appeared on the west side. With relief, Jobe steered them toward it and once again they dragged the boat undercover and built a makeshift shelter.

For Conn and Belle, the temptation to explore was too much. They'd been cooped up for too long and when no one was looking they seized their opportunity.

"Where are the girls?" Amos asked some minutes later.

Junip, wrapped in a blanket, looked up from her contemplations. "I don't know. Maybe they needed to go. The gods know I do." Junip stood, worried eyes telling that she was unconvinced by her own argument.

Amos clenched his jaw, exasperated. The mage didn't do much of anything it seemed; not even keeping an eye on the girls whilst they set up camp. He sighed heavily, realising he was being unfair. They were his responsibility and blaming Junip accomplished nothing. He waved her back down.

"You're probably right. Just the same I'd better go find them."

Amos searched the camp and soon found their tracks. No hunting skills needed here he smiled tightly. The footprints through the snow led him towards the river and his ire grew at the thought they may be spotted.

He spied them hiding in the bushes by the riverside, whispering to each other. *At least they've got the sense to stay quiet and undercover*, Amos thought crunching through the snow towards them.

They turned when they heard him coming and stared anxiously back at him. They looked so concerned, Amos held back on the lecture he was about to deliver deciding on a gentler approach.

"It's alright. I'm not mad at you. Just, you shouldn't wander off like that."

"Ssshhh!" Conn hissed, flapping a hand at him to get down.

Realisation dawned and Amos ducked, crouching low beside them. The bush at least was thick and he had to part it to look across to the far side. He feared the worst. "What is it?"

"Movement on the other side," Conn whispered.

"Urak?" Amos couldn't see anything.

"No, two men," Conn pointed towards a stand of trees and shrubs on the east side. "I think they saw us but they've not moved in a bit. They were wearing red cloaks."

"Red Cloaks?" Amos raised his eyebrows as a host of possibilities raced through his mind. If they were Red Cloaks then two probably meant they were scouts. Which meant there were more of them out here somewhere and a priest, they never went anywhere without the Red Fathers. "You're sure? Were they mounted?"

"No, on foot and I'm sure, they wore red cloaks and hoods. Belle saw too didn't you, Belle."

"Yes," Belle mumbled, nervous.

Amos rested a comforting hand on Belle's shoulder. Something didn't add up. Why would they be on foot in the middle of nowhere? "Do you think you could both do something for me?"

"Yes," the girls said in unison.

"Can you sneak, quiet as mice, back to camp? Tell Jobe and Jerkze. Ask them to come here," Amos said, "Then, very important, I need you to look after Junip. Have her think she looks after you but really you will be looking out for her. She's tired and cold so see she eats something. We may have need of her skill later so I want her fit and ready."

"Okay," the girls murmured agreement and scrambled through the snow back the way they had come.

It was minutes later before Amos heard Jobe and Jerkze approach. In that time he'd seen no movement from the trees on the far side of the river. There was a chance they had moved away he supposed but surely he would have seen a hint of red against the white shrouded background.

Jobe crawled up next to him. "Anything, boss?"

"Not a sign," Amos replied.

Jerkze joined them. He sniffed the air. "I smell horse!" The wind blew from the north, northeast and he scratched at his stubble, eyes scouring the brightening horizon. "At a guess, I'd say in that hill we passed a league back. It's faint but to smell it at all means there must be a lot of them."

"Maybe they're from the Defile," Jobe offered. "I was checking the map just as the girls came back. With this overcast, the fortress could be near and we'd never know it."

"Well, if they're not urak that's good enough for me," Amos said, "Can't sit here all day." He stood and stepped out from behind the bush and into plain sight. He waited, eyes roving the trees when he caught a flash of movement.

A figure emerged followed by another. They were, unmistakeably, Red Cloaks. Amos raised a hand and waved it over his head.

"There is someat off about that one on the left," Jobe murmured. He and Jerkze had remained hidden.

"We'll find out soon enough," Amos said. He cupped his hands and called, "Hellooo."

The Red Cloaks looked at each other before the one on the left raised his hands and lowered his hood. Long, blonde hair stirred in the breeze. It was so incongruous and unexpected it took Amos a second to register. It was Jerkze though that stated the obvious.

"That's a woman."

"Ai, that it is, didn't know the Red Cloaks took in women," Jobe quipped.

"They don't," Amos said, oblivious; what was a woman doing dressed as a Red Cloak? If the Red Church discovered her, the penalties would be severe.

The woman raised her hands to her mouth and shouted.

Amos turned to Jobe and Jerkze. "Did you get that?"

"Ai," Jobe said. "She's calling for help."

Jerkze stood up and tapped his friend on the shoulder. "Come on let's get the boat."

"What?" Jobe frowned. "Not sure that's a good idea."

"No, but knowing Amos like we do, he'll ruminate on it a minute, maybe two. Discuss with us what we think. Then ignore what we say and tell us to go get the boat. I'm just saving time. Besides, they ain't got horses and I can smell horses," Jerkze grinned as if that were explanation enough.

Jobe scowled that he'd not thought of it first and looked at Amos, who shrugged and gave a curt nod.

"I'll take Jerkze, you'll wait here. If things turn bad you're the best chance for getting Lady Constance and Belle to safety," Amos insisted.

Jobe glowered, unhappy. He didn't like it but couldn't argue the point.

So it was that Jerkze and Amos paddled the boat across the Oust. They had to fight against the current just to hold their line and by the time they neared the far bank, they could feel it in their arms.

"Ho there," Amos called. At his feet was his bow with an arrow in easy reach. Jerkze too had strung and set his. A precaution, but looking at the strangers close up, one they probably needn't have made. Both were young, seventeen eighteen summers at most. The woman was pretty, despite her appearance. She looked weary, her face red from wind bite, her golden hair dull and her eyes bloodshot. Had a rough time of it, Amos reflected.

Her companion had lowered his hood at their approach, revealing brown hair and brown eyes in a plain face. There was something about him though that made Amos leery. The soft downy fuzz on the lad's cheeks made him seem more boy than man but, like judging a horse, there was more to him than met the eye. But it nagged at Amos that he couldn't quite place what it was. One thing he wasn't though was a Red Cloak, of that Amos was convinced.

The youth's left hand was bound and fingers splinted but he seemed untroubled by it. He wore a sword strapped to his side but made no overt move towards it, keeping his hands at his side. In stark contrast to his companion, he seemed fresh and alert.

As the boat nestled against the bank the youth grabbed and held fast the stern rope Jerkze threw him, expertly looping and cinching it around a tree trunk. Amos climbed out holding the bowline and tied it to a bush before turning to the strangers.

The woman spoke. Her voice was lilting. "Thank you for coming, good sirs. We are in dire need."

"So it would seem," Amos said, he indicated Jerkze. "I'm Amos, and my friend here is Jerkze."

The woman licked her lips. Furtive eyes flicking to her companion before settling back on Amos.

"I'm Lett. This is Renco. We seek passage south on your boat if you can accommodate us." She picked nervously at her cloak as it fluttered in the breeze.

"I'm afraid we can't. The Defile is close though. Once this overcast blows through you'll see it. Maybe you can find the help you need there?"

"No," Lett's reply was instantaneous and Amos narrowed his eyes. "We would rather pass the Defile and move straight on to Rivercross."

She sounded crestfallen and the way she kept glancing over her shoulder told Amos more than her words.

"You're dressed as Red Cloaks which I can see you are not. And you're nervous. What are you running from… and," Amos held his hand up, "Before you think to lie to me do not tell me urak."

"Take your hand off your sword, lad. You don't want to do anything foolish now," Jerkze interrupted. He stepped closer, his hand firmly gripped on his hilt.

Renco stared at them both. Then slowly unfurled his fingers from his sword and rested his hand once again at his side.

"Good choice," Jerkze murmured. He stepped back but didn't release his sword, his eyes hawkish.

"We mean no harm," Amos said, directing his attention at the boy, brows furrowing at his silence.

"He doesn't speak," Lett said, "But he's smart. I wouldn't be here but for him."

"Where would you be?" Amos asked.

Lett ignored the question. "Can you take us across the river at least?"

"We can, but I don't know if urak roam the plains or not. It may be safer and quicker to take the south road to the Defile and then Rivercross."

Renco grunted and all eyes snapped to him. He signed with his hands and pointed to the north.

"Shit, shit, shit." Lett cursed, "Look. If you mean to help us, take us across the river. But we need to go now."

Amos glanced at Jerkze. "What do you think?"

Jerkze shrugged. "They're running, what matters if it's urak or Red Cloak. The lad knows someat's coming, so yeah, I think we should go. Up to you if you want to take them or no."

Lips tight, Amos nodded. "Okay, get in. You," he pointed at Renco, "untie the stern rope when I say."

Jerkze helped Lett board the boat, which rocked alarmingly causing her to sway back and forth until abruptly she sat. Hopping in at the back, Jerkze took up his paddle and dipped it into the water, swirling the blade as Amos untied the bow rope and clambered in.

"Okay lad, now," Amos called, back paddling to keep the boat tucked into the side. Watching as Renco untied the rope with a twist.

Immediately he was in, Amos pushed off into the river. He needed no encouragement to paddle, as a chill of premonition settled over him, and he pulled furiously for the opposite bank.

The river was a hundred paces wide and they were about halfway across when they heard sounds behind them; the nicker and snort of horses, followed moments later by men calling out. Their shouts clear, ordering them back.

Jerkze spared a glance over his shoulder "Red Cloaks," he grunted.

"How many?" Amos puffed, digging his paddle in deeper.

"Ten maybe," Jerkze said, just as something whirred past and splashed into the water five paces to his right. "Fuck… arrows. I think they want us to turn around."

A voice screamed out. "Return immediately. By order of Lord Commander, Archbishop Whent."

"Please, I'll throw myself in the river before you take me back," Lett threatened, her voice quivering.

"No one's taking anyone back," Amos panted with exertion.

Another arrow flew, this one a yard closer. On the near bank Jobe stood and set his feet, his bow was ready with an arrow on the string but he waited, eyes fixed across the river.

Jerkze pulled harder. He was a blind target and a hollow sensation crept up his back at the thought. An arrow skipped off the water and thunked into the back of the boat right on the waterline. The arrowhead passed right through the thin skin of the vessel and stuck fast in the wooden stanchion he sat on.

Jerkze swore. An inch or two to the side and a bit higher and it would have struck him in the ass. There was no time to dwell on it though, the bank was fast approaching.

The young man just in front of him, twisted about, brown eyes intense and deep. Face composed, he lunged. Jerkze flinched but the arm was already past followed by a flick of air as an arrow hummed over his right shoulder, cleared the gunwale, and hissed into the water.

Renco had phased, everything seeming to slow, as his senses heightened. Deflecting the arrow had been sloppy. He'd left it almost too late to act and had been forced to use his left hand. The splint securing his two broken fingers proved a hindrance, upsetting his timing and the arrowhead had sliced his palm as he deflected it away. It was a shallow cut. He felt no pain from it. That would come later.

His sudden movement had dislodged the man's bow and it rested against the boat's hull. On impulse, Renco picked it up and tested the tension on the string. It was awkward; his left hand unable to grasp the grip and blood from his weeping hand stained it.

Fitting an arrow, Renco drew, sighting past Jerkze's shoulder. He spied the bulky form of Comter on the far bank. The sergeant's mouth curled in the rictus of a snarl as he barked orders. Three Red Cloaks had unlimbered bows and were preparing to launch another volley.

Choosing his target, Renco released, watching the fletching spin as it fled from his bow. It was too high, his lack of hold on the bow causing the grip to slip in his hand. The arrow buried itself into one of the archers, piercing his gambeson.

The thrum of a bow sounded behind and an arrow fluttered high overhead. Renco followed its arc, watching as it landed between the feet of another bowman. Startled, the archer pulled his shot high and wide.

The boat canted round as it neared the bank. The last bowman was steady, his stance firm and he released. The shot was good. Still phased, Renco followed its flight. Picking up the bow had been a mistake; out of position, he could do nothing.

The arrow smacked into Jerkze with a wet thud. It threw him against the side of the boat and he would have gone over had Renco not grabbed a fistful of his tunic.

Jerkze screamed. The arrow had struck his left upper arm, piercing the fleshy meat and passing through it and into his side.

Amos shouted roughly. "Get ashore, now!" Leaping from the front of the boat, he scrambled up the bank holding the bow rope and started hauling on it.

Lett half fell, half tumbled out as the boat sluiced around. Renco rose, swaying at the motion before leaping for the side, one foot, dragging in the water. Ignoring the flare of pain in his left hand, he rushed to help Amos. Together they hauled the boat up the side with the wounded Jerkze, crying out but managing to hold on with his good arm.

They dragged the boat deep undercover and Jobe released a final arrow before coming to help.

"This is a fucking shit storm. What in seven hells happened?" Jobe raged. "Who the hells are they and why are Red Cloaks shooting at us?"

He glared at Lett and Renco, even as he leaned over with Amos and hefted Jerkze out of the boat. His friend squealed, crying through gritted teeth as they did. He was pale, blood oozing from his arm and side.

Jerkze screwed his face up. The arrow pinned his arm to his body and the pain was excruciating as the arrowhead scraped against a rib. Every step was torture as he was half dragged, half carried back to camp. Black spots swam before his eyes and he tasted blood in his mouth. He slumped, the strength leaving his legs. His vision grew blurry then dark and he collapsed.

## Chapter 42: Not All Is As It Seems

**Kingsholme, The Holme**

Tomas jumped back avoiding the sword by a good hand's length. It was only wooden, a training blade, weighted to simulate the heft and balance of a real sword. It wouldn't cut if it landed but that didn't mean it didn't hurt to seven hells and back when it struck, or leave a mark if it connected on an unpadded area. The bruises on his upper arm and left side torso bore testament to that.

"Come on, boy. Stop running and fight back." Herald lashed out just as he finished talking, but his blow missed again as Tomas dodged backwards before sidling to the right to find more space.

It's hardly fair, thought Tomas, glaring at Renix. The Order ambassador stood silent by the wall, seemingly paying them no mind. His eyes were closed for fucks sake.

Tomas hastily blocked a swipe from Herald that sent numb vibrations up his arm and he almost dropped his sword.

It had seemed such a good idea at the time, fighting Herald. Tomas had been sulking for days, crushed by images of Sparrow's torn and shredded body and aching with guilt. Her death was his fault. She'd looked out for him and he'd failed to do the same.

O'si hardly helped matters either. The Sháadretarch would sit on his shoulder like an evil dervish, whispering about opening the way and calling him the gods-damned Vox Léchtar Fai-ber all the time.

In the end, it was Renix that had broken him out of his stupor, pressing him to participate in Herald's training. The thought of whacking the smug bastard with a stick held much appeal. Something Renix played on. But it was a decision Tomas was coming to regret. The Prince might look overweight and soft but Tomas hadn't even come close to landing a blow on him.

The wooden training sword had seemed solid and comfortable when first he picked it up. But now, arm muscles throbbing with fatigue, the sword felt like a deadweight in his hand. With every block, Tomas was sure the weapon would be knocked from his grasp. It wasn't though. With dogged determination, he hung on to it.

Tomas dragged his sword upright, using both hands to steady the blade. He was lean and fit but this was a different kind of exercise, one he was ill accustomed to. He glowered darkly at Herald.

The prince looked angry, his red face glistening through a thin sheen of sweat. He'd been the aggressor throughout their bout, chasing Tomas around the training yard and raining blows on him. Tomas had been knocked onto his backside twice already and each time the prince gloated in triumph before standing back to let him regain his feet. Each time Tomas had dusted himself down and vowed to wipe the smirk off his pudgy royal face. Not now though. Now he'd had enough. His body ached, his arm felt like lead and his chest heaved as he sucked in air.

Herald circled Tomas. The boy was tired and he'd had enough, the defeat in his eyes conveyed as much. Why did Renix not call it? He'd beaten the sneak thief many times over already. What was the point? At seventeen he was a man and Tomas merely a boy and small for his age. The training sword, clumsy and unwieldy in his hands, was too heavy for him. Herald gritted his teeth; this was a waste of his time. He was learning nothing.

Knowing he should feel bad for the boy, Herald confessed to a smidgen of guilt but not enough to stay him. The cocky little gob-shite looked at him with such scorn and derision he deserved a good beating. He was the Crown Prince for god's sake. He squared his shoulders; maybe this lesson was for the boy, to teach him his place. Herald grinned, maybe he was the teacher; he'd gone easy on the lad till now but it was time to end this farce.

Tomas saw the prince sneer and his back straighten. He could read in Herald his intent even as he spun his blade back in an arc. This is going to be bad, thought Tomas, holding his sword upright and rising onto the balls of his feet. His calf muscles groaned in protest.

The blow when it came was telegraphed. Herald was surprisingly fast but drew his arm back so far, Tomas had time to step away out of reach. As the sword whistled by he shivered, knowing if it had landed it would have broken something. If the Prince had been toying with him before, he wasn't anymore.

The prince stepped in, feet shuffling, and closed the gap. Blade swinging, he struck again.

Tomas brought his sword up in a desperate block and the blades met with a loud clack. His fingers were gripped tightly on the pommel but it wasn't enough. Paralysing tremors erupted up his hands and arms and his sword was ripped from his grasp and sent spinning into the sawdust.

His mind screamed at him to get away and his body responded instinctively. Tomas was moving. Not away, out of Herald's reach but in close. He thrust outwards, hands splayed.

Tomas didn't feel the contact, couldn't feel his arms or hands. He looked on, incredulous, as Herald was sent sprawling backwards. His feet seemed to leave the ground before he landed, stumbled then tripped before crashing against the far wall five paces away.

There was a single loud clap.

"Enough," Renix called.

His eyes were open now, Tomas saw, as the Orderman walked across the sparring yard and knelt beside the Crown Prince. He huffed, seemingly satisfied, and stood. A shaken looking Herald reached out and gripped the hand Renix proffered and allowed himself to get pulled to his feet.

The prince groaned. Somehow he'd managed to hold on to his training sword. His free hand though felt his chest and he stooped slightly at the pain.

"What just happened?" Herald gasped. He was angry but couldn't quite focus on it as he tried to catch his breath.

Renix ignored his question. "The lesson is over. I have seen enough. Tomorrow I will instruct you."

The Orderman walked and picked up Tomas's fallen weapon before taking Herald's from his hand. "Come, my boy." He called to Tomas as he opened the door to the training yard.

Horyk Andersun stood outside it, looking anxiously in for his charge.

"You've been lax in your duties, Horyk. The prince is under-trained and ill-prepared. See you attend to it from now on." Renix drawled. Thrusting the training weapons at the tall Norderman, Renix walked briskly by, leaving Tomas scuttling behind.

They didn't speak as Renix led them across the training grounds and through the gate at the Royal Barracks; the guards on duty watching in silence.

The Royal Barracks was the largest of the four garrisons in Kingsholme. It was located close to Anglemere Castle which rose on an immense promontory just to the south. Like a hulking guardian, the castle sat atop the Iron Cliffs overlooking the azure waters of the Deeping Rift to the south and the sprawling expanse of the city to the north.

A wide boulevard, Kings Walk, connected Anglemere to Kingsholme and the Royal Barracks they'd just left was situated on the east side of the Walk. As Renix led them north, towards the Nobles, Tomas found himself marvelling, as he had on the way in, at the white paving stones. They were immaculately fitted and even smoother than the cobbled streets of the Nobles.

Sometimes, in the All-Ways, Tomas would find himself gazing south towards the castle and dreaming. He wanted to see it. To walk its walls. Explore its rooms. There were riches beyond imagination contained within, every guild thief knew that. To a young boy, the crisp, pure white road that led to the castle seemed almost magical. Walking it now in the real Tomas found it had lost none of that appeal.

His eyes turned west to the beatific splendour of Saint's Light Cathedral which rose like a jewel, its stained glass windows sparkling in the bright sunlight. Grand arches rose in sweeps from the ground, seeming to encase the holy palace in a protective embrace. Beyond it stood a complex of buildings and gardens and further again the impressive Convocation of the Trivium; church land, all of it, and it ran right up to the Iron cliffs.

Tomas had never been to church. 'There are no gods in the Stacks' was a saying he'd grown up with and he supposed it was true enough. Which was not to say the Trinity never went to the Stacks; Holy fathers and mothers of both the Lady and the Saint often came. They gave alms to the poor and brought their physikers for the sick and needy and were much loved by the people. But the gods and their ways meant nothing to Tomas. So, as awe-inspiring as it was, the Cathedral and Conclave of the Trinity held no interest. To him, they were otherworldly and supernatural. It was beyond his realm of existence or cognizance.

"It's a beautiful day, Tomas. Let us sit awhile." It was the first words Renix had spoken since leaving the sparring yard. He moved to a marble block near a tall plinth bearing the heroic statue of a man, fully armoured but for his head which looked north as if to watch over the city.

Somewhat reluctant, Tomas followed. His limbs ached and his body smarted still from where the prince had battered him. His thoughts had been on his bed. It made him smile. Until recently, a bed, a proper bed, was a luxury he could only dream of. He was growing soft.

"You seem inordinately pleased with yourself, my boy?"

"Yes, I enjoyed knocking his Royal Highness onto that pampered arse of his," Tomas said.

Inspecting the marble bench and satisfied it was clean, Renix turned and seated himself. "Did you now? I find that very interesting. Sit, Tomas."

Tomas sank onto the bench. He could feel a lecture coming his way, he usually got at least two a day and he'd not had one yet. No doubt humbling the royal ass was not something one did. He was surprised then when instead Renix pulled his satchel onto his lap. Opening the flap he pulled out a large, leather-bound volume.

Tomas's eyes flared in recognition. It was his book, taken from his room. Even if weren't for the title and wording announcing what it was, he would know it anywhere. The rippled leather cover was dry and cracked in several places, its edges hard, embossed in some strange metal.

"Why have you got my book?" Tomas accused. Renix's eyebrows rose up his forehead in response.

"You know what I mean," Tomas said defensively.

"Indeed I do. Sházáik Douné Táak, the Demon Book."

"It's the Book of Demons," Tomas corrected.

"Pardon me?" Renix said.

"Sházáik Douné Táak. It says the Book of Demons, not Demon Book."

Renix opened the book randomly and examined it. After a while, he touched a finger to the page. "And this word, what does this word say?"

Tomas sniffed. "Why? Think I can't read it?" He leant over to see the word that was pointed to.

"Shézarch." Tomas shrugged. "It's a name, a place."

He moved closer to read more. The strange symbols and glyphs manifested in his mind, rearranging and assembling. "It reads, *'Portals must be opened to the way between worlds, one at Sanctuary the other at Shézarch. Only then can the Sháadretarch be summoned.'* There is a whole bunch more but I've read that bit already."

"I see. Do you know what a Sháadretarch is?" Renix asked, closing the book and placing it back in his satchel.

"Of course, it's a type of demon, a powerful one. At least it's what we name them."

"We?"

"Us, humans; I mean they're not demons at all, we just call them that."

"So, can I talk to yours?" Renix asked.

*"Do not tell him anything more,"* O'si whispered urgently. Tomas blinked. Renix didn't appear to have heard anything. As if to confirm matters O'si hissed. *"He can't hear me. Tell him nothing. He's a practitioner."*

"My what?" Tomas stalled, rattled by O'si's interruption and decidedly uncomfortable under the Orderman's scrutiny. It was like Renix just knew, his grey-green eyes drilling into him as if he could fathom the truth.

"Let's not play games, Tomas. You can read archiárcik script, something that takes decades to learn and a lifetime to master. You're barely twelve, with no formal education and you just read a line of script that took me a full minute to decipher. Master Razholte is the only Wordsmith I know of still living, but now, I believe I have met another." Renix inclined his head then. Not a nod but a proper bow.

Tomas didn't know what to say. This man who had taken him in and shown him kindness and asked for nothing in return was bowing to him. Renix accorded to that oaf Herald nothing, not a bow nor a nod or even a blink of the eye. It all made Tomas uneasy. He was a no one, a thief, nothing more.

"Tomas?" Renix prompted. "I swear I mean no harm to your… guest."

"I… urm… I'm not sure," Tomas mumbled.

*"You're bloody useless,"* O'si rasped. *"Some thief and liar you turned out to be. Just swear you'll say nothing about P'uk."*

"P'uk?" Tomas said.

*"Bezalgets balls boy. I said, say nothing of P'uk,"* O'si scolded.

"Pardon me?" Renix raised a querying eyebrow.

"Sorry, didn't mean to swear," Tomas covered. "How did you know?"

"I've suspected for a while now but the training yard confirmed it. Herald had you well beaten, as well he should. But then you threw him across the arena and into the wall." Renix said. "I know you have no talent, I tested you when you slept that first night. What you did was more impossible than improbable. If I stand here now you could not push me over my boy, no matter how hard you tried. So it was not your fault, more your 'Sházáik's', when he or she or it interceded on your behalf."

"I did it myself, beat him fair and square. I confess I don't know how. It just happened; like something came over me. It felt… good," Tomas insisted.

"You did not make contact. You know that," Renix explained. "I was observing in the aether and saw the energy coalescing around your hands. It was not you that beat Herald. Of that I am certain."

Tomas sighed, his head sinking onto his chest. He didn't understand everything Renix said. He used big words a lot, but Tomas believed him and it hurt. He'd been pushed around his whole life. Beaten, bullied, and made to feel insignificant and worthless. As bad as all that was, the disappointment he felt right at that moment was ten times worse. Just for an instant, he had felt whole. He had hoped and believed that he wasn't a victim if he chose not to be. But it was all false, all a lie. This one he'd sold himself though and it was a bitter pill.

"Are you alright, Tomas? I did not mean to cause upset." Renix slipped a hand around the boy's shoulder only for Tomas to stand and shake it off.

"O'si. His name is O'si and he's a Sháadretarch. You two should get along well enough. You both peddle false hope," Tomas said and walked off.

Renix watched, concern lining his face. The boy was fragile that much was clear. A clean bed and safe roof had lowered the boy's guard and he'd built some measure of trust, but it would take more than that to fix him. He was a child and had witnessed the morbid, tortured remains of his only friend in the world, a child herself. What did you expect, he admonished himself, knowing he could have and should have handled things better. Renix frowned, wondering if he had undone it all.

* * *

Business had been good and Tasso enjoyed the work. It was clean and honest and she took a measure of pride in the fact that she did it well. Her fabrics had been laid out earlier in the morning, rolls of silk and cambric, woollen yarns of various grades, furs and linen.

Already she had seen eight customers and five had placed orders or made purchases. Now, with the early morning rush over, Tasso was at her bench near the front window where she could observe the square and any potential customers.

Wearing wooden paddles on each hand, Tasso worked at some wool that had been delivered the previous day. Raking it between the iron combs of each paddle, she separated and straightened the woollen fibres. It was tiresome work but work that needed doing.

From her window, she could see three of the four entrances leading into the plaza. There were rarely more than a dozen people wandering about at most times, so the man, when he entered the square was immediately obvious. He came from the direction of the Trades and wore a cloak and sword, both of which were unusual for the Nobles. It marked him as an outsider. His clothing, whilst well-made, looked practical and hardy rather than the lighter more expensive clothing she was used to seeing. He carried a large bag and from its heft, it was clear it carried something substantial.

Selling something or delivering, Tasso wondered. She watched as the man walked slowly into the centre. His head barely moved but move it did, casting fractionally side to side. It was clear he was looking for something. He stopped suddenly with his back to her and gazed up at the building opposite. Dropping his head, he spun around and eyed her shop before striding purposefully forwards.

Tasso carried on working as he approached. He spotted her through the window but his look gave nothing away. Opening the door he entered, eyes scanning the room.

"May I help you, sir?" Tasso asked.

"Marn Fabrics, you Marn?" The man's voice was gruff.

"I am indeed," Tasso deftly rolled the paddles in her hands to free them from the wool and stood.

"You work here alone?"

"I do. My husband has his own work to attend to. Fabric is not his thing." Tasso gave a warm smile.

The man grunted and nodded his head. Turning to the door he closed and bolted it.

"What are you doing? I'm open for business. If you're not here to buy anything I bid you leave," Tasso demanded. She moved from the window into the middle of the shop.

"I need your place, Marn." The man turned, a hand resting on his knife. Placing his bag on the floor he covered the gap between them in three strides. He peered down at her and leered. "I don't need you."

Tasso grimaced, annoyed but unfazed. As the man pulled his knife from its sheath, she whipped her arm around and slapped him hard in the face. The paddle sunk its tines deep. In the same movement and with a grunt of effort, Tasso raked her hand downward spinning away.

The man gave a high pitched cry as his cheek shredded into a mess of skin and blood. His harsh eyes were full of fear now. He brought his knife up but stepping in, Tasso batted it aside. She struck, raking his other cheek, feeling the metal combs pull through his flesh before she spun away again and out of reach.

This time she'd caught the edge of his eye, the side of his nose and left lip, and the man looked a tattered wreck with strips of skin hanging from his face. Wriggling her hands free from the paddles, Tasso dropped them to the floor. Lifting the hem of her skirt she slipped a thin-bladed stiletto from her boot.

Sobbing in pain, the man dropped to his knees.

"I'm sorry." Almost nonchalant, Tasso stepped forward and thrust the blade into the man's left eyeball; felt the orb pop as its point lodged deep entering his brain.

The man sunk back on his heels and was still.

Leaning in, Tasso felt for a pulse. Finding none, she grunted, satisfied. Leaving the knife in his eye she moved to his bag, opened it, and checked the contents. A long-handled crossbow and bolts, an assassin's weapon.

The door was already barred but it would not pay for a customer to glance in and see something they ought not to. Picking up a cloth, Tasso wiped the blood and eye pulp from her hands as she walked to the window. She glanced out. Patrick, a local shop holder, was in the square with a man she did not recognise. Both were facing towards her with quizzical, uncertain looks. Tasso raised the bloody cloth and waved.

"Caught myself," Tasso yelled. "Hurts like hells but I'm fine," she assured them.

Patrick held a hand up in return, gave a nod then turned back to his conversation.

Across the way, Tasso spied the boy. He walked in from the direction of the King's Way alone, and she wondered why. He'd left earlier that morning with the Order Ambassador. The boy dressed like a noble, same as every time she saw him, but it was obvious to her that he wasn't. He didn't wear the clothes as if he owned them. His walk and movement, the furtive way his head turned, always looking, always wary. It all told a different tale.

She watched as the boy disappeared through an archway directly opposite her shop. With a bang, Tasso pulled the shutters closed.

## Chapter 43: Knowledge Seed

**East of Fastain, The Rivers**

The wind was icy and fresh. It reddened Nihm's cheeks and nose and tugged at her hair. She stood in the bow of the *River Arrow* watching the banks of the river go by, happy to be alone with her thoughts and with only Ash and Snow for company.

She had much to ponder. She'd not thought beyond her Da and reaching him, but now they had found each other Nihm felt strangely out of sorts. Her Da was headed for Tankrit Isle with the ilfanum and would not part with her. Hiro though was against it, arguing that Nihm needed to find her own path rather than follow the one dictated by Keeper.

Inexplicably, Nihm's mind turned to Renco. She had dreamed of him again last night. It was not clear like in her waking dream. Then, she had projected herself somehow to see through his eyes. The dream last night was more vague; he was on horseback, as before, but struggling through wind and snow. The woman with sunlight hair rode beside him and they were surrounded by Red Cloaks. The foreboding danger was palpable, but that was all she could recall. The dream was real; she was sure of that and it bothered her.

Over the creak of the boat and the noise of the wind, Nihm heard footsteps approach, disturbing her solitude. A low rumble sounded from Ash, which Nihm stilled with a gesture. She thought it might be Morten but the weight and tread were all wrong. She didn't bother to wonder at how she knew, Sai would be all too keen to explain and she was not in the mood. She felt melancholy.

Turning, Nihm saw it was James Encoma. He started at her sudden motion, almost missing his step.

"Sorry, didn't mean ta bother you," James muttered.

Nihm didn't reply immediately. The last time she'd heard James speak it was to demand his father kick them out of their Holdstead. If they'd only listened to her Ma they might still be alive. Her eyes welled, and she wiped a sleeve across her face, angry at her tears.

Nihm sniffed. "I'm sorry about your family." She meant it. Bert and Hildi had always been nice to her.

"Thank you, and I about Marron." James looked awkward, unsure how to proceed and an uncomfortable silence descended.

Nihm returned to her vigil of the river. Did he look for comfort? If so, she had none to give.

"I was wrong," James stammered suddenly. "I wanted you to know."

Nihm took a long breath, letting the frigid air scour her lungs. She remained silent.

"For the longest time I was angry, still am I guess." His words stuttered behind her. "I treated you wrong. For that I'm sorry. I blamed you, ya see. Your Ma and Da were Order folk. I've behaved badly to Darion. Saw it as his fault when the truth is, all you were trying to do is help. That's what I'm sorry about. I just wanted you to know."

Nihm heard the tread of his boots as he turned and walked away. She knew she should say something, offer something in return, but no words would come.

\* \* \*

M'rika was not sure what to make of Nihm, daughter of Darion. Their connection was strong, that was plain to see. The angst and tension Darion carried with him had almost vanished at her arrival, that too was easy to see. But there was an otherness about his daughter that intrigued her.

She watched James Encoma approach Nihm and they conversed. M'rika closed her almond-shaped eyes and expanded her second sight. Nihm was shielded which was enough to tell M'rika she was gifted. Her shield was well-wrought and strong. She could not probe past it and could only sense the almost perfect aura of a human woman. Almost, but not quite, not for someone as attuned to tae'al as she. Despite the strength of the shield it was rudimentary at best and leaked infinitesimal wisps of tae'al. It hinted at much power. Power Nihm seemed not totally aware of. M'rika opened her eyes and waited.

This last day had been uneasy for her and R'ell. To be near so many of the Bonded was uncomfortable. Hiro was known to her. The knowledge of him conveyed at her seeding. So too was Ironside, but not the Order Knight named

Castigan. Tankrit Isle, home of the Order held many of the Bonded. She supposed she had better get used to it.

James Encoma left; whatever was said appeared to have been one way, for Nihm did not face him and instead was looking downriver. M'rika found herself smiling. It was a childish error the girl made. Still, Nihm was the daughter of Darion and a debt was owed, perhaps she could help correct it. Besides, she was curious.

Treading the boards bisecting the rowing benches, M'rika walked towards the bow. Although the oars were shipped, all of the benches were occupied. Many humans had been squeezed aboard, filling as much space as could be accommodated and most huddled beneath canvas covers to fend off the wind and cold.

As M'rika eased by James, who hardly seemed to notice her, she spared a glance at the overcast sky. A storm was brewing and with it would come snow, signalling the first lick of winter.

The wolfhounds stood guard, one on each side of Nihm, and they watched intently. They were pack and M'rika knew from their aura that they shared Bindu's blood. She held her hands out and let them sniff her.

"Will you speak with me?" M'rika asked.

Glancing back, Nihm looked surprised. She turned; they had spoken only in greeting the night before.

"I always dreamt of meeting the ilfanum. Grew up on tales my father told me. You were forbidden folk; magical, fae, and dangerous. What wasn't a girl to love about that? Of course I will."

"Your father is ilf-friend. First named so by De'Nestarin over ten years ago and affirmed by Da'Mari more recently. Do you know these names?"

"Da'Mari. It's another name for the Great Forest. An ilf name for ilf land, 'let not the touch of man sully it' an old saying my Da uses. I've never heard the other name."

"In a manner of speaking, you are correct," M'rika said, "though ilfanum do not own land. We are of it, Nihm."

Sai interjected. <This is a concept I am familiar with. Ilfanum it seems do not believe in ownership. The exclusivity of rights for the ownership and control of land or property is a human construct. It is a fundamental difference in philosophy and belief.>

"I think I understand," Nihm said. The ilf canted her head to the side. She was hooded in a white priest's robe but Nihm could see through the shadow of the cowl. She could see the dark, almond-shaped eyes staring back.

"Darion has told you his tale. A debt is owed and a debt must be paid." M'rika whispered this last, almost like a mantra.

"My father has paid enough. Lost enough," Nihm said, her tone rising, "He is taking you to Keeper, what more has he to give."

"Child of Darion, the debt owed is mine, not his," M'rika said.

"Ah," Nihm was taken aback, "Sorry, Da never mentioned that bit."

"I wish to help you but find myself conflicted. Who are you?" M'rika asked.

Nihm's eyes wrinkled. "Just Nihm; daughter of Darion and Marron Castell, it's all I've ever known. It's all I've ever been."

<I believe she is asking something fundamentally deeper. Perhaps, what sort of person you are?> Sai suggested.

"Your origin is of interest to me but that is not what I meant," M'rika confirmed. "Perhaps I should ask Hiro?"

<Beware. M'rika knows what you can do; what Hiro has taught you about aether and your new abilities. I do not think she knows of me,> Sai said. <Your father seems to trust and respect M'rika. It may be prudent to talk to him before saying anything further.>

Nihm felt a stab of guilt. She'd not told Darion of Sai, only of her awakening to aether and that Hiro was teaching her how to control it.

<You did not tell him of me because you thought he would see you differently. As being less than his daughter, a fear based on emotion and one I believe is unfounded.>

"Da says ilf do not lie. Is that true?" Nihm asked, not responding to Sai. His conjecture hit all too close to the mark, a mark she barely acknowledged.

"A lie has broad meaning and is a human trait. It is not one of ours. It is against our nature to speak an untruth," M'rika replied.

Nihm thought about the question. Who was she really? Did she even know Marron… or Darion? They were her Ma and Da but they were of the Order and yet never told her. Why? Why keep it from her and what else did they hide?

*<Too protect you,>* Sai said.

*<From what?>*

*<The Order is banned in the Rivers. It is the only premise I can conclude but there may be other reasons. I have insufficient data for my logic routines to run any accurate hypothesis.>*

Peering into the hood, Nihm took a deep breath. "Who am I, you ask? My life has changed beyond measure." She shrugged her shoulders, "I'm not sure I have an answer for myself let alone you. Can you help? Do you know what I am?"

Humans are very emotional, M'rika thought, reading the angst in the child's face.

"You have shielded yourself which means you are gifted. This I know. It means you can manipulate tae'al, what you humans call aether. Everything you see has its own tae'al and collectively this is known as their aura. I can read auras. Yours, however, is not true. It is a reflection of tae'al that you project through a shield."

Nihm shrugged, despondent. "It's something Hiro is teaching me. This all seems to have happened since my Ma saved me. I'm struggling to understand what it all means."

"Life is a journey that is ever moving. To choose your path you must first understand who you are. You must look within for the answer. It does not lie with me or Darion or anyone else. Remember that above all things," M'rika replied.

Nihm gave a crooked grin. "You almost sound like Hiro."

"Many of the Bonded are wise." M'rika's lip curled. "Hiro has taught you well but your shield is flawed. Its depiction is good but its projection is not anchored correctly. It does not move as your body moves. If you wish to hide your gift you should know how to do so properly."

"Bonded? Hiro is or was an Order Knight, is that what the ilfanum call them?" Nihm queried.

<*That is good. We should seek data to further our understanding,*> Sai intoned. Nihm ignored him.

"Yes, though not exclusively Order Knights. The Bonded become more than they were; they become other."

"Da says the ilf can bond with creatures. R'ell has his raven?" Nihm asked, finding herself intrigued at the conversation.

"That is different. That is a spiritual link of the mind, tae'al to tae'al. What one feels the other can experience. I believe your father told you some of this."

<*She speaks of her bond mate, Groldtigkah,*> Sai said.

M'rika continued. "Order Bonding is different, a perversion, where two beings assimilate as one. The Order Knights are no longer fully human. Keeper is not human."

<*She speaks of us.*> Nihm was not sure if the thought was her own or Sai's and found it mildly disturbing.

<*The ilfanum are purists. Perversion is a strong sentiment and in this they are wrong. Purism is an impossibility. Life evolves and evolution is change through mutation and natural selection. My nanotechnology is designed to enhance my host and make them better. With me you can adapt and be the best and strongest version of yourself,*> Sai said.

M'rika smiled. "But you digress. Do you want help with your shield?" M'rika asked. "If so, you must open to me so I can see you."

<*I don't know what to do?*> Nihm said. <*I don't know what she means about my shield but it seems she can detect a problem with it.*>

<*I sense the energy you manipulate around you but I have no understanding of how you do it and you appear unable to explain it logically, scientifically, or in any way that has meaning,*> Sai replied.

<*Can you hide or something? I don't know if she will be able to sense you but I don't think we can take that chance given what she has said.*>

<*I recommend against this course however my iterative routines indicate my argument will prove unsuccessful. Powering off for ten minutes. Make sure you are finished by then.*>

Nihm did not feel any different but somehow knew that Sai was gone. It felt… off. She looked deep into M'rika's cowl. The ilf was watching her intently. "Okay. What do I do?"

"I will reach and touch my fingers to your forehead. I want you to open your second sight and sense my tae'al. If you will it, you can accept my tae'al at the point of contact. I will then see past your shield. I must warn you that when I read your tae'al, I will see where it is strong and weak. Whether there is a taint."

"Taint?" Nihm said.

"It can be subtle but if your aura is corrupted, if it is not whole, I will not help you," M'rika said solemnly. "If that is the case it means your tae'al is compromised, you may be a danger."

Suddenly nervous, Nihm licked dried lips. I'm no danger, she thought. She'd never hurt anyone… her mind twisted to the fight with the urak and it stilled her thoughts.

M'rika could sense Nihm's nervousness. "Do not worry. I have read Darion and his aura is strong, his tae'al is whole. You are his daughter, I am sure it will be fine. Once I am satisfied, I will impart a knowledge seed. Upon consumption, you will gain an understanding of how to shield yourself, properly. This gift is rarely given to a human but I offer it freely. Are you ready?"

Nihm nodded her head. From deep within the sleeves of her robe, the ilf reached out a hand. Nihm marvelled at it. It was humanlike and delicate and covered in tiny leaf scales of green with flecks of mottled gold.

Extending her arm, M'rika lightly pressed her first two fingers against Nihm's brow. She closed her eyes and opened her second sight, "Now."

Her sense of Nihm changed. Tendrils of tae'al swirled around hers where her fingers touched. Suddenly, the tell-tale signature of a human woman flared. It was still there; only it had deepened, growing impossibly bright. If she saw with her eyes, M'rika would have had to guard them. The aura was so luminous as to appear almost white.

It was both shocking and awe-inspiring. She had never seen the like. M'rika adjusted her second sight. Nihm's core was strong and pure, tae'al connecting to every part of her being. It took M'rika only a moment to read it.

M'rika felt confused. Nihm's body was changed. It was stronger than it should be. The muscle and bone structure was subtlety different and her womb was gone, almost as if it had never been and the life flow through her body was changed as well. Her aura was pure, of that M'rika was assured, but there was a dichotomy. Nihm was both human and yet more. A bonded but different to any she had seen before.

That was not all though. Disturbingly, something else became clear and obvious as the weave of Nihm's aura told one last tale. Darion was not her father.

Feeling some reluctance, M'rika withdrew her sense. Breaking contact she let her hand drop to her side and opened her eyes to find Nihm peering back.

"So?"

"You are more than I expected," M'rika said.

"Is that good or bad?" Nihm prompted.

"I am not sure. You are like the Bonded in many ways, your body changed. Yet your aura is pure. It is a dilemma I am struggling to comprehend. I must go," M'rika said, but hesitated.

"I don't understand. I thought you would help me?" Nihm pleaded.

M'rika reached out and grasped Nihm's hand. "Your aura is so very strong. More than that, it is untainted. That is very good. I told you before that the answer you seek lies within. You must choose your own way, Nihm. Do not be tempted by the easy path. Instead, be swayed by the right one."

With that, the ilf walked away. Nihm watched, disconsolate. She was no nearer to understanding than before. She twisted her hand, realising it held something. Picking it up, Nihm looked closely, a seed. The ilf was being literal it seemed, for she knew instantly what it was. Nihm took several calming breaths as she considered whether to take the seed or not. Could the ilf be trusted?

She recalled their shared contact. As M'rika examined her aura, so Nihm had reciprocated. She could not read the ilf's tae'al, not clearly, not with any real understanding. But her sense was certain. The ilf was true, her aura good. Besides, ilf do not lie.

Popping the seed in her mouth, Nihm swallowed. She waited. Nothing happened. No burst of knowledge, no epiphany - no nothing really. It was all rather anticlimactic. Returning to the river, Nihm let her mind drift. At least the river knows where it goes, she thought.

A flake of snow settled on Nihm's hand and she looked at the sky. It had grown dark and heavy and more flakes started to fall, slowly at first then in earnest. Winter had arrived.

## Chapter 44: A Flame Of Hope

**Thorsten, The Rivers**

The Black Crow stood atop his keep, as he did every day, and looked out over his town. Bartsven, his first sword, stood unmoved at his back.

The town square below held the remnants of the survivors camp, and a sorry state it was in. It was half the size it had been. Those missing were the desperate, taking a chance on escaping, or the unfortunate, taken by urak on one of their infrequent raids.

The makeshift tents and lean-tos were covered over with a dusting of snow, hiding much of the squalor and filth under a white blanket. Richard swore under his breath, knowing many of the old and infirm would have perished in the night. Weak from hunger, the winter storm would have claimed many victims. It would only get worse now that winter was here.

His angst sat like a permanent companion in his chest. He felt worthless, unable to help the people below whilst he was safe behind his walls. It was a false security, he knew, it brought him nothing but time. It would not be enough.

A bird had arrived that morning bearing a message he had dreaded but anticipated. There was to be no relief. Twyford had retreated with forces intact to Rivercross. The urak were too many. He would come in the spring with the High King's war host at his back and a hundred war mages.

Hollow words and empty promises thought Richard. He'd seen the urak host. Felt the power as their mages, shamans Lutico named them, unleashed hellfire from the sky.

Stretching his eyes out past the walls, Richard surveyed the urak. Many yurts, large and small, were clumped surrounding the town. There were a dozen different encampments spread at every point of the compass. The urak in general seemed ambivalent towards them. Small parties would sometimes raid at night but they only ever took a handful of people. They showed no interest in attacking the keep or its walls.

Richard had studied each encampment many times with the aid of Lutico's viewing magic. Older urak and many females and young were predominant in the camps, but there were more than sufficient warriors protecting them. It was Lutico's speculation that the warriors were as much to guard against the other urak encampments as it was to keep them trapped, explaining that each housed a different tribe.

"They have no fear of us and with good reason. We do not have the numbers to trouble them," the mage had muttered.

He was likely right, Richard admitted, the pronouncement setting a deep malaise within him. For some reason though, Lutico's words would not leave him and like a stone in his boot, he could not ignore them. 'No fear', 'good reason', 'numbers to trouble' the mage's voice repeated, over and over.

"Damn you, Lutico." The mage was right but a thought had kindled in his mind.

"Did you say something, my Lord?" Bartsven asked.

"Just cussing, Bart. Just cussing," Richard said. He rolled the idea around some. It was idealistic and likely foolish but it was something.

\* \* \*

Captain Nathan Greigon shook his head. "It's a risk and for what benefit, my Lord?"

Greigon was newly promoted as First Captain and Richard Bouchemeax nodded silent approval at the question. He'd been worried at finding a suitable replacement for his old friend and comrade Mathew Lofthaus, who perished in the battle of the walls in a ball of hellfire; a loss that was still keenly felt. Greigon though was proving a revelation. More abrasive and abrupt than his friend, he brought a different dynamic. The captain had a mind for strategy that Matt had lacked and now Jacob was gone it was good to have someone to talk tactics with.

"Everything is a risk. Sitting here slowly starving is a risk. But this has a purpose, Captain," Richard said.

"And will you share this purpose?" Lutico groused from across the table.

"We know they send their young in to blood them. Bartsven assures me two trained men should take down one urak." Greigon and Lutico both glanced at the Norderman. Bartsven shrugged.

"We send out patrols, ten or twenty strong and we lay in ambush for when they come into town. They want blood, let's give them their own. We grow weaker the longer we sit and do nothing. At the same time we forage, let the people in the square find weapons, food, and shelter to bring back. Let's construct a barricade to protect them."

"You think that would help?" Greigon asked he looked thoughtful though as he said it, then nodded his head. "Maybe so, it would give hope and something to do other than await their fate."

"That is a reason but it is not a purpose." Richard leant forward placing a finger on the map. He traced the Oust as it ran, from Thorsten to Rivercross.

"We've no boats, my Lord. If you mean to run the river it's a long haul to Rivercross now winter is here," Greigon countered.

"True, though there are some boats to be found in the town, three and four-man skiffs and the like. But we've also the tools available to make them. We've plenty of woodsmith and leatherworking shops lying abandoned. Hells, we've Mackie's boat repair on Chandler Street. Mackie himself might even be in the camp below. We make what we don't have with whatever we do have." Richard's pale blue eyes looked erstwhile.

"So what, we make boats small enough to fit down the escape passage and send folk off downriver and hope they make it?" Lutico raised a quizzical eyebrow.

"Not seen one urak on the river, so why not? We've looked enough at their encampments. These are not war camps. Each, you tell me, is a different tribe and the warriors guarding them are not protecting against us but these other tribes. Your words, Lutico, not mine." Richard was impassioned. "There's a chance they won't risk sending warriors in pursuit if it means leaving their old, their young, and their females unguarded. And if we go at night when it's overcast, folk will be ten leagues away before anyone's the wiser. It's the best chance they will get."

Greigon nodded slowly as he listened. "I like it, my Lord."

\* \* \*

The hardest part turned out not to be the doing but the convincing. The keep was overcrowded with townsfolk and many feared it a ruse.

"You want rid of us. Savin' the food for ya 'selves, what little there is of it," shouted one man. "You'll shut us out to die with them others."

"Whether inside or outside the walls, this is a prison and we will all of us meet the same fate, starvation then death!" Richard raised his voice. Lutico, standing on the walls of the gatehouse, amplified it and, through some art projected the words down into the square below. "There is no help on the horizon. Twyford is not coming. We stand apart but we are not alone. We are Thorsten, we are one people and together we must save ourselves or die in the trying."

As the echo of his voice faded from the surrounding walls, Richard's call was met with stony silence.

"Open the gate," Richard commanded. Striding with purpose he forged a path through the crowd, Bartsven at his back. Greigon barked out orders and a hundred fully armed guards formed into a column.

The portcullis gave a metallic whine of protest as it raised and the gates creaked then rumbled as they cracked open. Richard strode through the widening gap, a flame of hope burning in his chest and determination written on his face.

© 2020 A D Green

## Chapter 44: The Easy Path

**Lower Rippleton, The Rivers**

The storm grew, sucking the light from the day. Visibility shrank and the way would soon be treacherous. Reluctantly, the boat master informed Lord Inigo it was unsafe to continue.

"The Ripples lay ahead, my Lord. Easy enough on a calm day but in this weather, it'd be a fool's gamble to run them."

The Ripples were a series of small islets that jutted from the Fossa like crooked teeth. They compressed the normally placid waters of the river into channels making the waterway fast. Running them in a storm would be perilous.

Idris glanced at Osiris Smee. His mage and counsellor had served his father before him. The young Lord relied heavily on his advice.

"Boat Master Hasan-bow speaks wisely. The villages of Upper and Lower Rippleton lie ahead. We can lay up overnight while this storm blows through," Osiris said agreeably. "Upper Rippleton is the larger and would be better suited to accommodate a personage of your standing. However, it resides upon the north bank. It makes more sense to wait the storm out at Lower Rippleton. At the very least it puts the river between you and any potential urak."

Idris agreed. "Very well, Master Hasan-bow, make for Lower Rippleton."

"Ai, my Lord." With a duck of his head and hiding his relief, the boat master left, leaving a troubled looking Idris alone with Osiris and the ever-present Si Manco.

"You fret, Idris. The High Lord's order was clear and unequivocal," Osiris said, knowing all too well what ailed his young Lord.

"Bah, orders. I have abandoned my people in their greatest hour of need. I should be with them, not running to Twyford because he cocks his little finger at me."

"You do not have to like it but he is your liege. It is a lawful order." Osiris's tone was low and measured.

"Mical Hanboek was given the same order, but still he marches to Rivercross with his people," Idris argued.

"Lord Hanboek is a fool. The High Lord is not. There will be consequences," Osiris said.

"Lord Hanboek is honourable at least. Something I am not feeling right now." Taking a deep breath, Idris waved his mage away. "Leave me, Osiris; I know you speak wise counsel. Counsel, I have accepted but that makes it no less bitter to taste."

"Lords must make difficult decisions all the time. You are doing well, Idris. Your father would be proud of you." With a bow of his head, Osiris left.

The young lord waited till the door was closed before releasing a long sullen breath. "Proud!"

\* \* \*

Darion found Nihm on deck in the bow, lost in reflection. Her face was red and her fingers blue from the cold but she seemed untroubled by it. At her feet, Ash and Snow sat like sentinels, one each side as the snow whipped about them.

They yipped at his approach. Darion reached out and ruffled their ears. Bindu, following on his heels, brushed up against them and they all touched noses in greeting.

"Thought you knew better than this?" Darion handed over some mittens and a scarf.

"Thanks and I do," Nihm said, winding the scarf about her neck and over her nose before pulling her hood up once more. She drew the mittens on and balled her hands into fists. Her fingers were like icicles. Sai had already admonished her but somehow it felt right coming from her Da.

Darion raised his voice above the wind. "Weather like this is raw. It can match a mood. It's numbing and sometimes that feels good. Trust me. It's not. It doesn't make anything go away, just masks the pain. What can I do?"

Chagrined, Nihm glanced ruefully up at her Da. "Don't know. I feel lost Da. I'm trying to work things out. I don't even know what to be honest. But it's for me to figure out."

Holding his arms out, Nihm came to him. Wrapping his arms around her, Darion hugged his daughter tight. He breathed in the crisp cold air and held it a while before blowing it out again in a warm cloud. It felt good to hold her but his heart lay heavy still.

"I'm sorry girl," His voice tremored. "I miss her fierce and when I thought I'd lost you too it broke me. I should never 'ave left ya."

"Why didn't you tell me about the Order?" Nihm mumbled into his shoulder.

"I was going to. We was waitin' for the right time, your Ma and me, but it just never seemed to come," Darion said.

"Why though? Why hide it at all?

"We convinced ourselves it was for the best, to protect you. Order folk is banished in the Rivers, you didn't need that worry. Thought we'd live our lives with no one the wiser, watchers with nought to watch. If the urak never came we'd be livin' there now like we've always done."

"So you might never have told me?" Nihm sniffed.

"Maybe not," Darion admitted. "If Keeper accepted you to the academy at Tankrit you'd have gone when you were six. I guess we'd have told you before then. It's what I wanted but your Ma was not so bothered. She thought ya could live a normal life without the burden of the Order."

"Ma didn't want me to go to this Order academy?" Nihm accused. Pulling away from the warmth of his comfort, she stared her Da in the eyes.

"When you was young, maybe two or three, Hiro came at Keeper's behest to test you. See if ya had the ability. Your Ma and I both did ya see, though neither of us to any great extent," Darion admitted. "You had none. Despite this, ya Ma asked Keeper every year for you to go. Every year he said no."

"Why'd he say no?"

"Keeper never said, but I have my thoughts." Darion brushed the snow off Nihm's shoulder where it had settled.

"See, your Ma and I would never 'ave sent you alone. If ya'd gone to Tankrit we'd a gone too. Keeper woulda lost two watchers. Maybe the urak would have gone unnoticed that bit longer. Certainly, word woulda got to him later than otherwise. In the end, Keeper decided what was best for the Order and that was us stayin' where we was."

"You and Hiro talk of this Keeper like he's a king or something. What's he like?" Nihm asked.

"He is ancient and very wise. Although to see him you would not think him so old. He is the head of our Order and has been as long as any can remember. His mind is unrivalled; his knowledge deep, yet despite that he is amenable. When you talk to him it is as old friends might talk."

"You sound almost as if you worship him," Nihm said. Her Da seemed impassioned and she had never heard him talk so before.

"Worship?" Darion's eyes widened in surprise, "No, but I respect him. He is as good and true as anything I know in this world."

Through the murky gloom and swirling snow, the faint outline of a jetty and outbuildings loomed into view. Calls rang out, rising above the wind as the *River Arrow's* boatmen sprang to life in a sudden frenzy of activity.

Nihm turned and together they watched as the boat glided closer. It cleared the jetty, the tillerman skilfully angling the vessel's prow in towards the shore, then out again to draw alongside a long stone wharf.

"It seems this storm has brought our journey to an end for today," Darion said. "Let's see if we can't get ashore and around a warm fire. These old bones are starting ta feel the cold."

It brought a smile to Nihm's face. Her Da looked as stout and solid as he always did. His bearded face and the crinkle of skin around his weather-wise eyes told Nihm 'his old bones' as he called them would not be bothered by this little tickle of a storm.

* * *

The village of Lower Rippleton occupied the south bank of the Fossa and consisted of two score houses with two inns and a town hall. Lying as it did, a day east of Fastain and just before the Ripples, its main trade was as a stopover for the river traders and boats carrying produce from Rivercross.

Its sister village, Upper Rippleton was larger and situated on the northern bank. As a general rule, it handled everything headed downriver. In normal times it would have berthed Lord Idris's flotilla. But these were not normal times.

The village was half abandoned. Some of its occupants had moved east to Rivercross but most had turned south. They weren't city folk and south lay Westlands and Midshire and safety. South, there were no urak hordes.

Lord Idris set his household and retainers up in the town hall. It was the only building large enough to accommodate them all.

Darion and Mercy with their respective parties took the larger of the two inns 'The Jaded Fish' for their accommodation.

The two Order Knights, Ironside and Castigan joined them having travelled on the *River Arrow* as well. However, they were alone. Unwilling to forsake the wains and horses which could not be brought aboard, it was left for their men Gatzinger and Regus to bring them by road with the two surviving grey knights riding guard.

Ironside paid the inn keep in gold coin. The innkeeper, pleased to see folk with real money and gold no less, rousted the refugees he'd put up moving them on to the other inn.

"Lower Rippleton is small and folks help each other out," he told Darion, reassuring the woodsman the refugees would have a roof over them.

The storm intensified. It was mid-afternoon but it was already dark, the sky hidden behind a dark grey fog of gusting snow, which settled in wind drifts on the ground and against buildings.

Inside the inn, the hearth fire was stacked and stoked until it roared sending a pleasant heat out over the room. The innkeeper served a basic but wholesome meal of flatbread and soup made from turnip and potatoes with vegetables and bits of chicken, bones and all.

"This is good fare," Morten announced, impressed. His Da would be happy to serve this at the Broken Axe. Thoughts of his parents made him sad and he abruptly sat, ignoring the joking banter alongside him between Stama and Crawley, one of the Black Crows that had come with Darion.

Lucky, sitting on Morten's other side, noted his silence, and glanced at him. Whatever he saw he seemed to understand. Laying a comforting hand on Morten's shoulder he slid a tankard of ale across the table in front of him.

In the far corner, the white priest, Father Melbroth was deep in discussion with Mercy and on the table next to them Darion sat with M'rika talking in hushed tones.

The other ilf, R'ell, sat silent and aloof beside them, his dark eyes taking in everything. They found Nihm's and his head canted slightly as they regarded each other; neither blinked.

<What is the purpose of this?> Sai asked.

<I've noticed R'ell rarely talks and mostly to M'rika and sometimes my da. I don't know. It's like he's looking down on all of us or something. I'm just looking back. If he blinks I win,> Nihm replied.

<A child's game.> Sai referenced a memory where Nihm played a similar game with Darion. She was six. <I do not think he understands the rules of the game.>

<Oh, he knows alright,> Nihm said. <I'm bored. All I've been doing is thinking and I'm no closer to knowing the questions let alone the answers. I need to do something.>

Breaking eye contact she rose. Did the ilf's lip move? If so it was marginal at best, barely the ghost of a smile but Nihm saw it. Unable to stop herself she scowled at R'ell before making her way upstairs. She needed to burn some energy and stop thinking for a bit.

In her room, she picked up Morten's old staff. The one fashioned for him by Lucky. Morten no longer needed it now that he had a proper war staff, so she'd acquired it. She shared the room with Mercy and Crawley but it was too small to train in. The two beds and a bed cot took up most of the available space. Instead, she grabbed a lantern and made her way outside. Shielding the light with her cloak she trudged through the swirling snow towards the large barn.

The cold was numbing and her recently thawed bones ached in protest. Ash and Snow barked and whined as she entered the shelter and Nihm grinned at their excitement. Simple and straight forward, they were inured, it seemed, to the everyday travails that beset her life.

Nihm hooked the lantern to a beam, its weak light barely casting to the box stalls on the far side. Moving to the wolfdog's stall, she unlatched it, and they brushed past the door before it was barely open. They cavorted around her and Nihm laughed at the sheer joy of them. Propping her staff against the wall she knelt and played with them a while. Rolling in the straw in a playful rough and tumble, she let their exuberance scour away her worry, at least for a time.

"Go on, away with you," She finally said, "I need to practise." But Nihm was unable to hide her cheer. The dogs seemed to understand, for they rolled to their feet and leapt away to go sniff and explore the barn.

Unclasping her cloak, Nihm draped it over the stall door. There were crates stacked against the opposite wall but the barn was clear in the middle.

Grabbing her staff, Nihm moved into the open space. She twirled the wood in her hands before going through a simple warm-up routine. It felt good to move and the dogs had warmed her blood already. She remembered the lessons her father taught and more recently, Master Hiro.

Weaving the staff into the defensive forms, she flowed from high guard to low guard and back, sweeping up to head guard then back into the three reverse guards. At first, she performed the exercise slowly for precision. Then gradually she increased the tempo, building speed and momentum and finding she could maintain the accuracy of the blocks.

Before Sai, it was easy for her to overextend and her Da would oft tap her staff with his own to throw her off balance before correcting stance or grip or offering some advice. Not anymore, her motor control was precise and her command of movement absolute.

Shifting her feet, Nihm changed stance and repeated the exercise but this time on the offensive, striking from the eight guards as she did so.

Midway through her third strike rotation, the dogs growled and Nihm became aware that someone approached the barn. Twirling the staff around her head, Nihm brought its end down to the ground with a thump then turned and faced the entranceway. She gave a short sharp whistle to still the dogs; they dropped to their bellies, eyes fastened on the barn door.

Lord Inigo stepped into the half-light, at his back the looming form of his swordmaster, Si Manco.

"I was on my way to the Inn when I saw the light," Idris said by way of explanation. "I didn't mean to interrupt."

Nihm's breath steamed from her exertions as she regarded him. He was a boy, fourteen though tall for his age and lean. She had spoken to him briefly the night before and he seemed, mature, was the word that sprang to her mind then but it was more than that.

"You're young for a Lord, my Lord," Nihm blurted, her eyes widening in horror at speaking her thoughts out loud.

His laugh was short and polite. His eyes told Nihm this was not the first time someone had stated the obvious to him.

"Sorry, I didn't mean to be quite so blunt as that."

<Or rude,> Sai prompted.

"Or rude," Nihm repeated.

"It seems everyone likes to remind me of my age as if somehow I'm unaware of it." This time when Idris smiled his eyes creased, taking the sting out of his comment.

"I could do with some exercise. Would you object if I joined you?" Idris asked.

<Yes, I would actually,> Nihm moaned inwardly.

"Sure," Nihm replied, watching as he unfastened his cloak. He wore a sword on his hip, its leather grip tarnished. He was practised. Nihm's assessment was confirmed as he walked to the centre to join her. There was grace in his movements. "You've no staff and mine is hardly fit for purpose. We will perform a mirror drill, no contact. I will lead."

Drawing his sword, Idris stood opposite, sufficiently back to avoid any inadvertent contact. With a grin, he swished his sword dramatically. "I'm ready."

Nihm's mouth tightened at his bravado. Nodding her readiness he returned it. Nihm glided immediately into low guard, watching as he mirrored her movement with his sword, but letting his free hand swing behind for balance.

Much to Nihm's annoyance he spoke.

"I've been Lord a little over a year now."

Nihm stepped back and brought her staff to the rest position. "What happened, my Lord, if you don't mind my asking?"

"When we're alone, Idris will do. I thought we were training?"

"So did I, but Da always says talk or train but never both at the same time. It seems to me you'd rather talk and I confess I am curious," Nihm replied. It brought a wry chuckle from Si Manco who lounged near the entrance, away from the wind.

"Sometimes all I seem to do is talk or listen," Idris complained. "My parents and sister died in a carriage accident in Rivercross a year past. I say accident but I believe they were murdered. Now I am headed there at the behest I suspect of the man that ordered their killings."

"Why would you do that?" Nihm asked.

Idris shrugged. "He is my liege lord and has commanded it. A lord must do their duty." He scowled suddenly. "In truth my lady I am conflicted. I feel I have abandoned my people and I burn at the order."

"I'm not a lady, just Nihm."

"But you think me a fool for going? I can sense it and I think it myself," Idris answered for her, "But I've no choice."

"I know nothing about Lords and such but my mother Marron taught me that I should always do the right thing. That often the doing was easier to know but harder to do. It sounds to me like you already know the right thing. The easiest path is not always the right one." Nihm dipped her head as she said this last. M'rika had said it to her only hours ago but she had not fully grasped its significance. Looking up again she met his eyes.

"Besides, surely a Lord's first duty is to his people, not his liege Lord. Especially one you suspect of murdering your family. I'd be going there to stick a knife in his heart."

With practised ease, Idris returned his sword to its scabbard without needing to look. "Thank you. I heard tell you lost your mother recently. I would like to have met her. I'm sorry for your loss."

Pain flashed across Nihm's face and in her eyes. Idris did not see it though, his gaze was thoughtful but his mind was turned inward as he considered her words.

Glancing at Nihm, he was suddenly energised. "Thank you."

To Nihm's surprise, he bowed to her. Before she could respond however, Idris spun on his heels and walked briskly from the barn. Si Manco hurriedly fetched his Lord's cloak from its hanging peg. He regarded Nihm as he did so, giving her a brusque nod before chasing after Idris.

## Chapter 45: Redwing

**Grimhold, The Rivers**

It's getting crowded in here, thought Tom. Hett's workroom and apothecary had always seemed quite large before but with a cot brought in for the burnt man and Wraith still lying on the table in the middle, now converted to a bed of sorts, it felt much more cramped.

The burnt man was Lord Sandford of Redford according to Black Jack. Though rumour said Redford was gone, destroyed by urak, its people killed or enslaved, some even said eaten. Tom shivered, the memory of the dead urak by the boat ramp was still clear in his mind, he could believe that last.

As for Wraith, she had shown no further sign of awakening, not since that time when her eyes had opened. Black as coal, they had regarded him, seeming to pierce his very soul. Strangely though, it hadn't bothered him. Wraith would never hurt him. The thought was fanciful. Everybody hurt him and there was darkness in Wraith. Hett said as much and the deep hunger in her gaze only reinforced that knowledge. It was frightening, only he was not fearful. He couldn't explain why.

The door latch slammed up and the door grated open. The hunched figure of Hett waddled through it.

"Stop ogling her, Tom. It was distasteful before. Now it's disturbing." The old crone said.

"I'm not ogling; I've just fed Wraith is all. The only thing disturbing is your mind," Tom replied.

"Is that so?" Hett said, fixing a rheumy, bloodshot eye on the boy and raising a tangled eyebrow. She huffed dismissively. Moving to a cluttered workbench she started clearing a space.

"Why isn't she waking up? You said her body is mended."

"You're startin' ta sound like Black Jack." Hett glared. "You heard what I told 'im. Ain't no different just cause you fancy ploughing her ya'self. Wraith may never wake up. Her mind is twisted and broke. You and I both know she ain't human, Tom."

Tom pursed his lips but held his peace. There was no arguing the point with Hett but Wraith would wake up. He knew it. The intensity of her look that day told him so.

"His Lordship was groaning earlier," Tom reported, changing the conversation. "I fed him water and he fell asleep again."

"Well, maybe you should have started with that, eh." Hett snapped. She dumped a bulky satchel on the bench, then moved to the cot and, crouching, examined her patient.

The faint noise of someone talking came from outside. The voice was high pitched, that of a child. It grew louder as it drew closer until it was right outside. There was a knock on the frame of the still-open doorway.

Tom knew who it was without looking. The voice belonged to Millie and her tone could only mean she chattered to her mother, Sofia Grainne. Sofia, Tom had learnt, was a scribe from Thorsten. The two had been 'rescued' by Torgrid and his band out near Longstretch along with a bunch of other people. Now they were Grimmers.

"Come," said Hett, not bothering to look up from her patient. "And shut ya hole, I need to concentrate."

Sofia entered, her steps furtive. She stopped just inside the entrance to wait, unwilling, it seemed, to leave its light. Millie held her hand and was quiet; a quick learner. Sofia glanced at Tom, giving a sad, lopsided smile. Her face was marked; her left eye swollen and her lip puffy. Unable to meet his stare her eyes slid away.

Tom said nothing. Hells, there was nothing to say. The haunted look told its own story as much as the lumps and bruises. Hett had warned her.

"Ma fell over and bashed her face," Millie blurted. "One of her eyes is red but she's alright though, aren't you."

Looking up at her mother for reassurance, she got it. "Yes, I'm fine Mils," Sofia said as she patted her daughter's hand.

"Bloody hells and damnfire, what part of shut ya hole do ya not understand?" Hett grated, levering herself onto her feet.

It drew a curious look from Tom. He'd felt the witch's venom more than anyone these last few months. Knew her well enough to know there was no bite in this bark.

The little girl knew it too, for it bothered her not in the least. "Aunt Hett, can you help? Ma says she's fine but it hurts. She was crying for the longest time last night."

"Hush, Mils. Aunt Hett is very busy. You mustn't disturb her." Sofia squeezed her daughter's hand as she looked across at Hett's scowling face. "Sorry, Black Jack wants you to meet him. In the holes he said. And you Tom."

"Well, ya have disturbed me." Hett moved back to her workbench. "Come. Let me take a look."

"But Black Jack…."

"Cocksucker can wait. Now come here, let me see," Hett ordered, waving her forward. Gripping Sofia's chin in one veined and wrinkled hand, the physiker pushed her head up and around, then peered one rheumy eye at its counterpart before assessing the bruised and swollen face; tutting away all the while.

"Torgrid or Jessop?"

"Torgrid," Sofia murmured, so softly no one but Hett heard it.

Hett grunted. She rummaged around her workbench, gathering several fresh leaves out of her satchel and taking a small wooden box out of a stack of boxes, each with a different symbol etched on their sides.

Opening the box she pinched two measures of the crushed brown powder it contained into a cup and mixed it with water. Lifting it, Hett thrust it out.

"Drink that."

Sofia sniffed it, her nose scrunching at the smell. "What is it exactly?"

Hett glanced briefly at Millie and quirked an eyebrow, "It'll kill any seed. It'll make you bleed and you'll get stomach cramps real bad. That's to be expected. Here."

Hett removed another of the boxes. This one contained seeds. She measured some out and placed them, along with the fresh leaves, onto a long flax leaf. She deftly folded it, with practised ease, into a small parcel.

"If it gets bad, steep the seeds in boiled water, let it cool, then drink. It'll help numb the pain. The leaves will help with the swelling. Wet them and lay them on your face at night. It has the added benefit of stainin' ya skin green, which, if you're lucky means ya won't suffer no more 'falls'. At least, not for a few nights, and with any luck, Torgrid'll think ya got the pox and shit hisself worryin' his cock'll fall off."

Reaching a hand out, Sofia took the package and tucked it into a pocket inside her over-vest. Then, with a grimace, she raised the wooden cup to her lips. Tilting it, she swallowed the contents in one go. Wiping her mouth on her sleeve she handed the cup back without a word.

"Thank you, Aunt Hett." Millie beamed.

Scowling, Hett thumped the cup down on the bench. "Ai, well ya can thank me by sortin' this lot out." She placed a hand on the bulky satchel, "Separate piles for each, mind. Do not open any of the pods, do not touch your face or lick your fingers else ya might get a rash or poisoned. Little runt ya are it might even kill you. So wash your hands when you're done."

"Yes, Aunt Hett," Millie said.

Hett walked stiffly to the door. "Come on, Tom. Let's see what Black Jack wants, eh. Nothing good I'm betting."

* * *

Jackson 'Black Jack' Tullock lied. He did not let anyone out of the hole the next day, nor the day after, or the next. He dangled hope but delivered cruelty. Jacob cursed him for it but he'd had much time to contemplate and he realised the cruelty had a purpose. Designed to break them and teach them. That there was only one rule and one master of the Black Keep.

Now though something was happening. His senses were highly condensed and attuned. He could hear it and he waited. Fearing to hope but unable not to.

Time in the hole passed differently, but Jacob knew it had been three days. Just three days. He felt old and crippled. His head throbbed and his eyes were sore and gritty with fatigue. His bones and muscles ached so badly they screamed in protest every time he moved. It was wretched.

The stone plinth he perched on, rising from the warm waters in the middle of his hole, was barely large enough to fit him. This tiny island though was his only sanctuary; for the water had things in it. Jacob could see them feasting on his excreta, picking at it in the faint light that filtered down.

His only triumph in this hell was the smell. He'd long become inured to it. The hole though, repaid this small victory a hundredfold. Tiny bites, itching continually, covered his body, piling yet another layer of misery on top of the rest. The worst was he couldn't stop from scratching them and his skin was red and bloody from his efforts.

Parched and starving, talk was infrequent. Talk required effort and took energy. That is, apart from Mahan. Mahan wouldn't shut up and oh how Jacob wished he would. That first day had been the worst. His constant babbling would be broken by screaming outbursts that melted into wracking sobs.

Jacob had tried to console and support Mahan but it was futile. After a time, he would neither listen nor respond. Thornhill to his credit had tried every day to coax his friend down from whatever hell his mind was in. *He's a better man than me*, Jacob admitted, disheartened.

With nothing too occupy his mind except his pains, Mahan's insanity, and the small circular wall of his cell, Jacob felt his own madness lurking just behind his eyes. What small hope he'd garnered had slowly been stripped away. Just three days. *Three days and I am no longer a man*. The thought was disturbing.

Their only respite came once a day when food and water were delivered. Hissings, one of their original captors, had assumed that duty from the youngster, Tom, who had seemed at least sympathetic to their plight. Hissings though was the polar opposite, taking pleasure in dropping their food in. Forcing their tortured limbs to try and catch it before it splashed into the warm, soiled waters of their cells. It was a game and Jacob hated him for it. His lisping voice became a boon and a bane, both looked for and hated.

But now something was happening. It was too early for Hissings and the sounds differed. More than one person approached.

The muffled, rhythmic thump of feet stopped outside. A thunk of a bolt and squeal of a hinge as the door was opened. More footsteps, drawing close.

"How goes it brother?" Black Jack's voice boomed echoing around the room.

"I've stayed in better establishments," Wynter said. His voice was hoarse and Jacob strained to hear it.

Mahan, who had not stopped muttering to himself, suddenly screamed. The sound was one of raw terror. The words were barely discernible but Jacob knew them well enough. They were always the same. "Let me out!" repeated, over and over, each word running into the next.

"Shut your trap," Black Jack ranted back. Boots moved. The screaming continued unabated.

Black Jack cussed. "By the Saint's holy asshole I swear I'll tear off your cock, rip out your balls then fed them you if you don't… shut… your fucking… hole." When his threat elicited no change, "Right, get that son of a whore out."

Jacob heard more movement. The metallic scrape of a grate as it was dragged open. Why didn't he say something? Guilt ate away at him but so did Mahan's screaming, digging into his brain like a worm. Gritting his teeth, Jacob sucked warm fetid air in through his nostrils and shook himself from his stupor. He let his anger kindle. Wiping a tongue over dried and cracked lips he spoke.

"Lord Tullock. Mahan is sick. You've broken his mind. He does not understand your words or actions." Footfalls, then the hard angled face of Jackson Tullock appeared above. He looked haggard and sported at least a day's growth of stubble.

"Sick or no, he's a price to pay now, Lord of Nothing. If'n his mind's truly broke he's a burden. A burden's no use to me nor anyone here. So you'd best pray you're wrong."

There was a howl and commotion followed by swearing. Jacob watched Tullock turn away, amusement writ on his face as he disappeared from view. It was followed moments later by a sickening thump, of something heavy hitting flesh. Then silence. Blessed silence.

"What have you done?" Thornhill husked. His voice was barely a whisper. No one heard.

"Varla, Baka, bind him and take him outside." Black Jack ordered. "Ah, Hett, what took ya so long, eh? I sent that bitch a half hour ago."

The noise of dealing with Mahan must have masked the physikers approach for Jacob hadn't heard her enter the room.

"Ai, Sofia was waiting for me when I got back. I came right away," Hett said.

"Sofia, eh. You ain't getting soft on me now, old witch?" Black Jack accused.

"You thrust her on me to teach. I'm doing it, whether I like it or no, but I'm telling ya now Jackson. She ain't no physiker. Don't have the gift for it, so you're stuck with this 'old witch'. Remember that next time you got the flux bad, eh."

"If she's no good I'll find another use for 'Sofia'." Black Jack promised. Jacob could hear the smirk in his voice.

"She's a scribe. That has its uses. I was thinking of writing a journal but my hands ain't what they used to be. Can't hold a quill long these days and my writing is hard to read, even for me."

"What use is a journal? I can't read. I'll move her," Black Jack pressed.

"If you know what's best you'll leave her be. Let her write my journal cos you're right about one thing; I'm old. My bones ache rotten in the mornings and worse at night. Gathering is getting harder and takes me longer. Life takes its dues. So, you'd better let her learn my ways as best she can cause when I'm gone, Sofia and my journal might be the only thing you got to replace me with."

There was a slight pause before Black Jack answered. "You're too mean and sour ta die, but fine have it your way."

Hett though wasn't done. "She's my property now, the little girl too. Tell Torgrid ta keep his mitts off her. The lass could hardly see out one eye and barely walk a straight line. She's no use to me broken." Hett's voice was firm and Black Jack laughed to hear it.

"Tell Torgrid yaself witch. Curse him with the black shits like you do me. I'm sure he'll listen up quick enough." Black Jack chuckled. Then, his voice turned serious. "Now, can we get down ta business? I didn't call you and Tom down here for a chit chat. Varla, Baka hold a minute."

For Jacob it was torturous. Listening but not seeing, unable to do anything. The sounds of movement and scuff of something heavy being dragged, a body. A man's groan sounded. Mahan lived still.

"Seems you lamped him one real good," Hett's voice sounded. "What are you askin?"

"Guy was screaming and yelling like a madman. So I shut him up," Black Jack replied. "Wanna know if he's broke. You know, in his head. Hissings says he's been like this for three days now."

"Ai, I've seen it afore, it's an unreasoning. Your father, may his rotting heart burn in hell, liked to use the holes a lot. Only some folk don't take to it as well as others."

"No one takes to the holes," Black Jack retorted.

"Ai, but an unreasoning is different. Folks sufferin' an unreasoning can be for all sorts of things. Hissings don't like heights, mewls like a baby if'n he's up higher than twenty feet or so."

"I do not," Hissings lisped. Hett ignored him.

"Others it might be deep water and some again darkness and small spaces. There is no understanding to be had with an unreasoning. It takes a person so it's all they can think about. The fear takes over, whether they will it or no."

There was the thud of a boot connecting with something soft, followed by a moan. "So is his mind broke?" Black Jack asked.

"Might be, three days is a long time to suffer an unreasoning. You've taken him out of the hole so he might come back to hisself. Put him in my workroom and I'll keep him under observation for a day. If he don't come back by then, he likely never will."

Listening on, Jacob thought Hett must have seen something in Black Jack's face, for her tone turned quizzical. "Lessen you don't want him to come back."

There was a pause but eventually, Black Jack answered. "I got plans, Hett. The world's changing and I need more people. This one's a soldier and I need fighters. But I need others too, builders maybe and crafters."

"So you want him fixed if he can be fixed?" Hett asked.

"He's no use to me crazy in the head. I'd sooner stake him in the Stench and watch the lizards eat him. I'll give you your day. Now tell me, how is little Lord Sandford doing? Will he live and what the fuck is wrong with him? How'd he do that to those critters in his hole?"

"His rate of recovery is astounding. Where the burnt flesh has flaked away the skin beneath is white and soft as a newborn. He's taking food and water but is not yet lucid. As for the how, well that is strangest of all. There is something lying within, a darkness," Hett said.

"Ai, in me as well," Black Jack replied.

"Yes, well your darkness is a stain on your soul and is part of you. His is something other. It's in him but apart from him. Strangest of all, it has the same congruence as Wraith."

"What does that mean exactly?" Black Jack asked.

"It means they are the same. What's in Wraith is also in Sandford," Hett explained.

"Might he be dangerous? Maybe I should slip a knife in him and be done with it."

"Maybe slip your blade into Wraith too whilst you're at it?" Hett suggested. "Only it's another knife you're wanting to stick her with isn't it, Jackson?"

"Fuck, you love to try my patience, witch," Black Jack snapped. There was another thud of a boot on flesh. "Baka, Varla take this sack a shit to Hett's place when she leaves. First though,"

"Tom lad, come here." Black Jack raised his voice followed by the shuffle of feet.

"Yes," Tom sounded tentative to Jacob's ears. He was scared.

"Folks have been sayin' I've treated ya harsh and I want you to know why. I want you to understand," Black Jack said. "You do want to understand don't you, Tom? I mean it coulda been different between us. Wouldn't you like ta know why?"

The quiet under menace in Black Jack's tone was apparent not only to Jacob but to Wynter, for he called out.

"You telling him here and now is for my benefit not his, Jack. If you're telling a truth you should at least start with it."

Black Jack chuckled. "Ai, mayhap brother you have the right of it. Or, perhaps my tale is for the both of you. After all, it's someat our father taught me."

"You learnt too much from that sadistic fuck. Just let the lad alone," Wynter said.

Ignoring him, Black Jack started. "Tom, this is a tale of loyalty. I wonder if you will understand it."

"I'll do my best," Tom mumbled.

"Good Tom, that's good. See, when I was a boy, no more than five, I had a bird."

"Fuck," Wynter said. "Not that bloody bird again."

"Interrupt again and I'll have Varla squat on your grate and take a shit on you," Black Jack said, his voice rising. "Now, ignore him, Tom lad. Where was I? Ah yes, the bird."

"The bird was our fathers, a Redwing grown from the egg. He fed and cared for it from a hatchling and named it Dashiell. When Dash grew big enough he trained her on the lure then in the hunt. My father loved that bird more than anything, more than me and certainly more than Ned. But he was often gone from the Black Hold and I had taken to feeding her. Dash was proud and fierce and I too came to love her. See, whatever she set her gaze upon she never failed in the kill. She was like death from above."

"One day, our father released the bird from her cage and held his arm out for Dash to sit upon. Instead, she flew to me. Dash loved me more than my father you see and I laughed, pleased, proud of my little Redwing. With a smile, my father approached, crooning to her and whistling, he stroked her head crest just how she liked. Then he snatched her in his fist and held Dash, squealing in front of me. He squeezed until her eyes burst and her bones crunched and she squealed no more."

"When I cried my father slapped me, hard. With Dash's blood and guts and feathers coating my cheek, he says to me 'Son, the bird forsook me. Me, who raised and nurtured her. I gave her life and yet she betrayed me, giving her loyalty ta another. Such is the price. I trust you will remember this lesson. For it comes at a grievous cost.' Father never spoke of Dash again nor raised another bird."

"Do you understand the lesson, Tom?" Black Jack murmured.

"Yes," the voice was high pitched as Tom gave the only answer he could.

"That pleases me," Black Jack said. There was a sudden scuffle of movement, followed by the sounds of a struggle.

"What are you doing?" Hett called out, followed immediately by Wynter screaming.

"Leave the boy, Jack. Take me, it's me you want. It's me that betrayed you, not Tom. By the god's he's your own blood!"

Black Jack's voice was tight and strained, "This is your doing, brother. This is on you. My bastard was more yours than ever he was mine."

The struggles grew fainter then ceased. Jacob found his breath was held. Black Jack was insane. Listening, he heard a thud as Tom's body crumpled to the floor, then stillness. The atmosphere was overlaid by heavy panting as Black Jack sucked in air. No one said a word. Not Hett and not Wynter. In the end, it was Black Jack that broke the silence.

"Leave him be, Hett. Get yourself back. Varla and Baka will go with you, take the crazy cunt with you."

*  *  *

The walk back to her place seemed longer than usual and Hett didn't speak, lost in bitter thoughts. Baka and Varla, dragging the listless body of the prisoner between them, showed no such reluctance.

"Black Jack never liked that boy but I never thought he'd kill him," Baka muttered. "Might be a bastard but Tom was his bastard, ya know."

Grunting with effort, Varla gasped. "Shut ya mouth, I don't wanna talk about it."

The snow that had arrived a day past covered the ground but was already melting. On the path they trod, it had already turned into a soiled slush. The Grim had its own distinct climate, Hett knew, and was warmer than the surrounding land, though she could not say why. The brown churned filth matched her mood as she listened.

"I know ya had a soft spot for the boy. I didn't mean nought by it, Var, the Lady knows I liked the lad meself but he was too soft for this place," Baka replied.

"He weren't soft. He just weren't mean, neither. Now shut it. I'm done talkin' about it."

"He's a crazy sonofabitch," Baka reflected. "As I recall you fucked him and his brother both, so you might wanna be careful, Var. That man, don't forget nothin'."

"Say another word and I swear I'll stick my knife in your eye." Varla adjusted her grip on the deadweight they carried. She was grateful when Baka heeded her.

A sudden, unbridled screech pierced the air. A woman's scream of horror. It broke Hett from her dark reflections, and her head came up. Her heart rate increased and fear seized her chest causing her to break into a shuffling, fast-paced walk, her body making the connection before her mind did.

Another heartbroken cry sounded. Louder this time, closer. Hett's place was as isolated as it could be on this island they called home. Shrubs and bushes lined the path; there was nothing else ahead but her cottage and workroom.

Hett didn't want it too but her mind caught up, it was the little girl, had to be. The cry was a woman's misery, a mother's anguish. She'd heard it before.

"Baka, take the man, Varla with me," Hett ordered. She scuttled on, not turning to see if they heeded her or not. The physiker wracked her mind, there was nothing in her satchel that would harm the girl, but there were plenty of things in the apothecary that could. Blast and hellfire, the girl was bold with a curious mind, what had she expected.

Her cottage came into view and then the adjoining workroom, the door to which was still ajar. She fairly flew through it and stopped so suddenly, Varla bumped against her back.

The scene inside was so unexpected it took Hett's breath.

Not so Varla, "Seven hells," She swore, her eyes casting about. The burnt man was on a cot against the wall. The torn body of a young girl was laid over him, her blood painting his face and chest. Her hair, matted red, was splayed covering her face, hiding her features. Neither man nor child moved. But, whereas there was a permanence to the girl's stillness, there wasn't the man's, given away by the frothy bubbles of blood beneath his nostrils.

Hett moved further into the room, the shock of Millie lying dead had twisted something inside her and a tear glistened on her cheek. The little girl was an innocent. Hett hardly dared admit it, even to herself, but Millie had got to her. In less than a week, her walls had been broken and her heart touched. A heart that was grizzled and old and bitter.

She wiped the tear away and returned to her observations. Sandford was alive, that much was clear. His black and white mottled skin was drenched in blood giving him a hellish appearance.

She saw the shadowed figure of Sofia sat on the floor in the opposite corner of the room. The light from the door barely reached and Hett's eyes had not yet adjusted to the dim light but it was she. Knees hugged tight to her chest, rocking gently back and forth.

It was wrong. Something was off. Sofia's behaviour was discordant and Hett knew it. No mother would abandon or leave their child like that. Her gaze had already raked over Wraith but her eyes settled upon her again.

Wraith was laid still on the table, in the same place in the same manner as before, except she wasn't. Her head was twisted, facing the door, facing her. Hett stepped closer, her blood sluggish through her veins and limbs heavy. She ground to a halt.

Wraith's eyes were open. In the half-light, Hett hadn't seen it immediately. They were inhuman and completely black, like Onyx. Dark pits that glinted in the reflected light of the doorway. The inky tendrils, spreading out from her eyes and across her pallid flesh, seemed almost vibrant and alive.

Finding her throat dry, Hett swallowed and forced her eyes away. They travelled down, to Wraith's mouth which was pulled into a rictus of a smile. White teeth showed as her lips parted.

Against her will, Hett found herself leaning closer to listen. Every sinew in her body screamed warning but she had to hear. Whatever it was, she had to know.

Hett stood bolt upright and stumbled back towards the door until she bumped against Varla.

"What is it? What did she say?" Varla asked. Her eyes were wide and her jaw slack at what she witnessed.

"I'm not sure. I think," Hett stuttered, she'd felt fear many times in her life but it was nothing like what she felt at that moment.

"I think. She said… Tom. I think she wants Tom."

## Chapter 46: A Glass Half Full

**Anglemere Castle, Kingsholme, The Holme**

The crisp staccato beat of Herald's boots was loud on the marble tiles, echoed by the softer more muted tones of Horyk Andersun. Herald liked the sound. Guards stood to attention when they heard it. Courtiers made way and servants scraped and bowed.

It soothed his ill-temper somewhat but not enough to assuage the bitter anger that simmered inside. He'd spent days avoiding Renix and his infernal lessons. The last one had been humiliating enough; he was determined not to face another. He could still see it now; that smug look of satisfaction on the sneak thief's face. The only saving grace from that indignity was that no one had witnessed it. No one except Renix and the boy and he'd deal with him soon enough.

Rounding the corner to his apartment, Herald slowed. The two guards stationed outside his rooms were there as always but someone was with them. Leaning languidly against the opposite wall was Sir Gart Vannen.

Something was unsettling about the man and Herald's eyes tightened. The look Vannen gave him was dismissive and it assaulted his already battered self-esteem. He seethed at the man's insolence. It wasn't until he was five paces away that Vannen pushed off the wall and straightened himself and then the inclined head was barely acceptable.

As intolerable as Herald found it, it was merely a distraction. That Vannen was here meant his sister must be inside, waiting for him. He groaned inwardly. He hated sparring with his little sister. Matrice was quick-tongued and didn't know her place. The combination always left him feeling like he was the younger since he invariably came out the worst from their exchanges.

Repaying Vannen's impertinence, Herald ignored him completely and swept into his rooms. Horyk waited outside, as was proper since the visitor was his sister. It was a relief. The big Norderman was unflinching in his duty and though he hated to admit it to himself, Herald didn't like to disappoint him. So it was better he stay outside.

Inside he found Matrice waiting in his solar. She rose elegantly from a recliner as he entered the room. She was dressed simply in a gown of blue silk with a red sash and matching hairband. It made him smile. A girl pretending to be a woman, trying so hard to be like their dead mother it was amusing.

"I am pleased to see you too, brother," Matrice said. "You look handsome when you smile so."

The compliment was enough to put Herald on his guard. "I must endeavour to smile more often then."

He took in the water glass on the side table. Grayson had seen to her needs then. That it was half full meant she'd not been waiting long, more's the pity.

Matrice's brows knitted. "Indeed you must. Though I confess I've not given you much cause recently to do so. I wish to rectify that and apologise for my behaviour."

Herald did not speak for a second, his suspicions well and truly aroused. "Why?"

His mouth tightened as she tilted her head as if his question perplexed her. It was a simple enough question. "You've never apologised to me before. Your behaviour toward me is unchanged, although murdering King's Champion was beyond the pale, even for you."

Matrice shook her head. "May I sit? Will you join me?"

Jaw clenched, Herald indicated she could and took a seat opposite. It grated to be recalled to his manners in his own apartment. Bitch.

Folding her skirt beneath her, Matrice settled back into the recliner. "You do not believe me and I've given you little cause to, I know, but King's Champion was an accident. You know I love horses. I would never willingly hurt one, Herald. You must know that."

"Grayson, some wine. Where are you? Must I find someone more reliable you old goat?" Herald shouted, turning towards the anteroom.

"Coming, Highness." The voice was clipped and precise.

"Would you like a glass?" Herald asked, turning back to Matrice, hoping to disarm her. Their father wouldn't approve of wine. He was protective of his little girl even though she was fifteen, old enough to marry and bear children.

"No, thank you," Matrice declined.

Herald raised an eyebrow. She was always pushing. She never liked to be told what she could or couldn't do. A rebellious spirit, father called it. Herald could hear his voice in his head even now, speaking proudly of it as if it was some great virtue.

Considering her words, Herald grudgingly found some measure of truth in them. The world knew Matrice adored horses. She had three to ride of her own and no man needed more than two according to Horyk.

"You do not seem yourself, sister. Are you alright?"

Matrice puffed her cheeks and blew a slow, exaggerated breath. "Following our latest altercation, father has had me spend time with her High Holiness, Maris Jenah. She has been teaching me on… many things." Matrice ended vaguely, giving a wry look.

Maris Jenah, high cardinal of the Church of the Lady. Herald laughed and slapped his knee. "Priceless. He has me seeing that Ord, Renix. No doubt for similar reasons." Her apology became suddenly clear to him. Maybe she even meant it. The thought set him laughing again and this time Matrice joined him.

An old man, immaculately groomed and attired, entered the solar with a tray bearing a wine goblet. "Your wine, highness."

Taking the proffered cup, Herald spared his steward a glance. Grayson had been with him for as long as he could remember. Fastidious and correct in everything, Grayson had taught him more about bearing and etiquette than the masters his father sent him to. He was slim, apart from a slight paunch around his middle, with a bald pate that was winning its battle against the silvered hair surrounding it. A wrinkled face with bright eyes regarded him back.

"Thank you, Grayson. That will be all." Grayson bowed and left the room as silently as he entered it.

The interruption broke their moment of levity. They only ever argued. Herald couldn't ever recall laughing with his sister before. Maybe the failing was his? He dismissed it.

"So, a few lessons with Maris Jenah and you wish to say sorry. Perhaps miracles do happen," Herald said, trying to recapture the moment. For a minute he had felt it, that bond of brother and sister. A bond they'd never truly shared. But it was gone and the yearning chasm he never knew he had, slammed shut.

"It's hard to argue with someone so unwavering in their goodness. It's damn frustrating, to be honest," Matrice admitted. "She is wise though and her teachings have opened my eyes. Made me look and ask myself, what is it that I want? I have come to realise that in order to achieve my desires it is I that needs to change."

Herald could see the hard set to her jaw and the stony, determined look in her eyes. She was serious, even though her last words were something dictated and regurgitated.

"Would that Lord Renix was so insightful, his lessons tend to the more painful and humbling than uplifting. Your words have moved me," Herald lied.

"I brought you a present to give our father." Matrice lent across the arm of her recliner and lifted a rectangular box from beneath her seat. She held it out and Herald took it. It was weighty.

"May I?" Herald asked, his curiosity getting the better of him.

A ghost of a smile crossed Matrice's face, "Of course."

Opening the box it contained a dark bottle, as Herald knew it must. Lifting it out he examined it. "Tankrit Red, father's favourite and rare as hen's teeth."

"Don't ask where I got it," Matrice gushed, pleased at his response. "I thought it might appease father somewhat. We both seem to be in his bad graces at the moment."

Herald regarded her, unconvinced by her sudden girlish exuberance. He'd seen it before, usually just before the sting.

"And you give it to me to gift. Why? You think this will make up for King's Champion. It doesn't." Herald dropped the bottle back in its box and closed the lid.

Matrice bowed her head slightly as if wounded by his response. She peeked at him through her lashes. "No, of course not, but it's a start, Herald, a peace offering. Besides, you need to be there not me and this might ease the way. Show father you have considered his words and that you're ready. You are the Crown Prince after all and war has come. It is only right and proper you take your place at our father's side."

Herald sniffed. "And where is there, exactly?"

"The Congress of Lords, father called a war council a month ago, remember. High Lord Dumac of Westlands arrived last night. With High Lords Twyford, Janis, and High Lady Montreau not attending for obvious reasons, Dumac is the last."

"Yes, of course." Herald waved a dismissive hand, "Of course, I will attend."

He looked thoughtfully at his sister. "Your information is more current than mine. Montreau not coming is news to me. Have the urak made it then to Cumbrenan?"

"I don't know," Matrice said. "I may be a princess but no one tells me anything. I only knew about Montreau because Sir Vannen heard some guards talking in the barracks."

A disgruntled Herald nodded, assuaged somewhat. Matrice was a girl and only fifteen. These were not matters to concern her. Still, the guards knowing about Montreau before him was infuriating. Matrice was right. He was the Crown Prince, he should have known before some guard.

"You did right to mention this and thank you. Your gift is very considerate. I hope this is a new start between us. For my part, I wish it so."

Her mouth curled. "It is. Things are changing. The world will soon be aflame. I can feel it. Take care, brother."

Rising from the recliner, Matrice glided from the room. Her bright countenance fading from her face the moment her back was turned.

## Chapter 47: Conclave Of The Cardinals

**Convocation of the Trivium, Kingsholme, The Holme**

*In the beginning, there was the One God. The One created everything. He created the ground beneath, the sky above, and everything in between. The One set his home in the heavens ablaze with light to warm this new world then filled it with life and watched.*

*He found no order, only chaos. The creatures of his world were wild. They existed at his whim but had not the wit to know it. They had the heart and the body but not the mind to understand. So he created humanity.*

*To them, he gave wisdom and knowledge and he watched.*

*At first, there was order. Humanity worshipped him and revered his teachings and he watched them for a while, content. After a time however, darkness from the cosmos seeped into the world. It corrupted, giving humanity wants and desires above what was needed. It made them cruel and selfish. They coveted more of the world and in their greed, the One was forgotten.*

*The One did not despair for he loved his creation. They were capable; he had witnessed the good in them before the corruption. But his children were weak of mind, body and heart. They had lost their faith and their way.*

*The One would not place them on the path again. To be worthy they must find it for themselves or be excised from the world. But the One was a caring and compassionate creator and devised a way to help them see the way.*

*The souls of all creatures possess the two pillars that govern the heart and body but only humanity possessed the third: the mind.*

*Scouring humanity, the One weighed each soul for what was needed. He looked for those adrift but who had not lost their faith and he was pleased. Not all had forsaken him, some still believed. The three most worthy and that suited his purpose were Ankor a holy man, Nihmrodel a wanderer, and Kildare a warrior.*

*Elevating them above all others, the One made the moons where the three could reside and watch over humanity. In his stead, they would guide them. They became the Trinity and to each he gave one of the three pillars, to guard and nurture.*

*Taken from the Holy Scriptures of the Trinity, First Passage of the Article of Truth, Book of Faith*

\* \* \*

The Conclave of Cardinals was held cyclically and in turn every two years for the churches of the Trinity. Its roots were said to be older than the Kingdoms and one of many religious traditions enshrined in ecclesiastical law. This year it was the turn of the church of Kildare, known more colloquially as the Red Conclave.

As prescribed in the book of Faith 'twelfth edition' from the Holy Scriptures of the Trinity, a Conclave's primary purpose was to elect a new High Cardinal. For the Red Conclave, this appointment was as the worldly representative of Kildare, to speak with his voice and spread his word.

The reality though was somewhat different.

Tradition dictated that once a High Cardinal was elected, so long as they were of sound mind and body, they would not be opposed by any of the remaining cardinals. The post effectively became for life. This had always been so.

To those unacquainted with church doctrine it might seem frivolous and a waste of time, travelling from across the Nine Kingdoms to attend a conclave that was preordained. They would be wrong. Each conclave lasted a ten-day and covered church business from the mundane, 'construction costs for new churches', the theological, 'interpretations of religious text' right up to religious law.

The previous two Red Conclaves had been fractious, with a strong debate over the heretical influence of the Order. It had culminated in the squeezing of High Lords to ban the Order from their realms, something that had initially met with stiff opposition but was now starting to gain traction. Once again, it was expected to be the hot topic at this year's conclave, that and the urak invasion. Once, tradition had been adhered to that was.

It was the first day of the conclave and it took place in the Convocation of the Trivium. The immense chamber was two thirds empty, but the remaining third was a sea of rippling red. Priests and bishops crammed into Kildare's wedge, their noise reverberating with a hollow deepness around the domed chamber.

On the central dais, rising above the congregation, sat the nine cardinals of the faith; Lords upon gilded thrones gazing out upon the red sea. Before them on the edge of the platform were nine ballot boxes, each of which was attended by an acolyte. Beside each of the boxes, incense burners threw pungent meditative fumes into the great chamber. To the side behind a table sat three scribes, all priests of the red, recorders for the conclave.

Of the nine thrones, the largest and most elaborate was perfectly centred and upon it sat his High Holiness, Worsten Lannik, High Cardinal of the Church of Kildare. He stood, raising his staff of office, and banged it three times against the stone floor.

Heavy booms rang out, filling every space. By the time the third note crashed and echoed it was the only sound.

"This is the one hundred and twenty-sixth conclave of the fourth age, so recorded. Welcome Brothers." Lannik's voice was deep and sonorous.

"As it is written, and so prescribed by the Book of Faith, a High Cardinal must be elected to serve in communion with, and as the earthly representative of, our Lord Kildare, Protector of the Pillar of the Body, God of War and Death. To carry out his holy will and serve his divine purpose, in the name of the One."

There was a rumble as the congregation intoned together the holy words. "Blessed is he."

"As laid out in the Order of Proceedings, the first round of ballots will now be cast," Lannik said.

As was customary, the current High Cardinal cast the first vote. Moving to the ballot boxes at the front of the dais, Lannik knelt upon aged knees and dropped his marker into the ballot for Kingsholme. Rising, he moved back to his throne and sat.

There were five rounds of ballots in the initial stage and anyone there present could be nominated, priest, bishop, or cardinal. At the end of each round, anyone that did not receive a nomination would retire from the Conclave, their day at an end.

It was ritualistic, in that each and everyone knew that after the fifth round only the nine cardinals would remain. But there was a point to it, however subtle. Like a well-choreographed dance, it gave an order to proceedings. It informed the church of who to look for in the years ahead. Whose star was rising and who's fallen away. It was an indicator of potential.

As expected, after the fifth ballot had been counted only the cardinals were left. Again, as prescribed by the Book of Faith, they retired to the Chamber of the Divine Representative. It would be here the remaining nine would pontificate and deliberate before appointing the next High Cardinal. Purely a formality, it was a foregone conclusion.

* * *

The Chamber of the Divine Representative was contained within the Convocation of the Trivium. It sat inside the Trivium's northern boundary, so the people could watch the smoke rising from their deliberations. The smoke was white but would change colour to red to signify once a High Cardinal for Kildare was anointed. Only at this time would the doors be unlocked and thrown wide for his High Holiness to come forth.

Tortuga never much cared for the Chamber of the Divine Representative. Foregoing the grandeur of the Hall of Convocation, it was small and windowless, the air musty and its only furnishings were a long wooden table and nine wooden chairs. A fireplace occupied one end of the room and the only door, locked and bolted from the outside, was on the internal sidewall.

For Tortuga, it felt restrictive and confining which was entirely the point he supposed, but he didn't have to like it. His size and girth singled him out as different. It always had, but in the dim, airlessness of the room, the walls seemed closer than they were. Oppressive, they offered no respite from the judgemental looks of his peers. Even now he could feel their eyes upon him. They tolerated him, barely. For tradition dictated they must.

It was amusing really, Tortuga thought. Kildare the Protector, Kildare the Warrior, Guardian of the Pillar of the Body, and yet here he was.

In keeping with doctrine, the other eight cardinals followed the morning training regimen prescribed by the Church and fasted twice a week. Despite their age, the eight were whip thin, and fit. When they looked at him, Tortuga knew they saw an aberration

The shade inside writhed, feeding on their disdain as if supping upon an apéritif.

© 2020 A D Green

Tortuga gave a grim smile. This was his third visit to the Chamber of the Divine Representative, a victory in and of itself. He'd invested much time over the years counteracting the external influences brought against him. Influences that sought to undermine his authority. To ultimately have him removed from office. And all of it, orchestrated by the men in this room.

All the Cardinals saw were his rolls of flesh and fat. An abomination, an affront to Kildare, they marginalised him. Never once did they stop and wonder how a man such as he could have risen so high in the Church.

"Tortuga, this is a worrying time for you." Worsten Lannik approached. In the grey light, he looked predatory. "I half expected you to forgo this year's conclave given the parlous state of the Rivers."

"It's a worrying time for all of us, High Cardinal. Long has the Rivers been the shield of the Kingdoms. Let us hope it is not entirely breached," Tortuga replied, enjoying the acerbic look on Lannik's face. Much like himself, the Rivers was not well regarded; never having quite shaken free from its history.

"Indeed. As you know, I've already sent Archbishop Whent and five thousand of the Faith Militant to the Rivers." Lannik indicated the long table, "Let's sit. Once matters are concluded here we can talk about what more we can do to help."

Tortuga allowed himself to be guided to the table. Most of the seats were occupied. Only the head and the two chairs furthest away from it were left free. It was another not so subtle byplay, to seat him farthest away from the head of the table, whilst allowing room for his bulk. The latter was unnecessary of course, as the table was large enough to seat a score of cardinals.

Taking the chair furthest from him, Tortuga sat, feeling and hearing the creak of wood as it stressed under his weight. It had already crossed his mind that the chair might collapse. The Cardinals were old but not beyond pettiness. It held.

As Lannik moved to the head of the table, Tortuga considered the empty chair opposite. It belonged to Per Torsten, Cardinal of Norderland. His eyes travelled to Torsten just as he straightened from his task. As the youngest and newest Cardinal, it was Torsten's duty to attend the fire and he was busy stoking the flames.

Satisfied the fire was burning as it should, Torsten filled a scoop from a bucket and cast pale nuggets onto the flames which flared and roared. Immediately the room filled with the scent of frankincense and dewslip. It was meant to aid their meditations but also served to emit a cloud of white smoke. It signalled to the world outside that their deliberations had begun.

The table was bare aside from a large pitcher of red wine and a long, thin loaf of bread. Both were ceremonial, the wine depicting the blood of Kildare and the bread the Pillar of the Body. The wine had been tested for purity and blessed before the conclave before being decanted into the jug. The loaf was one of three, hand-baked by the Mothers of Mercy. Of the other two, one was eaten to prove its purity, and the other was given to the faithful who watched and waited outside the Convocation of the Trivium.

Lannik waited for Torsten to be seated, then bowed his head, closed his eyes, and gave prayer.

"We thank the One for the three pillars, heart, body and mind. We thank our Lord, Kildare the Protector, guardian of the body, and follow his divine wisdom. God of War he protects us, God of Death he governs our passing. Only through him may we reach the One. Blessed is he."

"Blessed is he," The eight intoned.

"Today, through your divine guidance, the nine will choose one as your holy representative on this world. The chosen will carry your word and follow your teachings. Let none forsake him. Blessed is he."

"Blessed is he," The eight intoned.

Opening his eyes, Lannik regarded the table. "Has anyone anything to say? Else, we will drink the blood and eat the body and let Kildare chose."

It was a ritual. Once the smoke was sent no one spoke other than the High Cardinal. When next the eight cardinals did speak it would be with Kildare's voice as, through them, the chosen was appointed.

"I would raise an interesting point of note," Tortuga said, his voice wheezing but clear. Eight pairs of eyes swivelled to regard him. Only the fire and two sconces lit the room and in the greyness, it made their stares dark and forbidding.

"This is most irregular," Lannik said, "You forget yourself, Cardinal Tortuga."

Tortugas brows furrowed. "Hardly, and if I did, I am sure you would be quick to recall me. But I digress. I was researching the Book of Faith. We follow the 'twelfth edition' but did you know that the second part of your prayer is recited differently in the original scripture. It is almost identical. The only change is that 'become' has been usurped by 'choose'. The first line of the second stanza should read thus, 'Today through your divine guidance, the nine will become one as your holy representative on this world.' A small difference but an interesting one, I believe."

Lannik frowned. "I fail to see the relevance and like not your tone. The time to discuss Holy Scripture is not now. May we continue, Cardinal?"

Tortuga nodded his acceptance. "Of course, I thought it worthy of mention. That is all."

The atmosphere was stilted. The interruption had been unprecedented and was uncomfortable. The eight looked at Tortuga. He was lauded as a man of great intellect as well as great girth but this interruption in proceedings would be the end for him.

"Perhaps then you might break the bread and sup the wine," Lannik said.

Another ritual and another slight, the order of participation was another indicator of position. At the last conclave, he had been third in the order, sixth-ranked. Today he was first and last, despite this being both Torsten and Gambon's first conclave as Cardinals.

Rising, Tortuga lent forward reaching for the bread. It was slid towards him and he sensed the Cardinals wanted an end. The hostility around the table was tangible.

At least he was hungry. Tortuga tore a chunk off the loaf and ate it, shoving it whole into his mouth. As he chewed it around, he poured the wine into his goblet. Swirling it about, Tortuga raised it to his lips and sipped barely a mouthful before sitting again.

Cardinal Torsten, sat opposite was next to repeat the process, correctly this time, wine for his blood then bread for his body.

The loaf and wine were slowly passed up the table, each of the Cardinals completing the rite until it reached Lannik. The High Cardinal had barely shifted his steely-eyed gaze from Tortuga. He partook of the wine and ate the bread not tasting either.

Tortuga choked and then coughed. He raised a hand to his mouth and a small belch rumbled out.

Lannik frowned, this was intolerable. His lips tightened in annoyance as Tortuga sagged forward. It was hard to tell in the muted light but the High Cardinal thought he looked suddenly pallid.

Tortuga stared back at Lannik. He could see the High Cardinal's annoyance but he cared not for it. Something was wrong. His stomach rumbled, and his bellyached. A bitter, acidity coated his throat. His tongue felt swollen and his teeth tasted blood. Reaching a hand up he felt his nostril and his fingers came away red.

He saw the scowl on Lannik's face twist and his eyes shift around the table. There was a groan from Per Torsten and Tortuga glanced at him, pushing his rising pain and discomfort back so he could observe.

Abruptly, Torsten lurched forward. Opening his mouth, a violent stream of blood and vomit spewed forth. It covered the table reaching right across to Tortuga's side. There was fear in Torsten's eyes and sweat on his brow as he realised what was happening.

Staring back across at Tortuga, Torsten could see the fat man suffered too. Blood ran freely from his nose and leaked from his lips in rivulets that painted rivers on his jowls and chins. It was the eyes though; in the half-light, they were black, like pits of darkness. He reached a hand to his own and they came away red. Blood. It was blood that filled his eyes.

Groaning and cries rang out all up the table. Tortuga turned in fascination. Most of the Cardinals could control aether, mild practitioners of the art to one extent or another, but none were physikers. None could look inward and heal themselves. Even if they could, it was too late, all they would see were their insides melting as the poison spread its death.

Regurgitated food and blood coated the table. Three of the older Cardinals had already succumbed, collapsing across the newly created canvas. Their bodies convulsed and shuddered as the life left them. Lannik was not far behind them.

Tortuga rose painfully and stiffly to his feet. "I trust you see the relevance now, High Cardinal." A gob of blood landed on the table. A worry suffused him. He had taken barely a mouthful, but he could feel his death approaching.

He stumbled around the table towards the fire. Ironically, being the first to take the tainted wine, he and Torsten were the only two still showing any life. At that moment Torsten fell forward, his head clattered the wood with a crack before he slid from his chair and beneath the table.

A raking in his gut forced Tortuga to his knees. The shade of the Morhudrim shivered as it gorged. It had been uncaring of his pain until now but it sensed danger. Unfurling itself, it started to isolate and scour the poison from its host. The shade had become distracted. It should have acted sooner.

Tortuga reached a weak, trembling hand out. He gripped the bucket with the red incense in it and tipped it over, spilling the nuggets all over the floor.

His strength was failing fast. With a last desperate effort, his pudgy fist closed over a handful of the chunks and flung them into the flames. Exhausted, body spasming and dry heaving, Tortuga rolled onto his side and closed his eyes.

* * *

The crowd outside the north wall of the Convocation of the Trivium was a seething riot of sound and colour. It was rare commoners were allowed anywhere on the hallowed and sanctified church grounds. This, however, was one such occasion.

The Mothers of Mercy distributed bread and watered wine amongst the gathered host, adding to the festive atmosphere. Everyone here present was a devotee of the Trinity. By far though the majority favoured Kildare, for today his representative would be chosen. All expected to see High Cardinal Worsten Lannik stride forth reaffirmed. It was preordained and popular since he was admired and respected by his peers and the people both.

As was usual, the nobility and wealthy were in low attendance. Mixing with common folk was something to be avoided wherever possible. So an excited murmur rolled over the crowd when an ornate carriage, accompanied by a hundred mounted Kingsguard, rattled around the concourse outside the Trivium.

Royalty.

They watched expectantly to see who would alight. The High King with his young queen perhaps or maybe Crown Prince Herald. It was unheard of that royalty attend and it added a rising sense of drama. Something of import was about to happen, the crowd could feel it. The carriage door, however, remained firmly shut with the Kingsguard arrayed in a protective phalanx around it.

After a time, bored eyes moved away, back to the white plumes that puffed from a small chimney protruding from the side of the immense structure. They waited.

A roar went up. The smoke had changed to a deep red colour. A curtain in the carriage twitched. Engaged and excited as they were, most of the faithful barely noticed, when the door on the far side of the carriage cracked open and Sir Gart Vannen alighted. Holding a hand out, Princess Matrice took it and stepped down to the ground. Flanked by a score of guards she disappeared inside the building.

*** 

The festive jollity outside ended the moment Vannen opened the door and ushered the Princess inside. The place was in turmoil and broiled with Red Priests all in excited agitation.

Two priests, nominally guarding the door, stuttered and called out. Vannen ignored them, brushing past as he escorted the Princess into a wide corridor. It was clear from the raised voices and babble of noise that something untoward was occurring. The Kingsguard formed a protective cordon around their charge as Vannen led them down the corridor, the commotion growing louder with every step.

Outside a large open doorway, a thick knot of priests blocked the passage and Vannen cursed at them and forcibly pushed them aside. "Make way, damn you."

With the promise of violence in his voice and sheer brute strength, Vannen gained the entry. Through it was a large room, brightly lit, with many of the priests inside bearing torches. It reeked of sweet death, the lingering scent of incense mingling with that of blood and bowel.

A man dressed like his brethren but whose cassock was more richly appointed and embroidered turned and regarding Vannen, his face angry.

"In the name of Kildare who are you? You must leave at once." The priest signalled and several holy fathers moved to intercept.

With a crisp ring of steel, Vannen drew his sword. It cut through the din of noise, drawing everyone's attention and a hushed silence fell.

"If any man, be it a priest or otherwise, lays a hand upon her royal highness they shall lose that hand. I will ask once and once only. Step aside and let her highness through."

The calm menace that exuded Vannen left none in doubt. The priest made to speak again but startled as the sword tip kissed his throat, its point unwavering.

Vannen felt the princess at his back. Smelt her flowered perfume even through the cloying stink of the room. Her slight form pressed tightly against his as she reached around and laid a hand on his sword arm.

"Thank you, Sir Vannen. I will take things from here." Her voice was soft and lilting yet carried the room.

Slowly, Vannen removed his sword. With a deft flick and twist, he slammed it back into his scabbard. Reluctant, not wanting to break contact with the warmth at his back, he stood aside.

Matrice gave a polite smile. "Forgive us, Bishop. But this is no time for niceties. What happened here? Do any survive?"

Bishop Renton Barroso gazed into intense green eyes set in a heart-shaped face. The princess's dark hair, elaboratedly coiffed, framed delicate features. Slim, still to come fully into her shape, the princess was stunning. She should not be here. The Red Conclave did not allow women entry at this holiest of places at this most sacred of times.

Despite this, Barroso was drawn to her, his reply flowing from his lips without conscious thought.

"Highness, Cardinal Tortuga is the only one still breathing, the rest are dead. We are investigating, but it appears they were poisoned. We are trying to understand how. The wine and bread were consecrated and tested for purity."

Matrice could hear his fear and see the confoundment on his face. His every word was a hammer blow to his sensibilities as if, only now, speaking of what he witnessed made it real.

Her view no longer obscured by Vannen's broad back, Matrice turned away from the bishop, eyes scanning the room. The table was like a butcher's block. Cardinals decorated it, red robes of office blending in with the blood and vomit that covered its surface. Two Cardinals lay beneath the table, trailing rivers of blood and bile. Over by the fire was the huge, bloated form of Tortuga. He had been laid out on a wooden stretcher. He looked dead, excepting his chest expanded and compressed incrementally slowly.

Twisting about, Matrice looked at her guard Captain. "Take High Cardinal Tortuga and place him in my carriage."

"Highness." The Captain ducked his head and signalled a squad of guards forward.

"High Cardinal?" The Bishop's brows furrowed. "Highness, this is church business. You have no right and no jurisdiction here. I cannot allow it."

"Time is paramount so I will be brief," Matrice replied as her guardsmen bustled past to attend to her order. It felt good.

"Ancient scriptures say, do they not, that nine shall enter and one shall pass. Normally the High Cardinal is selected by his peers. That Tortuga lives is a miracle, even if only barely. Kildare has chosen. I do not profess to know his divine purpose but surely you, a man of faith, cannot question it."

The bishop looked like he had swallowed something distasteful but did not gainsay her and Matrice hurried on.

"Investigate Bishop. If it was poison then the High Cardinal is not safe here until you catch the perpetrators. If it was not poison but Kildare's will then no harm will come from it. In the meantime, I will guard him and have my own physiker look after him and aid his recovery. You may send a red priest to attend if you like but you personally must vouchsafe him."

"This is highly improper, Highness." The Bishop was sweating; his only superior lay prone, close to death. "The Red Church looks after its own. An outside force is clearly at play. Why are you even here?"

"Good, a pertinent question. You are competent at least," Matrice stated, staring unblinking into his eyes.

"A few days ago Cardinal Tortuga asked to see me and I attended him. He told me that Kildare had spoken to him in a vision. He'd already told High Cardinal Lannik who was scornful of his claim. Perhaps, if Lannik had not been so dismissive, Kildare might have saved his servant from this fate."

"What vision. What is it you speak of?" The Bishop's brows rose high on his forehead.

Matrice smiled. "Kildare sent a vision; that the blood of the chosen would be spared. Tortuga claimed not to know who this chosen was but said it was I that would save him, or at least play a part in it. Tortuga was very convincing. I believed him where Lannik did not."

"Although the vision was vague and unclear, Tortuga felt it was near. Portents were, and dare I say it, his own supposition, that the Conclave was a fulcrum and a likely time for the event. It is why I came and it looks like he was correct."

"That is very colourful and imaginative but surely you understand my position, highness," The Bishop argued. "You cannot be here. I'm sure your father the High King would agree. I'm afraid you must leave. By all means, send the royal physiker but really there is no need. Our brothers and sisters at the Church of Ankor have the best physikers in the realms."

Matrice returned a grim smile. "This is not a debate. I gave the courtesy of an explanation yet this is how you treat me."

She twisted her head slightly. "Sir Vannen, if the good Bishop speaks again as if to a child, please remove one of his fingers. Good day, Bishop."

Leaving the Bishop spluttering for words, Matrice turned and walked back through the doorway. The Captain hurriedly organised his guards, sending several ahead to clear the corridor.

Behind on a stretcher, followed Tortuga, four men straining under its burden.

## Chapter 48: The Red Queen

**Anglemere Castle, Kingsholme, The Holme**

Herald paced back and forth.

An amused Horyk Andersun watched on, idly picking at the fruit tray. The selection was good despite the harvest season being well gone. Fibrous ommi berries, just ripened, reminded him of home. They were edible and sweet but the nok-apples and bright red laer-grape from great Olme were more to his liking. For a Norderman, even after all these years in the capital, they seemed exotic.

"Why do you eat so, Horyk? Why hasn't he called for me?"

Popping a final grape into his mouth Horyk faced his Prince. His eyebrows crunched together and his mouth twisted playfully as he chewed and swallowed. "I will answer one of your questions. Which will it be? Choose wisely, my Prince."

An old game from his boyhood, it brought Herald a moment of respite from his pacing and worry. It even brought a hint of a smile to his lips.

Horyk had seemed a giant of a man when first they met. To his five-year-old self the Norderman's tales were outlandish and his demeanour rough and blunt. At the time, the Norderman treated him as a boy, not a prince. He hadn't wanted to like him, but somehow he couldn't help it.

"Okay, I have chosen," Herald recited the old words, stopping and staring at his first sword expectantly. "Why hasn't my father called me to the war council?"

"Are you sure? Wouldn't you rather know why it is I eat?" Horyk asked.

"Yes, I'm sure you big buffoon. Now answer."

"Pity," Horyk shrugged. "I know the answer to that one. The answer to the chosen, I don't."

Herald shook his head, trying to look cross but unable to stop a grin leaking out. With a heavy sigh, he resumed his pacing.

A knock resounded on the door to his apartments and Herald found himself rushing out of his solar. Brushing past Grayson he reached the door first.

"Yes,"

"Highness, Order ambassador Renix is here to see you." The guard's reply was muffled by the heavy oak.

The gods be damned, why had he spoken. This day could not get any worse. I should have let Grayson answer, he fumed. A deep chuckle from Horyk behind didn't help his mood. He glared daggers at his first sword whilst he thought about how to respond.

"You cannot hide from him forever. It is unbecoming of a prince," Horyk rumbled in his northern drawl. "Maybe the ambassador can answer your question."

"Bah, very well," Herald spat, raising his voice he called out. "Let him pass."

Herald retreated into his solar, leaving Grayson to attend his duty. Old fool, if Grayson wasn't so slow he wouldn't be in this pickle. His steward entered momentarily with Renix striding quietly behind. In his dark robes and with his aristocratic bearing he looked as self-assured and smug as ever.

"Your highness, Order Ambassador Renix is here to see you," Grayson said redundantly. He bowed formally before turning and retiring from the room.

"How can I help you, ambassador?" Herald asked pinching his lips.

"You've not attended your last three lessons, which is churlish of you," Renix began.

"Churlish," Herald's voice rose high, "Maybe I did not care for them. If beating on a young boy and making me feel inadequate is all you mean to teach me then I will not be taught. Not by you."

"Petulance is not a good trait in a future High King. Now come, time is wasting," Renix turned back for the door.

"I've told you. I am not coming," Herald snapped.

"I go to attend the congress of Lords. Am I to tell your father you are indisposed? Hiding in your rooms?" Turning, Renix disappeared from view.

Herald swore, "Self-righteous prig." Jumping up, he rushed to follow.

An amused Horyk Andersun grabbed a nok-apple as he sauntered past the table, taking a large bite.

© 2020 A D Green

\*\*\*

"I didn't know you were invited," Herald said, as they made their way through the corridors and halls of the great castle.

"I'm an advisor as well as an ambassador, Highness," Renix said.

"Well, I'm relieved he asked for me. Though I confess I am surprised he sent you," Herald continued.

"He didn't. This is your lesson for the day," Renix replied. "I suggest when we arrive you let me do the talking. In fact, it is best if you say nothing at all. Watch and listen."

Herald's face froze as the words sunk in. His father had not called for him. This was a lesson! It was a bitter blow and his temper kindled, "So much for the fucking wine, sister."

"Wine?" Renix raised an eyebrow and spared the prince a glance. The boy's face was red, his brow furrowed and his jaw clenched. 'He is incapable of hiding his emotion and he lacks control,' Renix thought.

"Matrice gave me a bottle of Tankrit Red, father's favourite," Herald explained, his voice sullen. "Don't know where she got it from but she thought it might bring father round if I gave it to him. We both thought as Crown Prince I must attend the war council. It is my right."

"Did she indeed?" Renix felt a deep foreboding. From his reading of Matrice, it seemed clear that she despised her brother. Evidently, she had just placed a piece upon the board in the game of lords and the piece did not even know it. The burning question was to what purpose?

Renix glanced again at Herald. Nothing good he surmised. He felt a momentary frustration wash over him. His friend had ill-prepared the prince. What was Edward thinking? How had he failed his son so spectacularly?

\*\*\*

Edward Blackstar, High King of the Nine Kingdoms sat contemplating in his study. It was a large chamber with a tall window that gave a stunning, panoramic view of the waters of the Deeping Rift to the south.

Several sconces burned, supplementing the light from the window, each casting a flicker of warmth around the room. The dribble of oily smoke lent a faint charcoal scent and had, over the years, marked the high stone ceiling above with black stains.

A fire was set in the hearth, its soft crackle and heat a comfort as Edward rubbed at his temples trying to ease the ache from behind his eyes.

The walls of his study were lined with bookcases but the rest of his furnishings and personal accoutrements had been removed. In replacement, several long tables had been constructed and pushed together to provide a large tableau upon which a canvas map was laid. It depicted the Nine Kingdoms in high detail and was, in and of itself, a work of art.

Markers denoting the Lords of various kingdoms and their estimated troop numbers were laid upon it. It looked impressive and formidable but it did not take much to see it was a veneer. Each High Lord ruled a Kingdom with every Kingdom Lord sworn and bound to them. Each Lord ruled their own land and retained their own armsmen. The chain of command from the lowest Earl to highest Lord all led back to him but that was too simplistic a view.

The reality was the Nine Kingdoms were a diverse and somewhat disparate mix of peoples and customs with different beliefs and ideals. Long-held enmity led to feuds and a complex politics existed to govern it all; the game of lords his father had called it and it was apt.

Seven hells, Edward recalled, only a few months ago the Rivers and Westlands had been all set for bloody conflict. Despite his intercession with Trenton Twyford and Henry Dumac, conflict in the spring had been all but assured. How he longed for those days. It had taken the urak invasion of the north to change what he could not. It instantly and dramatically turned the game on its head.

Add to that mix the Council of Mages and the Churches of the Trinity and it was a tangled discordant web he tried to weave and pull together. It was no wonder his head ached so.

The door to the chamber opened and Edward looked up as Harris Benvora and Rudy Valenta entered the room, two of his inner circle. They were early yet for the war council but it was natural they would want to arrive first.

As her mother before her, Benvora was magus to the Blackstars and had been since just before Edward became High King. He trusted her implicitly.

Valenta was chancellor. A political appointment but one well made. A deeply boring man, he was nevertheless good at his job. Insightful yet pedantic is a good combination for a keeper of the coin, Renix had told him once and it was true.

"You're early," Edward said, more for something to say than any other reason.

"I think my liege; you will find we are precisely on time," Valenta retorted, moving around the large table to join him.

"Well, early enough to join me for a quaff of wine," Edward lifted a box on top of the map table and opened it.

"I do not drink when I am working your majesty," Valenta said, somewhat stiffly.

"Harris?" Edward held the bottle up. "It's a Tankrit Red, a gift from Herald. Possibly the most thoughtful gift he has ever given me. I think he is trying hard to wheedle his way back into my affections and this council."

"Hmm, I'm tempted, Edward but I'm afraid the red disagrees with me. Gives me an awful head whether I sip one glass or drink a bottle, as well you know. I don't suppose you have a Branikshire white, that is more to my taste and High Lord Ostenbow would be mightily impressed."

Edward chuckled, "You know I do and you know where to find it. By all means, help yourself." Pulling the wax seal off the bottle he un-stoppered the cork with a satisfying pop and poured four fingers into a goblet.

Edward raised it to his lips but stopped.

There was a commotion outside the doors. Talking, but one of the voices was higher pitched and raised above the others. He lowered the goblet, disgruntled. He knew that voice. Elizabeth Hardcastle, High Lady of Midshire. The Shrew they named her, though it would not do to call her so in council.

\* \* \*

Princess Matrice hurried. The morning had passed quickly, too quickly. With five High Lords and their attendant entourages in residence, the castle was full of people, all of whom seemed determined to hinder her passage.

The main keep of the castle was immense but even so, with High Lords and Ladies taking over whole wings of it, Matrice had been forced to use one of the lesser rooms in the south tower for Tortuga's convalescence. She left him there lying like a cadaver, barely breathing. Death seemed imminent.

The detour to the south tower had meant a roundabout trip across the large assembly ground and then back again. A delay that meant she had to rush. Matrice knew her father would hold court in his study, newly repurposed as a war chamber, near to his throne room. She'd been there. Seen it for herself and it was impressive. He'd want to show it off.

Back inside the central keep, Matrice made her way up the grand staircase to the second floor. Here, Kingsguard were posted at every point and junction. Access was restricted but not to a princess of the realm. Flanked by Gart Vannen and the captain of her personal guard, none impeded her passage until she reached her father's war chambers. There the guards blocked her entry.

"Highness, the High King has ordered the doors barred. He is in council and only those invited to attend may pass." The princess glared and the guardswoman felt the heat from it. "You are not on the list. Perhaps I could pass on a message, your Highness?"

Matrice prepared to make her argument, the lines already drafted in her head but before she could plead her cause the guardswoman's eyes flicked past her shoulder and back down the corridor. At the same instant, she sensed Gart turn. She closed her mouth with a snap and twisted around to look.

Two men approached. They were both from Olme. Their deeply tanned skin and dark features proclaimed them so. The Southlands of Olme were vast and warm and divided predominantly from the rest of the kingdoms by the Deeping Rift in the east and the Inner Sea to the west.

The older of the two was completely bald, his head oiled and shiny. A vanity, Matrice surmised. She did not know him.

The other was High Lord Yanik Zacorik. Younger, no salt peppered his black hair or beard, and no worry lines marred his features. It was said in court he was insightful and intelligent, a dangerous man with dangerous ideals. His brown eyes, dark with intensity, fastened on hers.

"Princess Matrice, I have been three days in the city. It has been remiss of me not to seek you out and pay my respects. I knew your mother well, may her eternal soul rest in the heavens. Can you forgive me?" Zacorik inclined his head but his eyes never wavered.

"Of course, tell me Lord Zacorik. To arrive so quickly you must have crossed the Deeping Rift. A dangerous prospect, especially as autumn passes to winter, I am told storms and bad weather abides at the seasons' change." The risk tantalised her.

"That is so. I confess however the danger is much mitigated when travelling with a sea magus or two." His eyes twinkled playfully. "Perhaps later over dinner, I could recount my journey."

"Perhaps, though I'm afraid food is far from my mind," Matrice answered, casting a disdainful look towards the guards. "I have urgent news that is pertinent to your council, yet I cannot seem to gain entry to see my father."

Lord Zacorik smiled artfully; taking up her cause he addressed the guards. "Come now, the council has yet to begin. The High King would be displeased would he not if you were to deny his daughter entry when she comes bearing urgent news of state."

The guardswoman glanced at Matrice briefly, a hint of accusation in her eyes, then back to Lord Zacorik.

"I will bear full responsibility," Zacorik said.

The guard nodded acceptance and, standing back, pulled the door wide.

Haughtily, Matrice breezed through it. Her guard captain remained outside but Gart followed her, then High Lord Zacorik and his advisor.

Her father, Edward Blackstar stood in silhouette, the tall window behind him highlighting his frame. It was hard to read his face but Matrice could imagine the scowl upon it at her appearance. Beside him and arrayed about the map table stood the High Lords and High Ladies of five of the Nine Kingdoms and their advisors. The looks they gave varied from the amused, the bored, to the predatory, though which look was for her and which was directed at Lord Zacorik was harder to discern.

"High Lord Zacorik, welcome. I see you've encountered my daughter Matrice. The last time you saw her she'd have been a child," Edward said, his voice filling the room.

His tone was perfectly civil but Matrice knew him well enough to hear the mild rebuke in it. Mostly to remind her she was too young to be here but so too for Zacorik, who it was rumoured had five wives and many more concubines, some as young as she. It made her lip quirk at the thought.

If the High Lord of Olme picked up on it he showed no sign. "Indeed, she grows much like her mother. Her death was a sad loss for the Kingdoms; a woman of great vision, as well as great beauty."

Her mother had died a decade past. Matrice's only memories of her were vague but they were all warm happy ones. This was the second time Zacorik had mentioned her mother and Matrice wondered at that.

At the time of her mother's death, her father had grieved at the loss. At least she was told so. It was even said by some to have broken him but she had never seen it. Her father kept his pain isolated. Her five-year-old self never felt his comfort and he never shared his grief. In fact, they had never spoken about it. She was always too young and then, any chance evaporated when he married Lady Margot Warringal, niece of High Lady Elizabeth Hardcastle of Midshire. That had been six years ago; my, how time had passed.

Matrice recalled herself to the room; she had been lost in reflection and frowned in annoyance at her weakness. Her father had been speaking and, like an idiot child, she stood not responding. The pitch of his voice conveyed it was not the first time he had addressed her.

"Matrice, Lord Zacorik says you have something of import to divulge?" Edward prompted.

"I have come from the Red Conclave. Eight of the nine cardinals are dead. Only Tortuga lives and he lies gravely ill," Matrice said, brutally direct.

There was an explosion of noise at her announcement. Only Zacorik and his advisor remained quiet and considerate. A loud banging on the table drew silence back to the room.

"That is better," Edward announced. He turned and fixed a steel-eyed gaze on his daughter.

"Your brother gifts me a bottle of Tankrit Red," Edward tapped a ring against the wine bottle sat upon the table. "You gift me dire news. Unless you have anything further to add, wait for me in my chambers. There is much I would know, such as why you were at the Conclave."

"Surely knowledge is a precious gift father, whether it is favourable or not," Matrice fired back. "Besides, the news might not be as bad as you imagine."

Her pronouncement drew a chuckle from behind and a harsh glare from the High King. "Almost the entire hierarchy of the Red Church wiped out. The militant branch of the Trinity with their Red Cloaks is of vital import, yet you 'think' it may not be bad. Explain."

"That Tortuga survives means he is now High Cardinal of the Red Church. Nine enter, one will pass. He is the anointed, the chosen of Kildare. He is or was Cardinal of the Rivers. If he survives, surely he will not forsake the people of the north." Matrice looked at each of the High Lords and the High Lady as she spoke. That they considered her words was pleasing. She couldn't resist a parting dig, however.

"I will go father and await you as commanded. Enjoy Herald's wine. By the way, where is he? I thought my brother the Crown Prince would be in attendance."

Outwardly Edward remained calm. Only a slight tightening about the eyes gave any hint of his annoyance; both at the news and at his daughter's flagrant attempt to insinuate herself where she did not belong.

Zacorik was right; she was the spitting image of her mother. So much so it pained him to look at her. Did Matrice not understand he was trying to protect her? Did she not realise she played a dangerous game with ruthless people. In spite, he raised his goblet and downed the contents. It was beneath him but she had a way of getting under his skin. Even now, she stood and stared at him, her eyes flaring dramatically.

A sudden sharp pain stabbed through his abdomen. So severe it bent him over and only his hand on the table prevented him from keeling onto the floor. He coughed and a splatter of blood and wine landed over the Torns Mountains.

"Edward?"

The voice belonged to Harris but it was distant. He couldn't respond. A deep ache rolled through his gut and up into his chest and lungs. He looked up but his vision was blurred then faded to black.

The room watched in disbelief as Edward Blackstar collapsed over the table. Blood haemorrhaged from mouth and nose staining the map, inexorably slowly, he slid off the table and onto the floor.

Matrice screamed and it woke the room from their morbid shock. Zacorik called for the guards and everyone started moving and talking at once. Harris bent to attend Edward.

"I need the Royal Physiker, now!" she yelled.

Holding her hands apart over Edward's chest and abdomen, Harris closed her eyes and concentrated her mind. It had been over a hand of years since she had last incanted a shroud, it took her several attempts before she succeeded. The sconces flickered and hissed as she worked.

A blue nimbus of energy manifested. Wafer-thin, it formed between her fingers and she settled the shroud over Edward's body. It was not much, it could not heal. Its magic was external to the body, she was no physiker. What it provided was a window, sensing the ebb and flow of life energy beneath and reflecting it upon its surface. What Harris saw made her heart cold with dread.

"What's wrong with him? Why is he bleeding?" Matrice was there, kneeling beside her father. Hands shaking, she laid them on his chest as if to awaken him. "Save him, Harris."

A sob escaped the princess and it broke Harris. She could do nothing. "Don't watch, child." Only moments had passed but it seemed an eternity. "Where is the gods' damned physiker?"

Matrice rose, tears running freely down her cheeks as she gazed at her father and the deathly, torpid pallor of his face. Twisting away her eyes lingered over the table.

Claret lifeblood coated the map. It covered the Torn Mountains of the north and ran in rivulets of blood and regurgitated wine into the Norderlands and Rivers. It was a portent, an omen.

An image blossomed in her mind. It was of a Queen. Dressed all in red, hair and face smeared with blood, the same claret colour as her father's. Small of frame, with long dark hair framing a heart-shaped face and piercingly intense green eyes. The queen was strong and wicked and beautiful to behold. Matrice smiled.

* * *

Renix stopped so abruptly Herald walked right into his back making him curse.

"Hush, my prince." Horyk walked forward, his shoulder brushing against Herald. His head was cocked to the side and his hand was on his sword hilt.

Now Herald heard it too, the faint din of noise. A distant clamour of alarm, something was amiss but he could not reconcile it. "What is that about?"

"We should proceed carefully," Renix pronounced, "Horyk, stay behind me. Guard the prince."

Horyk directed a filthy look at the Orderman. What did he think he did?

Renix took the lead once again and they moved more guardedly down the corridor.

The rattle of armour and crump of boots announced the guards long before they rounded the corner. There were two of them and neither looked like stopping.

"Hold. What occurs here?" Renix called out.

They stopped, not at his words but at the sight of the Crown Prince. They addressed him directly.

"Highness, your father, the High King has been attacked in his war chambers. We've been sent for the Royal Physiker."

Herald spluttered in shock. "Attacked? By who? Does he live?"

"We don't know any detail, your highness, except we're to tell the Royal Physiker to bring what he needs to treat for poison."

"Go, do your duty. Time is critical," Renix commanded. "I will attend the Crown Prince." Blessedly, the guards heeded him and set off at once down the corridor.

"I must get to my father." Herald's face was pale and slack with shock.

"No, you must not," Renix retorted. "You must go elsewhere. It is crucial, for I suspect your life is in peril. Horyk, take the prince to my apartments before the castle is sealed."

"I will not run. I am no coward," Herald declared. "I am the Crown Prince and I will see my father. What if he dies?"

"You will shut up and you will listen. You must think like a King, not a boy, or a son. Time is short." Renix's tone brooked no argument.

Herald felt his ire build in an instant, rising ready to explode but it didn't. The sudden hard-edged look in Horyk's face and the solemn nod he gave were enough to make him bite back his reply. Closing his mouth, lips tight, Herald folded his arms.

"Good, there is hope for you yet," Renix said. "The Tankrit Red you gave your father is from my stock. I gave a bottle to Matrice to give your father. She has no love for you, boy. I suspect she has played you."

"It is hard to poison a king. Everything gets tasted and checked. Not so a gift from his son and heir. I hope I am wrong, but if I am not, the finger of blame will point squarely at you. Regicide, Herald, is a terrible crime. If proven they will kill you."

"I did not poison my father," Herald cried. "It's ludicrous and who are they?"

"Quietly my prince, walls have ears and corridors carry sound," Horyk whispered.

"They, I do not know for certain, but your sister has revealed her hand. If you go to your father I believe your next bed will be in a cell. For, if what I suspect is true, this has been meticulously planned."

"If? Suspect?" Herald snapped, his face contorting. "You want me to trust you but I don't."

"Good, it's the first wise thing you've said," Renix retorted. He glanced at both men, addressed both.

"Horyk, the castle will soon be sealed. You will need to hurry. Stop for no one. Hang a red cloth from my study window and wait. Someone called Tasso Marn will come. Tell her what I have told and you will be taken to a safe house. If I do not find you by morning I will be dead or captured. In that event, you must leave the city and make for Lord Duncan. He is your best hope and needs to know what is happening."

"What is happening? What the hells' is going on? My sister is spoiled and a brat but she would not do this… cannot do this!"

"A darker hand is at play, Herald. The Morhudrim sit in the shadows, manipulating, controlling. This has their taint." Renix said, "The kingdoms have ever been fractious. If the High King dies and you're implicated, you will be removed from the succession. Matrice is next in line but at fifteen many will not follow her. The High Lords and High Ladies have never bent a knee to a High Queen. Many will see her as a child and this as an opportunity to shake free from the Nine Kingdoms. History will be forgotten."

Renix grabbed Herald by the shoulders. "The urak attack the Kingdoms from without and now the Kingdoms are attacked from within. You are the best hope of uniting the realms. You must survive else I fear the Kingdoms fall.

In the end, it was Horyk that carried his decision. Horyk, believed the Orderman, even if he did not. But he believed in Horyk and trusted him.

"Come, my Prince. We must go, now."

His back stiff and shoulders square Herald was reluctant but allowed Horyk to guide him away.

Renix watched the two as they disappeared back the way they'd come. Closing his eyes Renix phased. Concentrating, he focused on his connection with Keeper and sent a burst of information down the link. As quick as thought, it took but moments.

<Tread careful my friend. You walk into danger. I have things in motion but we are not as prepared as we should be.> Keeper admitted.

<Time has made us lax,> Renix replied.

<Indeed. Help comes but it will be many days before it arrives and I am not sure it will be enough. What of the Vox Léchtar Fai-ber. Is he safe?> Keeper asked. <He's more important than the Prince. You must get him to safety.>

<That is out of my hands now. Tasso Marn watches,> Renix replied. Their link terminated and he phased back, the familiar, disconcerting nausea rinsing over his mind as he did so, it never got any less despite the years. Orienting himself, he set off down the corridor.

On approach to the king's study, Renix found the corridor filled with Kingsguard. Most knew who he was or of him and he was allowed to pass unhindered, though many, eyed him with a protective hostility that he recognised. Misplaced and too late, he thought bitterly.

At the entrance to the chambers, a guard captain stood watch over the door, issuing orders and overseeing entry and exit to the room beyond.

Even amongst the Order Knights, Renix's memory and recall was legendary. The man was familiar to him. He was guard Captain to Matrice.

The recognition was mutual and the slight nod he gave was not for his benefit as Renix sensed the guards behind form up and close him in.

"You're expected, ambassador." The captain pulled the door wide and Renix strode through it. The captain followed along with the guards but Renix was not mindful of them as he regarded the room.

The High Lords and High Ladies were all there, standing around the fireplace. Dumac and Hardcastle were in earnest yet hushed conversation with the rest. They looked guilty when they spied his entry and fell silent. Renix passed over them, his eyes searching.

A group of people was gathered at the head of the large map table. He recognised both Rudy Valenta and Harris Benvora both wearing worried frowns and there beside them, the slender frame of Matrice Blackstar.

As if sensing his gaze she turned and stared back. Her green eyes were piercingly cold and calculating. Lips tight she gave a curt nod of the head.

Renix started to turn as a slither of ice slipped into his lower back. It exploded into sharp pain and he cried out. Desperately, he phased, but it was too late. The pain fled, leaving him and his legs collapsed, unable to support his weight.

His head hit the ground hard and Renix was dazed. When he regained himself, Matrice was stood over him looking down. Her mask had slipped, showing Renix what he hadn't seen before. Wide predatory eyes, cruel lips curling, unable to disguise her pleasure or the crazed madness within. He read it all, each moment, each movement, every inflexion of face and body. It was all etched with excruciating clarity in his mind.

Renix blinked and tried to move but couldn't feel his legs or any pain. He heard a shout, "Matrice you cannot do this," Harris Benvora. More calls, though Renix found it hard to focus on them and pick them apart.

"Captain Loris, drag Lord Renix to the High King. Lay him so my father can see him. See, what his 'friend' has done to him." Matrice spun, and, raising her voice, addressed the High Lords and Lady's, anger dripping from every word.

"This is a personal matter. You will remain silent and bear witness. My brother did not contrive this betrayal alone. Any interruption will go badly." Holding eye contact with each, none looked away, but none challenged her either. Unwilling or indifferent it didn't matter.

"Sir Vannen, your knife," Matrice held her hand out flat. The blade, a thin razor-sharp stiletto, was laid in her palm still adorned with blood. Her fingers tightened around the hilt.

"Get everyone back," Matrice commanded Captain Loris as Renix was thrown none too gently beside her father.

Gathering her long skirts, Matrice stepped across the ambassador's body as if straddling a horse. Her eyes bored into his and a smile played across her face as she sank down on top of him, her legs pinning his arms to his sides.

Leaning forward, Matrice gently cradled his head. It was obscene yet intensely intimate as her lips brushed his cheeks and her hair tickled his face.

"I lied." She whispered, so soft only Renix could hear her. "It is nothing personal. You're just a loose end and too dangerous to be allowed to talk. A pity, I find you really rather interesting."

Renix blinked once, focusing on a black stain on the ceiling above. "I've lived a long life, seven hundred and sixty-four years to be precise. Longer than any man should or has a right to expect. To my credit, I have done more good than harm."

His eyes wavered, staring off now into nothing. "I lay here murdered by a fifteen-year-old child. She is young. It is not too late for redemption. I am ready."

He breathed deeply, lilac and jasmine caressing his senses. Her perfume was strong this close. It was not a bad last memory, Renix thought.

Matrice sat upright. Her lips parting as she ran her tongue between the edges of her teeth. "Thanks for telling me. But I don't want redeeming."

Raising the knife she placed its point beneath his jaw and smiled.

Renix returned it, "I wasn't talking to you."

The words came whispering out just as Matrice lent forward. The blade pierced with surprising ease through his skin and flesh as she thrust upwards.

Blood spurted and spat from his mouth as Renix choked. With a vicious final thrust, Matrice rammed the knife deeper until she lay over his face, the little cross guard tight against the flesh of his chin, the stiletto point penetrating through bone and cartilage to reach the brain.

Renix flopped lifelessly and Matrice sat back, releasing the knife. She stared at the ceiling and could feel his blood on her face and in her hair, dripping. She could taste it on her lips and in her mouth. It stained her dress.

Laughing, the Red Queen rose.

* * *

*Keeper bowed and tears, un-cried in a generation, fell as the connection was severed in an instant. The memory of those last moments, what was seen and witnessed would not be forgotten. That Renix asked forgiveness for Matrice was crazy but he expected no less from his friend, he'd always been sentimental.*

*The thought made Keeper smile but it was brief. The last words they had spoken together sitting like ash in his memory.*

# Epilogue

**Lower Rippleton, The Rivers**

Dreamwalking.

It was a good name, Nihm decided and it needed a name since she seemed to do it almost every time she slept recently. Unsurprisingly it was of him again. Somehow in some way she didn't understand, they were connected.

Renco. His name rolled around in her mind and Nihm shook herself, irritated. This time had been different. The girl with the sunlight hair was with him still, but there were others, not Red Cloaks but people she knew. It was time. She knew that now.

<You mean to go for him,> Sai stated.

Did she? Now that Sai said the words she realised they were true. Since Marron had died, her purpose had been to find her father, to be reunited. Now that they had found each other though, Nihm felt deeply unsettled.

Her Da wanted her to go with him to Tankrit Isle, to the Order. He expected it, assumed it and would insist upon it. But Hiro did not. The feeling she got was that Ma hadn't wanted her to go either. Da hadn't said as much but it was there between his words. She couldn't shake the feeling, as if the path she was on was not hers. Nothing felt right.

Nothing except Renco; which was madness, she didn't even know him. Saints sake, they'd never even met.

<You're procrastinating when you have already decided. It is a waste of energy and resource,> Sai told her.

It made her lip curl. Sai was so literal. <It's not as easy as that. My Da will be upset. He might forbid it and... well I've only just found him. I don't want to lose him again but he has the ilfanum to worry about and his mission.>

<If all humans are this indecisive it's a wonder your species has survived so long. You are creating obstacles where none exist. You are Nihm. Listen to those you trust but only you can decide and do,> Sai said.

*&lt;I thought you'd want me safe. If I go it will be dangerous,&gt;* Nihm prodded.

*&lt;My function is limited. I can only inform you, the decision ultimately is yours.&gt;*

*&lt;Well thanks,&gt;* Nihm said.

*&lt;For what?&gt;*

*&lt;For not saying the percentile chance of success is blah, blah, blah,&gt;* Nihm laughed.

*&lt;Your chance of locating the human called Renco is in the single digits. However, that does not include input for your Dreamwalk ability which I cannot experience and therefore quantify. It is irrelevant since my iterative logic routines indicate you would still go no matter the result,&gt;* Sai responded.

*&lt;Glad I mentioned it now,&gt;* Nihm retorted. She took a deep breath in through her nose and felt her lungs fill. She held it awhile before slowly releasing it.

"Okay, I'm ready."


Our Story continues in Darkness Resides, Book Three of the Morhudrim Cycle.

## Principal Characters

| | |
|---|---|
| Nihm | Pronounced Nim. Daughter of Darion and Marron Castell |
| Renco | Pronounced Ren-co. Apprentice to Hiro |
| Tasao Maohong | Pronounced – Taz-a-o Mow-hong. Hiro's companion. |

### The Order

| | |
|---|---|
| Darion Castell | Homesteader and Orderman. |
| Marron Castell | Homesteader and Orderwoman. |
| Keeper | Titular head of the Order. |
| Hiro | Order Knight (Sometimes) |
| Renix | Order Knight, Kingsholme ambassador |
| Chivalry | Order Knight |
| Ironside | Order Knight |
| Lyra Castigan | Order Knight |
| Attimus | Order Knight, Master at the academy |
| Tannon Crick | Order Knight at Norderland |
| Meredith Chancer | Clothier and Orderwoman in Confluence |
| David Chancer | Adopted son of Meredith |
| Regus | Orderman and manservant to Ironside |
| Gatzinger | Orderman and manservant to Castigan |
| Rutigard | Orderman and hand to Ironside |
| Ansel | Orderman and hand to Castigan |
| Tasso Marn | Shop Holder, Orderwoman in Kingsholme |
| Razholte | Wordsmith and Orderman, Tankrit isles |

### Lords of the Rivers Province

| | |
|---|---|
| Trenton Twyford | Pronounced Ty-Ford. Ducal Lord of the Rivers province |
| Richard Bouchemeax | Pronounced Bow-She-mow. Known as the Black Crow. Lord of Thorsten. |
| Jacob Bouchemeax | Son of Richard |
| Constance Bouchemeax | Daughter of Richard |
| William Bouchemeax | Lord of Redford – brother of Richard |

| | |
|---|---|
| Robert Bouchemeax | William's 1st son |
| Bruce Bouchemeax | William's 2nd son |
| Sandford Bouchemeax | William's 3rd son |
| Chadford | Lord of Greenholme |
| Menzies | Lord of Fallston |
| John Trant | Lord of Marston |
| Winston Brant | Lord Duke of Greentower |
| Victor Nesto | Lord of Charncross |
| Aric Nesto | Son of Victor, Captain of Charncross |
| Idris Inigo | Lord of Confluence |
| Mical Hanboek | Lord of Fastain |

## Men and Women of the Rivers

| | |
|---|---|
| Sir Anders Forstandt | Captain in the Black Crows guard. |
| Kronke | Sergeant in Forstandt's company |
| Pieterzon/Deadeye | guard in Forstandt's company |
| Sir John Stenson | Captain of Jacob Bouchemeax personal guard. |
| Greigon | Captain of the Black Crow's guard. |
| Mortimer | Sergeant on the Riversgate, Thorsten |
| Mathew Lebraun | Guard on Riversgate, Thorsten. |
| Geert Vanknell | Guard on Riversgate, Thorsten. |
| Lutico Ben Naris | Mage of the third order, master of the arts magical, emissary for the council of mages and councillor to Lord Richard Bouchemeax |
| Junip | Mage apprentice to Lutico. |
| Leticia Goodwill (Lett) | Bard apprentice. |
| Annabelle | Young girl, Thorsten, charge of Lord Amos Duncan |
| Ned Wynter | Bowmaster at Thorsten |
| Witter | Sergeant at Greentower |
| Nesbitt | Duke Brant's chamberlain |
| Sir Vincent Dulac | Commander for Lord Inigo, Confluence |
| Harton | Guard Captain, Confluence |
| Osiris Smee | Magus, Councillor to Lord Inigo, Confluence. |
| Si Manko | Swordmaster and First Sword to Lord Inigo, Confluence |

## Grimmers

| | |
|---|---|
| Jackson Tullock 'Black Jack' | Lord of the Grimhold |
| Hissings | Reaver |
| Tom Trickle | Hedge Mage |
| Hettingly | Physiker |
| Torgrid | Reaver Captain |
| Jessop | Reaver Captain |
| Odd-John | Reaver, Producer of Whiskey Mash |
| Nadine Varla | Reaver |
| Egg | Reaver |
| Busk | Reaver |

| | |
|---|---|
| Nils Baka | Reaver |
| Sofia Grainne | Captured scribe, from Thorsten |
| Millie Grainne | Sofia's daughter |

## The Duncans

| | |
|---|---|
| Atticus | Lord and Patriarch |
| Morgenni | Lady and Matriarch |
| Angus | First Son |
| Amos | Second Son |
| Mercy | First daughter and Fire Magus |
| Samuel | Third Son |
| Mori | Second daughter |
| Loris & Lucan | Twin Brothers, fourth and fifth sons |

## Red Priest's – Church of Kildare

| | |
|---|---|
| Worsten Lannik | High Cardinal |
| Henrik Zoller | Priest, protégé to the cardinal. |
| Maxim Tortuga | Cardinal and head of the Red Priests in the Rivers Province. |
| Eruk Mortim | Priest in charge of Thorsten chapter |
| Jon Whent | Archbishop of Killenhess, Lord Commander of the Faith Militant |
| Pieter Manning | Priest, Secretary to Tortuga |
| Per Torsten | Cardinal of Norderland |
| Renton Barroso | Principal Bishop, Order of Service. |

## Red Cloaks (Brothers all)

| | |
|---|---|
| Tuko | Zollers Guard |
| Holt | Zollers Guard |
| Thomas Perrick | Zollers Guard |
| Patrice | Zollers Guard, Physiker |
| Diadago | Zollers Guard |
| Hector Henreece | Wents Guard, Physkier |
| Comter | Sergeant, Wents Guard |
| Warwick | 1st Captain, Wents Guard |
| Maesons | Captain Wents Guard |
| Richard Morgan | Wents Guard |

| | |
|---|---|
| Hamish Johns | Whents Guard |
| Mackey | Whents Guard |
| Stokes | Whents Guard |
| Mercer | Tortuga's Guard |

## Men and Women of Kingsholme

| | |
|---|---|
| Edward Blackstar | High King |
| Margot Blackstar | High Queen |
| Herald Blackstar | Crown Prince |
| Matrice Blackstar | Princess |
| Rudy Valenta | Lord, Chancellor and Master of Coin |
| Malcolm Reibeck | Lord Chamberlain |
| Harris Benvora | Mage to The High King |
| Gart Vannen | Sir, First Sword to Princess Matrice |
| Horyk Andersun | First Sword to Herald |
| Grayson | Chamberlain to Herald |
| Loris | Captain of Matrice's Kingsguard |
| Bortillo Targus | Leader of the Syndicate, Thief Guild |
| Willie 'the Hand' | Fence in the Allways |
| Tomas 'The Mouse' | Child Thief and Wordsmith |
| Sparrow | Child Thief |

## Other Notables

| | |
|---|---|
| Arisa Montreau | High Lady, Cumbrenan |
| Costa Ostenbow | High Lord, Branikshire |
| Derek Travenon | High Lord, Eosland |
| Yanik Zacorik | High Lord, Southlands of Olme |
| Justin Janis | High Lord, Norderland |
| Henry Dumac | High Lord, Westlands |
| Elizabeth Hardcastle | High Lady, Midshire |

© 2020 A D Green

**Ilfanum**

| | |
|---|---|
| Da'Mari | Pronounced Da-Ma-re. A Nu'Rakauma – a world tree bordering the Rivers to the west.[1] |
| Eladrohim | Pronounced El-Ad-Ro-Him. A Nu'Rakauma – a world tree to the west of the kingdoms. |
| Elora | Pronounced El-Ora. Visok and K'raal[1] |
| M'rika | Pronounced Ma-Rik-ah. Visok and K'raal |
| Ruith | Pronounced Roo-ith. Healer |
| R'ell | Pronounced Ray-ell |
| Bezal | Pronounced Bez-al. R'ells bonded Crow |

**Sházáik (Demons)**

| | |
|---|---|
| O'si | Sháadretarch (Third Level Sházáik) |
| P'uk | Sháadretarch (Third Level Sházáik) |
| Q'tox | Tetriarché (Second Level Sházáik) |

---

[1] See Ilf Dictionary that follows for pronunciation guide and meaning.

## Urak

| | |
|---|---|
| Bartuk | Pronounced Bar-Tuck. Toreen, White Hand Clan – Scout |
| Mar-Dur | Pronounced Mar-duur. Clan Chief of the White Hand |
| Rimtaug | Pronounced Rim-Taag. Raid chief for the White Hand |
| Krol | Clan Chief of the Blood Skull |
| Tar-Tukh | Pronounced Tar- Tuck. Hurak-Hin (bodyguard) to Krol clan chieftain. |
| Nartak | Pronounced Nar-Tack. Hurak-Hin (bodyguard) to Krol Clan chief. |
| Grimpok | War Chief in the White Hand. |
| Muw-Tukh | Pronounced Mow-Tuck. Hurak-Hin (bodyguard) to Mar-Dur Clan Chief. |
| Baq-Dur | Pronounced Bak Dur) Bortaug tribe chief. White Hand Clan. |
| Nasqchuk | Pronounced Nas chuck. Raid Leader, White Hand |
| Karth-Dur | Tribal chieftain of the Manawarih, Blood Skull clan |
| Narpik-Dur | Tribal chieftain of the Toreen, White Hand clan |
| Grot-tuk | Pronounced Grow Tuk. Toreen, Warband leader, White Hand Clan |
| Murhtuk | Pronounced Meer tuck. Toreen, White Hand Clan |
| Rutgarpok | Pronounced Rut gar pok. White Hand Clan, Huntmaster |
| Makjatukh | Pronounced Mak jat uk. White Hand Clan, Scout |
| Maliktuk | pronounced Mal ik tuck. Toreen, White Hand Clan, Huntmaster |
| Orqis-tarn | Toreen Shaman, White Hand Clan |

## Ilf dictionary

| | |
|---|---|
| Ilf | Means child/children |
| Ilfanum | Means child of |
| Nu'Rakauma | Pronounced Nu-racka-uma means in literal terms giant tree mother |
| K'raal | A type of Lord/Lady |
| Visok | the term for a High Ilf |
| Anum | Means several things of/from |
| Umphathi | Means warden |
| Ka'harthi | Means, gatherer/gardener. |
| Fassarunewadaick | The name for the Fossa River near the Torns mountains. |
| Fassa | Means fast/quick |
| Rune | Means running/flowing/moving |
| Wada | Means water |
| Ick | Means ice/cold/frozen |
| Rokulinewaald | Means ward of the north forest |
| Rovalinewaald | Means ward of the south forest |
| Rohelinewaald | Means ward of the east forest |
| Ronilinewaald | Means ward of the west forest |
| Rokuline | Means north/northern |
| Rovaline | Means south/southern |
| Roheline | Means east/eastern |
| Roniline | Means west/western |
| Waald | Means Ward/Warden |
| Tae'al | Pronounced Taa – al (tail) Means essence or binding force |

© 2020 A D Green

© 2020 A D Green

**Look out for**

**Darkness Resides**

**Book Three of the Morhudrim Cycle**

**Due for release – December 2023**

I am hoping if you are reading this that you have read both Rivers Run Red and Shadows Fall. If so thank you. Reading is an investment of your time and I appreciate that you have given so much of it to me and my work.

If you can spare a little more, please could you leave a rating and/or review. It would mean a lot and help boost the visibility of my books so that others might find and enjoy them.

If you want updates on book three and beyond, or to give me honest feedback and suggestions, or want adding to my mailing list, then please check out my website https://adgreenauthor.com/ it is packed with information on my books, maps, lore and you can sign up for news.

You can also find me on:
Facebook @adgreentheauthor
Twitter @adgreenauthor


Thanks for reading.

A D Green

© 2020 A D Green

Printed in Great Britain
by Amazon